Praise for The Supremes at Earl s All-You-Can-Eat

'A funny, tender-hearted debut novel about the enduring friendship of three women, and the vividly drawn town in which their dramas take place.' *Shelf Awareness*

'Throughout the Supremes' intertwined stories is one constant – meeting and eating at Earl's All-You-Can-Eat, a place where relationships are forged, scandals are aired and copious amounts of chicken are consumed ... A novel of strong women, evocative memories and deep friendship' *Kirkus Reviews*

'Brimming with small-town warmth and idiosyncrasy ... a book of joy and tears' *Sainsbury's Magazine*

'There is no clue in the deliberately obscure title as to just how good this book is ... An excellent and unpreachy chance to learn how the [civil rights] movement affected ordinary women.' *Daily Mail*

'This beautifully written debut novel is a delightful tribute to friendship, full of wit and warmth and with a quirky twist' *Candis*

'Edward Kelsey Moore has written a novel jam-packed with warmth, honesty, wit, travail, and just enough madcap humor to keep us giddily off-balance. It teems with memorable characters, chief among them Odette, as unlikely and irresistible a protagonist as we are likely to meet. *The Supremes at Earl's All-You-Can-Eat* is that rare and happy find: a book that delivers not only good story, but good company.' Leah Hager Cohen, author of *The Grief in Others*

'Oprah is going to love this book ... warm and insightful.' *Sun Herald*

'With all the charm of Alexander McCall Smith, but a more acerbic wit, Moore's first full-length novel is rolling-on-the-floor funny.' *Adelaide Advertiser*

D0238570

About the Author

Edward Kelsey Moore lives in Chicago with his partner of many years. Having trained with some of the world's finest musicians, he has travelled widely and recorded extensively during his lengthy career as a professional cellist. Edward's literary work often reflects both his life as a musician and his upbringing as the backsliding son of a Baptist preacher. His short fiction has appeared in several literary magazines and on Public Radio. Like Dora in *The Supremes at Earl's All-You-Can-Eat*, Edward is also an avid gardener; like Odette, his horticultural projects are not always successful. *The Supremes at Earl's All-You-Can-Eat* is Edward Kelsey Moore's first novel.

Find out more on Edward's website at
www.edwardkelseymoore.com
or his Facebook page www.facebook.com/
EdwardKelseyMooreauthor
and follow him on Twitter @edkmoore.

The Supremes At EARL'S

ALL-YOU-CAN-EAT

Edward Kelsey Moore

HODDER

First published in the United States of America in 2013 by Alfred A. Knopf,
an imprint of The Knopf Doubleday Group
A division of Random House, Inc.
First published in Great Britain in 2013 by Hodder & Stoughton
An Hachette UK company

First published in paperback in 2014

1

A CIP catalogue record for this title is available from the British Library

ISBN 978 1 444 75731 6

Printed and bound by CPI Group (UK) Ltd, Croydon, CR0 4YY

Hodder & Stoughton policy is to use papers that are natural, renewable
and recyclable products and made from wood grown in sustainable forests.
The logging and manufacturing processes are expected to conform
to the environmental regulations of the country of origin.

Hodder & Stoughton Ltd
338 Euston Road
London NW1 3BH

www.hodder.co.uk

For Mom and Dad

The Supremes At EARL'S

ALL-YOU-CAN-EAT

Chapter 1

I woke up hot that morning. Came out of a sound sleep with my face tingling and my nightgown stuck to my body. Third time that week. The clock on the dresser on the other side of the bedroom glowed 4:45, and I could hear the hiss of the air conditioner and feel its breeze across my face. I had set the temperature to sixty before going to sleep. So common sense said that it had to be chilly in the room. Well, common sense and the fact that my husband, James, who lay snoring beside me, was outfitted for winter even though it was mid-July. He slept like a child – a six-foot, bald-headed, middle-aged child – wrapped in a cocoon he had fashioned for himself out of the sheet and blanket I had kicked off during the night. Just the top of his brown head was visible above the floral pattern of the linens. Still, every inch of me was screaming that the room was a hundred degrees.

I lifted my nightgown and let it fall, trying to fan cool air onto my skin. That accomplished nothing. My friend Clarice claimed that meditation and positive thinking eased her path through menopause, and she was forever after me to try it. So I lay still in the predawn darkness and thought cool thoughts. I summoned up an old summer memory of hopping with the kids through the cold water jetting from the clicking yellow sprinkler in our backyard. I pictured the ice that formed every winter on the creek that ran behind Mama and Daddy's house in Leaning Tree, making it look like it was wrapped up in cellophane.

I thought of my father, Wilbur Jackson. My earliest recollection of him is the delicious chill I got as a little girl whenever Daddy scooped me up in his arms after walking home on winter evenings from the carpentry shop he owned. I recalled how cold radiated from Daddy's coveralls and the way it felt to run my hands over the frost-coated hair of his beard.

But Daddy's shop had been gone for ages. The Leaning Tree property, creek and all, had been the domain of various renters for half a decade. And my children were each at least twenty years beyond dancing in the spray of a sprinkler.

No thoughts, at least not the ones I came up with, proved capable of icing down my burning skin. So I cussed Clarice for her bad advice and for making me think of the old days – a certain recipe for sleeplessness – and I decided to head for the kitchen. There was a pitcher of water in the Frigidaire and butter pecan ice cream in the freezer. I figured a treat would set me right.

I sat up in the bed, careful not to wake James. Normally, he was as easygoing a man as you'd ever meet. But if I woke him before dawn on a Sunday, he would look at me sideways all through morning service and right up until dinner. So, in order not to disturb him, I moved in slow motion as I stood, slipped my feet into my house shoes, and made my way to the bedroom door in the dark.

Even though I had made the trip from our bed to the kitchen thousands of times in pitch blackness, what with sick children and countless other nighttime emergencies during the decades of our marriage, and even though not a stick of furniture in our bedroom had been moved in twenty years, I rammed the little toe of my right foot into the corner of our old mahogany dresser not five steps into my journey. I cussed again, out loud this time. I looked over my shoulder to see if I had awakened James, but he was still snoring away in his linen wrappings. Hot and tired, my toe throbbing in my green terrycloth slip-ons, I had to fight the urge to run and wake James and insist that he sit up and suffer along with me. But I was good and continued to creep out of the room.

Other than the faint growl of James snoring three rooms away, the only sound in the kitchen was the bass whoosh made by the lopsided ceiling fan churning above my head. I turned on the kitchen light and looked up at that fan wobbling on its axis. With my toe smarting, and still longing to distribute my bad humor, I decided that even if I couldn't justify snapping at James about my hot flash or my sore toe, I could surely rationalize letting off some steam by yelling at him for improperly installing that fan eighteen years earlier. But, like my desire to wake him and demand empathy, I successfully fought off this temptation.

I opened the refrigerator door to get the water pitcher and decided to stick my head inside. I was in almost to my shoulders, enjoying the frosty temperature, when I got the giggles thinking how someone coming upon me, head stuffed into the refrigerator instead of the oven, would say, "Now there's a fat woman who is completely clueless about how a proper kitchen suicide works."

I grabbed the water pitcher and saw a bowl of grapes sitting next to it looking cool and delicious. I pulled the bowl out with the pitcher and set them on the kitchen table. Then I fetched a glass from the dish drainer and brought it to the table, kicking my house shoes off along the way in order to enjoy the feel of cold linoleum against the soles of my bare feet. I sat down at what had been my place at the table for three decades and poured a glass of water. Then I popped a handful of grapes into my mouth and started to feel better.

I loved that time of day, that time just before sunrise. Now that Jimmy, Eric, and Denise were all grown and out of the house, the early hours of the day were no longer linked to slow-passing minutes listening for coughs or cries or, later, teenage feet sneaking in or out of the house. I was free to appreciate the quiet and the way the yellowish-gray light of the rising sun entered the room, turning everything from black and white to color. The journey from Kansas to Oz right in my own kitchen.

That morning, when the daylight came it brought along a visitor, Dora Jackson. I clapped my hand over my mouth to stifle a squeak of surprise when I first caught sight of my mother strolling into the room. She came from the direction of the back door, her short, wide body waddling with an uneven stride from having her left leg badly set by a country doctor when she was a girl.

People used to call us "the twins," Mama and me. The two of us are round women – big in the chest, thick around the waist, and wide across the hips. We share what has often been charitably called an "interesting" face – narrow eyes, jowly cheeks, broad forehead, big but perfect teeth. I grew to be a few inches taller, five foot three. But if you were to look at pictures of us, you'd swear we were the same woman at different ages.

My mother loved the way she looked. She would strut through town on her uneven legs with her big breasts pointing the way forward, and you knew from looking at her that she figured she was just about the hottest thing going. I never came to love my tube-shaped body the way Mama loved hers, but learning to imitate that confident stride of hers was probably the single smartest thing I ever did.

Mama wore her best dress that Sunday morning, the one she usually brought out only for summer weddings and Easter. It was light blue with delicate yellow flowers and green vines embroidered around the collar and the cuffs of the short sleeves. Her hair was pulled up, the way she wore it for special occasions. She sat down across from me at the table and smiled.

Mama gestured with her hand toward the bowl of grapes on the table and said, "Are you outta ice cream, Odette?"

"I'm trying to eat healthier, maybe take off a few pounds this summer," I lied, not wanting to admit that I was thinking of the grapes as a first course.

Mama said, "Dietin' is a waste of energy. Nothin' wrong with having a few extra pounds on you. And you really shouldn't drink so much water at this time of day. You were a bedwetter."

I smiled and, in a childish show of independence, drank more water. Then I tried to change the subject. I asked, "What brings you by, Mama?"

"I just thought I'd come tell you about the fun I had with Earl and Thelma McIntyre. We was up all night goin' over old times and just laughin' up a storm. I had forgot just how funny Thelma was. Lord, that was a good time. And that Thelma can roll a joint like nobody's business, tight little sticks with just enough slack in the roach. I told her—"

"Mama, please," I interrupted. I looked over my shoulder the way I always did when she started talking about that stuff. My mother had been a dedicated marijuana smoker all of her adult life. She said it was for her glaucoma. And if you reminded her that she'd never had glaucoma, she would bend your ear about the virtues of her preventative vision care regimen.

Other than being against the law, the problem with Mama's habit, and the reason I automatically glanced over my shoulder when she started talking about that mess, was that James had worked for the Indiana State Police for thirty-five years. Mama got caught twenty years back buying a bag of dope on the state university campus on the north end of town, and as a favor to James, the head of campus security brought her home instead of arresting her. The campus security chief swore he'd keep it under wraps, but things like that never stay quiet in a little town like Plainview. Everybody knew about it by the next morning. It tickled Mama to no end when her getting busted became a sermon topic at church a week later. But James didn't see the humor in it when it happened, and he never would.

I was eager for Mama to get back on track with the story of her evening with the McIntyres, skipping any illegal parts, because foremost among my mother's many peculiarities was the fact that, for many years, the vast majority of her conversations had been with dead people. Thelma McIntyre, the excellent joint roller, had been dead for twenty-some years. Big Earl, on the other hand, had been just fine one day earlier when I'd seen him at Earl's All-You-Can-Eat buffet. If he had indeed been visiting with Mama, it was not good news for Big Earl.

"So, Big Earl's dead, is he?" I asked.

"I imagine so," she said.

I sat there for a while, not saying anything, just thinking about Big Earl gone from the earth. Mama gazed at me like she was reading my mind and said, "It's all right, baby. Really. He couldn't be happier."

We found out about Mama seeing ghosts at a Thanksgiving supper back in the 1970s. Mama, Daddy, my big brother Rudy, James, Jimmy, Eric, and me – I was pregnant with Denise that fall – were all gathered around the table. In keeping with tradition, I had done all of the cooking. Flowers Mama understood. She had the best garden in town, even before she devoted a plot to her prized marijuana plants. Food Mama never quite got the hang of. The last time Mama attempted to cook a holiday meal, we ended up feeding her black-and-gray glazed ham to the dog and dining on hardboiled eggs. The dog took one bite of Mama's ham and howled for six hours straight. The poor animal never quite recovered. So I became the family chef at age ten and we ended up with the only vegetarian dog in southern Indiana.

That Thanksgiving supper had started off real nice. I had cooked my best feast ever and everybody loved it. We joked and ate and celebrated having Rudy at home. My brother had run off to Indianapolis as soon as he graduated high school, so we didn't see much of him and my boys barely knew their uncle. Everyone was having a good time, except for Mama, who was testy and distracted all afternoon. She got more agitated as the meal went on, mumbling to herself and snapping at anyone who asked her what was wrong. Finally she stood up from the table and hurled the butter dish at an empty corner of the dining room. She shouted, "Goddammit to hell!" – my mother can cuss a blue streak when the inspiration hits her – "Goddammit to hell! I have had just about all I can take from you, Eleanor Roosevelt. Nobody invited you here and it's time for you to go." She shook an accusatory index finger at the corner of the room where the stick of butter, avocado-green plastic butter dish still adhered to it, slid down the wall, leaving a shiny trail like the path of a rectangular snail. Mama looked at the astonished faces around the table and said, "Don't give me that look. She may have been the perfect little lady when she was in the White House – all lace doilies and finger bowls – but since she died, she ain't done nothin' but show up here drunk as a skunk, tryin' to start some shit."

Later, Jackie Onassis came to see Mama, too, but she was much better behaved.

Daddy reacted to Mama's ghosts by trying, unsuccessfully, to persuade her to see a doctor. James and I worried about her in private, but pretended in front of the kids that there was nothing odd about their grandma. Rudy decided that Indianapolis wasn't nearly far enough from the craziness of his family, and he moved to California a month later. He has lived there ever since.

Mama reached across the kitchen table and poked at my arm. "You're gonna get a kick out of this," she said. "You know that woman Earl was livin' with?" "That woman" would be Big Earl's second wife, Minnie. Mama couldn't stand Minnie, and she refused to utter her name or acknowledge her marriage to Big Earl.

"Thelma says that woman set up a fountain in the front room where Thelma and Earl used to have the hi-fi. Can you imagine that? Do you remember how nice that hi-fi was? Best I ever heard. And they saved up for a year to get it. We sure had us some parties to remember in that house."

Mama watched me eat a few more grapes and then said, "Earl said the nicest things about you. He was always so crazy about you, you know. And I don't need to tell you how much he loved James."

James loved Big Earl, too. Earl McIntyre was the closest thing to a father James ever had. James's daddy was a low-down, dirty son of a bitch who ran out on him and his mother when James was barely more than a toddler. James's father stuck around just long enough to leave a few nasty scars and then hightailed it out of town a few steps ahead of the law to inflict more damage somewhere else. The visible scar on James was a half-moon-shaped raised leathery line along his jaw made by a razor slash intended for James's mother. The deeper, invisible scars he left on James, only I saw. Only me and Big Earl.

After James's father ran off, Big Earl and Miss Thelma

took it upon themselves to see that James's mother always had food on the table. When the All-You-Can-Eat, the first black-owned business in downtown Plainview, opened in the mid-1950s and Big Earl couldn't have been making a dime, he hired James's mother as his first employee. And they kept her on the payroll long after emphysema had made it impossible for her to work. More important, the McIntyres kept an eye on James, so he wouldn't end up like his daddy. I'll be forever grateful to them for that.

That's how Big Earl was, a good and strong man who helped other people to get stronger, too. All kinds of folks, and not just black, loved him. You could take a problem to Big Earl and he would sit there and listen to you spill out a lifetime's worth of troubles. He'd nod patiently like it was all new to him, even though he was a man who had seen a lot in his life and had probably heard your particular kind of blues a hundred times over. After you were done, he'd rub his huge hands across the white stubble that stood out against the coal black of his skin and he'd say, "Here's what we're gonna do." And if you had sense, you did whatever it was he said. He was a smart man. Made a little money, kept his dignity, and still managed to live to be old – something a black man his age in southern Indiana shouldn't have been able to do. Something many had tried to do, but failed at.

Now, if Mama's word was to be trusted, Big Earl was dead. But that was a mighty big "if."

Mama said, "What was I talkin' about? Oh yeah, the fountain. Thelma said the fountain in her front room was six feet tall, if it was an inch. And it was made up to look like a naked white girl pouring water out of a pitcher onto the head of another naked white girl. Who comes up with that kind of stuff?"

I poured another glass of water, and thought. Mama was often wrong when it came to her perceptions of the world, physical or ghostly. And she'd said many times herself that ghosts could be tricksters. The whole thing about Big Earl being dead could have been a prank played on Mama by a tipsy, belligerent Eleanor Roosevelt. I decided to put it out of my mind until later when we'd meet our friends for our standing after-church dinner date. We were gathering that Sunday, as we always did, at the All-You-Can-Eat. Little Earl and his wife, Erma Mae, had taken over running the restaurant several years back, but Big Earl still came in nearly every day to help out his son and daughter-in-law. One way or another, I'd have my answer come evening.

Mama asked, "So why are you up drinkin' all this water at this hour?"

"I woke up hot and needed to cool down," I said, taking another swig. "Hot flash."

"Hot flash? I thought you were done with the change."

"I thought so, too, but I guess I'm still changing."

"Well, you might wanna get that checked out. You don't wanna change too much. Your aunt Marjorie started changin' and kept it up till she changed into a man."

"Oh, she did not and you know it."

"Okay, maybe she didn't switch all the way over to a man, but Marjorie grew a mustache, shaved her head, and took to wearin' overalls to church. I'm not sayin' the look didn't suit her; I'm just sayin' you can draw a straight line between her first hot flash and that bar fight she died in."

I ate a grape and said, "Point taken."

We sat in silence, me thinking about Big Earl in spite of telling myself I wouldn't, and Mama thinking about God knows what. She stood up and walked to the window that looked out onto the side yard. She said, "It's gonna be a truly beautiful Sunday morning. I love it hot. You should get some rest before you go to church." She turned away from the window and said, talking to me like she used to when I was a kid, "Go on to bed now, git."

I obeyed. I put my glass in the sink and replaced the half-empty bowl of grapes and the water pitcher in the fridge and headed back toward my bedroom. I turned around and said, "Say hi to Daddy for me."

But Mama had already slipped out the back door. Through the window, I saw her slowly making her way through my sorry excuse for a garden. She stopped and shook her head with disapproval at the stunted stalks, insect-chewed vegetables, and pale blooms that made up my pitiful little plots. I knew what I would hear about on her next visit.

Back in the bedroom, I climbed into the bed and squeezed in close to my husband. I propped myself up on one elbow, leaned over James, and kissed the rough scar on his jaw. He grunted, but didn't wake up. I lay back down and pressed myself against his back. Then I reached around and brought my hand to rest on James's stomach. Squeezed against my man in the center of our king-size bed, I fell asleep listening to the rhythm of his breathing.

Throughout the year that followed, I thought about that Sunday morning and how Mama's visit had cooled me down and cheered me. Even during the worst of the troubles that came later, I smiled whenever I recalled that visit and how sweet it had been for her to come by, looking all done up in that cute sky-blue dress I hadn't seen in the six years since we buried her in it.

Chapter 2

I was born in a sycamore tree. That was fifty-five years ago, and it made me a bit of a local celebrity. My celebrity status was brief, though. Two baby girls, later my best friends, came along within months of me in ways that made my sycamore tree entrance seem less astonishing. I only mention the tree because I have been told all of my life that it explains how I ended up the way I am – brave and strong according to those who like me, mannish and pigheaded to those who don't. Also, it probably explains why, after the initial jolt passed, I wasn't much troubled when my dead mother showed up for a chat.

I started out life in that sycamore because my mother went to see a witch. Mama was smart and tough. She worked hard every day of her life right up until she dropped dead from a stroke while she was winding up to throw a rock at a squirrel that was digging up bulbs in her showplace of a garden. All of Mama's toughness had evaporated, though, when she found herself halfway through the tenth month of her pregnancy, wondering if it would ever end. Seven years earlier, Rudy had been born right on schedule. But three lost babies followed my brother, none of them managing to remain inside my mother's womb for longer than a few months. Now I had come along and refused to leave.

Before she went to see the witch, Mama tried all kinds of things her country relatives told her to do to get the baby to come. My grandmother advised her to eat hot peppers with every meal, claiming that the heat would drive the baby out. Mama did it for three days and ended up with indigestion so severe that she was fooled twice into thinking she was in labor. Two times, she and Daddy went to the colored hospital in Evansville, and both times she came home with no baby.

My mother's sister whispered to her that the only way to get the baby out was to have sex. Aunt Marjorie said, "That's how it got there, Dora. And that's the only sure way to get it out."

Mama liked the sex idea, if only just to pass the time while waiting, but Daddy was less than enthusiastic. She was twice his weight even before her pregnancy, and when she straddled him in his sleep one night demanding satisfaction, the terrified look in his eyes as she hovered over him made her back down from the sex solution and look to sorcery instead.

Like I said, that was 1950, and back then a fair number of people in Plainview, black and white, consulted a witch from time to time. Some still do, but nowadays it's only the poorest and most superstitious of folks, mostly the ones who live in the little Appalachian clusters outside of town, who will admit to it.

Mama went to the witch expecting a potion or a poultice – poultices were big among witches – but what she got instead were instructions. The witch told her that if she climbed up into the branches of a sycamore tree at straight-up noon and sang her favorite hymn, the baby would come.

Witches were like that. They almost always mixed in a touch of something approved by the Baptist church – a prayer, a spiritual, or a chant warning about the godless-ness of Lutherans – so people could go to a witch and not have to worry that they'd pay for it down the line with their immortal souls. It absolved the clients' guilt and kept the preachers off the witches' backs.

So, on a windy afternoon, my mother hauled a rickety old ladder out to a sycamore tree by the woods behind the house. Mama propped her ladder against the tree and climbed up. Then she nestled herself in the crook of two branches as comfortably as was possible considering her condition and began to sing.

Mama used to joke that if she had chosen something more sedate, something along the lines of "Mary, Don't You Weep" or "Calvary," she might not have given birth to such a peculiar daughter. But she dug her teeth into "Jesus Is a Rock" and swayed and kicked her feet with that good gospel spirit until she knocked over the ladder and couldn't get back down. I was born at one o'clock and spent the rest of the afternoon in the sycamore tree until my father rescued us when he got home from his shop at six. They named me Odette Breeze Jackson, in honor of my being born in the open air.

As it often happened when a child was born under unusual circumstances, old folks who claimed that they'd been schooled in the wisdom of the ancestors felt called upon to use the occasion to issue dire warnings. My grandma led the chorus in forecasting a dreary future for me. The way she explained it, if a baby was born off of the ground, that child was born without its first natural fear, the fear of falling. That set off a horrible chain reaction resulting in the child's being cursed with a life of fearlessness. She said a fearless boy had some hope of growing up to be a hero, but a fearless girl would more than likely be a reckless fool. My mother also accepted this as fact, although she leaned more toward the notion that I might become a hero. It should be remembered, of course, that Mama was a grown woman who thought climbing a tree in her tenth month of pregnancy was a good idea. Her judgment had to be looked at with suspicion.

Nearly everyone, it seemed to me, believed that coming into the world in any manner that could be seen as out of the ordinary was a bad omen. People never said, "Congratulations on managing to deliver a healthy baby while you were stuck in that rowboat in the middle of the lake." They just shook their heads and whispered to each other that the child would surely drown one day. No one ever said, "Aren't you a brave little thing, having your baby all alone in a chicken coop." They just said that the child would turn out to have bird shit for brains and then went on to treat the child that way even if the kid was clearly a tiny genius. Like the doomed child born on the water and the dummy arriving among fowl, I was born in a sycamore tree and would never have the good sense to know when to run scared.

Not knowing any better, I listened to what I was told about myself and grew up convinced I was a little brown warrior. I stomped my way through life like I was the Queen of the Amazons. I got in fights with grown men who were twice as big as and ten times meaner than me. I did things that got me talked about pretty bad and then went back and did them again. And that morning I first saw my dead mother in my kitchen, I accepted that I had inherited a strange legacy and visited with her over a bowl of grapes instead of screaming and heading for the hills.

I know the truth about myself, though. I have never been fearless. If I ever believed such a thing, motherhood banished that myth but quick. Still, whenever logic told me it was time to run, a little voice whispered in my ear, "You were born in a sycamore tree." And, for good or ill, the sound of that voice always made me stand my ground.

Chapter 3

Clarice and Richmond Baker claimed seats at opposite ends of the window table at Earl's All-You-Can-Eat and waited for their four friends to arrive. The restaurant was an easy walk from Calvary Baptist and they were always first to show up for after-church supper. Odette and James Henry's little country church, Holy Family Baptist, was farthest from the All-You-Can-Eat, but James was a fast driver and, being a cop, unafraid of getting speeding tickets. So they usually arrived next. Barbara Jean and Lester Maxberry were members of grand First Baptist, the rich people's church. It looked down on Plainview from its perch on Main Street and was closest to the restaurant, but Lester was twenty-five years older than the rest of the group and he often moved slowly.

Clarice caught her reflection in the window glass and imagined that she and Richmond must resemble a luminous peacock and his drab mate. She was hidden, neck to kneecaps, beneath a modest, well-tailored beige linen dress. Richmond, leaning back in his chair and waving hello to friends seated at other tables around the room, demanded attention in the pale gray summer suit Clarice had set out for him the night before along with his favorite shirt, a cotton button-down that was the vivid ultramarine of aquarium rocks.

He had always worn bold colors. Richmond had such a Ken-doll handsomeness about him that the women in his life, first his mother and then Clarice, couldn't resist the urge to dress him in bright hues and show him off. On the occasion of Richmond's first date with Clarice, his mother had adorned her teenage son in a peach jacket with white rope trim ornamenting the lapels. A getup like that would have gotten any other boy in town ridiculed and called a sissy – it was still the 1960s, after all. But Richmond Baker sauntered up Clarice's front walk and managed to make that outfit look as masculine as a rack of antlers. Clarice often pictured that loose, powerful way he walked back then before the surgeries stiffened him. It was as if he were constructed entirely of lean muscle strung together with taut rubber bands.

By coincidence, Clarice had chosen a peach skirt for that first date. Her skirt matched Richmond's prissy jacket so perfectly that everyone who saw them out on the town later assumed they had planned it that way. Clarice and her mother had peeked through the curtains and watched him step onto the front porch. Her mother, who was as excited as Clarice was, had dug her fingers into Clarice's arm until her daughter pulled away from her. All the while, her mother had gushed that their matching ensembles were a sign Clarice and Richmond were made for each other.

Clarice, though, had already seen all the signs she needed. Young Richmond had a handsome, almost pretty face with a small, well-shaped mouth and long eyelashes.

He had a football scholarship waiting for him at the university across town. He was a preacher's son, his father having been the pastor of their church before moving on to a larger congregation just across the state line in Louisville. And he had those beautiful hands.

She had been in awe of his hands long before they brought him glory for palming a football in high school, college, and a professional career that had lasted only one season.

By the time he was eleven years old, Richmond was using his already large paws to show off for the girls by pulling walnuts from the low-hanging branches of the trees that lined the streets between the schoolyard and their neighborhood. He would make a grunting, grimacing production of crushing the nuts between his palms until he tired of his solo act and joined in with the other boys who ran in his pack, tossing the walnuts at the girls as they ran home squealing and laughing.

The children had named the walnut trees "time bomb trees" because when the nuts were past their prime they turned black and made a quiet ticking sound on hot days. Years later, she often thought it was fitting that her earliest recollection of the boy who would become her husband was a memory of him lobbing time bombs in her direction.

Lit by the afternoon sun from the window at the All-You-Can-Eat, Richmond Baker still looked like a square-jawed young football hero. But Clarice was doing her best not to look his way at all. Every time she glanced at her husband, she thought back to the hours she had sat up worrying until he finally staggered in at 3:57 that morning. The sight of him brought to mind those horrible, slow-passing minutes of waiting and then the time spent lying in bed beside him after he finally got home, pretending to sleep and wondering whether she possessed sufficient upper-body strength to smother him with his pillow.

At breakfast, he had dragged himself into the kitchen, scratched his private parts, and told her a tale that she knew was a lie. It was the old reliable story of having to work late and finding that every phone within a ten-mile radius was broken. For the new millennium, he had updated his excuse to include cellular phones mysteriously losing their signals. He deserved some credit for keeping up with the times, she thought. After he told his lie, he had sat down at the kitchen table, blown a kiss in his wife's direction, and tucked himself into the breakfast she had prepared for him, attacking it as if he hadn't eaten a meal in weeks. Screwing around, Clarice thought, must stimulate the appetite.

Before church that morning, Clarice had mulled over her situation and decided that her problem was that she had gotten out of the habit of ignoring Richmond's little lapses; he had been on such good behavior for the past couple of years. She figured that if she just avoided looking at Richmond through breakfast, morning service, and maybe during the walk to Earl's, she could relocate that old wall in her brain she used to hide behind at times like this. Then she'd soon be back to merrily pretending things were just fine, as she had done for decades. She had gazed at the kitchen floor through breakfast. She had stared at the stained-glass windows during church. She counted the clouds in the sky and the cracks in the sidewalk on the way to the All-You-Can-Eat. But the remedy didn't work. The throbbing at her temples that bloomed each time she watched Richmond's pretty, lying mouth spread into a grin told her that she needed more time before she could step back into the old routine, the way her husband apparently had.

Clarice heard a deep male voice whisper, "Hey there, gorgeous." She looked to her right and saw that Ramsey Abrams had slithered up beside her. He placed one hand on the table and the other on the back of her chair, and then he leaned in until his face was just inches away from hers.

Ramsey had been Richmond's number one running buddy for years, the two of them continuing to sow their wild oats together long after they were married and the fathers of several children between them. With his nose nearly touching hers, Clarice could see that the whites of Ramsey's eyes were laced with bright red veins. She detected the odor of stale rum on his breath.

She began to create a picture in her head of how the previous evening had started. Richmond would have been in his office at the university where he and Ramsey both worked as recruiters for the football team. Ramsey shuffled in and said something along the lines of "Come on, Richmond. Just join me for a quick drink. I'll have you home by ten. You can stay out till ten, can't you? Your woman ain't got that tight a hold on your balls, does she?"

She had no real evidence that he had been the instigator of Richmond's night out, and she knew Richmond was perfectly capable of getting into mischief all on his own.

Still, Clarice itched to slap Ramsey's stupid face and tell him to get back across the room to the table where his son Clifton – the son who had been in and out of jail since he was thirteen, not the other son who sniffed airplane glue and touched himself inappropriately in women's shoe stores – and Ramsey's bucktoothed wife, Florence, sat glaring at each other.

She said, "Ramsey, you keep sweet-talking me like that and I'm going to have to try and steal you away from Florence."

He laughed. "Baby, I sure won't stop you from trying. Just don't tell Richmond."

Clarice said, "Ramsey, you are so naughty," and she slapped his hand in that way that men like him interpreted as *Please do go on, you sexy bad boy.* Then he leaned in closer and kissed her on the cheek. She let loose a kind of girlish squeal, the sound of which made her want to kick herself. No, not only herself, but her mother, too, for drumming this business of responding to male attention with adolescent giddiness so firmly into her head that it was automatic now.

She delivered another slap to Ramsey's hand. This time, she accidentally allowed her true feelings about him to creep into her gesture. He let out a very sincere "Ouch!" and snatched his hand away before walking toward Richmond's end of the table. As she watched Ramsey rubbing his knuckles, her headache eased just a bit.

Ramsey pulled a chair up close to Richmond and the two of them started whispering in each other's ears, stopping occasionally to bellow with laughter. Clarice imagined the content of the conversation passing between them and her thoughts turned violent again. She picked up her fork from the place setting, twirled it like a cheerleader's baton with her left thumb and forefinger, and thought about the sense of fulfillment she would gain if she walked to the other end of the table and plunged that fork into Richmond's forehead. She pictured the look of amazement that would spread over his face as she grabbed hold of his jaw to get better leverage, and then twisted the fork 180 degrees counterclockwise. That fantasy felt so dangerously good that she forced herself to put the fork back down on the table. She told herself, again, to look away.

Her gaze was drawn to the center of the table then, and she noticed the new tablecloth for the first time. The restaurant, apparently, had a new logo. At the center of the tablecloth, and all the others in the room, a painted wreath of fruits and vegetables spelled out "All-You-Can-Eat." Inside the circle of produce was a pair of shiny red lips with a bright pink tongue protruding from them.

Clarice could see Little Earl's tacky fingerprints all over this. He had inherited his father's kind disposition, but not much of his good taste. And she suspected that, even though the place was no longer legally his, Big Earl wasn't going to be happy with this innovation. Those nasty-looking lips and fruits and vegetables – particularly the suggestive cherry and cucumbers that spelled "All" – were going to have the more conservative patrons in an uproar. Clarice was thankful that her pastor wasn't a regular customer; she could easily imagine him calling for a boycott.

She couldn't believe she hadn't noticed the new table-cloths the instant she walked in. They definitely hadn't been there a day earlier when she had eaten lunch at this same table with Odette and Barbara Jean. She was so familiar with the All-You-Can-Eat, and it had changed so little over the years, that she could usually tell if one chair was out of place. This was how much Richmond had put her off her game.

Clarice and her friends had been meeting at the window table at Earl's for almost forty years – since right about the time they were nicknamed the Supremes. Little Earl had wild crushes on all three of them back then, and he had tried his best to seduce them with free Cokes and chicken wings. Clarice was sure that, if he had been a little more persistent, it would have eventually worked on Odette. That girl was always hungry. Even when she was a child, Odette ate like a grown man.

Clarice's first memory of Odette was of watching her stuff fistfuls of candy into her mouth and then wipe her sticky hands on her dress in kindergarten. Odette always wore hideous homemade dresses with crooked seams and mismatched patterns. Clarice still remembered their first conversation. Since Odette's maiden name was Jackson and Clarice's was Jordan, alphabetical order demanded that they sit next to each other throughout most of their education. Odette had reached over from her desk and passed Clarice a piece of taffy in class one day. Clarice said to her, "That's the ugliest dress in the whole world."

Odette replied, "My grandmama made it for me. She's real good at sewin', but she's blind." She popped another piece of candy into her mouth and added, "This ain't the ugliest dress in the world. I'm gonna wear that one tomorrow."

And she did. And it was. And they'd been friends ever since.

Little Earl's wife, Erma Mae, walked, ass first, through the swinging doors that led from the kitchen, carrying a tray of food. Erma Mae had the largest head Clarice had ever seen on a woman. When she was in high school, that huge, round head, coupled with her tall, bony body and flat chest, earned her the nickname Lollipop. Marriage to Little Earl, and access to all that good free food, had thickened her out from her hips on down, so the nickname hadn't stuck. Putting on all that extra weight was probably not the healthiest thing for her, but it did help to balance out that giant head, which Clarice supposed must bring Erma Mae some solace.

Erma Mae placed the tray on the buffet table and then plopped down on one of the two wooden stools next to the gleaming stainless-steel steam tables from which she and her husband oversaw their domain every day. She made eye contact with Clarice after she settled onto her stool, and she waved at her.

When Clarice waved back, Erma Mae stood and performed a little pirouette to display her new apron, which, like the tablecloths, had that awful lips logo on it. Clarice mouthed, "I love it," and thought, *Hope you're watching, Richmond. This is how you tell a convincing lie.*

Erma Mae yelled, "Belinda!" and her daughter rushed in from the kitchen. Erma Mae pointed toward Clarice and Richmond, and Belinda picked up a pitcher of iced tea and headed to their table. Clarice was fond of Belinda. She was a darling girl, and smart, too. She had won enough scholarship money to pay for a full ride at the university.

Unfortunately, she was also the mirror image of her big-headed mother at that age. If you squinted as she walked toward you, you'd swear a brown party balloon was floating your way.

After Belinda poured Richmond's tea, she accidentally nudged his glass with the pitcher, causing the glass to fall to the floor. She let out a yelp and said she was sorry. Then she started going on about how clumsy she was. Belinda pulled a kitchen rag from her apron pocket and moved to wipe up the spill, but Richmond stopped her. "And risk ruining that fancy new apron? I wouldn't be able to live with myself," he said as he took the rag from her. He dropped to his knees to clean up the mess. Belinda continued apologizing as he worked, and she poured him another tea using a glass taken from one of the other place settings at the table.

Watching Richmond kneel in his best summer suit at the feet of that awkward, plain girl just to make her feel good caused Clarice's bad memories of the previous night and morning to recede a little. That was Richmond. About the time she built up a good head of steam thinking of the many ways he had disappointed her, he'd go and remind her of what she loved about him. She watched him swirl that rag over the rutted oak floor and couldn't help but think of how those same wonderful hands had comforted their children and changed as many, if not more, of their diapers as hers had. Those hands had also spoon-fed her father – three times a day, every day – for the last weeks of her father's life, when he was too frail to lift a spoon and too proud to allow Clarice or her mother to feed him. *That* Richmond, the kind and selfless one, was the only

Richmond she had seen for two years. But the other Richmond, the one who lied and cheated, had reappeared, and no number of kind words or gallant gestures could erase him from her mind.

Belinda left, carrying the tea-soaked cloth and still looking flustered, but grinning. Richmond returned to his chair and gulped from his glass. Clarice tasted her tea and discovered that it was so sweet she couldn't stand more than a sip. Richmond, who was diabetic, had no business drinking any of it. But when she looked his way, she saw that Richmond was not only guzzling the sweet tea, he was using it to wash down a piece of pecan pie that someone, probably that damn Ramsey Abrams, had slipped to him.

This was part of the dance they did each Sunday. Richmond sneaked fatty, sugary treats that were off his diet and Clarice played the role of the frustrated mother, running to the other end of the table to pinch his ear and demand that he hand it over to her. The game always ended with Richmond batting those long lashes of his at her until she permitted him a spoonful of whatever he was sneaking. Then she would return to her chair, theatrically rolling her eyes about what an ill-disciplined boy her Richmond was.

But Clarice was in no mood to play along with him this time. She watched him chew the pie and wash it down with sweet tea, and she kept her mouth firmly shut. She told herself that this time she wasn't going to lift a finger to stop him. He could put himself in the hospital again, if he wanted to. If he didn't care, why should she?

Old habits evolve into reflexes, though, and Clarice found that she couldn't stop herself. She raised her tea glass high in the air with her right hand and then tapped it with the nail of her left ring finger to get his attention. She said, "Richmond, too sweet."

He pushed his lower lip out and unleashed the sad eyes, but he slid his glass of tea and the small plate containing the pie away from his place setting. Then, performing his part of their little ritual to perfection, he grabbed his fork and took one more quick bite of the pie. Then he winked at her.

Clarice had learned her husband was a diabetic two years earlier when she received a phone call from the hospital saying that he had been found in his university office in a coma and might not make it. He was in intensive care for weeks, and for months afterward he was nearly helpless – no feeling in his feet, no strength in his beautiful hands. When she finally got him home, she prayed, bullied, sweet-talked, and seduced, anything to get Richmond well again.

She succeeded magnificently. He was up and about far sooner than his doctors had anticipated. And when he recovered, he expressed his gratitude for the care she had given him to anyone who would listen. He would actually stop strangers on the street and say, "This woman saved my life; made me a new man."

And Richmond *was* a new man. For the first time in their marriage he was actually the husband Clarice had always pretended he was. All the love she had for him, the affection that had felt so inconvenient for so long, suddenly didn't seem misplaced. It was a second chance at life, a wonderful rebirth for both of them.

It lasted two years. Two fine years.

A petite woman in a knee-length tan dress and black patent leather pumps walked past Clarice and strode up to Richmond. She leaned over to say something into his ear, giving Clarice and half the dining room a view of her tiny backside.

The vise around Clarice's forehead tightened again. There she is, Clarice thought, the reason Richmond didn't make it home until nearly sunrise.

With her eyeglasses stowed away in her purse, Clarice couldn't identify the woman whispering to her husband. She reached to retrieve her glasses, but stopped herself. The only people who saw her bespectacled with any regularity were her piano students. That concession to middle age had come only after she had detected a slight decline in the general level of her students' playing that was caused, she came to realize, by her inability to see subtle technical lapses – an intermittently flattened finger, a wrist that dipped at just the wrong moment, a transient raised shoulder. Few people even knew that Clarice owned glasses, and she certainly wasn't about to give Richmond's latest partner in fornication the pleasure of seeing her looking matronly. Not today.

Clarice leaned back, hoping that a little more distance would bring the woman into better focus. She teetered on the rear legs of her chair until she felt that she was on the verge of toppling over backwards. Only the thought of Richmond's current bit on the side laughing at her as she lay with her back on the floor and her best Sunday pumps pointing at the ceiling forced Clarice to sit up straight again.

Attempting not to squint so blatantly that Richmond

and the stranger might notice, Clarice strained to see the other end of the table. Whoever the woman was, Richmond responded to her with a wide smile that displayed even, capped teeth that were the eye-straining white of new aluminum siding and took years off his face.

Right then, Clarice felt something crack inside of her. The look of admiration on Richmond's face as he flirted, right in front of her, with this skinny tramp in her polyester dress was just too damn much to take. Clarice had gone decades without making scenes, no matter how great the provocation. But now, at their window table at the All-You-Can-Eat, in front of some of their oldest friends, she was primed to leap into uncharted territory.

Before she had time to think about what she was doing, Clarice stood from her chair and shouted, "Richmond!" loud enough that the restaurant grew quieter as the people at the surrounding tables stopped their conversations to look her way. But her chance to let thirty-five years of pent-up outrage come flooding out evaporated when the woman whispering to Richmond turned in her direction and Clarice saw that it was Carmel Handy. She was good-looking, nicely shaped, well-groomed, and at least ninety years old. The schoolboy smile Clarice had seen on her husband's face had been just that. They'd both had Miss Carmel as their ninth grade English teacher.

That her prime suspect turned out to be Miss Carmel was, Clarice had to admit, one hell of an ironic twist. Carmel Handy was, at that time, Clarice's personal hero because of the local legend about her marriage.

The tale people told was that William Handy once took off on a weeklong whoring excursion. When he got home, Miss Carmel confronted him and told him the only excuse he could possibly have for disappearing like that was that he must have forgotten where he lived. So she recited their address, 10 Pine Street, aloud. And, to make it memorable, she punctuated the telling with three blows to Mr Handy's head with a cast-iron skillet. She didn't kill him, but she changed him from Big Bad Bill to Sweet William overnight.

That had happened before Clarice was born, if it happened at all. Rumor had a way of becoming permanently entangled with fact in small towns like Plainview. But, to this day, angry wives in southern Indiana evoke the legend of "the Skillet Lady" whenever they want to get their husbands' full attention.

Richmond and Miss Carmel both stared at Clarice, waiting for her to explain her outburst. She stared back at them, trying to come up with words. But no words would form. All she could think about was how satisfying it must have been for Miss Carmel to remind her no-count husband where he lived by clobbering him on the head once for each of the three syllables of their address. Since Richmond and Clarice lived at 1722 Prendergast Boulevard, she assumed that her satisfaction would be four times sweeter.

As she had so many times in the past, Odette came riding to Clarice's rescue. Through the window, Clarice saw James and Odette's car squeezing into a small space directly across the street, in front of the two-story white clapboard house Big Earl had moved his young family into not long after he opened the All-You-Can-Eat.

Clarice lowered herself into her chair and said, "Hi,

Miss Carmel, how are you, dear?" Then, to Richmond, "Honey, Odette and James are here."

Miss Carmel said hello to Clarice and then went back to chatting with Richmond, who was still teacher's pet after forty-three years. The customers seated nearby stopped staring and resumed their conversations when they saw that nothing exciting was going to happen.

For reasons Clarice could never understand, Odette and James insisted upon traveling around town in a microscopic ten-year-old Honda when James had full access to a much roomier and more presentable state police department vehicle. It looked even worse now because Odette had packed on at least ten more pounds that year; and that was on top of the extra fifty she'd been carrying since the Nixon years. The sight of them extricating themselves from that tiny car – Odette, as round as a berry and dressed in one of those shapeless muumuus she favored, and James, skeletal and over six feet tall – was such a spectacle that Clarice couldn't help but imagine she was taking in a circus act.

As she watched Odette and James walk toward the All-You-Can-Eat, Clarice asked herself how on earth she had ended up being the one Supreme who turned into her mother. Odette might look like Dora Jackson, but she was as different as she could be from her mother, who had always scared Clarice a bit with her talk of ghosts and her countrified brusqueness. And with all of her wealth, civic-mindedness, and charitable deeds, Barbara Jean was about as far as she could get from living the sad, desperate life her mother had lived.

Clarice had been the one to follow her mother's

example. She had become a pillar of her church, striving for biblical perfection at all costs. When her children came, first Ricky, then Abe, and, finally, the twins, Carolyn and Carl, Clarice had made sure that they were the cleanest, best-dressed, and most polite children in town. She had acted the part of a lady, even when every last particle of her being yearned to spit, curse, and kill. And she had grown up and married her father.

Chapter 4

Clarice Jordan Baker was the first black child born at University Hospital. It was reported in black newspapers as far away as Los Angeles. Clarice's mother, Beatrice Jordan, encased the news clippings of the glad tidings in ornate gold frames and placed them strategically around her house. No guest could sit at the Jordans' dining table or use their toilet without being aware that the family had once made history. The clipping over the mantel in the living room was snipped from the front page of the *Indianapolis Recorder.* The caption beneath the photo read "The New Negro Family." The article about Clarice's birth heralded the arrival of the "new Negro family of the desegregated 1950s." Her father, attorney Abraham Jordan, was missing from the picture.

Beatrice worked as a nursing assistant at University Hospital. She got it into her head one day that her child would be born there, instead of at the colored hospital an hour away in Evansville where everyone in Leaning Tree had their babies. Fortunately for her, this wild idea coincided with the arrival of Dr Samuel Snow, who had come to Indiana State University at Plainview from New York City that year to preside over the ob-gyn department. Dr Snow let it be known when he came to the hospital that, under his leadership, access to the department would no longer be restricted by race. The university agreed to his demand, believing he would get over that bit of New York-style eccentricity once he got settled in southern Indiana and gained an appreciation for how things worked there. But Dr Snow did not change his mind, and Beatrice, on the job well into her pregnancy, arranged to repeatedly waddle across his path and allow him to believe he had handpicked her – instead of the other way around – for the honor of making history at University Hospital.

In Beatrice's retelling, the minor complications of Clarice's birth were elevated to terrifying hours during which she and her baby balanced on a knife's edge between survival and doom. When Beatrice sensed in her daughter some resistance to acknowledging her mother's wisdom, she trotted out the tale of how her solid judgment was the only reason the two of them hadn't died in a substandard Evansville clinic. Clarice heard the story so often in her childhood that it became as familiar to her as "Cinderella" or "The Pied Piper." When relating the long version of the ordeal she suffered giving Clarice life, Beatrice often employed overripe fruit as stage props. For the short version, she simply pressed the back of her hand to her forehead and whispered, "It was a horror show."

Freshly snatched from death's door or not, an hour after Clarice was born her mother was fully made up, coiffed, dressed in a satin bed coat, and propped up in her hospital bed, ready for the photographers who had gathered to snap pictures of the inspirational middle-class colored family. But Mr Jordan couldn't be found. By the time he was located, sharing an intimate moment with one of the hospital cleaning ladies in a supply closet, the photographers had taken their snapshots and gone. That cleaning lady may or may not have been the woman who gave him the syphilis he passed on to his wife, sterilizing her and ensuring that Clarice would be an only child; Abraham was never quite certain.

And so it went, from the time Clarice was old enough to understand what was what until her father was too sick to get into trouble. Abraham Jordan cheated and lied. Beatrice prayed, consulted with her pastor, prayed again, and then accepted each deception with a smile. Clarice watched and learned.

Unlike her mother, who had been taken by surprise, Clarice had received fair warning about Richmond. Just before Clarice's marriage, Odette had a frank talk with her friend that forced Clarice to open her eyes and see just how much Richmond had in common with Abraham Jordan. Clarice had nearly called off the wedding, but, because she loved Richmond so, she chose to rely upon the counsel of her mother and the same pastor whose guidance would lead Beatrice into a life consumed by bitterness. Clarice had weighed her options and – like a fool, she later saw – she had decided to make a deal with Richmond that allowed her to clamp her eyes shut again. The deal was, so long as Richmond didn't embarrass her by being indiscreet the way her father had been, she would accept him as he was and go on as if everything were perfect.

They both stuck by the terms of their agreement, but Clarice's definition of indiscretion shifted over the years. At first, she told herself she could handle his missteps if he was at home and in bed beside her at a decent hour every night. But that didn't even make it through their first year. So she decided late nights were okay, as long as no strange women called the house. When she gave up on that, she settled for not being confronted with physical evidence.

As it turned out, Richmond was good about leaving no evidence. Clarice never had to scrub lipstick stains from his shorts or brush face powder from his lapels. She never contracted any diseases. And unlike her father, who had cast his seed around with the abandon of malfunctioning farm equipment, Richmond was careful. Clarice was never greeted at her front door by a younger woman clutching the hand of a child who had Richmond's pretty mouth.

That Sunday afternoon at the All-You-Can-Eat, between the ex-ample of her parents and the years she had spent honoring her part of her deal with Richmond, Clarice told herself that, given time, she could find her way back to that blissful state of mind in which the absence of sexually transmitted diseases and not having bastard children dropped off at her door were sufficient proof of her husband's love and respect. She was wrong.

Chapter 5

I did my best not to dwell on my sunrise conversation with Mama, but it was on my mind all through morning service and during the drive to the All-You-Can-Eat. When we got to the restaurant, I tried not to be obvious about it as I studied Big Earl's house, searching for signs of unusual activity. But everything was quiet. There were no cars in the driveway except Big Earl's Buick. No somber-faced men stood smoking on the front porch. No one was visible through the parted living room drapes.

Inside the restaurant, I scanned the room for Big Earl. It was his habit to spend Sundays zigzagging his way between the tables, chatting with the customers. I didn't see him, so I turned toward the buffet to look for Little Earl or Erma Mae. I caught sight of Erma Mae sliding off of her stool and walking into the kitchen. I decided to take her presence and the calm at the house across the street as good signs about Big Earl's well-being. Feeling optimistic and a little annoyed with Mama for getting me all riled up with her ghostly insider information, I followed James to our table.

Richmond was waving goodbye to Carmel Handy and Clarice sat staring at the cutlery with a peculiar look on her face when we joined them. James took a seat next to

Richmond and the two of them jumped right into a conversation. I didn't have to listen in to know what they were saying. They had been discussing the same two topics since 1972. They either talked about football or boxing. Specifically, they talked about famous athletes of the past and how they might fare against famous athletes of the present. When Lester arrived, the conversation would get heated. Each week he loudly declared that Joe Louis, the Brown Bomber, could have taken on Ali and Tyson together, and single-handedly whupped an entire football team. If Richmond or James disagreed with him, Lester would grow frustrated and begin to bang his walking stick against the nearest table leg, insisting that his age and wisdom made him the better judge.

Clarice perched on the edge of her chair, showing off her best charm school posture and wearing an expression that was supposed to be a smile. Clarice has a long, handsome face with lovely, round eyes and a wide, nicely shaped mouth. But that day her lower jaw was pushed forward, her eyes were squinted, and her lips were pressed together like she was trying hard to keep something in. I hadn't seen that face in a while, but I knew it well. And I had a good idea what its return meant. I had to fight to keep myself from going down to the other end of the table and slapping the shit out of Richmond. But it was none of my business. And I knew from experience that my interference would not be appreciated.

Before she married Richmond, I went to Clarice and told her some things that I thought she should know about her fiancé. No rumors, no guesses. I sat with my oldest friend on the couch in her parents' living room and described seeing Richmond late the night before kissing a woman who lived around the block from me and seeing his car still parked in front of her house that morning. It hurt me to say it, loving Clarice like I do. But Clarice used to claim that, when it came to matters of men, she wanted her friends to give her the cold and honest truth, even if it was painful. I was young then, just twenty-one, and I didn't understand yet that nearly all of the women who make that claim are lying.

Clarice being Clarice, she took my news about Richmond with such sweet grace and calm that I didn't realize I'd been relieved of my matron of honor duties and thrown out of her house until I was standing on her front porch with the door bumping against my ass. But the next day she was at my house holding an armful of bride magazines, acting like our conversation had never happened. I was her matron of honor after all, and I never said another word to her about any of Richmond's shenanigans from then on.

After we got through our kisses and hellos, I asked Clarice, "Seen Big Earl today?"

She said, "No, why do you ask?"

"No reason. He was just on my mind," I said, which was the truth, if not the whole truth.

Clarice said, "I'm sure he'll be in pretty soon. That's a man who truly does not understand the idea of retirement. Besides, I get the feeling he prefers being here on Sundays since *she* doesn't work on the Sabbath."

Clarice nodded toward the only vacant table in the room. It sat in a back corner and was covered with a shiny gold tablecloth that was decorated with silver stars and moons and symbols of the zodiac. At the center of the table sat a stack of tarot cards and a crystal ball the size of a large cantaloupe. A forty-year-old framed eight-by-ten photograph showing Minnie McIntyre decked out in sequins and feathers acting as a magician's assistant to her first husband, Charlemagne the Magnificent, was propped up behind the tarot cards and crystal ball. From that table in the back of the All-You-Can-Eat, Minnie operated her fortune-telling business. It was her claim that, since his death, Charlemagne had reversed their roles and was now working as her assistant and guide to the spirit world.

In spite of my own encounter with a traveler from the afterlife just that morning, I didn't believe for a second that Minnie had any such connections. It wasn't just that her predictions were famous for being way off; I knew just how inaccurate the dead could be from years of hearing Mama complain about how her ghosts often fed her a line of crap. The thing with Minnie was that her predictions almost always had a nasty edge to them that made it seem like she was more interested in delivering insults disguised as prophecies and manipulating her naïve customers than she was in communing with the other side.

Inaccurate and ornery as she was, Minnie had been in business for years and still had a steady stream of customers, many of whom were the sort of people you'd think would know better. Clarice doesn't like to admit it, but she was once one of those customers.

In a fit of bridal jitters, Clarice went to Minnie for a tarot reading the week before she married Richmond. Big Earl's first wife, Thelma, was still alive then, and Minnie hadn't yet sunk her teeth into Big Earl. So Clarice dragged

Barbara Jean and me to the run-down house out near the highway bypass where Minnie used to tell fortunes. She swore us both to secrecy, since seeing a fortune-teller was just a hair's breadth away from consorting with Satan to the folks at Clarice's church. Inside that nasty shack, we inhaled jasmine incense and listened while Minnie told Clarice that her marriage to Richmond would be joyful, but, having drawn an upright Hermit and a reverse Three of Cups, she would turn out to be barren and would look fat in her wedding gown. Clarice worried herself sick throughout her first pregnancy. And for years she couldn't bring herself to look at what turned out to be lovely wedding photos. Four healthy children and three decades later, Clarice still wasn't feeling inclined to forgive Minnie.

Clarice pointed her index finger at Minnie's table and said, "Stepmother or not, Little Earl shouldn't have that old fake in this place. There have got to be laws against that kind of thing. It's fraud, pure and simple." She took a swig of iced tea and twisted her mouth. "Too sweet," she said.

I prepared myself for one of Clarice's lectures on the moral failings of Minnie McIntyre. When Clarice was in the kind of mood she was in that day, she enjoyed identifying flaws, moral and otherwise, in everyone except the idiot in the blue shirt at the other end of the table. My friend had a multitude of gifts. She played the piano like an angel. She could cook, sew, sing, and speak French. And she was as kind and generous a friend as anyone could hope for. What she didn't have much of a knack for was placing blame where it should truly lie.

Clarice's church didn't help her disposition much.

Calvary Baptist wasn't full-blown Pentecostal, but it still managed to be the Bible-thumpingest and angriest church in town. So Sundays were bad for Clarice even without Richmond misbehaving or Minnie's name coming up in the conversation. Calvary's pastor, Reverend Peterson, yelled at his congregation every week that God was mad at them for a long list of wrongs they had committed and that He was even madder about whatever they were thinking of doing. If you weren't in a foul temper by the time you left a Calvary Baptist service, it meant you weren't listening.

At my church, Holy Family Baptist, the only hard-and-fast rule was that everyone should be kind to everybody. That view was way too casual for the Calvary congregation, and it drove them straight up the wall that we didn't take a harder line on sin and sinners. The Calvary crowd were equally disgusted with Barbara Jean's church, First Baptist, where the members proved their devotion to God by doing charity work and by dressing up like they were on a fashion runway every Sunday. The old joke was that Holy Family preached the good news gospel, Calvary Baptist preached the bad news gospel, and First Baptist preached the new clothes gospel.

Clarice didn't begin a recitation from her catalog of the ways Minnie's behavior offended her, though. A glance through the window provided her with something new to complain about. Pointing outside, she said, "There's Barbara Jean and Lester. You know, she really should call when she's going to be this late. It's not right to worry everybody like this."

Clarice was mostly letting off steam, but she had a point.

The summer heat tended to aggravate Lester's various health problems. And there was quite a list of problems. Heart, lungs, liver, kidneys. If it was still in Lester's body, it was going bad. They often appeared for supper an hour late after having to pull their car over for Barbara Jean to kick-start one of Lester's vital organs with a remedy from the portable clinic she kept in her pocketbook.

So, when I turned to watch Barbara Jean and Lester Maxberry making their way toward the restaurant, I was surprised to see Lester moving much more energetically than usual. Dressed in a white suit and matching white fedora, Lester's usually round back was straight, and he hardly leaned on his ivory walking stick at all. He lifted his knees high in that almost military way he did when he was feeling spry. It was Barbara Jean who slowly shuffled along, frowning with each step.

Barbara Jean wore a snug-fitting bright yellow dress and a yellow hat with a brim at least three feet wide. Her calves were encased in white go-go boots that had three-inch heels. Even from half a block away I could see that the boots were paining her. With every step she took, the corners of Barbara Jean's mouth turned down a little more, and she occasionally stopped walking altogether to take a deep breath before soldiering on.

Clarice said, "Oh, for heaven's sake, would you look at that." She pointed toward our approaching friend. "No wonder they're so late. She's wearing that yellow dress again. That thing is so tight she can barely breathe, much less take a full step. And would you look at the shoes she's trying to walk in. Those heels are six inches, if they're an inch. I tell you, Odette, Barbara Jean has got to accept the fact that she is a middle-aged woman and she can't wear the things she wore when she was twenty-two. It's unseemly. We really should have a talk with her about that. She needs an intervention real bad." She sat back in her chair and crossed her arms over her chest.

Clarice would never say a word to Barbara Jean about the way she dressed, and we both knew it. Just like she and Barbara Jean wouldn't tell me to my face that I was fat, and Barbara Jean and I wouldn't remind Clarice that her husband was a dog. These were the tender considerations that came with being a member of the Supremes. We overlooked each other's flaws and treated each other well, even when we didn't deserve it.

When Clarice got to carrying on the way she was, it always came back to one thing: Richmond. When he was up to no good, Clarice grew fangs that filled her mouth with bitterness. Mostly she swallowed the poison, but sometimes it came seeping out.

"I'll tell you one thing," Clarice said, "I wouldn't be caught dead in that dress." Clarice was nowhere near as big as me, but she was solidly built, no matter how she starved herself. If either of us was ever foolish enough to try and force ourselves into Barbara Jean's sexy little dress, death *would* most likely be the outcome.

The only thing I didn't like about Barbara Jean's and Lester's outfits was that they made my stomach growl. I was ravenous and, with her in that yellow dress and him in his cream-colored suit, they got me thinking about a slice of lemon meringue pie.

Truth was, Barbara Jean looked lovely in whatever she wore. She'd been the prettiest girl in our high school and she became the most beautiful woman I'd ever seen. In middle age, it's still difficult to look away from her. Every single feature of her face is striking and exotic. Looking at Barbara Jean makes you think that maybe God is a wonderful, ancient artist who decided one day to piece together all his loveliest creations and craft something that put his other works to shame. Unfortunately, God neglected to prepare men for his good work. Men had behaved very badly because of my friend's beauty, and, the world being unfair, Barbara Jean had often paid the price.

Barbara Jean and Lester came into the All-You-Can-Eat and brought along a gust of hot air that quickly overwhelmed the feeble air conditioner that hummed and sputtered above the doorway. People sitting near the door looked at Lester like they wanted to take a good whack at him with the walking stick he was using to hold the door open for his wife, who was several steps behind him on account of her impractical choices in wardrobe and footwear.

Barbara Jean came limping to the table issuing apologies. "I am so sorry we're late. Morning service went long today," she said as she sat down, unzipped her boots under the table, and sighed with relief.

Clarice interrupted her, saying, "Let's eat." Then she stood from her chair and marched toward the steam tables.

The men followed Clarice to the food while I waited for Barbara Jean to squeeze herself back into her boots. When she was done, we walked to the buffet line. Along the way, Barbara Jean leaned over and whispered in my ear, "Richmond back at it again?"

"That's my guess," I said.

We took plates from the carousel at the near end of the

four steam tables – one for main courses, two for side dishes, and the fourth for desserts. Then each of us did what we did every week. Skinny James piled his plate with some of everything. Richmond hid food that was off-limits to him because of his diabetes beneath layers of green beans and roasted carrots. Lester ate the old folks' selections, easy-to-chew dishes enhanced with added fiber. Clarice hadn't allowed herself a piece of anything fried since she was twenty-eight, and that day was no exception. She ate minuscule portions of low-fat items. Out of consideration for Clarice, Barbara Jean, who could eat anything and never gain a pound, ate only low-fat foods so it wouldn't seem like she was rubbing the difference in their metabolisms in Clarice's face. I, as always, divided my plate equally between main courses and desserts. Vegetables take up too much space on a small plate.

When we got to the end of the line, the men headed back to our table. The three of us women stopped to say hello to Little Earl and Erma Mae, who had come in from the kitchen and were sitting side by side on stools at the far end of the last steam table.

I said, "Hey, Little Earl. Hey, Erma Mae."

They answered together, "Hey, Supremes."

I inquired about their health, their children, and Erma Mae's elderly mother. I asked Little Earl for the latest on his sister Lydia and her husband, who ran a diner in Chicago that was almost identical to the All-You-Can-Eat. After being assured that all of those people were fine, I got around to the question I really wanted an answer to.

I asked, "How's your daddy doing, Little Earl?" trying to sound casual about it.

"Oh, he's great. Eighty-eight next month and gonna outlive us all, I 'spect. He should be comin' by sometime soon. Here lately he'll sometimes sleep in, but he won't miss an entire day's work, that's for certain."

"'Specially not on a Sunday," Erma Mae added, nodding her head toward Minnie's empty fortune-telling table. She said that for Clarice's benefit since the two of them were kindred spirits on the subject of Minnie.

At that moment the front door opened with a loud scrape. Little Earl looked toward the door with an expression of boyish expectation, like he really believed that just speaking of his father would conjure him up. But Big Earl didn't step into the restaurant. Instead, Minnie McIntyre stood in the threshold, holding the door open and letting a hot, moist draft into the room that made the nearby patrons groan in discomfort and give her the evil eye.

Minnie's costume of the day was a deep purple robe decorated with the same astrological signs that adorned her corner table. She wore gold Arabian-style slippers with curled-up toes, a necklace made of twelve large chunks of colored glass, each representing a birthstone, and a white turban with a silver bell jutting out from its top. The bell, she claimed, was for Charlemagne the Magnificent to ring whenever he had a message for her. He was very consistent. Charlemagne rang every time Minnie lowered her head to count a client's money.

Minnie walked into the restaurant, taking long, slow strides and holding her arms outstretched, palms toward the ceiling.

Little Earl left his stool and met her at the cash register. He sighed and said, "Miss Minnie, please, we talked about this. I just can't have you doing your readings on Sundays. The Pentecostals'll have my ass."

Minnie said, "You and your precious Pentecostals will be happy to know that you won't have to worry about me or my gift much longer." She wiggled her head from side to side as she spoke, making her bell ring repeatedly. She lowered the range of her normally high-pitched voice to a deep rumble and said, loud enough for nearly everyone in the place to hear, "Charlemagne says I'll be dead within a year."

Most people in the restaurant, having heard Minnie announce grave prophecies that failed to come to pass many times, paid her no mind. Clarice, Barbara Jean, and I stuck around and waited to hear what else she had to say.

Little Earl said, "Why don't I make you some tea, get you calmed down?"

"There's no calmin' me down; I'm facin' the end. And don't pretend you're sad to see it. You've wanted me out of the way ever since I married Earl." She pointed at Erma Mae and added, "You, too. I dare you to deny it."

Erma Mae was never one for lying. Instead of responding to Minnie, she yelled toward the kitchen, "Belinda, bring some hot tea for Grandma Minnie!"

Little Earl led Minnie behind the register and guided her onto his stool. In a soft, soothing tone of voice he said, "Yeah, that's right. Have a cup of tea, and then I'll walk you back across the street. You, me, and Daddy can talk this whole thing out."

She made a kind of a squawking noise and dismissed him with a wave of her hand. "There's nothin' to talk out. A year from now, I'll be dead."

Clarice was tired of listening to Minnie's ramblings. She whispered in my ear, "My food is getting cold. Are we about done listening to this old fake?"

Minnie screamed, "I heard that!" She was old; but you had to hand it to her, the woman still had excellent hearing. She leapt from the stool and lunged at Clarice, ready to dig her purple polished nails into Clarice's face.

Little Earl held her back and got her onto the stool again. She immediately burst into tears, sending black trails of mascara down her copper cheeks. Maybe she'd been faking it for so long that she'd started to believe herself. Or maybe she really had talked to Charlemagne. Fake or not, we all could clearly see that this was a woman who believed what she was saying. Even Clarice felt bad watching Minnie break down like that. She said, "Minnie, I'm sorry. I shouldn't have said that."

But Minnie wasn't ready to hear apologies or be consoled.

"I knew this was gonna happen. Nobody cares what happens to me. As soon as Charlemagne told me that I'd be dead within a year of Earl, I knew I'd get no sympathy."

Little Earl, who had been patting his stepmother on the back while she wailed, took a step away from her and said, "What?"

"Charlemagne came to me early this morning and said that I would follow Earl to the grave within a year. Those were his exact words."

Now the restaurant grew quiet as people began to catch the drift of what she was saying.

"Are you saying that Daddy is dead?"

"Yeah, he died last night while he was sayin' his prayers. Between that and my bad news from Charlemagne this morning, I've had a terrible, terrible Sunday, let me tell you."

Little Earl grabbed Minnie's shoulders and spun her on the stool so she faced him directly. "Daddy died last night . . . and you didn't call me?"

"I was gonna call you, but then I thought, *If I call 'em, they'll feel like they've got to come over. Then there'll be the preacher and the undertaker and maybe the grandkids. With everybody makin' such a fuss, I'll never get a lick of sleep.* So I thought it out and figured your daddy would be just as dead if I got a good night's rest as he'd be if I called you and didn't get my sleep. So I just let it be."

James, Richmond, and Lester came over from the window table then and joined us. No one said anything, and Minnie sensed that it wasn't an approving silence. She looked at Little Earl and Erma Mae and said, "I was just tryin' to be considerate. Y'all need your sleep, too."

When the crowd around her remained quiet, she let loose with another wail and a new round of tears. She said, "This is no way to treat a dyin' woman."

Little Earl began to untie his apron. He said, "Is he at Stewart's?" Stewart's is the largest black mortuary in town and it's where most of us are taken when our time comes.

"No," Minnie said, "I told you I let it be. He's upstairs beside the bed. And that wasn't easy on me, neither. I hardly got seven hours of sleep, him kneelin' there and starin' at me all night."

Little Earl threw his apron to the floor and ran out of the door toward his father's house across the road. James was right on his heels.

Erma Mae began to sob. She came around the buffet line and launched herself straight into Barbara Jean's arms, passing by Clarice and me even though we were both closer friends of hers than Barbara Jean. I wasn't surprised or offended, though. And I was sure Clarice wasn't either. Everyone knew Barbara Jean was the expert on grief.

As Barbara Jean held Erma Mae and patted her trembling back, I looked through the window and across the street. James and Little Earl were just arriving at Big Earl's home. They rushed up the front stairs and right past Mama, who stood near the porch swing. Big Earl and Thelma McIntyre sat on the swing holding hands, Miss Thelma's head on her husband's shoulder. I could tell from Mama's familiar gestures that she was telling one of her jokes. I had seen those particular movements a hundred times. I knew which joke she was telling and that she was now at the punch line. Right on cue, Big Earl and Miss Thelma doubled over laughing, stomping their feet on the painted boards of the porch floor and falling against each other on the swing. Even from dozens of yards away, I could see the sun reflecting off the tears that ran down the cheeks of Big Earl's grinning face.

Chapter 6

Erma Mae cried on Barbara Jean's shoulder as a crowd of friends surrounded them murmuring words of sympathy and support. Barbara Jean felt a hand stroke her back and she turned her head to see Carmel Handy standing behind her, shrunken and bony in her best Sunday dress. Barbara Jean knew what the first words out of Miss Carmel's mouth would be and she held her breath, bracing herself to hear them. Miss Carmel didn't disappoint. In her high-pitched, feathery voice she said, "Sweetheart, did you know you were born on my davenport?"

Barbara Jean's mother, Loretta Perdue, was drunk when she gave birth on the living room sofa of Miss Carmel, a woman she had never met. Her friends had thrown her a baby shower that day at Forrest Payne's Pink Slipper Gentlemen's Club, where she worked as a dancer. She often told Barbara Jean how she only drank whiskey sours when she was expecting because everyone knew that drinking beer during pregnancy would make your baby nappy-headed. "See, honey," she would say, "your mama was always lookin' out for you."

Loretta had plans to give her daughter, and herself, a leg up in life. After reading the news of Clarice's birth in the newspaper, and seeing how people went on about it, she decided that her child would be the second black baby born at University Hospital. Clarice's mother was just the wife of a shady lawyer and no better than she was, Loretta figured. Now that the color barrier had been broken, she would just show up at the hospital when the first pain hit and take her rightful place among a higher class of folk. Like most of Loretta's schemes, it didn't work out that way.

Things went wrong for Barbara Jean's mother when the man she had arranged to see that evening sprung a surprise on her. She'd told him five months earlier that he was going to be a father, and he had seemed to be pleased about it. Or rather, he was pleased Loretta was not going to tell his wife. She was content merely to accept a small monthly payment in exchange for her discretion. This same arrangement also suited each of the three other men Loretta had informed that they were the father of her unborn child.

Loretta had set up a meeting with Daddy no. 4 (going by the order in which she had told them about her pregnancy) at a quiet roadside diner in Leaning Tree after the baby shower. At the diner, she was going to remind him of just how fair she was being and then, when she had him feeling appropriately grateful to her for being such a good sport, she would casually mention just how much easier a new Chevrolet would make life for her and his child. If she worked it right, by sunset she would have a new car and he would travel back to his wife and family in Louisville thanking God that he had knocked up such a reasonable woman.

She seated herself at a booth and drank coffee to

come down from her whiskey sour buzz and waited for Daddy no. 4 to join her. When he stepped through the door with Daddy no. 2 right behind him, she knew that the jig was up.

As the men approached, Loretta, always quick on her feet when cornered, made one last desperate move to hold her plan together by playing one daddy against the other. She said, "I'm sorry, sweetheart. I've tried so many times to tell him that I love you and it's all over with him, but I was just too scared. He's so mean; I didn't know what he might do to me and our baby." She said it to both of them, hoping each would assume she was talking to him alone and that she could slip out of the diner while they fought over her. Later, she could separately thank both the conquering hero and the valiant loser for defending her honor, assuring each that she loved only him. With luck, after the dust settled, her plans could go forward unchanged.

Loretta was a stunning beauty, and she knew it. She thought it was only logical that men should fight over her, and they often did. When she got sick with the cirrhosis that killed her at thirty-five, the hardest thing for her – harder than dying, Barbara Jean thought – was saying goodbye to her beauty. Loretta died hard and she died ugly. Liver disease whittled away her cute, round face and bountiful figure to nothing – a mean turn of fate for a woman who, as one of her men described her, "looked like she was made out of basketballs and chocolate pudding."

Daddies no. 2 and no. 4 presented a united front in the diner, with Daddy no. 4 doing most of the talking. He told her she'd never get another dime from either of them, and he carried on as if he were some sort of genius detective for single-handedly figuring out her plot. The truth, blurted out by Daddy no. 2, was that Loretta had been the victim of her customary bad luck. The fathers had ended up seated next to each other at Forrest Payne's joint, and after they had sucked down enough of Forrest's watered-down liquor to loosen their tongues, they started bragging about their women. It didn't take them long to realize that they were each bragging about the same one.

Forrest Payne had pretensions of running a gentlemen's club instead of a country strip joint and whorehouse, so he greeted every customer at the door dressed up in his signature canary-yellow tuxedo. Then he escorted them to their seats with all the flourish of a French maitre d'. Since he didn't trust anyone else to handle the door and the cover charge money, Loretta knew it had to have been Forrest himself who had seated the daddies next to each other. This, in spite of the fact that she had left explicit instructions that none of her baby's fathers should be placed within ten feet of each other. For the rest of her short life, Loretta blamed Forrest Payne for ruining her.

Daddy no. 4 leaned across the table and wagged his finger at Loretta's nose. He said, "I was too smart for you, li'l girl. You been outplayed at your own game."

Loretta stared at Daddy no. 4, who had once been her favorite, and wondered what it was she had ever seen in him, with his wide, lopsided mouth and his strange, Egyptian-looking eyes. Then she thought about the ring he had bought for her, a decent-sized ruby with tiny azure sapphires arranged around it in a daisy pattern, and she recalled why she had put up with him. She slid her hands from the table so he wouldn't see the ring and get it in his head to demand its return. When she tried to pawn it a year later, she would find out the stones were glass.

Daddy no. 2 surprised Loretta by bursting into tears. He buried his face in his hands and wailed as if he'd been stuck with a sharp stick, blubbering on about his lost son. Daddy no. 4 put his arm around his new friend and then put both of their feelings about Loretta into words. He leaned toward her and launched into some very loud and creative name-calling. The other customers in the diner looked their way, wondering what the commotion was about.

Loretta was a firm believer that, if a woman was smart, she acted like a lady by the light of day no matter what she did after sunset. This situation, one daddy crying his eyes out and the other loudly exploring the limits of his vocabulary, was just the kind of thing that got you ostracized by decent folks – the kind of people she planned to be spending her time with as soon as she'd had her baby in University Hospital and elevated her status. Loretta hurried away from the booth and, for the benefit of anyone who might have been listening, said, "I can see that you two do not intend to behave like gentlemen. I shall not stay and risk losing my poise due to your crass behavior." What she said to herself was "Fuck this. I still got Daddy no. 1 and Daddy no. 3."

She headed back toward Forrest Payne's place to cuss him out, and was halfway there when her water broke. She made her way to the best-kept house on the block, thinking that its owners would be likely to have a telephone – not everyone did in 1950. Mrs Carmel Handy, a schoolteacher Loretta would have known if she hadn't left school in the sixth grade, owned the well-landscaped brick bungalow she chose to stop at. Miss Carmel answered the insistent knocking at her door and found herself confronted with a very attractive, massively pregnant young woman supporting herself against the doorjamb.

Between groans of discomfort, the girl said, "Hi, I'm Mrs Loretta Perdue, and I was admiring your front yard and thinking that whoever lived here must be a person of class and would surely have a telephone. I myself have a telephone, but I'm a ways from home and I'm not feeling well. So, if you don't mind, I need you to call my friend, Mr Forrest Payne, at his place of business and tell him to come get me and drive me to University Hospital where I plan to have my baby like folks of substance. It's the least Forrest could do since my situation is entirely his fault."

Because she had been in the middle of pressing her hair and she didn't want to stand there with her door open for any passersby to see her with her head half done, Carmel Handy permitted Loretta to enter her home. Careful not to burn Loretta with the still-smoking straightening comb, she helped her into the house. In her foyer, Miss Carmel listened politely as Loretta recited Forrest Payne's telephone number, all the while thinking how funny it was that this girl was trying so hard to make Forrest sound like anything but the pimp everyone in Plainview knew he was.

Miss Carmel led Loretta to her living room sofa to rest while she made the phone call. But instead of calling Forrest Payne – she wasn't about to have her neighbors see that man coming and going from her house, thank you very much – she called a nurse who lived down the block.

The nurse brought Barbara Jean into the world right

there on the sofa while Carmel Handy made the first of a dozen phone calls she would make that day to tell her friends what had happened in her home and to extol the benefits of plasticizing your furniture. That first call began "Some girl just popped out another of Forrest Payne's bastards right in my front room," starting a rumor that would follow Barbara Jean for the rest of her life.

The baby was named Barbara Jean – Barbara for Daddy no. 1's mother and Jean for Daddy no. 3's.

When Loretta's child was first handed to her, she took note of the infant's lopsided, half-smiling mouth and the almond-shaped eyes, already fully open, that were tilted up at the corners like an Egyptian's. Loretta recognized that face instantly and said to herself, "Ain't this some shit. It was No. 4 all along." Then she turned to Mrs Handy and said, "Got any whiskey?"

On a September morning fourteen years later, Miss Carmel read Barbara Jean's name aloud from the roster in her ninth grade English class. After placing her clipboard down on her desk, Miss Carmel walked over to Barbara Jean and, for the first time, uttered the words that would begin most of their encounters for the next four decades. "Girl, did you know you were born on my davenport?"

Once Barbara Jean had married Lester and his business had taken off, most of the town lined up to kiss her ass in order to get on Lester's good side. But Carmel Handy continued to greet her that same way. Barbara Jean supposed it spoke well of Miss Carmel's character that the wealth she came into didn't change her old teacher's behavior toward her one bit. But she still hated her for it. It shamed her to admit it, but Barbara Jean felt relieved when, in her eighties, Miss Carmel developed the habit of telling each black woman around Barbara Jean's age who crossed her path that she was born on her sofa. Eventually, the tale of the baby born in her front room became so bound up with Miss Carmel's short-circuiting brain that nearly everyone forgot that the story was rooted in fact or had anything to do with Barbara Jean.

Carmel Handy's block was one of the first to be demolished when housing developers and the university bought up most of Leaning Tree in the 1980s and '90s. On the day they bulldozed that little brick bungalow, Barbara Jean drove over to Miss Carmel's street and drank a champagne toast in the front seat of her new Mercedes.

As she stood in the All-You-Can-Eat at the center of an expanding circle of grief over Big Earl's passing, Barbara Jean listened to Carmel Handy reminding her, yet again, of her low origins. Barbara Jean thought then of the taste of the champagne she sipped that day in her car as she watched the workmen scratch Miss Carmel's home out of existence. That delicious memory helped her not to scream.

Chapter 7

The night before Big Earl's funeral, Barbara Jean dreamed that she and Lester were walking along a rutted dirt road on a cool fall day. They exhaled clouds of white mist while rust, yellow, and brown leaves floated around them in a circle, as if they were at the center of a cyclone. Because of the storm of leaves, Barbara Jean was just barely able to make out the path ahead of them. She held Lester's arm tight to keep from twisting her ankle in the tire tracks embedded in the road. Even in her dreams, she always wore heels.

After a time, the leaf storm around them thinned enough to reveal a river ahead. On the opposite shore, a small boy waved. Then, just as they lifted their hands to wave back, a woman in a silvery, iridescent gown appeared, hovering in the air above their heads. The woman said, "Lester, the water is frozen. Just walk on over and get him. He's waiting." But it was November or December in the dream and the river was clearly only half frozen. Barbara Jean could see the bubbling and churning current just beneath the brittle surface of the ice. She dug her fingers into the rough cloth of her husband's winter coat to keep him from going out onto the river. As Lester's sleeve escaped her grasp, Barbara Jean woke up with her pulse racing and both of her arms reaching out for Lester.

She'd had that dream, or one nearly identical to it, for years. Sometimes it was spring or summer in the dream and, instead of a dangerously thin layer of ice, it was a decrepit rope bridge with rotted wooden slats that spanned the water. But she always dreamed of the same road, the dirt trail that had once formed the western border of Leaning Tree. It had been paved ages ago, or so Barbara Jean had been told. She hadn't gone near it in years. She always dreamed of the same waving boy, her lost Adam. The woman in the air also never varied. It was always her mother.

Barbara Jean awakened from her dream with a sore back from being curled up for hours on one of the two Chippendale wingback chairs that sat by the fireplace in the library of her home. The chairs had been reupholstered, at frightful expense, with burgundy crushed-velvet fabric adorned with a fleur-de-lis pattern that matched the design of the library's hand-painted wallpaper. Every spring at the Plainview Home and Garden Walk, people made a big fuss over those chairs, and Barbara Jean loved them. But they were hell on her lower back if she sat in them for too long a time.

Barbara Jean and Lester's house stood at the intersection of Plainview Avenue and Main Street. A three-story Queen Anne giant with a turret at its northeast corner and six separate porches, it had once been called Ballard House, and still was by most of the inhabitants of Plainview over the age of fifty. It was built in 1870 by a local thief named Alfred Ballard who looted some of the best homes in the vanquished South during the Civil War and returned to Plainview a rich man. Mr Ballard's descendants lacked his business sense and his ruthlessness. They failed to add to their fortune, wasted the money Ballard had left them, and eventually lost the house to the tax man. In 1969, after he expanded his lawn care business to Kentucky and got a contract to tend all of the state-owned properties in the northern half of the state, Lester bought Ballard House for his young wife and their son, Adam. It was a gutted, falling-down mess at the time, and although she loved the house, Barbara Jean had no clue what needed to be done to put it back together. Clarice, though, had been raised by her mother with the assumption that she would one day oversee a grand home. So Barbara Jean turned every decision in the renovation process over to her friend. Barbara Jean stood back and watched as Clarice transformed her massive shell of a house into the kind of showplace Clarice would have lived in if fate, in the form of a three-hundred-pound, corn-fed Wisconsin linebacker with blood in his eye, hadn't stepped in and transformed Richmond from a potential NFL legend into a recruiter at a university whose football glory days were long past. Out of respect for her friend, Clarice never accepted a bit of credit for her hard work. Instead, she patiently tutored Barbara Jean, teaching her everything she knew about art, antiques, and architecture. Between the practical experience Barbara Jean gained from tending to the needs of her extravagant old home and from Clarice's guidance, she eventually surpassed her instructor's level of expertise.

When she stood from the antique chair to stretch her lower back, Barbara Jean's Bible tumbled to the floor. After she'd had dinner with Lester, counted out his pills, and put him to bed, the evening had become a blur. She didn't recall that she'd been reading the Bible before she fell asleep. It made sense, though. She tended to drag out the Good Book when she was in a dark mood, and the shadows had closed in around her that night, for sure.

Clarice had given Barbara Jean that Bible in 1977, just after Adam died. Lester had become frightened when his wife stopped speaking and eating and then refused to come out of Adam's room, so he called in Odette and Clarice. They got right to work, each of her friends administering the cures they trusted most. Odette mothered her, cooking wonderful-smelling meals which she fed to her by hand on the worst days. And, during the long hours she spent sitting in bed beside Barbara Jean while her friend cried onto her broad bosom, brave Odette whispered into Barbara Jean's ear that now was the time to be fearless.

Clarice came brandishing a brown suede-covered Bible. It was embossed with Barbara Jean's name in gold letters on its front cover and had "Salvation = Calvary Baptist Church" printed on the back. For weeks, Clarice read to her about the trials of Job and reminded her that the fifth chapter of Matthew promised "Blessed are they that mourn, for they shall be comforted."

But both of Barbara Jean's friends had come bearing medicine for the wrong illness. More than courage or piety, what she needed, what she would scour Clarice's Bible forwards and backwards searching for over the many years that followed, was a clue as to how to get out from under the boulder of guilt that rested on her chest and forced the breath out of her. Well intentioned as it was, Clarice's gift just armed Barbara Jean with a long list of good reasons to be seriously pissed off at God while the weight of her guilt ground her into powder.

Barbara Jean was finally able to leave Adam's room after she and God came to an understanding. She would continue to smile and nod through services every week at First Baptist just as she always had, and she wouldn't call Him out for being as demanding and capricious as the worst two-year-old child, ready at any moment to reach out with his greedy hands and snatch whatever shone brightest. In exchange for this consideration, Barbara Jean asked only that God leave her alone. For decades, the pact worked out fine. Then, with Big Earl's sudden passing, God reminded Barbara Jean of who He was. Bringer of death, master comedian, lightning bearer. He made it clear to her that He had no intentions of honoring the terms of their truce.

Barbara Jean put the Bible on the eighteenth-century candle table next to her chair and walked to the mirror above the fireplace to inspect herself. She didn't look too bad – a little puffy, but nothing some time with an ice pack wouldn't take care of. Also, the sun wasn't up yet, so she still had time to get a little rest to ensure she would look good for Big Earl. And she was determined to say goodbye to her friend looking her very best.

She had laid out her outfit for Big Earl's service earlier that evening, before heading into the library. Out of respect, she would wear a black dress. But she chose magenta shoes, a matching belt, and a white hat with clusters of red and black leather roses around its wide brim to go with it. The little black dress was cut well above the knee and had a tiny slit on the right seam. Clarice would hate it and would have to bite her tongue to keep from saying so. But Barbara Jean wasn't wearing it for Clarice. She was wearing it for Big Earl.

When she was a teenager and was ashamed of having to wear her mother's flashy, trashy hand-me-downs, Big Earl made a point of telling Barbara Jean that she looked pretty every time he saw her. Not in a dirty old man way or anything. He would just smile at her and say, "You look divine today," in a way that made her feel as if she were wearing haute couture. Or he would see her come into the restaurant in one of her mother's shiny, too-short skirts and he'd turn to Miss Thelma and say, "Don't Barbara Jean look exactly like a flower." Anywhere else in town, she might have been dirt, but inside the walls of the All-You-Can-Eat, she was a flower.

Long after Barbara Jean had choices and knew better, she would occasionally pick one of the brightest and the tightest from her closet and sashay into the All-You-Can-Eat on a Sunday afternoon just to give Big Earl a reason to grin and slap his knee and say, "That's my girl." On those days, she left the All-You-Can-Eat feeling twenty years younger than when she'd walked in. So, for Big Earl she was going to squeeze into a black dress she wouldn't be able to take more than a shallow breath in and she was going to look damn good in it, or die trying.

Barbara Jean knew she should get to bed, but she didn't feel sleepy, just a little woozy still from the vodka. She didn't remember getting the bottle from the liquor cabinet, but there it was on the table next to the Bible. That was her pattern. When her mind was too full of thoughts – usually about the old days, her mother or her son – she would reach for either the Bible or the bottle and end up with both in her lap before the night was over. She would sit in one of her burgundy chairs and drink vodka from one of the antique demitasse cups Clarice had found for the house. She sipped and read until the memories went away.

Barbara Jean always drank vodka, partly because whiskey had been her mother's drink and she swore she'd never touch it. Also, vodka was safe because people couldn't smell it on you. If you stuck to vodka and you knew how to control yourself, nobody talked trash about you, no matter how many times you filled your demitasse cup.

She put the cap back on the vodka bottle and returned it to the liquor cabinet. Then she took her cup and saucer to the kitchen and left them on the counter for the maid to deal with in the morning. When she returned to the library to turn out the lights, she contemplated reopening that troublesome Bible. She was in just that kind of mood, and it wouldn't take long. After a few vodkas, Barbara Jean's form of Bible study was to close her eyes, open the book on her lap, and let her index finger fall onto the open page. Then she would read whatever verse was nearest the tip of her nail. She had done this for years, telling herself that one day she would land on just the right thing to turn on some light inside her head. But, mostly, she spent countless nights learning who begat whom and reading of the endless, seemingly random smitings the Bible specialized in.

She thought about the day to come and decided to go on up to bed. Rather than disturb Lester, who was a light sleeper, she would lie down in one of the guest rooms. If he asked in the morning why she hadn't come to bed, she would tell him that she had gone straight to the guest room after staying up late to pick out her outfit for Big Earl. If she looked well rested enough, maybe he wouldn't suspect that she had spent yet another night in the library drinking and stocking up on ammunition for her ongoing battle with God.

Barbara Jean removed her shoes before she left the library so the sound of her steps wouldn't create a racket as she crossed the herringbone parquet floor of the grand foyer. She climbed the stairs slowly and carefully, recalling one of her mother's warnings about the missteps that could prevent Barbara Jean from accessing the better, more respectable life that Loretta had been cheated out of. Loretta had said that if a woman fell down the stairs, people would always gossip that either she was a drunk or her man beat her. And you couldn't have them saying either thing about you if you wanted to get chummy with the type of folks who could actually do something for you. That was the way Loretta had divided up the world, into those who could or could not do something for her. And she spent most of her life designing plots to wrest the things she wanted from the people who she believed possessed them. In the end, it did her no good.

In her stocking feet, Barbara Jean crept along the second-floor hallway of her house. She tiptoed past the bedroom she shared with Lester. Then she passed by the guest rooms. The door to Adam's room drew her to it as surely as if it had stretched out a pair of arms and pulled her into its embrace. She opened the door and stared into the room at the familiar low shelves crammed with out-of-date toys, the small desk strewn with faded crayon drawings, the miniature chair with a pale green sweater slung over it as if its owner might dash into the room at any second to retrieve it. Everywhere she looked there were things that she had sworn to her friends she had thrown away or given away decades earlier. She knew she shouldn't go into this room; it did her no good. But she still had a stagger in her step from the vodka. And she comforted herself with the knowledge that, in the morning, she probably wouldn't recall experiencing the ache in her soul and the fire in her brain that always led her to this same place.

Barbara Jean stepped inside and shut the door. She curled up on the short bed, atop cowboys and Indians on horseback engaged in endless pursuit of each other across the comforter. She closed her eyes – not to sleep, she told herself – just to rest and gather her thoughts before going to one of the guest rooms for the few remaining hours of the night. Moments later, Barbara Jean was on that dirt road again, clutching her husband's arm while her shimmering mother floated above their heads whispering, "He's waiting."

Chapter 8

Big Earl's funeral was held at Clarice's church, Calvary Baptist. He wasn't much of a churchgoer himself, but his daughter-in-law's family had worshipped at Calvary for almost as many generations as Clarice's people. It seemed like the perfect choice until the place started to fill up and it became clear that the university's football stadium was the only building in town that could have comfortably accommodated everyone.

Each pew of the church was packed with mourners. Hundreds of folks who couldn't get seats crowded the outer aisles, leaning against the white plaster walls. Small clusters of people who weren't able to squeeze inside the church stuck their heads into the opened side doors of the sanctuary, amen-ing Reverend Peterson's homily and bobbing their heads to the music along with those of us on the inside.

Denise, Jimmy, and Eric sat in the row behind their father and me. Without having to be asked, all three of our kids had arrived that morning to comfort James and to pay their respects to the man who was the only grandfather they'd ever really known, since my father passed when they were still little. They'd traveled to Plainview from their homes in Illinois, California, and Washington to be with us, and I was happy and proud that they'd come.

Although the Calvary Baptist approach to faith was a bit hard-assed for my taste, I was glad the service was there. For my money, that church is the prettiest in town. Calvary is only half the size of First Baptist, but it has a dozen beautiful stained-glass windows, each one portraying the life of an apostle. The windows extend from the floor all the way up to the vaulted ceiling and, when sunlight hits the glass, a rainbow is projected through the sanctuary onto a mural of the Crucifixion on the wall behind the baptismal pool.

The highlight of the mural is the sexiest picture of Jesus you've ever seen. He has high cheekbones and curly jet-black hair. His bronzed, outstretched arms bulge with muscles and He has the firm stomach of a Brazilian underwear model. His mouth seems to be blowing kisses to the congregation and His crown of thorns is tilted so He has a Frank Sinatra cool about Him. It all comes together in a way that makes you wonder if Jesus is about to ask you to join the church or to run outside for a game of beach volleyball with Him and a dozen of His hot biblical friends.

At Little Earl's request, Clarice played two pieces on the piano after Reverend Peterson's eulogy. One was an arrangement of "His Eye Is on the Sparrow," and the other was a piece that the program identified as a Brahms intermezzo. Both were lovely, but she had everyone in the church crying their eyes out at the end of the Brahms.

Clarice is one hell of a piano player. Beyond turning on the stereo, music has never been my thing, but even I can hear that something special happens when Clarice sits down at the piano.

When we were kids, we all thought she was going to be

famous. She won contests and got to play with the Indianapolis Symphony and the Louisville Symphony while she was still in high school. Conservatories across the country offered her full scholarships, but she stayed in Plainview because of Richmond. He repaid her by breaking her heart. He joined the NFL and left her behind without so much as a goodbye. Then, right after Clarice made plans to move to New York and launch her career, Richmond was back in town with a crushed ankle and no future in football. He swore his never-ending love for her and begged for forgiveness and nursing. The following year she was his wife, and ten months after the wedding she gave birth to their first child. Not long after that, the other children came and Clarice began her career as a local piano teacher.

Staying in Plainview and giving up on the future we'd all expected her to have was Clarice's choice. It wasn't some crime committed against her by her husband. And I never once heard her complain that she felt she'd missed out on anything. But as I watched my friend at the piano rocking to an internal beat below steamy Jesus, I couldn't help but think that we were all getting a peek at a great treasure Richmond Baker had selfishly snatched from the world to keep as his own.

Three of Clarice and Richmond's four children sat alongside mine. Like my kids, Carolyn, Ricky, and Abe had also come long distances. Only Carl, Carolyn's twin, didn't make an appearance, in spite of the fact that his wife, who he had told he would be in Plainview for the week, had called Clarice's house several times that morning trying to reach him. Even as she played, Clarice kept looking over her shoulder, searching for the face of her youngest son in the crowd. But I was sure that, deep down, she knew he wouldn't be coming. Carl could be anywhere. And wherever he was, he wasn't likely to be alone. Handsome Carl was the pretty apple that hadn't fallen far from Richmond's big, dumb tree.

After seeing Big Earl laid to rest next to Miss Thelma, we kissed our children goodbye and watched them hurry back to their busy lives. Then James and I drove home to pick up the food I'd made for the funeral dinner and headed over to Big Earl and Minnie's house.

No, just Minnie's house now. Big Earl had lived across the street from the All-You-Can-Eat since I could remember, and this sad, new reality was going to be tough to get used to.

We found the widow situated on the porch swing surrounded by sympathetic well-wishers. Minnie made it clear that no one would be granted admission without first being given a recounting of the visit from her spirit guide and the prediction that her death was coming sometime over the next 360 days. So we stood in the heat while she acted out the tale again. Then, as soon as decency allowed, James and I offered our condolences for her husband's passing and for her own upcoming demise and ran inside.

The place had changed a good deal since the days when I had spent a lot of time there. But that was to be expected. My memories were mostly from attending countless childhood parties in these rooms with Little Earl and our school friends. And the last time I'd stepped beyond the front door had probably been twenty years earlier, on the occasion of Miss Thelma's funeral.

The interior was now a combination of the old and the new. Everywhere I looked, decorations and furnishings from the era of the first Mrs McIntyre battled it out with things obviously brought in by the second wife. The old oak table I'd eaten at many times still took up most of the dining room's floor space, but an enormous, glittering gold-plated chandelier hung above it now. The chandelier had hundreds of clear glass lightbulbs with jittery orange lights bouncing around inside of them to suggest candle flames. It was definitely a Minnie addition.

Family pictures and framed needlepoint scenes crafted by Miss Thelma shared the walls with photographs and posters of young Minnie dressed in a sparkling one-piece bathing suit. In the photos, Minnie stood onstage flourishing a handful of playing cards or staring at the camera in open-mouthed pretend surprise as Charlemagne the Magnificent levitated her above his head.

I had never understood why Big Earl married Minnie. They couldn't have been more different in terms of their dispositions, and I never witnessed a moment of anything that looked like true affection between them. But looking at the old pictures of her that adorned the walls, the mantel, and just about every other visible surface, it made a little more sense to me. In those pictures, she was glamorous and desirable, an exotic and magical creature with an air of mystery. We had all thought of Big Earl as a father figure and a friend. But hadn't he been a man, like any other? Maybe when he saw Minnie, he didn't see the spiteful old woman who now sat on the front porch greeting guests with "Thank you for coming. Did you know I'll be dead in a year?" Maybe Big Earl looked at her and saw a gorgeous, smiling showgirl freeing a squirming rabbit from a hat. Maybe seeing Minnie that way had helped him get through those lonely years until he was back with Miss Thelma. I hoped that was the way it had been for him.

I caught sight of the fountain Mama had told me about during her visit to my kitchen earlier in the week. It took up a quarter of the floor space in the living room and was even more of an eyesore than Mama had made it out to be. It was six feet high, and the two naked maidens Mama had described – one crouching, the other standing over her dousing her with water from a pitcher – were life-size and realistically detailed. Rose-colored lights shone on the fountain from sconces on the wall above and behind it, giving the smooth marble surface of the statues the glow of pink skin. One of the lights submerged in the pool of water beneath the statues' feet was malfunctioning. The light flickered on and off and made it appear as if the statues were quivering.

A voice said, "Hard to look away, ain't it?" I turned and saw Thelma McIntyre standing next to me. Ever the lady, Miss Thelma was dressed for her husband's funeral in a tasteful black mourning dress. Her face was covered by a veil.

I nodded in agreement, but didn't say anything out loud to Miss Thelma. I had decided as soon as Mama left my house that first night that I was going to keep any ghost sightings to myself. I didn't want to put James through what we had all gone through with Mama, her driving us to distraction by keeping up an almost constant dialogue with one invisible friend or another. Also, I was perfectly happy to do without everybody thinking I was out of my mind and giving me that *poor thing, she can't help it* smile that the local folks had given my mother after word got around that she thought she was talking with the dead.

Another voice called out, "Over here, Odette" from the direction of the dining room. I turned, half expecting to see another dead friend. Instead, I saw Lydia, Big Earl's daughter, waving me over to a ten-foot-long table of food that sagged under the weight of countless covered dishes. With Miss Thelma tagging along, I brought my addition to the feast to Lydia in the dining room.

While I helped Lydia shift things around to make room on the table for my platter, James declared himself starving and began to pile food onto a plate. Mama, Big Earl, and a well-dressed white woman who I didn't recognize right away made their way through the crowded room toward Miss Thelma and me. People stood shoulder to shoulder in the room, but Mama and her friends glided across the space easily, squeezing between the guests in a way that made them appear to blink in and out of sight like Christmas tree lights.

When she got to the food table, Mama started to count. "One, two, three, four, five, six. That's six hams. Two smoked, two baked, a boiled, and a deep-fried. Very impressive." Mama was of the generation that believed you showed your respect for the deceased with a tribute of pork. She turned to Big Earl, who seemed to be genuinely moved by the pork shrine in his dining room, and said, "Six hams. Earl, you were truly loved."

Just then, Lydia pulled the foil off the dish I had brought. She bent over and took a long, deep sniff. She said, "Mmm, honey walnut glazed and spiral cut. Bless your heart."

Mama yelled, "Seven!" and Big Earl appeared to blush a little bit.

I realized that Barbara Jean and Lester were at the other end of the table when I heard Barbara Jean slap her husband's hand and say, "Stop right there. Strawberries make your throat close up." He received another slap when he reached for a different fruit platter and had to be warned about the countereffects of citrus on his ulcer medication.

Mama asked, "Has Lester been sick?"

I couldn't help but chuckle. Asking if Lester was sick was like asking if it was likely the sun would come up in the morning. His vital organs had gone into a state of semi-retirement ages ago. I was surprised that Mama had forgotten.

Seeing my reaction, Mama said, "I know he's been sick. I meant has he been extra bad off?" She pointed toward Lester as he and Barbara Jean sat down next to James in the living room. The strange white woman, who had just moments earlier been standing beside Mama and Big Earl, had followed Lester to his chair. She stood next to him, studying him closely as he began to eat his wife-approved plate of food. Mama said, "It's just that she's not usually interested in people unless they're about to pass over. She hovered around your daddy for an entire month before he died."

I recognized the woman then and let out a little squeak in spite of myself. Standing there in the living room in her fox stole was the regal former first lady, Mrs Eleanor Roosevelt. I suppose I shouldn't have been surprised to see Mrs Roosevelt. She moved in with my mother right after Daddy passed, so I heard about her antics nearly every day during the last nineteen years of Mama's life. And I had no reason to believe they'd parted company. Still, there are some people you just don't expect to come across in an old friend's living room.

Mama said, "Eleanor ain't good for much these days – can't be, the way she drinks and carries on – but she's got a real knack for knowin' who's about to go."

I whispered, "Well, tell her she's likely to have a long wait. Lester's been kicking at death's door for more than ten years, but it never opens up for him."

Clarice and Richmond came in burdened with yet another ham, and Clarice was immediately set upon by people eager to tell her how they had loved her piano playing at the service. After she escaped her admirers, Clarice came to the table and passed her ham to Lydia. Mama moved away then, presumably to tell Big Earl, who had wandered off somewhere with Miss Thelma, that the ham count was up to eight. Clarice saw the fountain in the living room and groaned. "Would you look at that? What that woman has done to this house is a crime." She stopped herself; her good upbringing wouldn't allow her to go on an anti-Minnie tirade in the woman's own home an hour after Minnie's husband had been put into the ground.

We filled our plates and joined Barbara Jean, Lester, and James in the living room. When we got there, Lester was complaining that the blinking light in the fountain's pool was beginning to give him a headache. "Probably a loose bulb. Wouldn't take but three seconds to fix." I expected Barbara Jean to warn Lester away from any notions he might have had about fixing the underwater light in the fountain. It would be just like Lester to splash around in that water and come up with some sort of microbe that landed him in the hospital for a week.

But Barbara Jean was staring at something else. Her eyes were locked on the picture window and on the crowd gathered around Minnie out on the porch. Something she saw there caused a look to come over her face that was a mixture of amazement and terror. I was certain for a moment that I wasn't the only person in the room newly able to see ghosts. Slowly, like she was a puppet being hauled upright by tightening strings, Barbara Jean began to rise from her chair. In her trance, she didn't seem to remember that she had a plate of food on her lap and I had to lunge and grab the plate before it slid onto the floor.

Clarice saw me snatch the plate from the air and asked, "What's going on?"

Then we looked to where Barbara Jean's gaze was focused, and we both understood. There, among the circle of cinnamon and mahogany faces surrounding Minnie on the front porch, was one white face. It was a face I recognized, one that I never thought I'd see again. Almost thirty years had passed since Clarice and I had last laid eyes on him, but we both knew it was Chick Carlson. His black hair was streaked with gray and he was thicker around the waist now. But he had just grown out of boyishness when he'd left Plainview, so that wasn't a surprise. Even from where I sat, I could see the pale blue of his eyes and see that he was, in middle age, a mature version of the beautiful kid Clarice had proclaimed "King of the Pretty White Boys" on the day we got our first look at him in 1967. Barbara Jean and Chick had loved each other deeply and foolishly, the way only young people can do. And it nearly killed them both.

As Chick leaned over to take Minnie's hand and offer condolences, Barbara Jean, wobbling a little on her red high heels, stepped away from us and toward the front window.

Then things got crazy.

A loud noise in the room drew everyone's attention. It was a kind of a low-pitched "whoop," like the short, insistent bark of a large dog. After that, there was a loud pop and the lights went out. It was still midafternoon and plenty of light came in from the windows, but the sudden dimness made people gasp anyway. Then we heard a series of thudding noises, another barking sound, and a splash.

Lester stood next to me now. His best black funeral suit was sopping wet and his sleeves were rolled up. He said, "I was just trying to fix that damn light in the fountain." He looked down at himself, dripping water onto the carpet. "I guess I fell in."

He held up his right hand for me to see. The tips of his fingers appeared to be singed. "Hurt my hand, too. That light must've had a short in it." Mama came up and stood between me and Lester. His brow wrinkled in confusion and he said, directly to Mama, "Dora, is that you?"

Mama said, "Hey Lester, nice to see you again."

I said, "Oh, shit."

Miss Thelma, Big Earl, and Mrs Roosevelt walked up to us then. Miss Thelma handed a lit joint to Mama, who offered it to Lester. "Take a hit, baby. It'll all make sense in a minute."

Lester, whose suit had completely dried in the previous

few seconds, continued to look uncertain about what had happened. But he said, "Yes, I think that sounds good," and took the joint from Mama.

Someone called, "Barbara Jean," and she turned around where she stood, just a few feet from the front window. The crowd parted between Barbara Jean and the corner of the room that contained the fountain. Now she and I both saw what most of the people in the room had already seen. Lester was on the floor, half in and half out of the now-darkened fountain, the two marble statues lying on top of him.

Barbara Jean ran to Lester's side as Richmond threw the large statues off of him like they were made of cotton balls instead of stone. James shouted for someone to call 9-1-1 and moved in to start CPR. I knew it was too late. Lester – the true Lester, not the wet shell being pounded on by my well-meaning husband – was already shaking hands with Eleanor Roosevelt and telling her how much he had always admired her good works.

Mama turned to me and said, "I gotta tell ya, I'm surprised."

No one was looking my way, so I answered her out loud. "Well, you said Mrs Roosevelt was good at picking out who was about to die."

"Oh, not that. I figured all along she was right about that. I just always assumed it would be Richmond who'd die underneath two naked white girls." Mama walked away then, not interested in the commotion taking place at the foot of the fountain.

I went over and joined my friends. Clarice had her arms around Barbara Jean, both of them seated on the floor. I got down on my knees beside them and grabbed ahold of Barbara Jean's hand. She stared at Lester's body as it rocked under James's futile effort to revive him. She shook her head slowly from side to side and said, in the soft tone of a mother gently scolding a much-loved, naughty child, "I can't take my eyes off you, can I? Not for two seconds."

Chapter 9

Clarice and Odette moved in with Barbara Jean after Lester died. For the last bit of July and on into August, they made sure she got dressed and ate something every day. They slept on either side of her in bed for the first few nights. Not that Barbara Jean slept much. Every night, they heard her creep out of her room and down the stairs to sit alone in her library. She would return to the bed just before sunrise and pretend later that she'd slept through the night.

Barbara Jean hardly spoke at all. And, when she did, not a word of it was about Lester. Most of her time was spent pacing the house, stopping in her tracks every so often to shake her head like a sleeper trying to wake up from a nightmare. She was in no shape to be left alone or to make any decisions. And there was so much that had to be done.

Clarice and Odette were surprised to learn that, although Lester had spent many years fighting off various near-fatal illnesses, the only preparation he had made for his passing was a short will leaving everything to Barbara Jean. So while Odette saw to Barbara Jean, Clarice could be depended on to organize the service and interment. She planned everything from Lester's burial suit to the menu for the funeral dinner. She accomplished it all with a gracious smile, even swallowing her temper when dealing with the pastor and higher-ups of First Baptist Church – a piss-elegant crowd if ever there was one, all of them eager to demonstrate to his widow just how deeply they adored the wealthy deceased. It was quite an undertaking, but burying any signs of contention and making sure that everything moved smoothly and looked exactly as it should was what Clarice had been raised to do. And Clarice was glad that her unique skills, gained at considerable personal expense, could be put to use to help her friend.

When a rich man dies, the vultures descend quickly. And Lester had been wealthier than anyone had imagined. He'd been Plainview-rich back when he was courting Barbara Jean. He became Louisville-rich not long after they got married. And, it was learned, he died Chicago-rich/New York-comfortable. Lester's greedier relatives were knocking on Barbara Jean's door for a handout well before the first fistful of dirt hit the lid of Lester's coffin. One previously unknown cousin came by claiming Lester had promised to fund her Hawaiian vacation. A great-niece wanted to interest Barbara Jean in "a surefire business opportunity" that just needed "a little start-up money." Several of Lester's leering male relations dropped by, basted in Old Spice, all prepared to provide guidance and a strong shoulder for the beautiful widow to weep upon.

This sort of situation, Clarice thought, was precisely why God made Odette. When the corners of Odette's mouth turned downward and her eyes narrowed, nobody stuck around to see what was coming next. She stood guard over Barbara Jean, sending anyone who posed a potential threat running for their lives with just a glance. And she did it all while battling through hot flashes that set her on fire almost every night.

The Supremes were in residence at Barbara Jean's for three weeks. Odette left each day to spend time with James, but always came back to be with Barbara Jean at night. Clarice went to check on Richmond a few times that first week, intending to cook his dinner and monitor his diabetes. But the fifth time she stopped by the house and failed to find him in or see any sign that he had come home at all since she'd been at Barbara Jean's, she asked herself why she was doing it, and couldn't come up with a good answer. So that day Clarice made sure the freezer was stocked with a month of meals, then she left Richmond a note saying she would return when Barbara Jean was okay. She stayed away for the next two weeks, limiting her contact with Richmond to one daily phone message that always went unanswered.

The morning after declaring temporary independence from Richmond, Clarice sat down at the piano in Barbara Jean's sitting room after breakfast. The piano was a Victorian beauty, a Steinway square grand with a rosewood cabinet. Clarice had ordered it herself during the initial renovation of Barbara Jean's mansion. It was a fine instrument and Clarice thought it was a shame that its role of late was merely decorative. She ran a finger over the white keys and then the black and was pleased to discover that it was in tune. She began to play.

The music drew Barbara Jean to the room, closely followed by Odette. They listened and then applauded when she finished. "That was nice," Barbara Jean said. "Sort of happy and sad at the same time."

"Chopin. Perfect for any occasion," Clarice said.

Barbara Jean rested her elbows on the piano. "Remember how Adam used to imitate you?"

"I sure do," Clarice said, twisting her mouth to feign offense.

Barbara Jean turned to Odette. "Adam used to do the best imitation of Clarice after his lessons. He would hunch over the keys and sway and moan. It was the funniest thing in the world, watching him work up all that passion while he played – what was it? 'Chopsticks'?"

"'Heart and Soul,'" Clarice said.

"That's right. 'Heart and Soul.' The first time he did it, Clarice and I both laughed so hard we ended up on our knees crying. It was a hoot."

Odette had heard that story on the day it happened and hundreds of times since, but Barbara Jean was laughing and it sounded too good to put a stop to it.

Barbara Jean said, "He loved music. I bet he could've been really good."

"Absolutely. He was musical. He had a natural facility. Adam had it all."

"Yes, he did," Barbara Jean said.

Barbara Jean talked about Adam for the rest of that morning. "Remember how he loved to draw? He'd spend hours up in his room with his crayons and colored pencils." "I'll never forget how he taught Odette's boys to dance like James Brown. I can still see Eric shuffling across the floor in his training pants." "Wasn't he the most dapper little boy you ever saw? Never knew a boy to fuss over his clothes like he did. One scuff on his shoes and he'd pout all day."

The following morning and the next few began the same way. They had breakfast, and then Clarice played the piano. Then Barbara Jean talked about Adam, allowing memories of him to pull her back into her life. Eventually, there was so much conversation and laughter that it seemed as if the three of them were guests at an extended slumber party. Except, at this party, talking about men was carefully avoided. No Lester Maxberry. No Richmond Baker, which suited Clarice fine. And definitely no Chick Carlson, whom Clarice and Odette were both pretending they hadn't seen at Big Earl's house after the funeral.

In spite of the circumstances, on the mid-August morning when Barbara Jean thanked Odette and Clarice for their support and kindly, but firmly, ordered them out, Clarice was sorry to leave. She told herself at the time that her reluctance to end the slumber party was because she'd had such fun with her friends, reliving a part of their shared youth. Later, she admitted to herself that she was frightened of what she knew in her heart she would find when she got home.

When Clarice stepped inside her front door after two weeks away, she called out Richmond's name to empty walls. None of the food she had prepared for him had been touched. And the sheets on their bed were as fresh as they'd been when she had put them on over a fortnight earlier.

When Richmond came home two days later, he gave her a peck on the cheek and inquired about Barbara Jean.

"She's better," Clarice answered. "Are you hungry?"

He answered yes, and then kissed his wife's cheek again after she told him that she would prepare ham steak and roasted potatoes, one of his favorite meals.

Richmond showered while Clarice hummed "Für Elise" and cooked his dinner. He never offered an explanation about where he'd been sleeping, and Clarice never asked him for one.

Chapter 10

Odette, Clarice, and Barbara Jean became the Supremes in the summer of 1967, just after the end of their junior year of high school. Classes had been out for only a couple of weeks and Clarice was at Odette's house preparing to go to the All-You-Can-Eat. Big Earl occasionally opened up the restaurant to his son's friends on Saturday nights. The kids thought of it as adventurous and grown-up, getting out of Leaning Tree and into downtown Plainview for an evening. A night at the All-You-Can-Eat was their first taste of adult liberty. In truth, they had escaped their homes and their parents to sip Coca-Cola and eat chicken wings under the most watchful eyes in town. They couldn't have been more strictly monitored anywhere else on the planet. Big Earl and Miss Thelma had a talent for identifying and neutralizing troublemakers, and no kind of teenage mischief got past them.

Mrs Jackson tapped on Odette's bedroom door as Clarice rummaged through her best friend's chest of drawers searching for something to liven up, or cover up, those dreadful dresses Odette always wore. The blind grandmother who had made her clothes back when she was a little girl was dead, but her grandma's style and taste lived on in Odette's sorry closet. Mrs Jackson said, "Before y'all go to Earl's, I want you to run this over to Mrs Perdue's house for me."

She held out a cardboard box wrapped with twine. Grease stains covered most of the box's surface, and it emitted an aroma of burnt toast and raw garlic. Even Odette's three cats, all strays that had sensed her true nature beneath her get-the-hell-away-from-me exterior and followed her home to be adopted, shrank away from the odor of the package. They yowled and bolted out of the open doorway.

Odette took the box from her mother and asked, "Who is Mrs Perdue?"

Mrs Jackson said, "You know, your little friend Barbara Jean's mother. Her funeral was today, so I baked a chicken for the family."

Clarice looked at the clock and felt that she had to say something. She had made plans to meet Richmond and one of his buddies at 7:00. It was only 5:30, but Clarice knew from experience how long it could take to transform Odette from her usual self into someone a boy might want to wrap his arm around. There simply wasn't time for anything else.

Clarice was indignant. She was a good girl. She got excellent grades. Hardly a season passed without her piano playing winning her a prize or affording her a mention in the newspaper that would join the articles about her birth that adorned the walls of her parents' home. Still, she was monitored every hour of her day. All of her socializing took a backseat to the four hours of piano practice she did daily in preparation for the two lessons she had each week with Zara Olavsky, an internationally renowned piano pedagogue who taught at the university's music school. She was required to check in hourly whenever she was away from home. And she had the earliest curfew of any teenager in town.

Her parents grew even more vigilant that year, with Richmond in college and Clarice still in high school. There were no dates at all unless she double-dated with Odette. Clarice was certain that, with Odette's gruff personality around boys and those horrible outfits she wore that growled "*keep away*," her parents viewed Odette as walking, talking virginity insurance. Not that Odette's face was all that bad. She could be cute in the right light. And her figure was decent, top-heavy and round. Lord knows there were plenty of boys who longed to slip a hand down her blouse. But no boy wanted to cop a feel off the fearless girl. She was just more trouble than she was worth. Richmond had called in all kinds of favors to get his college friends to go out with her. Pretty soon he was going to have to start paying them.

But Richmond had a date for Odette that night and Clarice's parents had agreed to allow her to stay out an hour later than usual. It was going to be a perfect evening. Now Odette's mother was trying to ruin it.

Whining often worked on her own mother when she wanted out of an unpleasant chore or wanted her curfew extended, so Clarice gave it a try with Dora Jackson. She said, "But, Mrs Jackson, we're going to the All-You-Can-Eat and Barbara Jean lives the other direction and I've got on heels."

Odette mouthed, "Shut up." But even though she knew

from the look on Mrs Jackson's face that she should stop talking, Clarice piped up with "And besides, Barbara Jean is not our friend. She's nobody's friend, except the boys she runs around with. And she stinks, Mrs Jackson. She really does. She drowns herself in cheap perfume every day. And my cousin Veronica saw her combing her hair in the bathroom at school last year and a roach fell out."

Mrs Jackson narrowed her eyes at Clarice and said, slow and low, "Odette's gonna take this chicken over to Barbara Jean to show that child some kindness on the day of her mother's funeral. If you don't wanna go, then don't. If you're worried about your feet, borrow some sneakers from Odette. If you're worried about roaches fallin' off of her, then step back if she gets to flingin' her head around. Or maybe you should just go on home."

The only thing Clarice could think of that was worse than delaying her date with Richmond to run this ridiculous errand Mrs Jackson couldn't be dissuaded from was the idea of going back home and, with her chaperone otherwise occupied, being forced to stay in and keep her mother company all evening. Seeing her plans with Richmond fading away, Clarice rushed to save them. Speaking quickly, she said, "No, ma'am. I'll go with Odette. I didn't really believe that roach story. Veronica likes to make stuff up."

Mrs Jackson left the room without another word, and Odette and Clarice headed to Barbara Jean's.

Plainview is shaped like a triangle. Leaning Tree comprises its southeast section. To get to Barbara Jean's house, the two girls had to walk south along Wall Road and then along side streets into the very tip of the triangle's corner.

The wall that gave the road its name was built by the town when freed blacks started settling in Plainview after the Civil War. A group of town leaders led by Alfred Ballard – whose house Barbara Jean would one day own – decided to build a ten-foot-high, five-mile-long stone wall to protect the wealthy whites who lived downtown when the race war they expected finally came. Though further north, the poor whites were on the east side of the wall with the blacks, but the town leaders figured they could fend for themselves. When the new inhabitants proved less frightening than predicted, commitment to the wall project faded. The only section of Ballard's Wall that made it to the full ten-foot goal was the portion that divided Leaning Tree from downtown. The rest of the proposed wall ended up as isolated piles of rocks, creating a dotted dividing line through town.

That part of the story of Leaning Tree was pretty well accepted as fact by everyone. Plainview's children were taught that bit of local history in school, with the aesthetic aspects of the wall replacing much of the racial politics. But the history taught in school and what black children were taught at home took off in radically different directions at the subject of the naming of Leaning Tree.

In school, they learned that early settlers called the southeast area of town Leaning Tree because of a mysterious natural phenomenon – something about the position of the river and the hills – that caused the trees to lean toward the west.

At their dinner tables, the children of Leaning Tree were told that there was no mystery at all to the crooked trees. Their parents told them that, because downtown was on higher ground, Ballard's Wall cast a shadow over the black area of town. The trees there needed sunlight, so they bent. Every tree that didn't die in the shadow of that wall grew tall, top-heavy, and visibly tilted. A name was born.

Barbara Jean's house was on the worst street in the worst neighborhood in Leaning Tree. Her street was only eight blocks from Clarice's house, only five from Odette's. But as they turned onto Barbara Jean's block, Clarice surveyed her surroundings and thought that this place might as well have been on the far side of the moon for all the resemblance it held to the landscaped, middle-class order of her street or the quaint charm of Odette's old farmhouse, with its fanciful octagonal windows and scalloped picket fence, courtesy of Odette's carpenter father. In this neighborhood, people lived in tiny boxes with warped and splintering siding, peeling paint, and no gutters. Noisy, nappy-headed children ran naked over lawns that were mostly dirt accented with patches of weeds.

Barbara Jean's house was the best on her block, but that wasn't saying much. It was a little brown shack whose paint had faded to a chalky tan color. This house was only better than its neighbors because, unlike every other house on the street, the glass in all of its windows seemed to be intact.

Odette climbed up the two steps from the walkway and rang the bell. No one answered, and Clarice said, "Let's just leave it on the stoop and get going." But Odette started banging on the door with her fist.

A few seconds later, the door opened just wide enough for Clarice and Odette to see a big man with red eyes and blotchy, grayish-brown skin staring at them. His nose was flat and crooked, as if it had been broken a few times. He had no discernible neck, and most of his face was occupied by an unusually wide mouth. His shirt strained against his belly to stay fastened. He topped it all off with hair that had been straightened and lacquered until it resembled a plastic wig from an Elvis Presley Halloween costume.

He squinted against the sunlight and said, "Y'all want somethin'?" His words whistled through a gap between his front teeth.

Odette lifted the box and said, "My mama sent this for Barbara Jean."

The man opened the door fully then. He stretched his mouth into a smile that caused a prickly sensation to travel across the back of Clarice's neck and gave her the feeling he was about to take a bite out of her. She was relieved that they could finally hand off the box and get the hell out of this neighborhood. But the man stepped back into the dark beyond the doorway and said, "Come on in." Then he yelled, "Barbara Jean, your friends is here to see you."

Clarice wanted to stand on the front stoop and wait for Barbara Jean to come outside, but Odette was already walking through the front door and waving at her to follow. When they stepped into the front room, they saw Barbara Jean looking surprised and embarrassed to have two girls from school she hardly knew walking into her house.

Barbara Jean wore her funeral clothes, a too-tight black skirt and a clinging, shiny black blouse. Shameless, Clarice thought. During the walk to Barbara Jean's, Clarice had admitted to herself that this mission of mercy really was the only right thing to do. But as she silently critiqued Barbara Jean's sexy mourning outfit, another side of Clarice's nature leapt to the forefront and she began to eagerly anticipate describing Barbara Jean's getup to her mother and her cousin Veronica. Their reactions would be priceless.

The living room was crowded with showy, ornate furniture that was all well past its prime. With each step, a plastic runner protecting the bright orange carpet crunched beneath their feet. The place looked as if someone with a little money, but not much taste or good sense, had once lived there and left behind all their stuff.

Odette walked over to Barbara Jean and held out the box. "We were sorry to hear about your loss. My mama sent this. It's a roast chicken."

Barbara Jean said, "Thank you," and reached for the box, looking eager to hasten her visitors' departure. But the man grabbed the box away just as Odette handed it to her. He said, "Y'all come on into the kitchen," and walked toward the back of the house. The girls didn't move, and from the next room the man shouted, "Come on now." Obedient girls that they were, they followed.

The kitchen was in worse shape than the two rooms Clarice and Odette had passed through to get to it. The floor was so chipped they could see the tar paper underneath the linoleum. Dirty dishes were heaped in the rusted metal sink and piled on the cracked wooden countertop. The red patent leather seat covers of the kitchen chairs had all split open and dingy white stuffing bulged out of the open seams.

Where, Clarice wondered, were the aunts, female

friends, and cousins who were supposed to descend en masse to cook, clean, and comfort after a tragedy? Even the lowliest, most despised second or third cousin in her family would have merited at least one afternoon of attention on the day of their burial. But no one had bothered to come here.

The man sat at the table and motioned for them to sit with him. The three girls sat down and stared at each other, not knowing what to say. He turned toward Odette and said, "Tell your mama that me and my stepdaughter sure appreciate her kindness." He reached out then and patted Barbara Jean's arm, causing her to flinch and scoot away from him, her chair making a loud scraping noise as the metal feet dug into the scarred floor.

Clarice wanted to get out worse than ever, but Odette wasn't doing anything to move the process along. Odette just watched the man and Barbara Jean closely, as if she were trying to decipher a riddle.

The man poured a shot of whiskey from a bottle of Old Crow that sat in front of him on the table. Then he picked up his smudged glass and drained it in one swallow. Clarice had never seen a man drink straight whiskey and she couldn't help gawking. When he noticed her staring, he said, "Sorry, girls. Where's my manners? Barbara Jean, get some glasses for our guests."

Barbara Jean put her hand to her forehead and sank a little lower in her chair.

Odette said, "No, thank you, sir. We just came to drop off the food and get Barbara Jean. My mother said to bring her back to our house for dinner and not to take no for an answer."

Barbara Jean looked at Odette and wondered if she was crazy. Clarice kicked Odette hard under the table with the point of her shoe. Odette didn't yelp or react at all. She just sat there smiling at the man, who was pouring his second drink.

"Nah, I don't think she should go anywhere tonight," he said, his wide mouth twisting into a nasty expression that made Clarice's stomach tighten up. She got the feeling that something bad was about to happen, and she set her feet beneath her so she could run if she needed to. But the man relaxed his mouth back into his cannibal grin and said, "Barbara Jean's been through a lot today and she should stay home with her family." He looked around the room and made an expansive, circular motion with the whiskey bottle as if he were indicating a corps of relatives scampering and fussing around them. Then he put the bottle down and touched Barbara Jean's arm again. Again, she recoiled from him.

Odette said, "Please let her come. If we come back without her, Mama'll have Daddy drive us back over to get her. And I hate riding around town in the back of that police cruiser. It's embarrassing."

"Your daddy's a cop, huh?"

"Yes, sir. In Louisville," Odette said.

Clarice couldn't stop her jaw from dropping open at the sound of Odette lying with such conviction.

The man thought for a few seconds and had a change of heart. He rose from his chair, staggered badly, and stood just behind Barbara Jean. He leaned forward and squeezed her upper arms with his large hands. Then he rested his chin on the top of her head. He said, "No need to put your daddy through the trouble of comin' by. Your mama's right. My little girl should be around women tonight. Jus' don't stay out too late. I don't like to worry."

He stood there for a while holding on to Barbara Jean's arms and swaying while she looked straight ahead. Finally, she said, "I've got to change," and she slid sideways out of his grasp. The man was thrown off balance and had to grip the chair to keep from toppling forward onto the table.

Barbara Jean walked just a few steps away and opened a door off the kitchen. She went into the smallest bedroom Clarice had ever seen. It was really just a pantry with a bed and a battered old dresser in it. And the bed was a child's bed, far too small for a teenager. Clarice watched through the partially opened door as Barbara Jean pulled off her tacky black blouse. Then she picked up a bottle of perfume from the dresser and repeatedly squeezed the bulb, spraying her arms where the man had touched her as if she were applying an antiseptic. When she caught Clarice's reflection in the mirror above her dresser, she slammed shut the door.

The man straightened up and said, "Y'all scuse me. I gotta take a leak." He shuffled away, but stopped at the kitchen door and turned back to Clarice and Odette. He winked and said, "Be good and don't drink up all my whiskey while I'm gone." Then he continued out of the room. A few seconds later, they heard him relieving himself and humming from down the hallway.

When they were alone, Clarice took the opportunity to kick Odette again. This time Odette said, "Ouch, quit it."

"Why did you do that? We could've been out of here and gone."

Odette said, "We can't just leave her here with him."

"Yes, we can. This is her house."

"Maybe, but we're not leaving her alone with him right after she buried her mother."

There was no use arguing with Odette once she got a notion stuck in her head, so Clarice said nothing more. It was clear to her that Odette had looked at this cat-eyed, stray girl and set her mind on adoption.

When Barbara Jean emerged from her cramped cell, she was wearing a glittery red blouse and the same black skirt. Her hair, which had been pulled back and pinned up, now fell around her shoulders in waves, and she had applied lipstick to match her blouse. She may have stunk of cheap perfume, but she looked like a movie star.

The man came back into the room. He said, "You look just like your sweet mama," and Barbara Jean looked at him with a hatred so strong that Clarice and Odette felt it like a hot wind sweeping through the room.

As the man fell into his chair and reached for the bottle, Barbara Jean said, "Bye, Vondell." She was out of the kitchen and headed down the hallway before Clarice and Odette had begun their farewells to the bleary-eyed man at the table.

Outside, they stood in front of the house looking at each other. Clarice couldn't stand the silence. She lied the way she'd been taught to do after meeting someone's unpleasant relative. "Your stepfather seems nice."

Odette rolled her eyes.

Barbara Jean said, "He's not my stepfather. He's my mother's . . . He's nothing is what he is."

They walked about a half a block together, quiet again.

Barbara Jean spoke after a while. "Listen, I appreciate you getting me out of the house. I really do. But you don't have to take me anywhere. I can just walk around for a while." She looked at her watch, a dime-store accessory with yellow rhinestones surrounding its face and a cracked, white patent leather band. "Vondell's likely to be asleep in another couple hours. I can go back then." To Odette she said, "Thank your mother for making the chicken. It was real nice of her."

Odette hooked an arm under Barbara Jean's elbow and said, "If you're gonna walk, you might as well walk with us. You can meet the latest victim Clarice's boyfriend has dragged over from the college to distract me while he tries to get down her pants."

"Odette!" Clarice screamed.

Odette said, "It's true and you know it." Then she tugged Barbara Jean in the direction of the All-You-Can-Eat. "Oh, and Barbara Jean, whatever you do, don't eat any of my mama's chicken."

When her mother and her cousin later asked Clarice why she had become friendly with Barbara Jean that summer, she would say that it was because she got to know and appreciate Barbara Jean's sweetness and sense of humor and because she had felt a welling up of Christian sympathy after gaining a deeper understanding of the difficulties of Barbara Jean's life – her dead mother, her dreadful neighborhood, her sad little hole of a bedroom, that man Vondell. And those things would one day be true. Within months, Clarice's mother and cousin would learn that any petty criticism or harsh judgment of Barbara Jean would be met with icy silence or an uncharacteristically blunt rebuke from Clarice. And Clarice would eventually confess to Odette that she felt tremendous guilt about having been the source of many of the rumors about Barbara Jean. Her cousin might have started the rumor about the roach in Barbara Jean's hair, but Clarice had been the main one spreading it around.

But at the time, even as she listed in her mind the more noble reasons for making this new friend, she knew that there was more to it. At seventeen, Clarice was unable to see the true extent to which she was ruled by a slavish devotion to her own self-interest, but she understood that her primary reason for becoming friends with Barbara Jean was that it had benefited her. On the night she and Odette dropped off that putrid-smelling chicken, Clarice discovered that Barbara Jean's presence was surprisingly convenient.

When Clarice, Odette, and Barbara Jean walked into the All-You-Can-Eat, Little Earl ushered them to the coveted window table for the first time. A group of his pals was sitting there, but he chased them off, saying, "Make way. This table is reserved for the Supremes." After that, every boy in the place, even those who Clarice knew had told some of the most outlandish lies about Barbara Jean and what she'd supposedly done with them, came to the window table to stutter and stammer through their best adolescent pickup lines.

Richmond showed up with James Henry in tow a few minutes after the girls had been seated. Clarice made a mental note to give Richmond hell later for bringing him. James was the worst of all the regular guys Richmond had scrounged up for Odette. He was nice enough, and he'd had a fondness for Odette ever since she'd beaten two teenage boys bloody when she was ten after they'd called him "Frankenstein" because of that ugly knife scar on his face. But he was, Clarice thought, the most boring boy on the face of the earth. He barely made conversation at all. And when he did, it was pathetic.

The only topic James talked with Odette about at any length was her mother's garden. He worked for Lester Maxberry's lawn care business and he came to their dates armed with helpful hints for Odette to pass along to Mrs Jackson. James was the only boy Clarice knew who could sit in the back of a car parked on the side of a dark road with a girl and talk to her about nothing but composted manure.

Worst of all, James was always exhausted. He had to be at work early in the mornings, and he took classes at the university in the afternoons. So just when the evening got going, James would start nodding off. Odette would see his head droop and she would announce, "My date's asleep. Time to go home." It was intolerable.

Odette had a slightly different view of James Henry. He might have been the worst double-date choice for Clarice's purposes, but Odette was content with him. She thought it was kind of sweet how he dropped off to sleep during their dates. How many other boys would let themselves be that vulnerable in front of a girl – mouth open and snoring? And he had excellent manners. James had become a frequent visitor, never failing to come by and personally convey his thanks to Dora Jackson for the food she regularly brought to his home after his mother became housebound with emphysema. This in spite of the fact that Odette had witnessed James wisely burying her mother's half-raw, half-burned pork chops beside his house one day. She assumed, hoped, that all of the meals her mother gave the Henrys ended up underground as well. Still, each inedible bundle was greeted with undeserved gratitude from James.

Odette knew just enough about men to have her guard up at all times. So she hadn't eliminated the possibility that, underneath it all, James might be as horny and stupid as his friend Richmond. But she was willing to tolerate his head falling onto her shoulder occasionally while she figured him out.

Richmond and James wound through the crowd of boys gathered around the window table. James behaved the same way he always did. He sat next to Odette, complimented her homemade dress, inquired about her mother's garden, and then yawned. Richmond was another story. To Clarice's surprise and enjoyment, Richmond, by then a college football hero, felt threatened by all of the testosterone-dizzy boys surrounding his girl, even though they were really there for Barbara Jean. Ordinarily, he was content to sit in the center of the throng, entertaining the boys who came by the table to laugh at his jokes and to hear tales of his record-breaking freshman year on the team. Clarice felt that she had his full attention only in those brief moments when they found themselves alone. That night, though, Richmond spent the entire evening with his arm draped around her shoulders, whispering in her ear and being extra attentive to her in order to clearly stake out his claim.

Barbara Jean was like magic, Clarice thought. The more boys came by to get a close look at her, the more territorial Richmond became. That night was a wonderful evening of flirting, dancing, and nonstop free malts and Coca-Colas from admirers. When James drifted off to sleep and it came time to leave, Big Earl had to intercede to forestall a fistfight over who would see the Supremes home.

As they left the All-You-Can-Eat and headed for Richmond's car, Clarice whispered to Odette, "Barbara Jean is our new best friend, okay?"

Odette said, "Okay." And by the end of the summer, that's the way it was.

Chapter 11

Six weeks after Big Earl's funeral, my summer break ended and I returned to my job. I was food services manager at James Whitcomb Riley Elementary School, which was a fancy way of saying "head lunch lady." Normally, I enjoyed getting back to work and starting the new school year. But that fall was a tough one.

James was still adjusting to life without Big Earl being there for him. I often caught him reaching for the phone, only to set it back down again as a brief shadow of pain traveled across his face. Whenever that happened, I knew who he'd been thinking of calling. I'd done the same thing for months after losing Mama so suddenly. James's mother had died relatively young, but she had wasted away for years and James had learned to live without her long before she passed. Losing a parent, and that's what Big Earl had been to James, in the blink of an eye was a new kind of loss for James and it was going to take him some time to work it through.

Barbara Jean was bad off, too. She tried to put up a good front. She wasn't hysterical or even teary-eyed, and she looked as perfectly put together as ever. But it was easy to see that Lester and Big Earl passing right up on top of each other like they'd done had laid her low. She was living deep in her own thoughts and pulling herself further away from Clarice and me every day.

Clarice had her hands full with Richmond. He was back to his cheating ways with a vengeance. It was like the old days. Richmond catted around, not caring who knew. People barely acquainted with him and Clarice openly gossiped about it. Clarice pretended not to notice, but she burned so hot with anger at him some days that I hoped, for both of their sakes, that Richmond was sleeping with one eye open.

And me. After slacking off for a while, my hot flashes were back big time. More nights than not, the early hours of the day found me cooling myself in the kitchen and shooting the breeze with Mama, instead of sleeping. I loved Mama's company, but the lack of sleep was taking a toll on me. I felt run-down and I looked, as my mother bluntly put it, "like shit on a cracker."

By the middle of October, I'd had my fill of feeling bad, so I went to my doctor and rattled off a long list of symptoms. I told him about my hot flashes and my fatigue. I complained that I was getting forgetful and, James claimed, irritable. I wasn't willing to tell him the main reason I had decided to see him. I had no desire whatsoever to explain to my doctor that I'd made my appointment because former first lady Eleanor Roosevelt had been showing an awful lot of interest in me lately. I remembered, all too well, how she'd orbited around Lester right before he electrocuted himself, and it had me feeling antsy.

At first Mrs Roosevelt had only visited me along with Mama, but then she started turning up by herself. Some mornings I would walk into my cramped office off of the cafeteria at Riley Elementary and there she'd be, asleep in one of the rusty metal folding chairs or stretched out on the floor. Occasionally she'd pop up out of nowhere and lean over my shoulder as I did the food orders over the phone. I made up my mind to see the doctor after Mrs Roosevelt greeted me every morning for a solid week, grinning wide and offering me a swig from her flask. (Mama had been right about Mrs Roosevelt and the drinking. That woman was at her flask morning, noon, and night.)

Mrs Roosevelt and Mama sat in the corner of the examining room during my checkup and during the tests that came afterwards. They came with me again a week after that first appointment and listened in as my doctor, Dr Alex Soo, told me that I had non-Hodgkin's lymphoma.

Alex was my friend. He was a chubby Korean man, about a year younger than my son Jimmy. When he took over my old doctor's practice several years back, I had been his very first patient.

Alex came to town just after my Denise left the house, and as soon as I laid eyes on Alex's round, smooth face I decided to mother the hell out of him, whether he wanted it or not. When I found out that he lived alone and had no relatives nearby, I badgered him into spending the holidays with me and my family. It was an annual tradition now. Sometimes, if Alex wasn't careful, he'd slip and call me "Ma."

Now this kind young man sat twisting his fingers behind a mahogany desk that seemed too large for him. He worked hard at not looking me in the eye while he rattled off the details of what was happening within my body and what needed to be done to stop it. The next step, he said, was to get a second opinion. He'd already made an appointment for me with an oncologist at University Hospital who was "one of the most highly regarded in his field." He used terms like "five-year survival rate" and "well-tolerated chemotherapy cycles." I felt sorry for him. He was trying so hard to remain calm that his voice came out robotic and full of bottled-up emotion at the same time, like a bad actor playing a soap opera doctor.

After he got done with his speech, he let out a long sigh of relief. The corners of his mouth curled up slightly, like he was proud of himself for making it over a big hurdle. When he was able to look at me again, he started in offering his most optimistic prognosis. He said, "Your general level of health is very good. And we know a lot about this kind of cancer." He went on to say that I might be lucky. I might be one of those rare people who sailed on through chemotherapy with hardly any side effects.

His words were meant to comfort me, and I appreciated it. But part of my mind had already left the office. In my head, I was telling my anguished kids not to worry about me. They were adults now and scattered all over the country, but still in need of parenting. Denise was a young mother, still filled with fear and worry over each stage of her children's development that defied the books she had believed would bring order to motherhood. Jimmy and his wife were both hell-bent on getting ahead and would work themselves to death if I didn't nag them into taking an occasional vacation. And Eric, he was as quiet as his father, and no one but me, who had listened over the phone as he cried his heart out over lost love more than once, knew that he felt everything twice as deep as his brother or sister.

From the moment I told the Supremes I was sick, Clarice would try to take over my life. First she'd want to take charge of my medical treatment. Then she'd get on my very last nerve by trying to drag me to her church for anointings and such. And Barbara Jean would just get all quiet and accept that I was as good as dead. Seeing her grieving for me ahead of time would bring back memories of all she's lost in her life, and it would depress the hell out of me.

My brother, in spite of being raised by our mother, had grown up and become a man who believed that women were helpless victims of our emotions and hormones. When he found out I was sick, he would talk to me like I was a child and pester me just like he used to when we were children.

And James. I thought of the look I used to see on James's face in that horrible, gray-yellow emergency room light whenever one of the kids suffered some childhood injury. The smallest pain for them meant despair for him. Whenever I came down with a cold or flu, he was at my side with a thermometer, medicine, and an expression of agony on his face for the duration. It was like he'd pooled up all the love and caring his father had denied him and his mother and was determined to shower it onto me and our children ten times over.

I made up my mind right then that I'd keep this whole thing to myself for as long as I could. There was still an outside chance that it was all a false alarm, wasn't there? And, if this chemo was indeed "well-tolerated," I might be able to tell everyone about it at my leisure. If I was lucky, in five or six months I could turn to James and my friends one Sunday at the All-You-Can-Eat and say, "Hey, did I ever tell you all about the time I had cancer?"

When I didn't say anything for a while, Alex spoke faster. believing he had to provide me with some sort of consolation. But I wasn't the one who needed to be consoled. Behind him on the windowsill of his office, Mama sat with both of her hands pressed to her face. She was crying like I had never seen before.

Mama muttered, "No, no, this can't be right. It's too soon."

Mrs Roosevelt, who had been lying on the sofa against the wall of Alex's office, rose and walked over to Mama. She patted Mama on the back and whispered in her ear, but whatever she said didn't do the trick. Mama continued to cry. She was crying so loud now that I could barely hear the doctor.

Finally, forgetting my vow not to talk to the dead in the presence of the living, I said, "It's all right. Really, it's all right. There's nothing to cry about."

Alex stopped talking and stared at me for a moment, assuming I was talking to him. He apparently took my words as permission for him to let go because within seconds he was out of his chair and crouching in front of me. He buried his face in my lap, and I soon felt his tears soak through my skirt. He said, "I'm so sorry, Ma." Then he apologized for not being more professional as he blew his nose into a tissue I pulled from the box on the corner of his desk and handed to him.

I rubbed his back, pleased to be comforting him instead of him comforting me. I bent forward and whispered,

"Shh, shh, don't cry," into Alex's ear. But I said it staring ahead at my mother as she sobbed into Eleanor Roosevelt's fox stole. "I'm not afraid. Can't be, remember? I was born in a sycamore tree."

Chapter 12

Clarice turned around in her chair to get a good look at the newly redecorated All-You-Can-Eat. It was just before Halloween and the restaurant was dressed up for the holiday. The windows were draped with cotton cobwebs. A garland of crepe-paper skulls surrounded the cash register. Each table was decorated with a centerpiece of tiny orange pumpkins, gold-and-green striped gourds, and a small wicker basket filled with candy corn. It wasn't the prettiest display Clarice had ever seen, but it did at least cover up that awful restaurant logo on the tablecloth.

No matter how she felt about the new logo, it was clear that this affront to her sensibilities wasn't going anywhere anytime soon. The kids from the university had discovered Little Earl's T-shirts with the big red lips, pink tongue, and suggestive fruits on them. Now a constant stream of young people came into the All-You-Can-Eat to giggle and buy the risqué restaurant merchandise. Little Earl was making a small fortune.

The Supremes, Richmond, and James were all in their usual places by the front window. For Barbara Jean's sake, they had tried shuffling things around after Lester died – moving the men to the opposite end one week, shifting

James to the center and Richmond to Lester's seat the next. But it was no use. The more they tried to avoid seeing it, the stronger they felt Lester's absence. Barbara Jean finally called a halt to the musical chairs, saying that she preferred to keep things the way they had always been.

Everyone was tired that week. Richmond yawned every few minutes – which was no surprise to Clarice since he'd been out all night again. Barbara Jean hadn't been fully awake since Lester died. She pretended that she was okay, but her mind wandered constantly and Clarice always had the feeling when she talked to her that Barbara Jean was only half there. James had been sleepy since childhood. And Odette actually fell asleep at the table that afternoon.

Clarice was exhausted from having spent most of the night playing the piano. She had begun to rely on music to get her through those nights when Richmond did his disappearing act. Instead of sitting up stewing over where her husband was, she had taken to playing the piano until she was too worn out to think. The previous night Clarice had begun playing Beethoven sonatas at midnight, and the next thing she knew she was under-scoring Richmond's arrival home at six in the morning with an angry fugue. Now her fingers ached and she could hardly lift her arms.

She poked Odette on her shoulder with her fork and said, "Wake up. You're starting to snore."

Odette said, "I wasn't sleeping. And I certainly wasn't snoring. I never snore." James heard her say that and let out a snort. "I heard every word you said. You were talking about how you surprised yourself yesterday with how much Beethoven you could still play from memory. See, I was listening."

"I finished telling that story ten minutes ago, Odette. Since then I've just been watching you sleep. Are you feeling okay?"

Odette sidestepped Clarice's question. "I'm sorry," she said. "Work is really taking it out of me. The children get unrulier every year. And the parents, well, they're just impossible. It seems like all the kids are on some sort of restricted diet that their parents have to come in and explain to me. And you'd better believe they make sure I know they'll sue me and the school district, too, if their little darlings ever get near a peanut or a grain of refined sugar. It's like they were bred in a lab somewhere, all of them allergic to this and intolerant of that. And try keeping those kids from trading candy loaded with chocolate and nuts this close to Halloween. It's enough to drive you crazy."

Barbara Jean said, "The kids haven't changed, Odette, you have. You're getting old."

"Thank you both. It's such a joy to come have Sunday supper and find out I'm a decrepit old woman who snores. Why I continue to hang out with you witches I will never understand."

Clarice laughed and said, "You hang out with us because we're the only ones not too scared of you to tell you that you snore and that you're old. But don't feel bad about it. We're all in the same boat."

At the other end of the table Richmond said, "Now *that* is a nice car."

Everyone turned and saw the car Richmond was

admiring. It was a steel-gray Lexus, polished to perfection, with windows tinted so dark you couldn't see who was behind the wheel.

No one spoke, each person at the table feeling the absence of Lester right then. He would surely have taken over the conversation at that moment. Lester had loved cars. He would have said that the Lexus was okay to look at, but way too small. From the 1970s onward he complained that luxury cars were disappointing now that they'd "taken the size out of 'em." Every year, he took a tape measure with him to the Cadillac dealer and bought the longest one on the lot regardless of color or style.

The Lexus moved forward at no more than three miles per hour. Just a few steps in front of the car, a heavyset young woman in a blue sweatshirt and blue sweatpants that were darkened to black from perspiration jogged in slow motion, struggling to lift her feet from the pavement.

Barbara Jean asked, "Isn't that your cousin's girl?"

Clarice said, "Yes, that's Sharon." The driver's-side window of the Lexus slid down and Veronica stuck her head out of the window. She yelled something at her daughter that the spectators in the restaurant couldn't hear.

"What on earth is Sharon doing?" Odette asked.

"I think she's exercising," Barbara Jean said.

Clarice said, "A big girl like that shouldn't run. It's suicidal."

The car stopped and they watched as Veronica double-parked and got out. She walked up to her daughter, who stood doubled over gasping for air in the street, and wagged a finger at her. Sharon poked out her lower lip and then began to run in place in front of her mother's car. Veronica gave her panting daughter a thumbs-up and headed toward the All-You-Can-Eat.

Odette groaned. "Oh, Lord, not her. Your cousin is the last thing I want to deal with today."

Odette had longed to strangle Veronica since 1965. But she had resisted the impulse, for Clarice's sake. Clarice didn't feel much fondness for Veronica, but they were blood. She was stuck with her, in spite of the fact that her cousin had been a thorn in her rear as far back as Clarice could remember. And now she was worse than ever, the perfect example, Clarice thought, of what happens when a pile of cash gets thrown on top of a raging blaze of ignorance.

Veronica's family had been the last of the Leaning Tree old-timers to sell out to the developers and it paid off big for them. Given half a chance, Veronica would expound for hours about what a visionary her father had been for holding out the way he did. The truth was, Veronica's father hated his wife so much that he preferred to keep the family poor rather than sell the property and see her live comfortably. Like Clarice's mother and many of the devout women of her generation, Clarice's aunt Glory had believed divorcing her husband and taking her rightful half of everything he owned would buy her a trip to hell, so her husband knew he had her stuck. He planned to torture her with his presence for decades. What he didn't plan on was dropping dead of a heart attack in the middle of one of their nightly arguments. Glory skipped her husband's funeral service to meet with a real estate lawyer.

She moved next door to her sister Beatrice in an Arkansas retirement village a week later.

Now Glory, Veronica, and Veronica's family were all living off the big chunk of money that they had received for the property, which Clarice hoped Veronica thanked the Lord for every night since she was married to a man who was borderline retarded and couldn't feed a bowl of goldfish, much less an entire family, on the piddling amount of money he made. Of course, like most of the poor folks from Leaning Tree who had lucked into the first real money of their lives when they sold their land, Veronica's clan of morons were burning through the money as quickly as they could. Clarice had no doubt Veronica would show up on her doorstep pleading for a handout sometime in the near future.

Veronica had a distinctive walk that was characterized by rigidly straight legs and jerky movements. She took fast, short steps – not quite running, not quite walking. Just the sight of her cousin trotting toward the window table that afternoon made Clarice ache to slap Veronica with her open palm. But instead of slapping her, Clarice said, "Veronica, darling, what a lovely surprise." Then the two of them made kissing noises at each other.

Clarice prepared herself to hear Veronica brag about her new car, but Veronica had other fish to fry. Without saying a word of hello to anybody – that was *so* like her – she started talking.

"I figured I'd catch you here. I've got wonderful news. Guess what it is." Clarice was about to say that she couldn't possibly guess what her cousin's news was when Veronica yelled out, "Sharon's getting married!"

Clarice said, "Congratulations. I didn't even know she was seeing anybody."

"It was a whirlwind romance. She met him four weeks back and the two of them hit it off right away. And here's the amazing thing, it was all foretold. I went to see Miss Minnie for a reading last month, and she told me that Sharon would meet a man and fall in love that very week. And wouldn't you know it, she met the man of her dreams at church the next Sunday." She wrinkled up her nose at Clarice and said, "That'll teach you to doubt Miss Minnie's powers. She hit the nail right on the head with this one. He was just who she described to me, tall, handsome, well-dressed. I took one look at him and told Sharon, 'Go introduce yourself. That man is your future husband.' A few dates later, she was asked to become Mrs Abrams."

Veronica had been a true believer in Minnie's abilities since she'd gone to see her for the first of many readings a few years earlier. Clarice was convinced her cousin went to see Minnie that first time for the specific purpose of getting under Clarice's skin, since Veronica knew full well how Clarice felt about the fortune-teller. At that reading, Minnie predicted that Veronica's husband, Clement, would have an accident of some sort. As it happened, Clement ended up in the hospital that same day after injuring himself at work. That was all the proof Veronica needed. Now she took everything Minnie said as the complete gospel truth. Clarice had reminded her, as nicely as she could, that predicting an accident for Clement wasn't such an impressive feat. He worked construction and, being a blithering idiot, he sliced, punctured, or burned himself on a weekly basis. It was the inevitable result of putting that fool in the same room with band saws, nail guns, and blowtorches. You didn't have to have second sight to see it coming. But Veronica was convinced that fate, having already showered her with much-deserved cash, had now provided her with her own oracle to go along with her imagined social prominence, and she wasn't hearing anything to the contrary.

Richmond said, "Sharon's marrying Ramsey Abrams's boy?" When Veronica nodded yes, Richmond looked right and left to see if anyone was within earshot and then whispered, "I don't want to talk bad about the boy, but does Sharon know about the stuff with him and the ladies' shoes?"

"Not *that* Abrams boy," she snapped. "Sharon's marrying the other brother." Clifton, the Abrams boy now engaged to Sharon, had spent his teenage years getting stoned and committing petty theft. As an adult, he had spent more time in jail than out. It seemed likely to Clarice that, if the Abrams boy had proposed to Sharon, it was because he was trying to get his hands on her mother's money before it ran out.

When no one said anything, Veronica seemed to guess what was on all of their minds. She added, "Clifton's changed. Been saved by the Lord and the love of a good woman."

Veronica looked over at Minnie's fortune-telling table. "I was hoping to catch Miss Minnie between appointments to get a quick reading. I want to find out what her spirit guide says before I pick the wedding date. I told Sharon I'd take care of all the plans so she can concentrate on losing weight. I want her to look just like her sisters did at their weddings."

Clarice said, "That's so sweet of you," but she thought something else. She thought of how Sharon's older sisters were two of the ugliest women she had ever seen, having inherited their mother's heavy brow and too-close eyes and their father's huge ears and sunken chin. Thin as the older girls were, Veronica would be doing her youngest no favor by making her look like her sisters.

The door opened again and Minnie McIntyre, draped in a black cape with dozens of silver eyes pasted all over it, swaggered into the All-You-Can-Eat. Since her husband's funeral she had taken advantage of Little Earl's soft heart and guilted him into allowing her to do Sunday readings. Of course, he was also less concerned about offending his more conservative customers than he had been before, now that his All-You-Can-Eat merchandise was such a big hit with the college crowd.

Veronica said, "I'm glad you're here, Miss Minnie. I was hoping you had a few minutes free today."

Minnie didn't answer Veronica. She turned to the occupants of the table and said, "I suppose y'all have heard about my latest prediction coming true. Charlemagne has opened the gates to the world of shadows to me now that he knows I'll be coming to join him soon." She crossed her arms over her chest and looked toward heaven the way she always did now when she talked about her approaching death.

Clarice couldn't stop herself from rolling her eyes. Minnie saw her, and she looked for a moment as if she might punch Clarice. But just then, a woman waved at her and called her name from the client chair at Minnie's table.

Minnie said, "Veronica darlin', I've got this one readin' to do and I can help you right after."

She took two steps away in the direction of her table, but then turned around, forcing her cape to swirl dramatically around her. She said, "You know, Clarice, I had a vision last night that I was all set to tell you about. I saw Richmond embracing you on a foggy beach, and I was sure that there was a romantic journey in your future. Funny thing is, when the fog cleared up, I saw that the man in my vision was Richmond, but the woman wasn't you. Isn't that strange?"

She stood there grinning, both she and Veronica waiting to see how Clarice would respond. But Clarice didn't tear up or even do Minnie the honor of casting an angry glance at Richmond, who was busy dragging a spoon across his empty plate and pretending not to hear what was being said just a few feet away. So the fortune-teller twisted her mouth in annoyance and marched off across the room toward her client.

Veronica raised her right arm in the air and snapped her fingers several times. When she attracted Erma Mae's attention she mouthed, "Iced tea." As she seated herself in the table's empty chair, she muttered, "And don't take a year to bring it." Then she turned to Clarice and said, "I didn't just come here to see Miss Minnie. I wanted to ask you to help me with the wedding, Clarice. You did such a nice job on your daughter's wedding that I thought of you immediately when Sharon got engaged. The first thing I said to Sharon was 'Let's call Clarice and have her do your wedding the exact same way she did Carolyn's, except without the shoestring budget.'"

Clarice exhaled slowly, smiled, and said, "You're a doll to think of me, Veronica. But I'm sure you and Sharon will be able to plan a beautiful wedding without my help."

Odette, who had been unusually quiet all afternoon, spoke up. She said, "Yes, Veronica, none of us will forget that Easter pageant you organized over at First Baptist. It was spectacular." Barbara Jean put her head down and covered her laughter by pretending she was coughing. And Clarice made a mental note to buy Odette an extra nice Christmas gift for bringing up Veronica's Easter pageant just then.

A couple of years earlier, Veronica had played on the fears of the board at First Baptist that their Easter pageant would be outshined by the white folks at Plainview Lutheran. The Lutherans had recently started adding some real sparkle to their Easter show – live lambs and a candlelight processional. She promised them that, if they handed the event over to her, she would produce an extravaganza that would leave the demoralized Lutherans hanging their heads in shame.

From the moment Veronica's daughters started the show with an interpretive dance, the whole thing was a disaster. Veronica's older girls were no more coordinated than they were pretty. And poor Sharon, who had been known to become out of breath just lifting a two-liter Pepsi bottle to her lips, got heart palpitations and had to sit down and rest in the middle of the routine.

The highlight of Veronica's show, a dramatization of Christ's ascension into heaven, was ruined when the winch used to carry Reverend Biggs up into the rafters got stuck and left him dangling in a harness thirty feet in the air. It took hours for the fire department to get him down. And the worst part was that no one had any doubt the Lutherans would hear all about the whole debacle.

Veronica slid her glass of iced tea, untouched since Erma Mae brought it to her, a few inches further away from her so she could rest her elbow on the table as she presented her back to Odette. To Clarice, she said, "I was thinking you could come with me tomorrow to look at invitations and some swatches for the girls' dresses."

Clarice didn't want to spend an extra minute with Veronica. The holidays weren't that far off and she would be stuck with her at family gatherings soon enough. But she also had an awful feeling that this was a little taste of justice coming her way. She had sought Odette's counsel when helping to put together Carolyn's wedding, and she had initially been sincere in asking for it. Denise's ceremony, which Odette had helped to plan, had been lovely. But once Clarice got going, she hadn't been able to stop herself from taking note of each detail of Denise's wedding and then doing her best to ostentatiously outdo them all. Now Veronica was asking for advice, and Clarice knew without a doubt that her cousin would one-up everything Clarice had done for her Carolyn's nuptials.

Clarice was reminded then of what she found most insufferable about Veronica. Her cousin had an awful way of making her look at her own worst traits just when she didn't want to see them. Whenever Clarice was around Veronica, she had to acknowledge that in Veronica she saw herself. It frightened her a little to think that the primary difference between them was the moderating influence of Odette and Barbara Jean.

Thanks to Odette stepping in again, Clarice didn't have to commit to helping her cousin that afternoon. "Veronica," Odette said, "I think maybe Sharon's ready to get back to her run." They looked outside and saw that Sharon had left the car behind and was moving down the block with renewed determination in her stride.

Veronica said, "You can't keep that girl away from her jogging. I had some trouble persuading her to get with the program at first, but now she's devoted."

Not a second later, Sharon veered off the street and straight into the front door of Donut Heaven bakery.

Veronica grumbled, "That girl," and ran out of the restaurant. She hopped into her new car and drove a third of a block up the street to the donut shop. She dashed inside and came out seconds later, dragging Sharon with her. As her mother wrestled her into the car, Sharon cradled one of Donut Heaven's bright pink boxes against her chest as if it were a newborn baby.

Odette cleaned the last bit of gravy from her plate with a dinner roll and said, "That woman ruins my appetite." Then she gnawed the gristle from the end of a pork chop bone.

They left the All-You-Can-Eat earlier than usual that day, all of them pleading fatigue. For the rest of the evening Clarice thought about Minnie's vision. She wasn't becoming a convert or anything like that. She knew that it took no psychic ability to envision Richmond with another woman. Hell, it didn't even take a good pair of eyes. What she thought about was how peculiar it was that having that nasty woman rub Richmond's behavior in her face in public had hardly had any effect on her. If such an incident had occurred a few months earlier, she'd have taken to her bed for days. But, even as it happened, the only sensation Clarice had been aware of was a fierce desire to be alone with her piano.

Chapter 13

After Lester's business was sold and all of the money issues had been seen to, Barbara Jean decided that she needed some sort of regular activity to give shape to her days. So she found a job. Then she found another. And another. All three were volunteer positions; still, it was the first time she'd had to report to work since she'd polished nails and administered shampoos at a hair salon when she was a teenager. On Mondays and Wednesdays, she delivered flowers to patients at University Hospital. Out of respect for her recent loss, the volunteer coordinator assigned her to the maternity ward, where she mostly encountered happy new parents and avoided the terminally ill. It wouldn't have mattered, though. They could have thrown death in her face all day and Barbara Jean wouldn't have blinked. With the help of an occasional sip from the thermos of spiked tea she always kept with her – it wasn't practical to bring her demitasse cups from home – she had turned off the part of her that grieved. And she wasn't about to turn it back on.

Every Friday morning, Barbara Jean went to First Baptist and did office work. She answered the phone, filed and made copies, all the things she had once done for Lester when his business first took off. After the office closed, she went downstairs to the church school and led Bible study class for new members. Even her pastor, Reverend Biggs, was impressed with Barbara Jean's biblical knowledge. Finally, she thought, all of those drunken nights in her library with Clarice's gift Bible were of some use to her.

On Tuesdays, Thursdays, and Saturdays, she worked at the Plainview Historical Society Museum. The museum, which consisted of a greeting area and three small rooms, each dedicated to a period of Plainview history – Indian Territory, Civil War, and Modern – was a twenty-minute walk up Plainview Avenue from her house. Her primary responsibilities were to sit at a desk in the greeting area, hand out brochures, and say, "Please wait beneath the Indiana state flag generously donated to the museum by the descendants of famed Hoosier president Benjamin Harrison. A tour guide will be with you momentarily."

Sometimes she was called upon to don a frontier wife costume and pretend to churn butter or stir imaginary food in a plastic pot over a papier-mâché fire, if the usual frontier wife volunteer couldn't make it. When no guests were at the museum, which was most of the time, she sat, sipped from her thermos, and read fashion magazines.

There were many days when her two sentences guiding the museum guests to their waiting place beneath the flag were the only words to cross her lips from sunrise to sunset. Those days were her favorites. She saw the other Supremes two or three times a week, and that was all the conversation she felt she could handle.

Walking back to her house from the museum, she followed Plainview Avenue as it rose toward the center of town and the intersection of Plainview and Main, where her house stood. If she turned her head to the left and peered downhill, she had a perfect view of the remnants of Ballard's Wall and the entrance to Leaning Tree Estates, as the housing development that now occupied her old neighborhood was called.

One early November day as she left the museum for home, she looked down at Leaning Tree. The tall, contorted trees of her old stomping grounds lent even more drama to the landscape now that they'd shed their leaves. She stared at their hunched-over skeletons. They were more impressive to her now than ever. Those trees had all adapted and thrived in the face of the grave insult that had been done to them. If she'd been inclined to ask God for anything, it would have been to make her more like the leaning trees.

She had done her best to adapt. In the three months since Lester's death, she had organized her time so that she was on the move nearly all day, every day. And wasn't that what everyone said widows should do?

But now, studying those crooked, old trees, Barbara Jean had to admit to herself that she had failed to thrive. No matter how activity-filled her days were, it was her nights that owned her. That night, she entered her fine home and heard the voice of her mother whispering bad advice and viperous recriminations in her ear. And after managing to fall asleep in her bed, she was wide awake within an hour, believing that she had felt Lester shift positions in the bed and then heard his congested cough coming from the bathroom. *Was it pneumonia again?*

She got out of bed and wandered the three floors of her

house, hoping that she might find it calming. But it didn't work; it never did. Adam filled the space every bit as much now as he had when he was alive. She heard his footsteps running from room to room on the third floor, where Lester's home office had been before the stairs became too much for him. Adam played up there that night just as he had thirty years earlier. The dark, cluttered storage rooms and mazes of filing cabinets held no menace for an adventurous boy who was never frightened, even when he should have been. The sound of Adam humming to himself in the TV room off of the kitchen as he polished that collection of shoes he was so fond of echoed through the first floor. She caught sight of him at the piano in the sitting room, waiting for his aunt Clarice to come by to give him his lesson. The museum that his bedroom had become seemed to have taken over the second floor. All of the other bedrooms were merely anterooms ushering her into the one room on the floor that mattered.

Only the library, with its waiting bottle and book, was a sanctuary from the spirits that haunted her. And that room offered no refuge after she collapsed into a drunken, exhausted sleep in her Chippendale chair. As soon as she nodded off, they returned. Loretta, Lester, Adam, and now Chick.

By the start of her senior year of high school, Barbara Jean was spending most of her time with Clarice and Odette. She hung out at one of their houses every day after school, doing homework, listening to records, and gossiping until at least eight. That way, when she got home she could tiptoe past Vondell, who was pretty much guaranteed to be passed out on the couch by then. On weekends, when it was harder to avoid Vondell, she worked at a hair salon that one of her mother's old friends owned, and slept at Odette's.

Barbara Jean never stayed over at Clarice's house. Mrs Jordan always went out of her way to be polite and kind to Barbara Jean, but she couldn't go so far as to allow the daughter of Loretta Perdue to spend an entire night in her home. Barbara Jean was initially surprised that Clarice's mother even allowed her to enter her front door, as Mrs Jordan was widely thought to be equal parts sanctimonious and stuck up. But she welcomed Barbara Jean's visits. When Barbara Jean better understood the workings of Mr and Mrs Jordan's marriage, she felt comfortable in assuming that Mrs Jordan's friendliness was the result of her relief at seeing that at least one of the town's bastards looked nothing like her husband.

It was a Saturday night. The three girls were at Clarice's house listening to records when the phone rang. Mrs Jordan called up the stairs for Clarice, saying that her cousin Veronica was on the line. Odette and Barbara Jean followed Clarice down to the kitchen where the phone was and watched as she listened. She hardly spoke at all, just shook her head and gasped, "No," and "You're kidding." When she hung up the phone, she turned to Odette and Barbara Jean and said, "Veronica says there's a white boy working at the All-You-Can-Eat."

Back then, no white people ever wandered into the All-You-Can-Eat. And it was unheard of for a white person, even a teenager, to work for a black man. So this was major news indeed. Five minutes after Clarice hung up the phone, the Supremes were on their way to Earl's.

When they arrived at the restaurant, they found the largest Saturday night crowd they had ever seen. Every table was full, except for the window table that, on weekends, was now permanently reserved for them. They had to squeeze through the crowd to get to their station. What with Clarice's music prizes, Richmond being the local football hero, and Barbara Jean looking the way she did, the window table was normally the center of attention at Earl's. But that night nobody glanced their way. Everyone was there to see the white boy.

When he stepped out of the kitchen with Big Earl, the crowd grew quiet. All that could be heard was an occasional whisper and the voice of Diana Ross cooing "Reflections" on the jukebox.

The white boy did not disappoint. He was tall and thin with wide shoulders and narrow hips. His skin was so pale that he looked as if he hadn't been in the sun in years. His hair was Shinola black and somewhere between wavy and curly. His pronounced cheekbones and high-bridged nose reminded Barbara Jean of the faces of statues she had seen in school art books. His round eyes were an icy blue. Later, Barbara Jean would remember looking at those eyes and thinking, *This must be what the sky looks like if you see it through a diamond.* He followed Big Earl from table to table, taking drink orders, clearing dishes, and wiping up spills. All the while, no one in the entire restaurant made a sound. They just watched him.

It was Odette, never embarrassed to say what she thought, who broke the silence. "That," she said, "is one pretty white boy." Several people heard her and began to

snicker. Then conversations started again and the atmosphere returned to something closer to normal.

Clarice said, "I have to disagree with you, Odette.
What we have here is the King of the Pretty White
Boys." Barbara Jean giggled, but she thought that maybe
it was true. It made perfect sense to her that, if she
stared at him for long enough, a jeweled crown would
appear on top of his head, maybe with an accompany-
ing trumpet salute, like in the Imperial Margarine
commercial on TV.

When Big Earl came to the window table accompanied
by the King of the Pretty White Boys, he said, "Hey girls,
let me introduce you to Ray Carlson. He's gonna be
workin' here."

The boy mumbled, "Hi," and gave the table a wipe,
even though it was clean.

The Supremes were saying hi to him when Ramsey
Abrams, who had overheard Big Earl's introduction,
hollered out from a couple of tables away, "You related to
Desmond Carlson?" And the place went quiet again.

Desmond Carlson and a few other rednecks were the
reason blacks couldn't walk along Wall Road any further
north than Leaning Tree. Desmond and his crew drove
their pickup trucks over the northern end of Wall Road on
their way from their houses to downtown and to the back-
country bars that dotted the landscape outside of
Plainview's town limits. Poor, uneducated, and faced with
a world that was changing in ways they couldn't understand, Desmond and his buddies were perpetually one or
two whiskey shots away from stupidity and violence. It
was their habit to hurl insults and beer bottles from their

cars at anyone with dark skin they found on the section of the road they had laid claim to.

His friends were content to cause trouble at night. But if Desmond encountered a Leaning Tree resident on Wall Road at any time of the day, he would yell out, "Get off my fuckin' road, jig," or some other comment that made his viewpoint clear. Then, laughing, he would aim his truck at whomever he had caught trespassing on his road so that they had to jump into the ditch at the side of the road to avoid being sideswiped.

Half of the town was scared to death of Desmond, who was always drunk, always angry, and – rumor had it – always armed. The Plainview police were in the scared half. They used the fact that Wall Road was university property and therefore technically under the jurisdiction of the Indiana State Police as an excuse to avoid having to confront Desmond and his buddies, who all had much bigger guns and were much tougher than the police. The university cops were only equipped to deal with drunken frat boys and they weren't about to get in the middle of a local squabble that might ignite a civil rights battle. So the residents of Leaning Tree walked a half mile out of their way, around the southern end of Wall Road and onto side streets that led to Plainview Avenue, whenever they left home for downtown.

Ramsey Abrams asked again, "So, what is it? You related to him, or not?"

Ray Carlson said, "He's my brother," and a wave of cursing and grumbling moved through the room.

Ramsey said, "Damn, Big Earl, what'd you go and let him in here for?"

Big Earl turned a hard eye on Ramsey and said, "Ramsey, both your brothers is in jail and you don't see me checkin' your pockets for silverware every time you leave here, do ya? I figure Ray here deserves the same chance."

That was that. Big Earl had told everyone how it was going to go down, and there was to be no arguing. Ramsey made a loud snorting noise to show his disapproval and went back to his food. Everyone else returned to eating, dancing, and flirting, the business of being teenagers.

Every so often someone came to the window table to whisper about the white boy. Little Earl told the girls that Ray had come by the restaurant trying to sell chickens he had raised. He said his father gave Ray a meal and then offered him a job on the spot, without the boy even asking. Ramsey came over to repeat his belief that it was a shame Big Earl had given a job to a white man that a black man should have had. Veronica came by and said that the girls at her table agreed he was cute, but thought he had no ass. Odette replied, "Who cares what he looks like walking away when he looks that good coming at you." And the night went on that way.

Later in the evening, Barbara Jean watched Ray Carlson as he cleared the table next to hers. As he worked, small white feathers began to fly through the air around him. Every time he moved his arm, another feather flew. She wasn't sure what was going on at first, but finally she saw that the feathers were coming from him. Hundreds of tiny white chicken feathers were stuck to his shirt and pants. Did he sleep with those chickens he raised?

Ray shed so much as he wiped the table that Richmond

Baker made his entrance through a cloud of white. Richmond reached out with one of his big hands and snatched a floating feather out of the air, then another. In addition to being a college football star, Richmond was a twenty-four-hour smartass. He took a look at the molting boy and cracked, "Hey, Big Earl, I see you went and hired yourself a chicken." From that day forward, Ray was Chick.

All evening long, Barbara Jean watched Chick work. He was a sight to see. He moved quickly and gracefully, gliding between the tables and maneuvering around the whirling couples as they spun in front of the jukebox in the corner where Big Earl had rearranged the tables to make room for dancing.

The only time Chick and Barbara Jean acknowledged each other directly after their introduction at the table came just before the girls went home that night. Clarice wanted to have one more dance with Richmond before leaving, so Barbara Jean was sent up to the jukebox to choose a song. She had just picked a tune and turned around to go back to her table when she found herself staring right into Chick's face.

Both of his arms were loaded with dirty dishes as he headed toward the kitchen door just a few feet away. The strain of lifting the plates made the muscles of his skinny arms stand out. Barbara Jean noticed for the first time that he had a dimple in his chin. She had to clasp her hands behind her back to keep from reaching out and pressing that delicate indentation with her forefinger.

Neither of them said anything for a few seconds. Then he said, "Hi," and smiled at her. She said hi back and took in that face of his again.

That was the end of their conversation. Just then, a dancer bumped him from behind and the stacks of dirty plates, silverware, and cups that he had balanced on his arms tilted forward and headed straight for the floor. Barbara Jean had to jump back to keep from being hit by the bits of food and shards of broken ceramics that went flying. The noise was tremendous, and when they saw what had happened, several boys cackled and pointed as if it were the funniest thing they had ever seen.

Big Earl came rushing over then. And that was when Barbara Jean saw something. It was just the briefest exchange, but it taught her lessons about both Big Earl and Chick, the first men she would love. Chick was already on his knees piling up the plates and garbage when Big Earl got to him, all six and a half feet of him still moving fast. Chick's reaction was to bring his forearm up defensively over his face and say, "I'm sorry. I'm sorry."

Barbara Jean recognized that posture and that reflexive apology and the feeling of waiting to be hit that went along with it. She understood then at least one part of Chick's story.

Big Earl knelt down beside him and used his great paw of a hand to pull Chick's arm away from his face. He wrapped an arm around the King of the Pretty White Boys and gave him a quick squeeze. Though the music was loud, Barbara Jean heard him clearly say, "It's all right. You're all right here. Ain't nobody here gonna hurt you." Then he helped Chick pick up the dishes.

The entire scene took less time to play out than it took Aretha to spell out "R-E-S-P-E-C-T" and Barbara Jean stood a few feet away watching it all. As Big Earl and Chick cleaned up the mess and then headed into the kitchen together, Barbara Jean thought for the first time in her life that she had truly been cheated by not having had a father.

More than three decades later, after she saw Chick standing on the porch at Big Earl's funeral dinner and after Lester was dead and gone, Barbara Jean had every evening to sit alone and think. She used many of those hours to return to the night she first saw Chick at the All-You-Can-Eat. She played it over countless times in her head in a way she hadn't done in ages. Every time she thought about it, she asked herself whether things might have turned out differently if she hadn't gone to the jukebox that night, or if she had just walked away when those plates hit the floor instead of standing there and learning just enough of Ray Carlson's story to set in motion the schoolgirl process that transformed pity into love. She asked herself if maybe there was some way she could have seen what was coming and avoided it. After each round of those thoughts, she would end up in her chair in the library curled up with her vodka bottle, wondering if she would ever be able to stop rolling that same old stone up the hill and just accept that what had happened was her fate. She had inherited her mother's luck.

Chapter 14

I got a second opinion about my condition on the Friday after Halloween. Again, Mama, Mrs Roosevelt, and I had to sit through a speech about non-Hodgkin's lymphoma. This time nobody cried, though.

Mama said I should talk to James as soon as I got back home, but I ignored her advice. I still wanted to hold on to the fantasy that maybe I could get through my treatment and never have to tell him. Hadn't Alex Soo said that some rare patients got through chemo like they were taking an aspirin? Well, maybe he hadn't said exactly that, but I decided to believe he had. I made up my mind to put my trust in the part of James's nature that never noticed when I got new clothes or when I gained pounds or lost them. Okay, so far only *gained* pounds, but the opposite was likely to be true, too. I decided to count on the same clue-lessness that used to make me want to shake James by the throat to be my friend now.

I slept late that next morning. Life being funny the way it is, the hot flashes that had been keeping me awake at night for months stopped the day after Alex Soo told me I might be dying. When I walked into the kitchen, the first surprise was the smell of coffee. I had learned decades ago that James didn't understand the science of coffee making.

Whenever he brewed up a batch, he ended up with sludge or piss water, nothing in between. So he was forbidden to touch the coffee machine.

But that morning a glass carafe full of coffee rested on a cork trivet in the center of the kitchen table. My mug, a brown and white mess of clay coils fashioned by the tiny fingers of the grandkids and presented to me the previous Christmas, was there on the table, too. And at his usual spot at the table, behind a coffee mug that matched mine, sat James, who was supposed to be working that day.

He sat at attention with his back completely straight and his hands clasped together in front of him atop a wicker placemat. He stared at me for a moment and then said, "What's wrong?"

I started to say, "Nothing," but he held up a hand to stop me. He asked again, slower this time, "Odette, what's wrong?"

I never lie to James – well, not often, at least. I poured a cup of pale brown coffee for myself and I sat down next to him. I exhaled and began, "You know those hot spells I was having? Turns out it was more than the change."

Then I told him everything that both of the doctors had told me. James listened to me without saying a word. The only time he interrupted me was when he scooted his chair back from the table and patted his thighs with his palms, a gesture that had been a signal for me to climb into his lap in the early days of our marriage.

I laughed. "It's been a long time since I sat in your lap, honey." Running my hand over my round stomach, I said, "This might be the end of that chair."

But James didn't laugh at my little joke. He patted his

thighs again and I went over to him and sat. As I talked, he squeezed me tighter and tighter against his body. By the time I reached the end, explaining what I knew of my treatment, our faces were pressed together and I could feel tears rolling down my cheeks.

I cried for the first time since hearing Dr Soo tell me I had cancer. I wasn't crying for the life I might be leaving. Months of talking to Mama had taught me that death didn't have to mean leaving at all. I cried for James, whose heart I might break, for my beautiful, scarred husband who continued to hold me even though his legs must surely have already gone numb under my weight. My tears fell for this strong man who surprised me by managing not to weep, even though I knew from our decades together that he must be screaming inside. I cried for James, who never expected, or needed, me to be that fearless girl from the tree, just me.

He wiped my face with a paper napkin and asked, "So, when do we start treatment?"

"Tuesday," I said. I had made plans to start on Tuesday because that was usually James's late day at work. I wanted as much time as possible to get myself together afterwards, in case my first day was rough.

He caught on immediately that I had planned to use his work schedule as a way to maneuver around him. He said, "Decided to do it on my late day, huh? Sneaky. And a little cowardly, I've got to say." But he didn't look too angry. And he didn't let go of me.

He asked, "What time do we go to the hospital?"

"James, you don't have to come. There's a service at University Hospital that'll drive me home if I don't feel good."

He acted like he hadn't heard me. "What time on Tuesday?"

I told him, and it was settled. He would take Tuesday off from work and go with me to the hospital for my first treatment.

James said, "If you don't tell Clarice and Barbara Jean soon, you won't have to worry about any cancer. They'll kill you themselves when they find out. You wanna call 'em now, or do you wanna call the kids and Rudy first?"

I said. "I've got a better idea. When do you have to go in to work?"

"I told 'em I'd be in around noon, but I'll call in and stay here with you."

"No, I won't need you for the whole day, the morning'll do." Then I began to unbutton his shirt.

James might sometimes be slow on the uptake, but he read my intentions right away. "Really?" he said.

"Sure. Who knows how I'm going to feel after Tuesday. We'd better get it while the gettin' is good." I kissed James hard on his mouth. Then I slipped off of his lap and reached out for his hand to pull him up from his chair.

As we walked to our bedroom, our hands clasped together so tight that it hurt, I thought, *How on earth could I ever have underestimated this man?*

After I told Clarice about my chemotherapy routine – each cycle would be five days long, followed by a few weeks of rest before the next cycle started – she drew up a chemo calendar that designated who – James, Barbara Jean, or Clarice – would be in charge of me on each treatment day. She did several hours of research to determine the best foods for fighting cancer and designed a diet for me. Then she arranged for weekly deliveries of vitamin- and antioxidant-rich groceries to my house. She hired a personal trainer for me. A thick-necked former marine sergeant who worked on injured football players at the university, he showed up at my door one afternoon barking out orders and vowing to whip me into shape. And she penciled me in for a laying on of hands at Calvary Baptist's Wednesday night prayer meeting, which was no small feat seeing as Reverend Peterson didn't even consider the members of my church to be Christians, and felt that praying over us was a waste of energy.

I appreciated her efforts. But I had to show Clarice that she wasn't going to boss me through cancer the way she wanted to, even if I had to be a bit childish and ornery about it. I shifted my appointments around until Clarice's detailed schedule became meaningless. I blanketed the healthy foods Clarice chose for me with butter and bacon crumbles. And the personal trainer, well, he yelled at me one time too many. The last I saw of Sergeant Pete, he was running from my family room with tears in his eyes. Of course, I outright refused to go to Calvary Baptist for the laying on of hands. I tried explaining to Clarice that I always felt worse leaving her church than I did when I walked in and I didn't think that boded well for the healing process. Thoroughly exasperated, Clarice looked at me like I was crazy and said, "Feeling bad about yourself is the entire point of going to church, Odette. Don't you know that?"

I stopped by Barbara Jean's house and told her about my diagnosis over a cup of tea in her library. She was silent for so long that I asked, "Are you all right?"

She started to say "How long have you got?" or "How long do they give you?" But she thought better of it after the first two words came out and she turned it into "How long . . . have you known?"

We talked for an hour, and I think, by the time I left, she had come around to believing I had at least a small chance of surviving.

My brother, Rudy, said that he would come to take care of me as soon as he could get away. I told him it wasn't necessary, that I was fine and had plenty of people looking after me. And I joked with him, as I did each year, that Southern California had thinned his blood too much for him to handle Indiana in the fall or winter. But my brother, who is old-fashioned to the point of annoyance, kept insisting that he would come. He only relented after I handed the phone over to James and let my husband convince Rudy that a levelheaded man was in charge of me.

Denise cried for just a minute or two, but she soon calmed herself and accepted my word that things weren't too bad. Then she took my cue and settled in to talking about the grandchildren. I heard Jimmy's fingers tapping at the keyboard of his computer as I told him. Facts had always comforted him, and he was on his way to becoming a lymphoma expert by the time we said goodbye. Eric hardly said a word to me over the phone, but he was in Plainview for a surprise visit a few days later. Eric was at my side every second for a week and, even as I snapped at him to quit breathing down my neck, I loved having him at home again.

Everything considered, they all took the news of my

illness as well as possible. Even as I grew sicker, proving to everyone, and ultimately to myself, that I wasn't going to be that rare patient who sailed through chemotherapy without so much as a tummy ache, my people propped me up. I think it made everybody feel more optimistic about my chances for recovery to see that I was determined to charge through my disease just like I charged through everything else in life. My friends and family found few things more comforting than the sight of me with my fists up and ready for battle.

Chapter 15

A month before Little Earl's eighteenth birthday, a cute girl at school told him that he looked like Martin Luther King. Then she let him put his hand under her blouse in the name of Negro solidarity. That led Little Earl to celebrate his birthday that November with a costume party so he could dress up as Dr King in hopes of encountering more young women who were passionately devoted to the civil rights movement.

Clarice, Odette, and Barbara Jean made plans to dress up as the Supremes since their friends, families, and even some of the teachers at school were now calling them by that name. They spent weeks working on their costumes. Odette did most of the sewing, stitching together glossy, gold, sleeveless gowns. They used hot glue to attach glitter to old shoes. And Barbara Jean's boss at the salon loaned them three acrylic wigs with identical bouffants for the occasion.

On the night of the party, the plan was that they would each get dressed at home. Clarice had been given a used Buick after a third piano lesson with Mrs Olavsky was added to her weekly schedule and her mother decided that she'd had enough of chauffeur duty, so Clarice was to pick up the other girls at their houses for the ride to the All-You-Can-Eat. Clarice parked in front of Barbara Jean's house and she and Odette went to the door to fetch her and some accessories for their costumes. Barbara Jean had offered to dip into her inheritance of fake furs and oversized plastic jewelry to help them complete their ensembles.

They were standing on the porch when Clarice saw an odd expression come over Odette's face. She didn't know what Odette was reacting to. Maybe it was a sound or a smell. But Clarice had just raised her hand to knock on the door when Odette said, "Something's wrong."

Before Clarice could say anything, Odette pushed right past her and turned the knob. The door opened and she rushed inside. Not taking the time to think about the possible consequences, Clarice followed her, both of them moving in a kind of a shimmying shuffle because of the restrictions of their outfits.

Barbara Jean, wearing her shiny gold gown, sat in a threadbare maroon overstuffed chair in a corner of the living room. Her bare feet were tucked beneath her and she clutched her wig in both hands, pressing it to her chest. The fake furs and costume jewelry she and her friends were going to wear that evening rested in a pile on the floor in front of the chair. She didn't look up as Odette and Clarice came into the room.

Vondell, her stepfather or whatever he was, stood beside Barbara Jean's chair. He had disappeared a month earlier, making Barbara Jean's life easier and giving her the hope that she might not have to deal with him anymore. Between free meals at Odette's and Clarice's houses, the tips she made at the salon, and the low rent on the dump she lived in, Barbara Jean had been able to afford a teenager's dream. She had a house of her own and complete independence.

But now Vondell was back and he looked even worse than he had the last time they had seen him. His stubbly graying beard had grown thicker, and his processed hair had grown out so it was nappy at the roots and matted at the ends. And then there was that odor of his that permeated the room, that sharp blend of cigarettes, whiskey, and poor personal hygiene.

He glared at Odette and Clarice for a minute. Then he said, "Barbara Jean, you didn't tell me we was gonna have company this evenin'." That wide, froglike mouth of his broadened into a grin as he talked, but no one in the room sensed a bit of goodwill in him.

Odette said, "Hello, sir, we're going to a birthday party tonight and we just came to get Barbara Jean." She looked at Barbara Jean in the chair and said, "Come on, Barbara Jean. We don't wanna be late."

But Barbara Jean didn't move. She just glanced up at Vondell and then stared at her knees again. The big man had lost his smile now. He glared at her, daring her to rise from the chair.

Clarice joined in and said, "Yeah, we have to finish up our hair and nails at my house and . . ." She lost her nerve and didn't finish. No one was listening to her anyway. The battle was on, and it was being fought between the other three people in the room.

There was a long silence during which Clarice heard only the big man's breathing and the sound of the plastic carpet runner crunching beneath her feet as she inched backwards toward the front door. Then Vondell said, "I think y'all best get movin'. Barbara Jean ain't goin' out tonight."

The tone of his voice scared Clarice half to death and she ran to the door. But Odette stayed put. Odette looked back and forth from Barbara Jean, still cowering in the shabby chair like a scared two-year-old, to the hulking man who had moved closer to Barbara Jean and was now stroking her hair in an imitation of fatherly affection that caused acid to rise in Clarice's stomach.

Odette said, "I haven't heard what Barbara Jean wants us to do. If she wants us to go, she can say it herself."

Vondell took a step toward Odette and put his hands on his hips to puff himself up. He was careful to keep a smile on his face so she would know he wasn't taking her seriously. "Li'l girl, I told you to leave *my* house. And, believe me, you don't want me to have to say it again. Now, get a move on before I put you over my knee and teach you some manners."

Vondell had Clarice scared, but the look Odette gave him now frightened her almost as much. Odette's eyes narrowed and her mouth twisted. She lowered her head as if she were preparing to ram into him headfirst. Clarice could see that even if Odette didn't scare Vondell, she definitely surprised him. When he saw the change in her posture, he jerked back away from her a little before he could stop himself.

Odette, talking louder now, said, "Barbara Jean, do you want to stay here or come with us?"

Barbara Jean didn't answer at first. Then, almost too quietly for anyone to hear, she whispered, "I want to go with you."

Odette said, "Well, that settles it. She's coming with us."

Vondell didn't speak to Odette, but turned his attention to Barbara Jean instead. He moved beside her again and grasped her right forearm in his big hand, pulling her halfway out of the chair so awkwardly that she would have fallen to the floor if he had not been supporting her with the strength of his hold. She let out a gasp of pain and Vondell growled, "You best tell these girls to go on home, or you gonna be in some real trouble. I fixed your mama's uppity ways and I can do the same wit' you."

Odette's voice dropped an octave and she very slowly said, "If you don't want that hand broke, you'd better get it off of her right now."

Clarice got swept up in the moment and put in her two cents. "She's coming with us," she said, trying to act like Odette.

But Clarice wasn't born in a tree. When he took a couple of quick steps in her direction, she hopped backwards and let out a squeal. Odette moved, too, but she moved sideways to stand between Vondell and Clarice.

He said, "What you gonna do, call your daddy? You know, I asked around about your daddy after the last time you was here, and I heard he ain't no cop at all. What I heard was that you was that child born in a tree and you ain't supposed to be 'fraid of nothin'. Maybe it's time somebody gave you somethin' to be scared of." He moved closer to her and pushed out his chin.

Odette stepped away from him then and came over to where Clarice stood with her fist clinched around the handle of the door, ready to escape. Vondell laughed at her and said, "That's a good girl. Run on home." Then to

Clarice he said, "You can come back sometime if you wanna, baby. But leave that crazy fat bitch at home."

A few feet away from Clarice, Odette stopped, yanked the wig from her head, and tossed it to her. Clarice caught it out of reflex and then watched in bewilderment as Odette spun away from her and said, "Clarice, unzip me."

When Clarice didn't say anything or do as Odette had told her, she said it again. "Unzip me. I spent too much time making this dress to get this asshole's blood all over it."

She fixed her eyes on Vondell and said, "You're right about me. I am the girl who was born in a tree. And you're right about my father. He's not a cop. But he was the 1947 welterweight Golden Gloves champion. And from the time I was a little girl my boxer daddy has been teaching me how to deal with dumb-ass men who want me to be afraid. So let me thank you now, while you're still conscious, for giving me the opportunity to demonstrate some of the special shit my daddy taught me to use on occasions like this.

"Now, Clarice, unzip me so I can take care of this big bag of stink and ignorance, once and for all."

With fingers that shook so badly she could hardly grab hold of the zipper, Clarice did as she had been commanded. She pulled the zipper down and Odette's shiny gown slid off of her and formed a shimmering pool at her feet. Wearing just a white bra and floral-patterned panties, Odette lifted her fists and danced her way toward Vondell, already floating like a butterfly and apparently prepared to sting like a bee.

For a moment, Vondell stood gaping at her, eyes wide,

mouth open. Then, to Clarice's amazement, he started to back up. First one step, then another. He tried to act as if he were in charge, calling her a string of filthy names and threatening to hurt her. But Clarice could see from the way his eyes darted left and right searching out an escape route that this short, chubby teenage girl had him unnerved.

Odette kept moving toward him and he kept backing away. He moved across the living room floor, his feet shuffling across the orange carpet. His hands gripped the backs of the heavy, mismatched furniture he was careful to keep between himself and Odette. When he had backed completely out of the room and into the hallway that led to the kitchen, he yelled out, "I ain't got time to be dealin' with this crazy shit. Go on, get out. I don't care where you go. You ain't none of my concern." He moved out of sight then, and a few seconds later they heard the rear door of the house open and slam shut.

Odette maintained her Golden Gloves stance for what seemed like an hour, but was probably less than a minute. When Vondell didn't return, she brought her fists down, shaking out her shoulders as if she'd just gone ten rounds. Then she walked toward Clarice, who was still frozen at the front door. Stepping into the circle of golden fabric she had shed onto the floor earlier, Odette said, "Clarice, could you give me a hand getting back into my dress?"

After Clarice packed Odette into her gown, the two girls went to Barbara Jean, who sat in the maroon chair staring at Odette with awe. Clarice picked up the imitation fur stoles and dime-store jewelry from the floor while Odette helped Barbara Jean up from the chair. Odette said, "Come on, Barbara Jean, we've got us a party to go to."

The three girls squeezed into the front seat of Clarice's car for the drive to Little Earl's party. They were about a third of the way there when Clarice finally found words. She said, "That was incredible, Odette. I had no idea your father taught you how to box."

Odette snorted and said, "Box? Daddy's never weighed more than a hundred ten pounds his entire life. Who the hell was he gonna box? Vondell would've broken my neck if he'd decided to fight me."

During the rest of the ride to the All-You-Can-Eat, Clarice fought to keep her eyes on the road and not stare at her insane friend in disbelief. Barbara Jean gazed out of the car window and periodically gasped, "Holy shit."

They had fun at the party that night. They flirted and lip-synched Supremes songs. They watched Little Earl, in a costume consisting of his best Sunday suit and a Bible, try to use the "I Have a Dream" speech as a pickup line. They admired Chick Carlson.

Girls approached Chick all night. Freed from convention by their costumes, they forgot for that evening that they were on opposite sides of a racial divide and constantly interrupted his busboy duties by asking him to dance. Clarice, Barbara Jean, and Odette got a kick out of watching him hop across the floor in his cowboy costume – his everyday clothes plus a bandana. And they giggled as, regardless of the song, he treated each girl to a two-step – the only dance that country white boys knew back then.

Late in the evening, Odette went missing for a while. She returned to the window table with Big Earl and Miss Thelma, who promptly shooed away all of the kids, except Barbara Jean, Odette, and Clarice. Then, after seating themselves on either side of Barbara Jean, they told her that she would be moving into the room that their daughter, Lydia, had vacated when she left Plainview two years earlier. They didn't ask her opinion or entertain other options. Each of them held one of Barbara Jean's hands and informed her that Lydia's room was hers that night and for as long as she wanted.

Barbara Jean protested just long enough to show that she had good manners. Then she agreed. So that evening, courtesy of Big Earl, Miss Thelma, and Odette, Barbara Jean had a family for the first time in her life. And Clarice came to understand that she had a friend who could perform miracles.

Chapter 16

Between them, Lester and Barbara Jean owned four vehicles when he died. When she learned that Odette was sick, Barbara Jean donated Lester's truck and his year-old car to the American Cancer Society. She thought it might buy her friend some good luck. That left her with her Mercedes and an old Cadillac.

Lester had bought the Cadillac new in 1967, the first in a long string of Caddies he bought over the years. He babied it, keeping it looking as if it had just rolled off the dealer's showroom floor until the day he died. It was the only one of his cars he never sold or gave away when newer models came out. The car hadn't been touched since the last time Lester drove it. It just sat in the garage taking up space and reminding Barbara Jean of the past.

One day when she arrived at the museum to work a volunteer shift in her butter-churning outfit, Barbara Jean discovered that a sign had been posted near Benjamin Harrison's flag. The sign asked for volunteers to contribute something to the annual Christmas auction. She offered the Cadillac.

Judging from the shocked reaction she received when she contacted the committee putting together the auction, a mint condition 1967 Fleetwood was a little more than they had in mind. They had been expecting donations more along the lines of handcrafted needlepoint chair cushions, beeswax candles, or gift baskets full of homemade strawberry preserves in quaintly bonneted jars. But once they understood that Barbara Jean really intended to donate the car itself, not a ride in it or some sort of leasing arrangement, they eagerly accepted her gift. In return, she took them up on their offer to have a room of the museum, the one with the Indian artifacts, renamed the Lester Maxberry Exhibition Hall. They had wanted to name the room after Barbara Jean, but she declined the honor. The Fleetwood had been Lester's baby. And he had been the one with happy memories of it, not her.

Barbara Jean had been living at Big Earl and Miss Thelma's house for about a month when she first saw the car. She was walking home from her job at the salon when she saw a crowd gathered across the street outside the All-You-Can-Eat. Clarice stepped out of the knot of people and called her name.

When she got closer, she saw that the dozen or so people in the street were clustered around the nicest Cadillac she had ever seen. In fact, it was the only brand-new Cadillac Barbara Jean had ever seen outside of TV commercials. It was a beauty, so shiny that it was hard to look directly at it in the afternoon sun. It was sky blue, and the brilliant gloss of the car's paint job reflected the clouds above so perfectly that looking down at the hood almost made you feel dizzy, as if you didn't know which way was up. The back end of the car was long and so sleek that it seemed likely you would cut your finger if you ran it along the sharp fins. Occasionally one of the people circling the car in admiration would lean in to exhale on the bright finish and watch the oval of their condensed breath appear and then evaporate.

Only one person in the crowd dared make any real physical contact with the car. That was the Cadillac's owner, Mr Lester Maxberry.

Barbara Jean knew Lester, of course. He was famous. At one time or another, he had employed half of the boys in her high school in his landscaping business. James Henry worked for him all through high school and his two years of college. James worked for Lester so long that everyone expected him to take over the business one day. They went on expecting it until James surprised them all by becoming a cop.

Lester sometimes came into the All-You-Can-Eat with James and sat with the young people at the window table. He was always nice, courteous, and charming in an avuncular way. He would talk sports with the guys, or dispense advice, or compliment the girls. But he usually didn't stick around for long. He would say, "Let me get going, so you young people can enjoy your evening," and then he'd tip the fedora he always wore and leave while they objected.

Barbara Jean enjoyed Lester's company, but she never thought of him in a romantic way, even though just about every other woman she knew did. He had a small, compact body and a long face with droopy eyes that most of the girls thought were sexy. He also had a slight hesitation in his stride from an injury he had received while he was in the service, but he layered it over with so much cool and self-confidence that it seemed like a stylish accessory. Lester was light-skinned and had curly, but not kinky, hair at a time when there weren't many attributes considered more important than fair skin and good hair.

Lester stood at the prow of his automobile with one foot on the front bumper and his hip leaning onto the driver's-side quarter panel. He wore navy blue pinstriped pants, a dress shirt the same sky blue as his new car, and a black fedora with a blue feather in its band. He must have been cold. It couldn't have been more than forty-five degrees on that December day. But he looked perfectly comfortable posing there, smiling and showing off his car.

When he saw Barbara Jean, Lester stood and said, "Hey, Barbie, what do you think?"

She said, "It's slick, real slick." She immediately regretted that answer. "Slick" sounded so stupid and childish, just the wrong thing to say to a man like Lester Maxberry. She corrected herself. She said, "It's a gorgeous car, truly gorgeous," and felt better.

"Wait till you see this. This is the best part." He walked around to the driver's side of the car and then leaned into the open window. He pressed the horn, and after it sounded he turned around with a big grin on his face. The horn had been modified so that it honked out the first three notes from the chorus of Smokey Robinson's "Ooo Baby, Baby." The crowd gathered around the car went nuts, some of them singing, "Ooo, *Ooo*-ooo."

Barbara Jean was squeezed off to the edges of the crowd by the boys who pushed forward to ask car questions or just to hear the horn again, so she went into the All-You-Can-Eat to say hi to Miss Thelma. By this time on a Saturday she could usually be found in the kitchen of the restaurant starting the baking for Sunday's after-church rush.

Barbara Jean walked through the dining room and headed down the hallway that led to the storeroom and the rear of the kitchen where the baking table and ovens were. Before she got to the kitchen, the door to the storeroom opened and Chick Carlson stepped out. She acknowledged him with a nod and kept walking. But when she came closer to him, she saw that he had a cut on his forehead.

She knew that she shouldn't ask. She knew that it was none of her business. But she asked anyway.

She pointed to the cut just below his hairline. "What happened?"

He said, "My brother, he gets mad and . . ." He stopped himself and looked embarrassed, as if he hadn't intended to say what he had said. He bit his lip and stood there turning redder and redder.

She didn't recognize it at the time, but something started between them at that moment, an irresistible need to say and do things before common sense could intervene and hold them back. That need would stretch out over far too many years. And she would live to regret it.

Barbara Jean slipped off her jacket and rolled up the sleeve of her blouse. She pointed to three small scars on her arm and said, "My mother hit me with a belt buckle."

He said, "I'm sure she didn't mean it."

"Yes, she did. She used to hit me a lot when she was drunk. But you're half right; she didn't mean to give me the scars. She was just so drunk that time that she didn't realize she'd grabbed the wrong end of the belt when she swung it."

He came closer to her then and reached out and touched

her scars with the tip of his finger. "It looks like a face. See?" He ran his finger over the longer arc-shaped scar on the bottom, "That line looks like a mouth and these two smaller ones up here are like eyes."

With that slight touch, suddenly they couldn't stop talking. Words that they had kept bottled up while they stared at each other across the dining room of the All-You-Can-Eat came rushing forward. They didn't flirt or tease each other with coy chitchat the way other teenagers might have done in the same situation. The things they told each other were the things that only they could share.

She said, "My mother drank herself to death."

He said, "My father died in jail. When I was a kid they told me it was a heart attack, but I found out later he got knifed in a fight. My mother ran off about the same time. I barely remember her."

"I never met my father, but there are two guys who think I'm their daughter."

"You can't see it because of my hair, but I've got a five-inch scar on top of my head from getting stitches after my brother hit me with a brick for taking food from his refrigerator."

"When I was fourteen, my mother twisted my arm until she dislocated it because I left the house with no makeup on."

Chick said, "Big Earl lets me stay in the storeroom here because he found out I was living in the shed at my brother's place and sharing it with the chickens."

She held up her hand and said, "Okay, you win." Then they both started laughing.

That was when she did it. She took a step toward him

and kissed him on his mouth. She leaned into him until he fell back against the wall. Then she kept pressing against him, wanting to be as close to him as she could be.

She didn't know why she was kissing him, she just knew that she had to, the same way she had to tell him things she hadn't yet told Odette or Clarice, stuff about her mother and her various fathers. With him, those truths just came tumbling out.

When she started to think about the foolishness of what she was doing and began to pull away, he wrapped his arm around her waist and squeezed her even tighter to him. They stood there in the back hallway of the All-You-Can-Eat kissing each other until they were both dizzy from not breathing. They only stopped when they heard someone calling Barbara Jean's name.

Chick released her waist and Barbara Jean stepped away from him until her back met the opposite wall. They were there, grinning at each other across the hallway, when Clarice ran in and shouted, "Barbara Jean, come on! Lester wants to take us for a ride in his new car. He asked especially about you."

She said, "Hi, Chick," and then pulled Barbara Jean down the hallway, stopping only long enough to give Barbara Jean a chance to pick up the coat she had cast off in order to show her scars. As she grabbed her coat, Barbara Jean glanced back for one more look at Chick's beautiful, smiling face. Then she was off to take her first ride in Lester's blue Fleetwood.

The chairman of the museum's Christmas auction committee was Phyllis Feeney. She was a nervous, pear-shaped woman who used her hands so much when she talked that she looked as if she were speaking sign language. When Phyllis came to get the Cadillac, she brought along her husband, Andy, who was stocky and jumpy like her. Phyllis was even more animated than usual that day, fidgeting and playing with her hair. She relaxed quite a bit when the title to the car was handed over and she was assured that Barbara Jean wasn't going to back out of the deal at the last second.

Barbara Jean escorted them to the garage, where Phyllis handed the keys to Lester's blue Cadillac over to her husband. Then Phyllis climbed back into the Ford they had arrived in and drove off. Andy slid behind the wheel of the Fleetwood and brought the giant engine to life. He rolled down the window and said, "She purrs like a kitten."

He put the car in reverse and drove out of the garage. Just as he got to the end of the driveway, Barbara Jean called out, "Andy, hit the horn!"

"What?" he asked.

"Hit the horn. It's the best part."

He did it, and when he heard the three notes of the horn rise and fall he said, "Oh man, I love this car. I'm gonna have to bid on it myself." He waved at Barbara Jean and turned down Plainview Avenue.

For a good five minutes after he was out of sight, Barbara Jean could still hear Lester's car off in the distance singing, "Ooo, *Ooo*-ooo."

Chapter 17

Odette, Barbara Jean, and Clarice sat talking in the infusion room of the hospital. Clarice, who couldn't resist judging décor wherever she was, approved of the room. It was pretty, if you ignored the medical equipment. The lighting was less harsh than in the rest of the hospital. And the muted pastel flowers on the wallpaper complemented the comfortable cherry wood and brown leather chairs that stood beside the treatment lounges. Unfortunately, there wasn't much that could be done to beautify an IV pole. Looking in any direction reminded you of precisely why you were there.

It was just before Christmas, but the room wasn't decorated. The only signs of the holidays were the red Santa Claus hat worn by the gum-popping duty nurse who kept watch from a desk in the corner and the blinking Christmas tree pin on the collar of Barbara Jean's yellow hospital volunteer smock.

Barbara Jean wore her smock even though she wasn't working that day. There was a limit of one visitor per patient during chemo, so Barbara Jean wore her volunteer outfit to look official enough to get around the rule. Clarice sometimes borrowed the smock from Barbara Jean so she could visit along with James on the days he came with Odette.

To pass the time that morning and to distract Odette during her treatment, Clarice showed the other Supremes the twelve fabric swatches Veronica had dropped off at her house the previous evening. Veronica had begged and flattered Clarice into agreeing to assist her in planning Sharon's wedding, and she had given Clarice a list of tedious chores to perform. In spite of herself and in spite of Veronica, Clarice found that she was pleased to have this wedding-related work to do. She needed as many diversions as possible to keep her from dwelling on Odette's health and Richmond's errant penis. And there were only so many hours a day she could practice the piano before her knuckles complained. Her latest job was to submit her written opinion on each of the fabric swatches Veronica had brought to her. Every single one of the swatches was a subtly different shade of green crushed velvet.

Clarice said, "I'm supposed to help choose the material for the bridesmaids' dresses from these. Can you imagine? Wrapping up Veronica's unfortunate-looking daughters in any of these fabrics is just plain cruel. And green is Veronica's favorite color, by the way, not Sharon's. Sharon wanted peach, but Veronica told her nobody could tell the difference between peach and pink, so it would look like just a run-of-the-mill pink wedding. Veronica decided the wedding would be green and white, and that was that."

Odette and Barbara Jean agreed that slapping green crushed velvet on the homeliest girls in town was an insane notion. Barbara Jean pronounced it "child abuse" and Odette, enjoying her curious-bystander-to-a-highway-pileup role, said, "I can't wait for that wedding." Even the duty nurse, who had been pretending not to listen in, stared at the swatches as Clarice waved them in the air. She stopped chomping her gum long enough to mouth "Pitiful."

Clarice explained that she had to get the fabric judging out of the way quickly in order to concentrate on a more complicated chore. She was supposed to find a flock of white doves to be released as Sharon walked down the aisle.

"Veronica saw it on TV and now she just has to have it. Have you any idea how hard it is to find trained white doves? And of course it's all because I had that bubble machine at Carolyn's wedding. Everything's like that with Veronica. Carolyn had bubbles; Sharon has to have white doves. Carolyn had a broom-jumping; Sharon's going to have laser lights that spell out 'Clifton and Sharon' above their heads during the ceremony and then switch to read 'Hallelujah!' when they're pronounced husband and wife."

Barbara Jean said, "Lasers? Really? You'd think she'd want to steer away from special effects after that Easter pageant went so wrong."

"I guess she feels like she's safe since there are no plans for any of the wedding party to fly through the air. Not yet, at least."

They were laughing so loudly at the memory of poor Reverend Biggs hovering in the rafters of First Baptist that they just barely heard the hiss of the automatic door to the infusion room announcing that someone had entered. Odette looked up and smiled. Barbara Jean and Clarice turned around and saw Chick Carlson.

Chick wore a tan overcoat with a university ID clipped to the collar. He lifted the ID in the direction of the nurse when she approached him to ask who he was there to see, and she nodded at him and let him pass. He walked toward the Supremes until he stood at the foot of Odette's lounge. He said, "Hey, everybody," greeting them as if it were just another day at the All-You-Can-Eat in 1968.

Odette said, "Hey, Chick. I can't get up and hug you, so you'd better come to me." He stepped closer to Odette, leaned down, and kissed her on the cheek. He turned toward Clarice and she reached out and shook his hand. Then, after a pause that was just a little too long to feel comfortable, Barbara Jean said, "Hello, Ray. It's been a long time."

Odette sat up as much as she could on the infusion lounge and took in her old friend, getting her first good look at him in almost thirty years. He reminded her of a seasoned hiker who had just stepped in from a brisk stroll on the mountainside. His cheeks were red and his gray and black waves of hair had either been tousled by the wind or he had spent hours with a stylist that morning to give him the air of a gracefully aging action-movie star. Odette caused his cheeks to redden even more by saying, "All these years and you still look good enough to eat."

She told him to pull up a seat, but he claimed that he was already running late and couldn't stay long. Chick said he had seen James on his way in to work that morning. James had filled him in on Odette's condition and told him where he'd find her.

Odette asked, "So what brings you back to us after all this time?"

"I'm in charge of a research project," he said. "We're working with birds. Raptors, actually – hawks, owls, falcons. They converted the old tower for us." He waved his hand in the direction of the tower even though there was no window in the room and in spite of the fact that the Supremes, like everyone else in town, knew exactly what tower he was talking about.

The tower was all that was left of a tuberculosis sanatorium that had once occupied the land where the hospital now stood. TB patients had been brought there to take the fresh air cure. Five stories tall, it stood atop a rise at the edge of the campus and was visible from nearly any vantage point in town. Now Chick, the boy who had always been covered with feathers, kept birds there.

"You really should see what the university has done with it," he said. "The facility is incredible. Twice as big as the space I had in Oregon."

"Oregon?" Odette said. "I thought you went off to school in Florida."

"I did, but I only lasted a few months there. Too hot for me. After a year, I transferred to a graduate program in Oregon. The college offered me a teaching job after I finished and I ended up staying till I came back here."

Odette, who was never shy about obtaining information, proceeded to grill him. Within a minute or two, she'd found out that Chick had lived in Plainview since the summer, had been married and divorced twice with no children from either marriage, and lived in one of the new houses in Leaning Tree.

Chick felt himself beginning to sweat. Since the day he accepted the job that meant returning to his hometown, he had thought about what he would say when he crossed paths with the Supremes. He prepared a short speech, a few sentences about his life in the Northwest followed by a brief description of the work that had brought him back to Plainview. But he had envisioned reciting his carefully practiced patter to the Supremes in a safe environment like a grocery store loaded with distracted, chatting customers or a busy street corner. Now, because of a chance meeting with his old buddy James that morning, he found himself fumbling through a scattered version of his little speech in a hospital room whose walls seemed to be inching toward him more quickly with each passing second. He had been thrown hopelessly off balance by Odette's questions, this place, and the presence of Barbara Jean, still painfully beautiful after what seemed like a million years and like no time at all.

Chick veered away from his prepared remarks, speaking faster and faster. He described, floor by floor, the state-of-the-art veterinary facility that was housed in the tower. He told them about the two graduate-level courses he taught at the university and how the brightest of his students now formed the eager young staff that assisted him in his work with the raptor project. He detailed the plans for releasing the first breeding pair of rehabbed falcons sometime that coming summer. After he had listed the names of each of the eight birds in the project and related the story of how each name was chosen, he realized that he had been talking for ten minutes straight and he stopped himself. He said, "I'm sorry. You get me started talking about my project and I don't shut up."

Odette said, "No need to apologize, it's nice to hear that you like your work." Then she laughed. "But tell me, Chick, what is it with you and birds?"

He grinned, then stuffed his hands inside the pockets of his coat and shrugged his shoulders. For a moment, he was once more the shy, pretty boy they had met almost forty years earlier.

No one said anything for a few seconds. Barbara Jean, Odette, and Clarice did some throat-clearing and fidgeting. Chick stood staring down at the floor, making it apparent that he had prepared only a few lines of dialogue for this meeting and, having exhausted them and followed them up with some nervous rambling, had no more conversation left in him.

Barbara Jean filled the silence with something that surprised them all. She said, "I saw you after Big Earl's funeral."

Startled by her own words, Barbara Jean let out a little gasp and her eyes grew large. She looked back and forth from Odette to Clarice several times in quick succession. Clarice thought for a moment Barbara Jean might ask which one of them had spoken. Of course, it would never have crossed either of her friends' lips. Clarice and Odette had carefully avoided discussing the day of Big Earl's funeral – the day of Lester's death – for months. And they had never once told Barbara Jean that they had seen her staring out of the window at Chick just before Lester decided to perform those ill-fated electrical repairs.

Chick and Barbara Jean locked eyes, but said nothing. Clarice began to prattle on about what a good friend Big Earl had been to all of them. Odette nodded in agreement. Barbara Jean clasped her hands together in her lap to stop them from shaking.

Finally, Chick said, "Well, I'd better get going."

Odette made him promise that he would come by her house for a visit, and polite goodbyes were exchanged. Then Chick took a couple of steps in the direction of the door that led out to the hallway. Before leaving the room, he turned around and added, "It's really nice to see you all looking so lovely."

It seemed to both Clarice and Odette that his last remark was aimed directly at Barbara Jean.

As soon as Chick left the room, Barbara Jean slumped forward in her chair and buried her face in her hands. She took two or three deep breaths and then sat up straight again. She announced, "I'm going to get some coffee. Anybody else want some?" Before either of her friends could answer her, she rose and rushed toward the door. Odette gestured with her head for Clarice to follow, and she did.

Clarice found Barbara Jean standing with her forehead pressed against a window just down the hall, her breath fogging the glass with each exhalation. She walked up to Barbara Jean and stood beside her.

Clarice asked, "Are you all right?"

Barbara Jean replied, "He looked good, didn't he?"

"Yes, he did look good. Grew up to be a handsome man."

"No, I mean he looked like his life was okay. He didn't look like his life was sad or ruined or anything."

Clarice said that yes, Chick looked as if his life had been fine, not knowing where Barbara Jean was going with all this.

Barbara Jean said, "Yes, he's done all right. He's done real well. Works for the university now. Teaches. Likes his work. Ray's all right." It sounded to Clarice as if Barbara Jean were trying to convince herself.

It is truly a wonder, Clarice thought, how that old devil inconvenient love can rear its head and start messing with you when you least expect it. She'd have bet a million dollars Barbara Jean didn't want to feel anything for Chick, the man she'd loved before she was old enough to know any better. But it was written all across her face. Game over, story ended. Barbara Jean was stuck with affection that just wouldn't die, no matter how hard life and time had tried to kill it. Oh sister, Clarice thought, I know just how you feel. Barbara Jean and Clarice stayed there for several minutes gazing out of the window. They had a view of the hospital parking lot and the redbrick tower where Chick was presumably now settling in for a day of tending to his birds. Clarice watched clusters of students walk up the hill toward the main part of the campus, the vapor of their breath rising around them in the cold December air. In the distance, she could see the crosses atop the steeples of First Baptist and Plainview Lutheran. She saw the preening copper rooster on the weather vane that capped the turret at the northeast corner of Barbara Jean's house rising over the tops of trees that had lost all but the most tenacious of their leaves. Further off, she could see the remains of Ballard's Wall and the tidy roofs of the new houses of Leaning Tree.

Plainview was lovely. A sprinkling of snow had fallen and turned the town into a postcard-perfect scene, ready to be photographed for the university's catalog or committed to needlepoint. She was about to say as much to Barbara Jean when something new came into view that caused them both to stiffen.

A white Chrysler, its sunroof open in spite of the chill, pulled into the parking lot and stopped at the doors just below where they stood. A man got out of the car and greeted the young woman who ran out of the building to meet him. He walked around to the passenger side of the Chrysler and opened the door for the woman. She lost her hat – a replica of the wide-brimmed, floppy style popular in the 1970s – to a gust of wind as she bent to climb into the car. The man caught the hat for her, gracefully snatching it from midair. He glanced left and right, like a criminal checking for witnesses. Then he playfully swatted the woman on her behind with the hat. She took her hat from him and, with a toss of her long black hair, hopped into the Chrysler.

The man was Clarice's husband.

Barbara Jean kept her face pointed forward and said nothing. But she watched Clarice out of the corner of her eye.

Clarice stared at the car as it left the parking lot. She felt more embarrassed for Richmond than for herself as she watched him roar out of the lot and onto the road that led downhill to the highway, peeling rubber like a rowdy high school boy. The sound of his screeching tires was so loud that they heard it through the thick plate-glass window.

After the car had disappeared from sight, Clarice said, "He claimed he was going to be in Atlanta to scout recruits with Ramsey Abrams for the next two days."

Barbara Jean, still not looking directly at her, said, "The girl works in the hospital gift shop. The flowers I take to patients on my volunteer days get delivered to the gift shop first. I see her at least two times a week when I go there to sort the flowers. Her name is Cherokee."

"Cherokee? Like the Indian tribe?"

"No, Cherokee like the Jeep. Her father owns a car repair shop and he takes his work home, apparently. She has brothers named Tercel and Seville."

"You're kidding me."

"Nope. Cherokee, Tercel, and Seville Robinson."

Clarice said, "You see? This is why I can't hate Richmond, no matter what he does. Just when I want to break his neck, the man always finds a way to make me laugh."

Barbara Jean reached out and grabbed hold of Clarice's hand, saying, "Let's go back and see if Odette's finished." They left the window and walked back down the hallway toward the infusion room swinging their clutched hands like a pair of five-year-olds.

Just before they got to the door, Clarice said, "Chick Carlson and this Cherokee woman both in one day. I swear, Barbara Jean, sometimes this town is just too damn small."

"Clarice, honey," she responded, "you have just said a mouthful."

Chapter 18

On the evening of December twenty-first, Clarice answered the ringing telephone in her living room and heard a familiar voice. It was a sweet, tenor sound with a subtle lisp, like a choirboy who had been born with the tongue of a snake. It was the voice of Mr Forrest Payne.

Instead of hello, he said, "She's here."

Clarice didn't need to ask what or whom he was talking about. She answered, "I'm sorry. I'll be right over."

From the other end of the line, she heard the *snick-snick* of a cigarette lighter being struck. Then Mr Payne, the vile whoremonger with the lovely speaking voice, said, "Merry Christmas, Clarice. God bless you and your family." He hung up before she was forced to return his kind wishes.

Clarice arrived at the Pink Slipper Gentlemen's Club fifteen minutes after receiving Forrest Payne's call. Her mother stood on a small hill just east of the parking lot. Tall and thin, Beatrice Jordan looked elegant in the black, sable-trimmed sheared mink coat that Clarice's father had given her twenty years earlier after doing something especially humiliating to her, the details of which Clarice was never privy to. In hands covered by her bright red leather Christmas gloves, Beatrice held a megaphone. She bellowed, "You are a child of God. Stop what you're doing. Your sinful ways will bring a storm of hellfire down upon you. Come to the Lord and you will be saved."

Clarice had heard her mother's hilltop sermon dozens of times. It always began the same way, "You are a child of God. Stop what you're doing. Your sinful ways will bring a storm of hellfire down upon you. Come to the Lord and you will be saved." After that, a Bible verse. As Clarice approached her on her hill, her mother broadcast Romans 8:13. "For if you live according to the sinful nature, you will die; but if by the Spirit you put to death the misdeeds of the body, you will live." Beatrice was especially fond of the more ominous verses.

Clarice's mother's first Pink Slipper bullhorn sermon occurred during a visit home not long after she'd moved away following her husband's death. Clarice had been at home awaiting her mother's arrival. Anticipation had just transformed into worry, causing her to station herself at the front window to watch for her mother's rental car, when the phone rang. Pretty-voiced Forrest Payne had told her that her mother was at his place with a megaphone. She hadn't believed him until he carried his phone outside so she could hear her mother's amplified voice crackling out warnings of damnation.

Mr Payne had said, "Clarice, I'm calling you instead of the police out of respect for the many years your daddy, God rest his soul, served as my attorney." But she suspected it was really out of respect for the fact that her father had spent so much money at the Pink Slipper that Forrest Payne should have named a room, or at least a memorial stripper pole, in Abraham Jordan's honor.

After Clarice persuaded her mother to stop sermonizing that first time and got her back to her house, Beatrice informed her daughter that she was finally ready to openly acknowledge her deceased husband's infidelities. But she also made it clear that she had entered into a new type of denial. She refused to hold Abraham responsible for any of his misbehavior. Instead, she blamed his cheating on the loose women and poorly chosen male friends who she believed had led him down a sinful path. She focused her righteous fury on Forrest Payne and his little den of iniquity out on the edge of town.

So, once or twice a year, Clarice's mother, the epitome of all things ladylike and proper, stopped by Forrest Payne's Pink Slipper Gentlemen's Club armed with a megaphone and an unquenchable thirst for revenge. It is terrifying, Clarice thought, what marriage can do to a woman.

Making the situation even worse, Beatrice didn't recognize Clarice at first. When she saw that Clarice was walking toward her instead of going into the club, she took her daughter for a fresh convert. She pointed the megaphone at Clarice and said, "That's right, sister, turn your back on that house of evil and listen to the Word." Seeing, finally, that it was Clarice, Beatrice said, unamplified, "Hi, sweetheart, I suppose he called you again."

Clarice nodded yes.

"Well, I was just about finished here anyway." But she wasn't done quite yet. A truck pulled into the parking lot just then and the driver, a heavyset, bearded man in a cowboy hat who moved as if he had already had a few drinks, walked falteringly from his vehicle toward the fuchsia front door of the club. Beatrice lifted her megaphone again and squawked out, "You are a child of God. Stop what you're doing. Your sinful ways will bring a storm of hellfire down upon you. Come to the Lord and you will be saved." When the man disappeared inside the Pink Slipper, she tucked the bullhorn under her arm and descended her hill.

She stopped just in front of Clarice and looked her up and down. Clarice was wearing the gray down parka and snow boots she had thrown on to go fetch her mother after receiving Forrest Payne's phone call. Beatrice frowned as she took in her daughter's ensemble. She said, "I can't believe you allow yourself to be seen in public like this. These people may be the lowest of God's creatures, but that doesn't mean they won't talk."

Clarice quietly mumbled to herself, "I love my mother. I love my mother." She knew she was going to have to remind herself of that often over the next several days. This Christmas season was going to be rough, with Odette being sick, Barbara Jean walking around half in a coma, and Richmond behaving more like Richmond than ever. She wasn't in the mood to have her mother's special brand of crazy piled on top of it all. Clarice gave serious thought to marching into the Pink Slipper and doing her best to persuade Forrest Payne to have Beatrice locked up for trespassing and disturbing the peace. Let the county jail have her for the holidays. That would serve her right.

Clarice hugged her mother and said, "Merry Christmas."

The following morning as she cooked breakfast, Clarice discussed the day's itinerary with her mother. She had scheduled several things: hair appointments for them both, visits to old family friends, shopping excursions for last-minute gifts, and a grocery store trip for the meal they had to prepare for Clarice's children and their families. There were also all sorts of holiday events going on at Calvary Baptist if more was required to keep Beatrice busy. It was important that Beatrice always have something to do. Left to her own devices, her fingers began to itch for her bullhorn.

Things would become easier when the kids arrived the next day. Ricky would be with his wife's family this year, but Clarice and Richmond's other children were coming. Abe was bringing along a new girlfriend for his grandmother to exhaustively interview and disapprove of. Carl would have dozens of pictures to show Beatrice from the latest exotic vacation spot he had taken his wife to as penance for his latest transgression. Carolyn's four-year-old son, Esai, who had inherited Clarice's musical genes, could be relied upon to occupy his great-grandmother with hours of singing and dancing. God bless him. The child could go all day, if needed.

Beatrice wore dark red lipstick that left a vivid imprint on the white mug from which she sipped Earl Grey tea. She always came to breakfast in full makeup. Because it involved a rare excursion into the use of coarse language, Clarice never forgot her mother's opinion about being seen, even in your own home, without your face done. "Honey, it's the equivalent of dropping your pants and taking a dump in the fountain outside of Town Hall." As a goodwill gesture toward her mother and to avoid aggravation, Clarice had been sure to apply lipstick herself that morning.

Her mother asked, "What were you playing last night?"

Clarice apologized for waking her. The piano was in a music room that was off the living room. The bedrooms were upstairs at the opposite end of the house – far out of earshot, she thought.

"No, no, you didn't wake me. I just got up in the night to go to the bathroom and I heard you. I sat on the stairs for a while and listened to you play. It was beautiful. Took me back to when you were a youngster. I used to sit on the stairs at the old house for hours listening to you practice. I have never been as proud of you as I was then, listening to my baby girl overpower that big piano. You really had a gift."

Her mother seldom passed out compliments, even backhanded ones. Clarice took a moment to enjoy it. Then she said, "It was Beethoven, the *Waldstein* Sonata. I've gotten into a habit lately of practicing Beethoven in the middle of the night when I can't sleep."

Beatrice took another sip of tea and said, "You know, I've always thought it was a terrible shame that you gave up on your music."

Here we go, Clarice thought. "I hardly gave up on music, Mother. I have two dozen piano students, and I have former students performing all around the world."

Her mother dabbed at her lips with a napkin and said, "That's nice, I suppose. But what I meant was that it's a shame you never did more, after showing such promise. You never made those recordings when that man asked you to. What was his name? Albert-something, right?"

"Albertson. Wendell Albertson."

"That's right. You really should have made those records."

When Clarice was a sophomore at the university, she won a major national competition. Wendell Albertson, who was the head producer at what was at that time the leading classical music label in the country, was one of the judges. He talked to Clarice after the competition and told her that he wanted to record her. His idea was that she should record all of the Beethoven sonatas over the coming year. He had wanted to market her as a female André Watts, a pianist version of Leontyne Price. But Richmond was injured not long after the competition, so the recording was put off until later. Then Richmond and Clarice became engaged and the recording was delayed again. Then there were the children. Her piano teacher, Mrs Olavsky, had greeted the news of Clarice's first pregnancy by shaking her head and saying, "All these years, wasted," before slamming the door to her studio in Clarice's face.

Clarice hadn't wanted to believe that it was over for her, but time had proved her teacher right. All those years of work, both hers and Mrs Olavsky's, had been wasted. Though she tried not to, Clarice thought of the career she had thrown away whenever she suffered through a sloppy, poorly phrased performance from one of her weaker students. And she mourned that lost life even more keenly each time she watched one of her especially gifted pupils escape Plainview for a fine conservatory, leaving her behind to ruminate over her missed opportunities.

Beatrice said, "You know, I often wonder what would have happened if you'd gone ahead and made those records."

"I haven't given it a thought in years," Clarice said. That was only half a lie because there *had* been years, mostly when the kids were young, when she hardly ever thought about having passed up her big chance. But now it was on her mind during each one of those nights when she sat up playing the piano. Lately, as she charged through the angriest Beethoven passages, she found herself wondering what would have happened if she had been stronger or braver and walked away from Richmond when she'd had the opportunity. But then there wouldn't have been the children, and what would her life have been without them? She stirred the grits in the saucepan and tried to think of Christmas shopping.

The phone rang and Clarice pulled the last strips of bacon from the skillet before going to answer it. After she said hello, she heard a young woman ask, "May I please speak to Richmond?"

Clarice was about to call him to the phone, but she heard the sound of water running in the bathroom at the top of the stairs, so she said, "I'm sorry, Richmond isn't available right now. Who may I tell him called?"

There was a pause, and then the woman said, "I was just calling to confirm my meeting with him today." Another pause. "This is Mrs Jones."

Mrs Jones. Clarice had to roll her eyes at that one.

Clarice said, "I'll be sure to deliver the message, Mrs Jones." She hung up and went back to stirring the already overcooked grits.

Her mother had tired of discussing Clarice's failed musical career. She began to complain about her Arkansas neighbor, Clarice's aunt Glory, another of her favorite topics of conversation. Aunt Glory was petty. Aunt Glory was ill-tempered. Aunt Glory was unwilling to listen to constructive criticism. And, worst of all, Aunt Glory had set such a bad Christian example in her own home that Veronica had fallen under the satanic influence of a fortune-teller.

She said, "Veronica hasn't been right since she left Calvary and went over to First Baptist. Those First Baptist folks are all show and no substance. Watch and see how fast they drop her after she burns through that money she got from the Leaning Tree place. Mind you, they're still a step ahead of that primitive Holy Family bunch. I know your friend Odette goes there, but honestly, they might as well be snake handlers."

The ache behind Clarice's eyes that had started when Forrest Payne called a day earlier throbbed a little harder with each word that came from her mother's mouth. What made it worse was the fact that Clarice had expressed similar sentiments about her cousin and about her friends' churches countless times. Just like Veronica, her mother had a way of reminding Clarice of how alike their thinking was, and seeing the similarities between them made her more and more uncomfortable as time passed.

Richmond burst into the kitchen with a wide, welcoming grin on his handsome face. He was dressed in black slacks and a maroon knit shirt that was tight enough to display the muscles he worked so hard at maintaining. He kissed his mother-in-law on her forehead and sat down next to her.

He winked and said, "Good morning, Bea. How's the second-prettiest girl in the world doing today?"

Beatrice giggled and said, "You are a darling man, taking the time to sweet-talk an old woman like me."

"You haven't aged a day since I met you, and that's the truth," he said, gaining another giggle in reply.

To Clarice, Richmond said, "Sweetheart, I have to spend the day in Louisville with Ramsey talking to a football coach and a kid we're scouting. Depending on how things go, I might not make it back for dinner."

She nodded and brought Richmond his bowl of grits and a plate with two scrambled eggs and bacon. He said, "Thanks, babe," and began to eat.

She walked across the kitchen and got the pot of coffee from the machine and brought it back to the table to pour it into his mug. Maybe it was because her mother distracted her from her task by asking about Odette's health, or perhaps because her mind wandered off to her plans for the day, or because she caught a glimpse of the self-satisfied smirk on Richmond's face, but the coffee Clarice poured missed Richmond's mug entirely. Half of the pot spread onto the table and the other half splashed into Richmond's lap. It wasn't until he screamed, "Damn it!" and jumped up from his chair that she realized what she had done.

In a voice so high-pitched and breathless from shock that she sounded as if she had been the one doused with steaming hot coffee, Clarice cried out, "I'm so sorry! Are you okay? Let me get something to wipe that off."

He pulled the steaming fabric of his pants away from his thighs with both thumbs and forefingers. "Don't bother. I've got to get out of these. Jesus Christ, Clarice." He left the kitchen and hurried up the stairs.

Beatrice didn't say anything to Clarice as she watched her daughter clean up the mess she had made. She just finished her cup of tea and ate her breakfast – one slice of dry toast and one poached egg, the same breakfast she'd eaten every morning Clarice could recall.

Clarice, having lost her appetite, placed the food she had planned to eat into a plastic tub and tucked it into the refrigerator along with the eggs and milk.

Richmond came down again as Clarice put the last of her breakfast away. He was wearing gray pants and an annoyed expression now. He said, "I'm running late. I've got to go."

"But you've hardly had anything to eat," Clarice said.

He pulled his coat from the rack by the garage door. "That's okay. I'll get something later."

"Richmond, I really am sorry about the coffee."

He blew a kiss at his wife from across the room and went through the door.

Beatrice retrieved her compact from the pocket of her red-and-green Christmas cardigan and reapplied her lipstick. Then she said, "Clarice, I think you should have a talk with Reverend Peterson. That always helped me when things were bad with your father and our little problem."

Clarice's mother called her father's serial infidelities their "little problem." It bugged Clarice to no end whenever she described it that way, but she felt that she couldn't rightfully say anything about it. She knew it was hypocritical of her to be bothered by her mother giving Abraham Jordan's cheating a comfortable euphemism when Clarice herself had spent decades pretending Richmond's "little problem" didn't even exist. But that didn't stop her from wanting to shout at her mother to shut the hell up.

Beatrice said, "Reverend Peterson has had a lot of experience. Believe me, there isn't a thing you can say that'll shock him. He can help you deal with all this anger."

"I'm not angry."

"Clarice, what you have to concentrate on is that this is all a part of God's plan. Sometimes we women have to suffer an unfair amount to gain the Lord's favor. Just remember that you're paying the toll for your entrance into the Kingdom. Reverend Peterson explained that to me years ago, and I haven't had a moment of anger since."

That just about beat all, Clarice thought. Her father was long dead and her mother still felt sufficiently irate about his behavior to warrant traveling with her holy megaphone. And *she* was passing out anger-management advice? *Watch out, old woman, or I'll brew an extra hot pot of coffee just for you.*

Clarice said, "Thank you for your advice, Mother, but I'm really not angry. Things are the same with Richmond as they've always been. We're fine."

"Clarice, dear, you just scalded the man's crotch and threw away his insulin."

"Threw away his insulin? What are you talking about?"

Her mother pointed at the trash can. Clarice went to it and pressed the foot pedal that lifted the lid. Sure enough, atop eggshells, coffee grounds, and discarded wrappings of different sorts was the box that contained Richmond's insulin supply, the box that sometime during the past ten minutes she must have removed from its place in the refrigerator door and tossed into the trash.

She picked up the insulin and stared at it for several seconds. Then she put the box back into the fridge. She took off her apron then and said, "Mother, I think we'll go shopping a little bit later."

Clarice left the kitchen and walked through the dining room, past the living room, into the music room, and to her piano. She ripped into Beethoven's *Appassionata* Sonata and forgot about everything, for a while.

Chapter 19

During the week after she saw Chick at the hospital, Barbara Jean couldn't keep her mind in the present day. She chatted with Erma Mae at the All-You-Can-Eat on Wednesday afternoon and found herself glancing down, fully expecting to see Erma Mae's son, Earl III, clinging to his mother's apron with sticky hands. It was only after several seconds of bewilderment that Barbara Jean recalled that Earl III – or Three, as everyone called him – had long since grown up and said goodbye to Plainview, like most of his generation. That Friday evening, a pack of laughing college students passed her on the street as she walked home from the museum, and she ogled them until they noticed that she was watching and returned her stare while chuckling and whispering to each other. In her embarrassment, she nearly chased after them to explain that she had momentarily misplaced a few decades and had been searching through their crowd for the younger faces of her middle-aged friends. The sight of a young interracial couple strolling, hand in hand, down Plainview Avenue on Saturday night spun her into a state of near hysteria, fretting over threats to the couple's safety that had largely vanished years earlier. Each memory triggered by these encounters pushed her toward a bottle, a flask, or her thermos of spiked tea. The good memories weighed her down just as heavily as the bad, and they all demanded to be drunk away, even though some of those memories really were wonderful.

After Barbara Jean kissed Chick in the back hallway of the All-You-Can-Eat, she fell into a pattern. She would wait until Big Earl, Miss Thelma, and Little Earl were asleep, and then she would look out of her bedroom window to see if the light in the storeroom across the street at the restaurant was on. If it was, she slipped out of the house and went to see Chick.

They sat on his bed, surrounded by sixty-four-ounce cans of green beans and corn, and they talked until one or both of them couldn't keep their eyes open any longer. When they weren't talking, they were kissing – it was just kissing, at first. And every moment was heavenly.

If they couldn't meet at the All-You-Can-Eat, they would sneak over to the backyard of Odette's house and press themselves together in the seclusion of the vine-covered gazebo in her mother's garden. At Barbara Jean's insistence, they even traveled over shadowed routes to his bully of a brother's property a few times. They went into the shed where Chick had lived with his chickens and they kissed passionately on his old feather-covered cot. It was like a purification ritual, and the danger of the situation made it all the more irresistible.

Chick was a year out of high school then and he was thinking about college, mostly because Big Earl kept telling him that he was too smart not to. Big Earl said the same thing to Barbara Jean.

Barbara Jean liked the idea of college, but she couldn't imagine what she would study. She didn't have a passion like Clarice had with her piano. She got okay grades and she liked school enough. But Loretta had drummed it into her head since she was a child that she was going to marry a rich man. And that required a specific kind of preparation, a kind that you didn't need college to achieve.

Barbara Jean's mother taught her to dress in the manner that she associated with glamour – everything shiny and/or revealing. To make sure Barbara Jean talked like a high-class woman, her mother put belt lashes across her back if she dropped *g*s from the ends of her words, the way Loretta did. Barbara Jean and her mother joined First Baptist Church because the richest and lightest-skinned black people in town went there. Her mother weighed her every week to make sure her weight was always within man-catching range – something she and Clarice shared in common, Barbara Jean later discovered.

Barbara Jean thought it was funny that, when she finally did find a rich man, Loretta's life lessons had proved useless. All that had mattered was that she pass his family's skin color test. When she was introduced to Lester's mother, the old woman held a brown paper bag up to Barbara Jean's cheek and, judging her just a smidge lighter in comparison, said, "Welcome to the family."

During the winter of Barbara Jean's senior year, she wasn't thinking about her education, or marrying rich, or anything. She was crazy in love with a white boy who was poorer than anybody she knew. Loretta must have been spinning in her grave.

Even as she fell more deeply in love with Chick, Barbara

Jean saw more of Lester. She was too naïve and too blinded by her feelings for Chick to even notice that the hours she spent with Lester were also a kind of dating. He often showed up at the All-You-Can-Eat with James and sat for a while at the window table with Barbara Jean and her friends. But Barbara Jean never thought anything of it. Everyone, it seemed, put in time at the window table. Little Earl, that obnoxious Ramsey Abrams, Clarice's silly cousin Veronica. Even Chick became a regular guest at the table when he wasn't on duty, since he and James had become good buddies.

Sometimes Lester drove his young friends to Evansville and other nearby towns in his beautiful blue Cadillac, treating them to dinners they could never have afforded on their own. Always, he was a perfect gentleman. Lester never so much as held Barbara Jean's hand, much less made any sort of advances. She enjoyed his company and was flattered that he wanted to be her friend.

Clarice told Barbara Jean several times that Lester was interested in her, but Barbara Jean didn't pay much attention to her. Barbara Jean shared Odette's opinion that Clarice, already having scripted her own happy ending with Richmond, was now eager to write one for everybody else.

On a January night in 1968, Lester took James, Richmond, and the Supremes out for a ride in his Cadillac and then to dinner at a nice place in Louisville to celebrate Richmond having broken a passing record at the university. Barbara Jean enjoyed herself. The food was good and the restaurant was the most glamorous place she had ever stepped inside of. But she couldn't wait to get back to Chick. It was Chick's birthday and she had saved up to buy him a Timex wristwatch with a genuine leather band, which she thought back then was the height of elegance. She kept an eye on James all through dinner, waiting for his yawning to signal that the evening was over. But James didn't start to fade until 10:00, and it was nearly 10:30 when they began the forty-minute drive back to Plainview.

When Lester dropped Barbara Jean off, she found Odette's parents in Big Earl and Miss Thelma's living room. Laughing and bobbing their heads to a scratchy old record playing on the stereo, they waved hello to Barbara Jean through a haze of bluish-gray smoke as she climbed the stairs to her bedroom. The four of them stayed up late that night, the way they always did when they got together. When the Jacksons finally went home at around 2:00, Big Earl and Miss Thelma went straight to bed. They fell into loud snoring not five minutes after their bedroom door closed. For the thousandth time that night, Barbara Jean looked out the window to see if the storeroom light at the All-You-Can-Eat was still on. It was, so she tiptoed down the stairs and went to see Chick.

He was sitting on his narrow bed looking down when Barbara Jean walked into the room with the gift box in her outstretched hands. She rushed over and sat beside him. She said, "I'm sorry. I couldn't get over here any sooner." She was going to explain about the Jacksons visiting until late, but he looked up then and she stopped talking.

Chick had a red-and-blue bruise on his chin and his lower lip was split. She didn't need to ask who had done it.

She said, "Why'd you go over there?" and then immediately wished she hadn't said it.

She reached out and wrapped her arms around his shoulders. He tried to pull away at first, but then he relaxed and laid his head against her neck. He talked quietly in her ear.

"I ran into my brother's girlfriend, Liz, this morning. She said Desmond had been talking about how he wanted me to come back home. She said he'd been in a good mood for a while, not drinking as much and stuff. Plus, Liz's got this little girl. She's not my brother's kid, but she calls me Uncle Ray. And Liz said her daughter was asking why her Uncle Ray didn't come see her over Christmas." Chick shrugged. "She asked me to come by for supper. So, I went.

"Desmond was already pretty drunk when I got to the house, but he was joking and kidding around like we used to do sometimes. Then he lost it halfway through supper. He's like that. Changes real quick."

From years with Loretta, Barbara Jean knew how a drunken meal could go all crazy with no warning. One sip too much and a switch inside got flipped from off to on, and then things went bad fast.

"Nothing really started it, but all of a sudden he was yelling at Liz that she was a whore and was cheating on him. He threw his plate at her, so Liz grabbed her kid and took off before he could throw another one. Then he started in on me. He said he heard a rumor that I was working for a – a colored man."

Chick said it in a way that made it clear to Barbara Jean that "colored man" hadn't been the term his brother had used.

"Desmond said he wasn't gonna let me shame him in front of his friends. And then he started swinging.

"I'm getting better, though," Chick said. He raised his hands and showed her his scraped and bleeding knuckles. "I got in a few good ones myself this time." He tried to smile and grimaced because of his busted lip.

All the air seemed to go out of him then. He pulled away from Barbara Jean and stared down at his hands as they rested in his lap. Shaking his head, he said, "It's all shit. It's all just a bunch of shit."

She reached out and lightly stroked the bruise on his chin, remembering how the touch of his fingers had forever transformed the belt buckle scars on her arm into a smiling face. She kissed his mouth, avoiding the swollen part of his lip. She kissed him again and again. Then she put her hands on his waist and carefully pulled his T-shirt up over his head. There were more bruises on his chest and on his skinny arms and she leaned over and kissed those, too.

Chick put his hands on the sides of her face and kissed her now. Then he reached down and began to unbutton her blouse.

They undressed each other as if they had been doing it for years, no fumbling or rushing. And when they were both naked, they slid beneath the covers of his bed.

Barbara Jean was more experienced than Chick was. But her knowledge of intimacy had come too early and under bad circumstances, courtesy of evil men. She realized from the moment that she and Chick pulled the blankets over their bodies that this was as different from those other times as it could be. And that difference made it seem like her first time, too.

They wound themselves together over and over again, in a blur of arms and legs, lips and hands. When, finally, they were so ragged from exhaustion that they could do no more than lie with their mouths inches apart, each inhaling the other's breath, Barbara Jean forgot all about the passing of time and fell asleep in his arms under the pile of tangled linens.

When Barbara Jean awakened, he was gone. She sat up in the bed and looked around the tiny room, at the giant cans of corn, lard, and beans that were stacked to the ceiling against slatted wood walls, at the lamp he'd made from a Coca-Cola bottle and other bits scavenged from the trash cans behind the hardware store. She began to panic, thinking that she had made an awful mistake. She heard her mother's voice in her head saying, "I told you, girl. That's how men are. They get what they want, and then they run."

The panic fled when Chick tiptoed back into the room, still naked, carrying a big dish of ice cream with two spoons sticking out of it.

Seeing that Barbara Jean was awake, he grinned at her. "It's my birthday. We've got to have ice cream."

His smile fell away when he saw Barbara Jean's face. He said, "Are you okay? You aren't sorry, are you? You aren't sorry we did – you know, what we did, are you?"

"I'm not sorry. I just thought for a second that you'd left, that's all."

Chick sat on the edge of the bed and kissed her. He tasted like vanilla and cream. "Why would I go anywhere? You're here."

She took the ice cream dish from him and placed it on

the bedside table he had made by stacking old fruit crates. She kicked off the blankets and pulled him toward her. They both laughed as she sang, "Happy birthday to you, happy birthday to you," into his ear while he settled his weight on top of her again.

Barbara Jean and Chick were sharing melted ice cream when they heard the back door of the restaurant open. Someone rattled around in the kitchen as they listened. Then the radio came on and they heard Miss Thelma humming.

Barbara Jean knew she should have been frightened of being discovered there with Chick. And she knew that she should have thought she had done something wrong. She had learned at least that much from Sundays at First Baptist Church. But she couldn't manage to feel the slightest bit bad about the best night of her life.

They stayed there in bed together listening to the clanking of pots and pans and enjoying the sound of Miss Thelma's out-of-tune vocalizing. They finished the melted ice cream and kissed, silently celebrating their new lives on a planet all their own.

An old-timey blues song came on the radio and Miss Thelma began to sing along: "My baby love to rock, my baby love to roll. What she do to me just soothe my soul. Ye-ye-yes, my baby love me . . ."

Chick threw back the covers and hopped out of the bed. He stood beside the bed and began to dance, slowly moving his narrow hips in a widening circle while turning away from Barbara Jean to wave his tiny ass in her direction. He grinned back at her over his shoulder, mouthing the words of the song as he moved.

Barbara Jean had to pick up the pillow and press it against her mouth to keep Miss Thelma from hearing her laugh as Ray Carlson, the King of the Pretty White Boys, danced for her. She laughed so hard she cried. All the while her spinning, seventeen-year-old brain replayed the same thoughts: *My Ray. Ray of light. Ray of sunshine. Ray of hope.*

Barbara Jean thought of her mother. But now, for the first time ever, thinking of Loretta didn't make her feel bad. She thought about what Loretta would say if she had been able to tell her about this night. Her mother would have said, "Well, it looks like you are your mama's daughter after all. Your stuff was so good you done made a white boy jump up naked and dance the blues."

Chapter 20

I didn't exactly sail through my treatments the way I'd fantasized, but the side effects weren't as bad as I'd been warned they could be. My stomach was a mess sometimes, but mostly I was able to eat like I always had. My skin dried out, but didn't crack and bleed. I was tired, but not so weary that I had to quit my job or even miss a Sunday at the All-You-Can-Eat. Though it was brittle and broke off with the slightest tug, I kept a fair amount of my hair. Best of all, I celebrated Christmas week without a single visit from Eleanor Roosevelt. By the time of our New Year's Day party, I was full of optimism and ready to kick up my heels.

Our annual January get-together was a long-running tradition, going back to the first year of our marriage. The truth, even though he denies this, is that the first party was an attempt by James to prove to his friends that I wasn't as bad a choice of a mate as I seemed. Richmond and Ramsey – and others, most likely – had warned James that a big-mouthed, hot-tempered woman like me could never be properly tamed. But James was determined to show them that I could, on occasion, be as domestic and wifely as any other woman. I suspect that he's still trying to convince them.

What James *has* proved is that people will flock to a party hosted by a troublesome woman as long as she lays out a good spread. The party got a little bigger with each passing year, and lately we can count on seventy-five to a hundred folks showing up throughout the course of the day.

I normally cooked for a solid week in anticipation of my guests arriving, but that year James fought me, insisting that I conserve my strength and have the whole thing catered by Little Earl. We battled it out until we finally came to a compromise. Little Earl covered the savory. I did the sweet, with some help from Barbara Jean and Clarice.

My friends worked harder than I did to put the party together. Clarice even brought her mother by to lend a hand with the baking. Mrs Jordan – who, with her bullhorn nonsense, was giving Mama a run for her money in the race to be considered the nuttiest woman Plainview had ever produced – was a real asset in the kitchen once she got past her revulsion over the cheapness of my serving platters. I appreciated her coming by to help, but her habit of stopping to thank Jesus at every step of the cooking process got old real fast. We thanked Him for every ingredient, the utensils, even the oven timer. Being around her reminded me of something Mama liked to say: "I love Jesus, but some of his representatives sure make my ass tired."

On New Year's Day, the guests started showing up around three o'clock. My sons, my daughter, and my grandkids did all of the greeting. Denise was bossy, ordering her older brothers around like she always had. Jimmy argued with his sister over the slightest thing: "The coats go in the middle bedroom." "No, they don't. They go in the guest bedroom." Eric ignored them both and acted just as thrilled to be having company over as he did when he was six years old. I half expected him to grab one of the guests by the hand and demand that they accompany him to his room to see his train set. Seeing my fully grown offspring together, falling back into the roles they had played as children, was a load of fun for me, although I'm sure my son-in-law and daughter-in-law were counting the seconds until they could escape my house and get back the adults they'd married.

James's police friends arrived first. The younger men who worked under James came at the precise moment the party was scheduled to start, like they were appearing for morning roll call. Mostly fresh-faced, beefy white boys – there were still no women in his unit – they came bearing flowers, in the company of skinny girlfriends who wore extremely low-cut blouses. As always, the first-timers looked stiff and uncomfortable until the good food, plentiful beer, and a few country songs mixed in with the R&B on the stereo loosened them up.

My brother stomped through the living room and threw himself on me like an overly friendly Labrador. Rudy spun me around and inspected me. "You don't look much worse than usual," he said. Then he gave me a brotherly punch in the arm and a kiss on each cheek.

Rudy's wife, Inez, stepped closer, slapped him on the wrist, and chastised him for being too rough with me. Then she hugged me so tight she squeezed the breath out of me. Inez might be a dainty thing – she's my height and no more than a hundred pounds – but every last bit of what's there is muscle. Rudy likes to pretend his wife is helpless, and she plays along. But I wouldn't want to be the one to make Inez mad. The three of us did some fast catching up before I passed them along to James and said hello to the newest guests.

Richmond, Clarice, and her mother, Beatrice, arrived at the same time as Veronica and her mother, Glory. Beatrice, Glory, and Veronica all wore elaborate, floor-length gowns. It was their habit to overdress for every occasion. They came to picnics dressed for a day on a yacht. They showed up at graduation ceremonies done up as if they were attending a coronation. They always wanted their hosts to understand that they were either on their way to or on their way from a much more important gathering.

Beatrice and Glory made a big show of not speaking to each other due to an argument they'd had on the phone that morning. Whenever the two elderly sisters came within five feet of each other, they snorted and sniffed like riled-up horses before stalking off in opposite directions.

Barbara Jean caused a stir when she sashayed in packed into a hot pink dress with a plunging neckline. The young cops looked away from their dates and stared in appreciation at this woman twice the age of their girlfriends. Barbara Jean went straight to the drinks table and hit the vodka with an intensity that worried me.

My doctor, Alex Soo, came in with a hefty woman on his arm. She was as loud as he was quiet, and she had a laugh like a rooster's crow. She parked herself beside one of the food tables and soon made it clear that her goal for the day was to break the world record for consuming the most deviled eggs in one sitting. I liked her right off.

Ramsey Abrams and his always angry wife, Florence, arrived with their sons, Clifton and Stevie, and their future daughter-in-law. Like her mother, grandmother, and great-aunt, Sharon was dressed in the style of touring royalty. From the moment she stepped in the door, she signaled her intent to spend the evening flouncing around in her party dress while gesturing wildly with her left hand to show off the expensive engagement ring Clifton had given her. The naïve girl was completely oblivious to the way her shady fiancé broke out in a sweat when she brandished that rock anywhere near one of the many cops in attendance.

I sure wished Ramsey and Florence had used common sense and left Stevie at home. He clearly wasn't over that shoe thing of his, or his airplane glue habit either, judging from his glassy eyes. He stared at the feet of every woman who walked past with an expression on his face that reminded you of a stray dog outside of a butcher shop. It gave people the creeps.

Clarice's daughter, Carolyn, who is good friends with my Denise, stretched her Christmas visit out a few extra days and came to the party with her husband and her son, who was carried in already sound asleep in his father's arms. Carolyn had gone way out of her way to find a man who wasn't the least bit like her father. She married a Latino intellectual who teaches physics at a college in Massachusetts. He's small, much shorter than Carolyn, and he's had the doughy body of an idle middle-aged man since he was twenty-two.

When Richmond realized that Carolyn was getting

serious about the intellectual, he did everything he could to divert Carolyn's interest in the direction of someone he thought would be more suitable for her. He scoured the campus until he found two replicas of himself in his virile prime. Then he dragged both men to a big Memorial Day picnic at his house, where he paraded them in front of Carolyn like a couple of prize bulls. In a turn of events that I'm sure Richmond will still be trying to sort out on the day he dies, Carolyn stayed with her egghead while the two Richmond clones began a romance with each other on that Memorial Day that is still going strong more than a decade later.

Mama appeared, along with Mrs Roosevelt, late in the evening. They both looked like they'd been to several other parties already that day. Mama's eyes were bloodshot and Mrs Roosevelt, who was wearing a cone-shaped silver and gold paper hat that was attached to her head with an elastic band, seemed to have forgotten her usual good manners. She waved in my general direction as she staggered in. Then she plopped down onto a footstool and began to snore.

When Mama spotted Rudy, she squealed, "Look at my boy. Ain't he the handsomest thing?" Rudy's a dear, but he's mostly ears, nose, and belly. Pretty, my brother is not. I said nothing.

After Mama finished making a fuss over Rudy, she commenced to making a nuisance of herself by following me around the house as I performed my hostess duties. "Oh, there's the Abrams boy," she said when she saw Ramsey. He was standing much too close to the girlfriend of one of the young cops and getting dirty looks from the girl's date and from his wife, who scowled at him from a few feet away.

Mama said, "You know, it's sad when you think about it. He's probably just overcompensatin' for a very small penis. All of the Abrams men have little dicks. That's why they're so short-tempered. His poor father and uncle were the same way, had practically nothin' down there at all."

I silently prayed that my mother would spare me the details of just how she'd come across that bit of information about the Abrams men.

I noticed Clarice sitting on the couch next to her mother and aunt. She was frowning like she had a toothache and her attention was focused on some point way off in the distance. The fingers of both her hands were tapping away on her lap like she was playing an invisible piano. If her mother didn't get out of town soon, Clarice was going to snap.

When I came over to offer to freshen up their drinks, I saw that Clarice's mother and her aunt Glory had started speaking to each other again. They were having a good time now, arguing about who would be more surprised to be left behind after the Rapture, the Catholics or the Mormons.

Mama sneered at them. "I know you and Clarice are friends, but you can't tell me you don't wanna slap the livin' shit outta that mother of hers. Talk about somebody with her head stuffed way up her own ass. And that sister of hers is just as bad. As far back as I can remember, Beatrice and Glory been usin' Jesus as an excuse to be bitches." She wagged her finger at them and, like they could hear her, said, "That's right, I said it!"

Veronica waved me over to where she was holding court, showing Sharon's wedding planning book to a group of women who were too polite to walk away. She pointed to a page in the book that held a magazine clipping with a picture of a bride floating on a rug in midair down the center aisle of a church. Veronica said, "I'm thinking Sharon should make a magic carpet entrance. It's all done with lights and mirrors. Isn't it something?"

I agreed that it was something, all right, and tried to ignore the fact that my mother was next to me shrieking with laughter at the idea of big Sharon floating to the altar.

Over Mama's continued cackling, I heard Veronica discussing the trouble she was having finding a suitable affordable home for the newlyweds. Sharon had another year at the university, and her fiancé, Clifton, Veronica claimed, would be going back to school soon. So after the wedding, which Veronica and her psychic had determined should happen on the first Saturday in July, she would settle them into something nice, but reasonably priced, here in town.

James, ever helpful, walked by just then and said, "You know, Veronica, we don't have a tenant in the house in Leaning Tree."

If I hadn't been holding a tray of pigs in blankets, I'd have knocked James upside his head. I had nothing against Sharon. It wasn't her fault that she'd inherited her father's intelligence and her mother's personality. It was the thought of Veronica traipsing in and out of Mama and Daddy's house that made my pressure rise.

I gave James my *back away quickly* look. But he'd been immune to my hostile glances for ages, so he wasn't put off his stride for a second. He just went right on being helpful.

He said, "We just put a new roof on it and painted it. And the last tenant took good care of the garden. It's not like it was when Miss Dora was living, but it's not bad."

It turned out I didn't have to worry about the prospect of having more Veronica in my life. Veronica wrinkled her nose and said, "Thanks, James, but I didn't spend all those years working to get out of Leaning Tree just to send my baby daughter back there."

Mama let out a snort. "Talk about a nerve. I guess she's too good for my house now. She oughta try to sell that bullshit to some folks who don't remember where she came from. And what kind of 'working' did she do to get outta Leanin' Tree? All she did was outlive her lowlife daddy. Odette, tell her your mama's back and that she's fixin' to haunt the fuck outta her. Go on, tell 'er."

I hadn't seen Minnie McIntyre come in, but I heard the tinkling of a bell and turned to see her standing just behind me. Minnie had taken to wearing her fortune-telling turban with its tiny silver bell all the time. She said that, because she was so near death, Charlemagne the Magnificent had more messages for her than ever. So she wouldn't miss one of those messages, she made sure to always have her bell at the ready. My first thought was *Oh great, now Mama will never shut up.*

When Mama was alive, just the sight of Minnie McIntyre was enough to start her cussing and spitting. I prepared myself to hear her let loose with a foul-mouthed tirade. But Mama was watching Denise as she attempted to corral my grandkids. She wasn't thinking about Minnie. Mama heard Denise call her daughter by her name, Dora, and I thought she was going to fall out on the floor.

Mama was in my business so much that I had forgotten she wasn't a daily part of my children's lives, too. She hadn't seen them in years and didn't know her great-grandchildren at all. Now she'd discovered that she had a cute little namesake running around and it had knocked the wind out of her sails. She went silent and tottered off behind the kids. After all the shocks she'd handed me, it was kind of nice to see Mama taken by surprise for a change.

Barbara Jean stood talking with Erma Mae on the other side of the living room from me. She nodded her head and pretended to listen to whatever Erma Mae was saying to her. But I could see that she was staring at my grandkids, especially my grandson William, just as hard as Mama was. Barbara Jean did that from time to time, saw boys around eight or nine years old and couldn't draw her eyes away from them. I knew she was thinking of Adam. How could she not? Sure, Adam and William looked nothing alike. My grandson inherited my roundness and cocoa skin, and Adam was a buttercream-colored string bean. But they shared that same wild energy and heartbreaking sweetness that little boys have in those brief years before your presence bores and annoys them and they can't abide an embrace. Barbara Jean's boy would never grow out of that phase.

Barbara Jean watched my grandson as he zipped through the room, tormenting my cats with an overabundance of affection and charming guests with his big smile. When my son-in-law sensed that William was becoming too rambunctious for the crowd and carried his giggling and squirming son out of the room under his arm, Barbara Jean looked like she might cry. I'd have bet good money that she was seeing Lester and Adam just like I was, remembering how Lester couldn't resist hoisting Adam in the air whenever that boy was within reach. If Lester'd had his way, Adam's feet would never have touched the ground. Barbara Jean walked away from Erma Mae then, heading in the direction of the vodka.

That year's party was the biggest ever. It was like everybody we'd ever met came by to say hello. Or, more likely, they came to say goodbye. Nothing like a little touch of cancer to get folks to feel all sentimental about you, whether they cared for you or not. But by midnight most of the guests had left. Mama retired to the family room to coo over her great-grandkids, who had collapsed on the couch alongside Clarice's grandson by then. I was dead on my feet and longed to stretch out and rest, but I went into the kitchen to do some cleaning up. I opened the kitchen door to find my Denise and Clarice's Carolyn washing dishes, laughing and talking the same way they had done when they were girls. I stood there for a few seconds watching them – both of them smart, strong, and happy. Well, I thought, looks like Clarice and I did at least one thing right.

A hand touched my shoulder and I turned to see Richmond. He whispered into my ear, "Listen, Odette, Clarice and I are leaving, and we're taking Barbara Jean. She's had a little too much to drink."

I followed him out of the kitchen, through the living room, and into the front hallway, where Clarice was helping Barbara Jean into her coat. The quiet mood Barbara Jean had been in all day had given way to gloominess. Her watery eyes and the haunted expression on her face seemed even bleaker because of the pink dress that mocked her now with its youthful cheeriness.

I gave her a quick hug and said, "I'll call you tomorrow."

Barbara Jean tried to say good night, but her words came out in a jumble. Clarice and Richmond each grabbed one of her arms and guided her out. They were followed by the oh-so-proper Mrs Jordan, who glared at Barbara Jean and clucked, "Unseemly. Entirely unseemly."

I stepped out onto the front porch and watched as Clarice and her mother got into the front seat of Richmond's Chrysler while he helped Barbara Jean into the back. After he got Barbara Jean settled in, he shut the door and trotted over to her car and hopped inside. They drove off, Richmond leading the way in Barbara Jean's Mercedes.

I stayed on the porch for a few minutes, enjoying the cold air after so many hours inside the warm, crowded house. Mama joined me, and Mrs Roosevelt came out just after Mama. The former first lady had sobered up and her famous warm, toothy smile was firmly in place as she snuggled up against me.

Mama said, "I hate to see Barbara Jean like that. I think maybe there's trouble comin', don't you?"

I didn't answer for a moment. I was distracted because, for the first time in all of her visits, Mrs Roosevelt seemed to have actual physical presence. I felt the weight of her body leaning against mine. And, in the chilly air of the evening, the warmth that emanated from her was almost uncomfortably hot. She and I now truly shared the same world. *This can't be good,* I thought.

When I finally answered Mama, I said, "Yeah, I believe trouble's coming."

Chapter 21

If you ever wanted evidence that I wasn't as fearless as the rumors made me out to be, all you had to do was look at the way I handled Barbara Jean's drinking. Without even discussing it, I joined in a coward's pact with Clarice and didn't say a word about it for years. Both of us were afraid that if we confronted it head-on we'd find our friendship toppling over like a tower of children's blocks.

Not dealing with Barbara Jean's drinking turned it into an invisible fourth member of our trio, a pesky, out-of-tune singer who Clarice and I just adjusted to over time. We learned not to call Barbara Jean on the phone after nine at night because she wasn't likely to remember the conversation. If she was going through a bad spell, we would say that she was "tired" and we rescheduled anything that we might have had planned so we could do it when she was feeling more energetic. It went on like that for years, and the whole time I convinced myself that we weren't doing her any harm by not confronting her about it. She would go through periods when she was tired more days than not, but those episodes were always followed by longer periods when she was fine.

I told myself that it was Lester's place to step in and say something if it was going to be said. He was her husband.

But Lester was gone now, and for the first time in ages, Barbara Jean had been drunk in public. I tried to tell myself that what had happened at my party had been typical New Year's Day excess. Who hadn't tied one on celebrating a new year at some point in their lives?

But this was different. And Clarice and I both knew it, even if we hadn't said anything. Barbara Jean had that darkness about her in a way that I hadn't seen since she lost Adam. And it didn't seem like she was going to shake it anytime soon.

I entered 2005 recognizing that one day soon, while I still had the chance to do it, I was going to have to risk toppling that tower of blocks.

Barbara Jean's drinking got bad for the first time in 1977, during that horrible year after little Adam died. For a long stretch of months she was drunk more than she was sober. I would stop by her house and find her hardly able to stand. She maintained a good front when she was out among strangers, though; people talked about how well she was holding up. If I hadn't known her like I did, I'd have agreed. But I heard the occasional slurred word coming into her speech earlier and earlier in the day. I saw how she wobbled on those high heels she loved to wear.

And poor Lester. World War II had only succeeded in adding a hitch to his step, but his son's death defeated him. He turned into an old man that year. The first in a long list of chronic ailments – a kidney problem, if memory serves – made its appearance just a month after Adam's funeral.

Lester dosed himself with work the same way Barbara

Jean medicated her sorrow with alcohol. With Adam gone, Lester started taking more business trips, staying away from home longer. And when he returned, he looked more exhausted and more miserable.

When he had Adam, Lester's work energized him and kept him young. Barbara Jean might have seen her son as a future painter because of his elaborate crayon drawings or a musician because he was such a natural at the piano, but Lester knew that his boy was meant to work with the land like his daddy. On the weekends and during Adam's summer break from school, Lester brought his son with him whenever he had jobs around Plainview. Lester joined in doing the sort of grunt work that was customarily left to low-level employees so that Adam could see and understand every aspect of the business he would inherit one day. And Adam had loved every minute of it. Dressed in his overalls, he followed his father everywhere, planting, digging, and raking with his miniature tools.

Now that he wasn't creating something to hand over to his son, there was no reason for Lester to touch a shovel or lift a rake. His body withered along with his spirit, and his life's work turned into a numbers game. He made deal after deal and piled up cash like he thought it might make him and Barbara Jean happy one day.

Even though they were from different generations and even though the one thing, or so it had always seemed to me, that bound them as a couple was gone, Lester and Barbara Jean stayed together and sometimes managed to look like all that money really was bringing them happiness. Richer, sicker, sadder, and older, as the shock of Adam's death faded, they built new lives.

It was during that awful first year that the Supremes and the fragile new life Barbara Jean and Lester were building nearly came to an end, with some help from Richmond Baker.

We were at our table at the All-You-Can-Eat on a Sunday afternoon. Clarice's twins were seated in their highchairs between her and Richmond. Denise was on James's lap, making a macaroni and cheese sculpture. The other children were at a table of their own just a few feet away, within snatching distance.

Clarice tried to keep up a conversation between yawns. The twins had really knocked the stuffing out of Clarice in a way the older two hadn't. She could barely keep her eyes open some days.

Barbara Jean looked divine that Sunday in a dress of layered taffeta that was traffic-cone orange. Big Earl stood and applauded her when she walked into the restaurant. Lester was out of town again, so she was alone. She was relatively steady on her feet, but she talked in an uneven, overly careful way that telegraphed her drunken state to those of us who really knew her.

During that meal I watched as a curious and troubling scene played out. We were discussing the latest round of renovations going on at Barbara Jean's house. It was one of the few activities that seemed to really interest Barbara Jean around that time. Things started going funny when she said, "What I need to do right now is get a carpenter in there to do some work in the bedroom closets. Somebody put in metal shelves at some point, and those things are coming down practically every day. One of them almost took my head off last night."

Richmond said, "You don't need to hire anybody to do that. Lester can take care of that with an electric drill and some masonry screws in no time."

Barbara Jean shook her head no. "Lester's gone for the next two weeks and I've got to do something about it right away." She laughed and said, "I think that for everyone's safety I'd better not try to do it myself."

Richmond, the charitable Mr Fix-it, said, "I'd be happy to come over and help you out."

Barbara Jean leaned across James to pat Richmond's arm. "Richmond, you are a lifesaver."

The thing with Richmond was that he *would* help a friend in need without giving it a second thought. As much as he annoyed me, I had to admit that he really was that guy who'd hand you the shirt off his back. Unfortunately, when an attractive woman was involved, Richmond would hand her the shirt off his back and then toss her his pants and underwear, too.

Alarm bells went off in my head when Richmond turned his *at your service* smile on Barbara Jean. I looked at Clarice and James to see if they were hearing the same warning signal I was. But Clarice was focused on the twins, not her husband. And James was bouncing Denise on his knee and not paying a bit of attention to anything else that was happening at the table.

That night at home I stewed over what I'd heard earlier at the All-You-Can-Eat. I told myself it wasn't any of my business and that my friends were responsible adults. They would come to the right decisions on their own. And even if they didn't do the right thing, it wasn't my place to step in. Finally, when it was clear that turning things over in my mind was going to ruin *Kojak* for me, I told James that I had an errand to run and I left the house to act upon my true nature.

I smelled Richmond before I saw him. Since he was a teenager, he'd worn the same lemony, woody cologne. It always marched into the room several seconds before he did. I was waiting in the shadows, sitting in one of the wicker rockers on Barbara Jean's front porch when he stepped up to the door.

I said, "Hello there, Richmond," just loud enough for him to hear me.

He jumped, put his hand to his chest, and said, "Odette, you damn near scared me to death." Then he asked, "What are you doing here?"

"Just enjoying the night air. What about you, Richmond? What brings you by Barbara Jean's tonight?"

He produced a smile that I would have believed was innocent through and through if I hadn't known him better. He said, "I told Barbara Jean I'd come by and take a look at those shelves of hers that keep falling."

"That's truly sweet, Richmond. But I've got some bad news for you."

"What's that?"

I pointed to the sack in his hand and said, "Looks like you were in such a rush to come over here and be a Good Samaritan that you went and picked up the wrong bag. Instead of your drill, you accidentally grabbed a bottle of wine. Must be the stress of dealing with the twins."

He lost his smile then and said, "Listen, Odette, it's not what you're thinking. I was just—"

I interrupted him. "Richmond, why don't you come over here and sit with me for a minute."

He hemmed and hawed, saying that he should probably get back home.

"Just for a minute, Richmond. Really, I insist."

He groaned and then took a seat in the chair next to mine, falling into it like a teenager who'd been called into the vice-principal's office.

He placed the bottle of wine on the floor between his feet and said, "Odette, I was just paying a friendly visit. Nothing's happened and nothing's going to happen. But Clarice might get things mixed up. You aren't going to tell her, are you?"

"No, Richmond, I'm not going to tell Clarice. But you and I have to have a conversation because there's something I need to tell you."

I rocked back and forth in the chair a few times to think about what I wanted to say. Then I said, "If I weren't married to a man everyone loves, I probably wouldn't have a true friend in this world, except Barbara Jean and Clarice."

He said, "That's not true. You're a perfectly charming woman."

I waved off the compliment, saying, "Richmond, you have lovely manners. I've always admired that about you. But you don't need to waste time blowing smoke up my ass. I know who I am."

I continued, "I'm a tough woman to be around. I don't try to be, I just am. I don't know how James deals with me. And to top it off, I was never pretty enough for people to overlook me being a pain in the ass."

He started to interrupt once more, but again I stopped him. "Please, Richmond, let me go on. I promise to get to the point.

"I know that you probably think I don't like you. Maybe Clarice told you that I warned her not to marry you." In the dim light from the street lamps out on Main Street, I saw an expression of surprise on his face. "She didn't tell you, huh? Well, I did. I told her you'd always be a cheater no matter how hard she tried to change you and that she was better off without you. I shouldn't have said it, but I did. That's kind of my way.

"But I want you to know that I really don't have anything against you. And I understand why Clarice loves you. You're polite. You're funny. When I watch you with your children, I see a kind, warm side of you that is absolutely beautiful. And, even though I hate to admit it, you are one of the best-looking men I've ever laid eyes on."

He relaxed then. A discussion of his physical attractiveness was something Richmond had always been comfortable with. "And I love Clarice, I really do."

"I believe you. But what you need to understand is I'll do absolutely anything to protect the handful of people in this world who truly love me. And, Richmond, if you follow your dick and go in this house with Barbara Jean, she'll never be able to see herself as a decent human being again. She'll come to her senses tomorrow and hate herself for letting it happen. It'll eat her alive, almost as bad as losing Adam. Clarice will eventually figure it out and feel more humiliated than she has ever felt with any of your other women. And then, Richmond" – I reached out and placed my hand on his muscular forearm – "I will have to kill you."

Richmond laughed and then said, "Okay, Odette, I get it. I'll stay away from Barbara Jean."

"No, Richmond, I don't think you really get it yet." I squeezed his arm tighter and said, very slowly, "I am as serious as a heart attack. If you ever come sniffing around Barbara Jean again, I will kill you dead."

I held his gaze and added, "I won't want to. And it will bring me no pleasure to do it. But, still, I will kill you."

Our eyes locked for several seconds and I watched the last traces of a smile leave his face as he took in that I was telling him God's honest truth.

He nodded. "I understand."

I patted his arm and said, "Well, this has been real nice. I don't know about you, but I feel a whole lot better."

I pushed the sleeve of his shirt a few inches higher on his wrist and read his watch in the faint light. "And would you look at that," I said, "I can still catch the end of *Kojak*." I stood and stepped to the edge of the porch. "Why don't you walk me home?"

Richmond picked up the bottle and came along with me, down the stairs and onto the stone walkway that led to Main Street. I looped my arm around his and said, "It really is a lovely evening, isn't it?"

I looked over my shoulder as we turned onto the sidewalk. Just for a second, I caught sight of Barbara Jean peeking out of an upstairs window at me and Richmond, a man who now understood me in a way that even James didn't, as we strolled away from her magnificent house.

Chapter 22

After saying goodbye to her last piano student of the day, Clarice went to visit Odette. Late February had brought with it a spell of false spring. Temperatures were almost twenty degrees above normal and she felt energized by the warm weather.

Odette was having a bad month. She didn't complain, but Clarice could see that she had practically no energy. The previous Sunday at the All-You-Can-Eat, Odette had terrified everyone at the table by leaving an entire pork chop untouched on her plate at the end of supper. So Clarice decided to drop by bearing a slice of peach cobbler, a bag of gifts, and some decent local gossip she'd picked up. (Rumor had it that Clifton Abrams, less than five months from marrying Sharon, had something going on the side.)

Everyone in town was celebrating the unexpected warm weather by airing out their homes. For the first time in months, Clarice passed by open door after open door as Plainview's residents welcomed in the unseasonable breeze. Odette and James's front door was also open, and standing on their porch, Clarice peered through the screen door and saw them in their living room. James sat on the sofa and Odette sat on the floor in front of him with her back to him and her legs stretched out on the rag rug. She petted an enormous calico cat that Clarice didn't recognize. Odette still picked up strays, so this one could have been added just that day. Two other cats lounged across her shins. Her eyes were closed and her head was tilted back. James, who had half a dozen bobby pins squeezed between his lips, attempted to coax Odette's hair into a semblance of the style she'd worn it in most days for the last three decades, pulled into a tight bun on the back of her skull.

Odette had lost a lot of hair by that time, and what was left didn't want to cooperate with the twisting and tugging of James's long, clumsy fingers. Repeatedly, he would lift one of the remaining tendrils of hair only to have it slip away from him or simply break off at the root and float down onto Odette's shoulder.

When a particularly large clump of hair came off in his hand, he spat out the bobby pins and said, "I'm sorry."

She said, "That's okay. Most of it's already come out anyway." Then she reached back and grabbed his shirt and pulled him down toward her. She kissed him on the mouth.

When Odette released her husband, she looked at him with a softness in her face that Clarice only saw when Odette looked at James. It was a warm glow that never failed to make her look pretty.

Through the screen, Clarice watched James redouble his efforts to style Odette's hair. She had just raised her hand to knock when she heard Odette chuckle and say, "Clarice is gonna be thrilled when I go bald. She's been wanting me to cover up this mess on my head with a wig since we were in the eighth grade."

Clarice knew that Odette hadn't meant anything unkind by that remark. She knew that Odette would happily say the same thing directly to her with a broad smile on her face. But that knowledge didn't help her at that moment. All she wanted to do was rush inside and shout to Odette that she loved the sight of her just as she was – good hair, bad hair, or no hair. But Clarice didn't move. She couldn't.

Was it possible that she had allowed the person she loved most in the world to believe that she saw her as something other than beautiful? And she did love Odette most of all. More than she loved Richmond. And, she asked the Lord to forgive her even as she thought it, as much as she loved her own children. Words Clarice had spoken to Odette over the decades rang in her ears, obliterating any other sounds or thoughts. "Do something about your clothes." "Fix your hair." "Let me help you with your makeup." "If you could just take off twenty pounds, you'd have such a cute figure."

A wave of shame struck her so hard that she pulled her knuckles away from the wood frame of the door and backed off of the porch. She walked to her car as quickly as she could and drove away with the shopping bag containing two pre-styled wigs, now destined for the Salvation Army, resting on the passenger seat.

Clarice was at her piano, trying not to think, when Richmond came home a couple of hours later. He surprised her by announcing that he would be spending the evening in, something he hadn't done on a Saturday night in months. They had dinner – leftovers since she had thought she would be dining alone and hadn't cooked anything that day. Then they cuddled together under a throw blanket on the living room sofa and watched a movie he had picked up from the video store. Later, Clarice would recall that the movie had probably been a comedy. She would carry with her a hazy memory of Richmond laughing just before things took a turn.

Clarice couldn't concentrate on the movie enough to laugh or cry. She was still dwelling on her visit to Odette and James's house. She watched her handsome husband and thought, *Would you do that for me? Would you do my hair for me if I was too sick to lift my arms and do it myself?*

The answer she came up with was a decisive yes.

Yes, Richmond would style her hair if she was sick. He would do it for her and do it with no complaints. And he would probably do it well. Those big, beautiful hands of his were capable of anything he put his mind to doing with them.

But she also knew that one night, as Richmond combed through her hair, their phone would ring and he would go to answer it. After he hung up, he would return to her with a lie already worked out to explain why he had to leave for just a little while. She would sit, hair half done, smiling in her sickbed, and pretend to believe his lie as he scooted out the door. If she was lucky, there would be no mirror in the room in which she might catch a glimpse of her face contorted into an imitation of that lovely, soft expression that came over Odette's face so naturally when she gazed at James.

That vision was in Clarice's head when she stood up from the sofa, walked over to the television, and turned it off.

Richmond said, "Hey, what are you doing?" He lifted

the remote from where it rested on his lap and pointed it at the television. But Clarice was standing in the way and the set wouldn't respond.

When she didn't move, he asked, "What's going on?"

She said, "Richmond, I can't live with you anymore." It came out easily and sounded totally natural, even though her heart was pounding so hard she could barely hear her own voice.

He said, "What do you mean?"

"I mean I'm tired. I'm tired of you, tired of us. Mostly I'm tired of me. And I know I can't live with you anymore."

He let out a long sigh and set down the remote. Then he spoke to her in the low, calming tone people reserve for interactions with hysterical children and brain-damaged adults. "Now, Clarice, I'm not sure what's gotten into you that you think you need to make this fuss right now, but I want you to know that I'm sympathetic. You've gone through a lot lately with Odette being sick, your mother's problems, and whatever's going on with Barbara Jean. And I understand that the change can hit some women extra hard, mess up your hormones and everything. But I think you should remember what the truth is. And the truth is, I've never pretended to be anything other than the man I am.

"Not that I'm claiming to be perfect. Listen, I'm more than willing to accept my portion of the blame for a situation or two that may have hurt you. But I have to say that I believe most women would envy the honesty we have between us. At least you know who your husband is."

She nodded. "You're right, Richmond. You never pretended to be anyone other than the man you are. And that might be the saddest part for me. I really should have helped you be a better man than this. Because, sweetheart, the man you are just isn't good enough."

That came out meaner than she had intended it to. She really wasn't angry – well, no angrier than usual. She wasn't sure what she felt. She had always assumed that if this moment ever came she would be yelling and crying and trying to decide whether to burn his clothes or glue his testicles to his thighs while he slept, the way women on afternoon TV always seemed to be doing to their unfaithful men. Now mostly she felt fatigue and a sadness that left no room for histrionics.

Richmond shook his head in disbelief and said, "Something's not right about this. Really, I'm worried about you. You should get a checkup or something. This could be a symptom of something bad."

"No, it's not a symptom," Clarice said, "but it might be the cure."

Richmond hopped up from the sofa. His shock and confusion had faded. Now he was only mad. He started to pace back and forth. "This is Odette's idea, isn't it? It's got to be her idea, all the time you've been spending with her."

"No, this idea is all mine. Odette's idea was to castrate you back in 1971. Since then she's kept quiet on the subject of you."

He stopped pacing then and tried a different approach. He walked over until he stood close to her. Smiling his slickest, most seductive smile, he put his hands on her arms and began to stroke them up and down.

"Clarice, Clarice," he whispered, "there's no need to go on like this. We can work this out."

He pulled her to him, saying, "Here's what I think. Let's plan a little trip together. Maybe go see Carolyn in Massachusetts. Would you enjoy that? I could buy you a new car and we could make it a road trip. Just you and me."

His mouth was at her ear now. "Just tell me what you want me to do, baby. Tell me what I can do." This was Richmond at his best, Richmond the lover. That part of their relationship had always been perfect. But now, when she thought about his extraordinary abilities in the arena of lovemaking, she was forced to think about the countless hours he'd spent honing those skills with other women.

Clarice put her hand on his chest and pushed him away. She shoved him harder than she meant to and he lost his balance for a second. She was shocked by how good it felt to see him stagger, on the brink of crashing ass-backwards into the glass-topped coffee table.

She said, "Evolve, Richmond. What I want you to do is *evolve*."

He started pacing again, faster this time. "I don't get it. All these years and you pull this on me now. You had plenty of time to say something if you weren't happy. This is on you, Clarice." And more softly, to himself, "This is not my fault."

She could see the gears turning as he tried to figure a way out of this. When he couldn't come up with a way to turn things around, he settled on rage. He stalked up to her and bent over so his square chin was just inches from her nose. His breath hot on his wife's face, Richmond said, "And I'll tell you something, Clarice, I'm not moving out. This is my house every bit as much as it is yours. More, actually, since *I* paid for it. So, you'd better think this foolishness through a little more."

He crossed his arms over his broad chest and stood up straight, looking satisfied that he'd made his point successfully and put her tantrum in its proper place.

Clarice walked out of the living room then, and headed toward the stairs and their bedroom. She said, "That's okay, Richmond. You're welcome to stay here. I'll leave."

That night, after stopping by Odette's place to pick up the keys, Clarice carried a suitcase of clothes and a cosmetics bag into the front door of Mr and Mrs Jackson's old house in Leaning Tree. When her piano was delivered two days later, Clarice inaugurated this new phase of her life by playing Beethoven's melancholy, powerful, and joyful *Les Adieux* Sonata and allowed the second love of her life to reassure her that she'd done the right thing in leaving the first.

Chapter 23

Despite Clarice's pleas, her parents maintained their insistence that Odette chaperone all of their daughter's dates throughout her senior year of high school. Barbara Jean was as disinterested in dating boys as boys were eager to date her, or so it appeared at the time. So she often came along to keep Odette company. From Clarice's standpoint, the situation was tolerable when it was just the Supremes and Richmond out for the evening. Richmond, the lone male among a group of females, enjoyed the appearance that he was keeping a harem. And Odette and Barbara Jean were good about giving her some time alone with Richmond. The arrangement was upended when Barbara Jean began to decline Clarice's invitations in order to spend more time with Chick. Claiming she had taken on extra hours at the salon, Barbara Jean withdrew from the foursome.

So Richmond dragged James Henry along again. Late nights out came to an end and conversations about topsoil resumed. Even on the rare occasions when Clarice was granted an extended curfew, usually as a reward for a well-reviewed piano performance or as a way to end her relentless begging, the presence of sleepy James was guaranteed to cut the evening short. Finally, after one too many nights of getting back home before ten o'clock, Clarice put her foot down and demanded that Richmond find someone for Odette who kept grown-up hours. That was when Richmond began bringing Ramsey Abrams along to serve as Odette's date.

Ramsey was a night owl, but he was also an idiot. Odette spent the evenings she was paired up with him cruelly mocking the stream of inane blather that poured out of him. And if Ramsey noticed her sharpening her claws on him, he was content to ignore it for the opportunity to spend a few hours ogling Odette's breasts.

Odette didn't appear to be bothered by James's absence from date nights. She only asked Richmond once what had become of James, and that single inquiry was phrased as a question about the health of James's mother. After Richmond told her that Mrs Henry was no better or worse as far as he knew, Odette didn't ask about James again.

Switching out James for Ramsey worked fine as far as Clarice was concerned. She and Richmond saw more of each other than they'd been able to for a long time. They stayed out later, usually meeting at Earl's and then going for a ride or to a party or somewhere in Louisville when they had time. Ramsey had just enough sense not to make the potentially fatal mistake of copping a feel off Odette, and she seemed amused to have Ramsey around to insult. Everybody won.

After several late nights with Ramsey, Odette and Clarice showed up at the All-You-Can-Eat one Friday night in March assuming that Ramsey and Richmond would be waiting for them at the window table. Instead, James Henry sat in the chair to Richmond's left.

Clarice walked over to the table and said hello. Then she took Richmond aside to express her disapproval. She said, "What is *he* doing here?"

Richmond said, "It'll be all right, I swear." In response to her raised eyebrow, he added, "The thing is, James really likes her. He found out I'd been bringing Ramsey along for Odette and he got so mad I was scared he was gonna take a swing at me."

He was exaggerating just a bit. Richmond hadn't really worried that he'd be attacked when James barged into Richmond's dorm room the night before. Either of Richmond's biceps was nearly as big around as James's waist, so even if James had violence on his mind, Richmond knew any danger posed by him was minimal. Still, Richmond had been amazed to see James that agitated. It wasn't James's way.

James had worked like a grown man to help support himself and his mother since he was thirteen years old. In high school, when Richmond and the other guys were playing sports or sharing a bottle of rotgut whiskey in the woods, James was likely to be at home cooking and cleaning. And James never showed any sign of being justifiably pissed off about any of it or even seemed to notice that he was being cheated, not that Richmond saw, at least. But there James had been, jabbing his bony finger into Richmond's chest and yelling about Odette Jackson, of all things. Richmond had wanted to laugh, but instead he promised James he would help him.

Richmond put his big hands on Clarice's arms and slowly slid them from her shoulders to her elbows and back again, trying to massage away her anger.

He said, "It'll be good, really. I told James exactly what to say to her. I gave him some great lines to use. And I filled him up with coffee before we got here. It's going to work. Trust me."

When they got back to the table, James was saying, "So tell your mother she should put herbs in her perennial border to keep pests down." Then James sat back and began silently studying Odette the way he always did after he had run out of gardening talk, as if he were a scientist and she was something rare he'd spotted growing in a petri dish. Odette stared back at James, her mouth set in a scowl. If he had tried any of those good lines Richmond claimed to have given him, Clarice assumed that they must not have worked.

As they sipped pop and ate chicken wings, Richmond and Clarice tried to keep some sort of conversation going. But neither Odette nor James talked. James just watched Odette with a mixture of affection and curiosity while she squinted back at him with an expression that approached fury.

Richmond talked about maybe driving down to Louisville and checking out a dance club he had heard about. Clarice suggested that they stop by a secluded place by the river on the way back.

The plans for the evening were just about finalized when Odette blew up. "What the hell is wrong with you, James Henry?" She leaned toward him until their noses were just inches apart and said, "I'm so sick of you staring at me like I'm gonna sprout another head all of a sudden. This is how I look, James. If you don't like it, you can just go stare at somebody else." She sat back in her chair then.

"Now, you got something to say? Or do you just wanna stare some more?"

James looked surprised and then embarrassed. He broke eye contact with Odette and watched the tabletop for a few seconds. Then James said, "I love you. And I've been thinkin' that if you ever get married, it should be to me."

Odette, Richmond, and Clarice all said, "What?"

He said it again, "I love you, Odette, and I've been thinkin' that if you ever get married it should be to me."

Richmond threw both of his hands in the air in disgust. He said, "I swear to God, Clarice, that is *not* one of the things I told him to say."

Odette narrowed her eyes at James. Clarice could tell that Odette thought he was making fun of her.

But James just sat there, still watching her. Only now he sported a grin on his face, as if he were proud of himself for finally having his say.

Right then, at their table at the All-You-Can-Eat, Clarice saw Odette rendered speechless for the first and last time of their long friendship. Clarice watched as Odette scrutinized James for a good long while. That was when she saw it for the first time, that softness in Odette's face. The lines on Odette's forehead disappeared, her jaw relaxed, and the corners of her mouth tilted up just the tiniest bit. Clarice understood then that she had witnessed more than one unusual sight that evening. She had also seen something Odette was afraid of. All this time, her tough friend had been frightened that this scarred boy might not love her the way she loved him.

Odette had seen enough movies and heard Clarice rhapsodize over Richmond often enough to know that there were things a young woman was supposed to say at a time like this. She tried her hardest to think of one of those things, but nothing came to her. Her mouth dry and her pulse racing, she sensed the onset of what she guessed was panic. But when Odette looked at James's satisfied smile, she was comforted by the certainty that he wasn't a man who would ever need long-winded reassurances or grand pronouncements of affection. And that made her want to wrap her arms around him and hold on till he begged her to let him go.

Odette covered James's hand with hers and nodded her head a couple of times. She said, "Okay then, James, just so's we understand each other."

Chapter 24

Barbara Jean knew that Clarice leaving Richmond and returning to Leaning Tree didn't have anything to do with her; it had been a long time coming. Still, it felt like another piece in the conspiracy the whole world was engaged in, a sinister plot to drag her back into the past and lock her up there. Here they were, the Supremes, gathering again in Leaning Tree, in the same house where they had talked, laughed, and sung along to records on Odette's pink and violet portable record player forty years earlier.

Driving to and from Odette's old house – Clarice's house, now – Barbara Jean saw the Leaning Tree of her girlhood all around her, instead of the one that existed in the present day. Out of the corner of her eye, she spotted landmarks that hadn't stood in decades – Abraham Jordan's law office, the five-and-dime where her mother bought her cosmetics, the carpentry shop Odette's father had once owned. They were there, more real than the large homes and cute, overpriced boutiques that had replaced them, until she blinked her eyes and made them vanish.

The people of the past continued to visit her as well. And when they came – Lester, Adam, Loretta, Chick, Big Earl, Miss Thelma, the other Supremes and herself as young girls – Barbara Jean gave in completely to the past and let the force of it pull her drunken mind along as if it were caught in the tide under the surface of the frozen river she now dreamed about every night.

Lester asked Barbara Jean to marry him on April Fool's Day in 1968. At first she thought he was kidding.

Lester had taken the Supremes, Richmond, and James out to dinner. Being a Monday, it had been an early night. James worked mornings. The girls had school.

Barbara Jean was the last to be dropped off at home that night. Lester parked outside Big Earl and Miss Thelma's house, and she waited for him to jump out of the car and come around to open her door the way he always did. But Lester sat gazing forward as the Cadillac idled. So she said, "Well, good night, Lester," and she reached for the handle to open the door.

Lester put a hand on her shoulder and said, "Hold on a minute, Barbara Jean. There's something I want to talk to you about." He left his hand on her shoulder, the most physical contact they'd ever had, and began to speak.

"Barbara Jean," he said, "I've been trying hard not to make a fool of myself about this, but I'm sure by now you know that I have feelings for you."

She expected him to grin and shout "April Fool!" But he continued with a straight face, and she realized, with as much fear as interest, that he was serious.

"You probably think of me as an old man—"

"No, I don't, Lester," she interrupted.

"It's okay. You're young. When I was your age I thought forty-two was ancient. But, here's the thing. Forty-two isn't really all that old. And you've always seemed like someone more mature than your years. So, I've been thinking that maybe you and me could spend more time together."

When she didn't respond, he added, "Just so you understand, I'm not talking about just messing around or something. I'm talking about you and me really being together. What I want is a wife, Barbara Jean."

She didn't know what to say, so she just nodded and thought, *Boy, were you right about this one, Clarice.*

"You'll be done with school in a couple months and you've probably been thinking about what's ahead for you."

Lester was wrong about that. While Barbara Jean had been raised to always have an eye out for the next opportunity – "You got to be a forward-thinkin' woman if you wanna get anywhere in this world," her mother always said – she had done nothing but try *not* to think about the future since the day she first kissed Chick Carlson in the hallway of the All-You-Can-Eat. And it was becoming increasingly difficult to do. Practically every night, Chick whispered his dreams to her as she lay in his bed with her head resting on his chest. Chick had been reading about cities where they could be together. He made it sound so easy, so possible. They would slip off together to one of the mixed-marriage Promised Lands, maybe Chicago or Detroit, and everything would be perfect. Barbara Jean wanted to fantasize along with him, but where Chick imagined minor inconveniences that they could link arms and breeze right past, Barbara Jean saw impassable obstacles of race, ignorance, and rage. So she let Chick talk about an idyllic tomorrow, but she blocked out his words and only listened to the sound of his heartbeat.

Lester continued, "I just want you to know that I'd like to be a part of your thinking. I've got a fair amount of money. And if things go the way I believe they will, I'll have a lot more soon. I could certainly take care of you and give you anything you might want. Not that I'm trying to buy you, or anything like that. I just thought you should know that I can take care of you right. I could even buy you Ballard House and fix it up for you, if you want. I remember how much you said you liked it."

"I did?" Barbara Jean asked, not recalling having said any such thing.

"Yeah, that first time you rode in my car, when we passed by the house you said, 'Look at that place. I'd love to live in something like that.'"

Barbara Jean had thought that very thing every time she passed the house, but she didn't realize she had ever said it out loud. But Lester had heard her and remembered all these months later. It touched her heart.

"You don't have to decide anything right now. I know this probably isn't what you were expecting to hear from me today," he said. "I'm going to be away in Indianapolis for the next week and a half to do some business. You can think about it and give me an answer when I get back."

The only words Barbara Jean could think to say were "Thank you, Lester." So she left it at that.

Lester took his hand away from her shoulder. Then he leaned in and planted a kiss on her cheek. He slid away from her and hopped out of the car. Then he walked around to the passenger side and opened it. Again, she said, "Thank you, Lester."

She hurried up the walkway to Big Earl and Miss Thelma's house without glancing back and she let herself in. As she climbed the stairs to her room, Barbara Jean thought of her mother. When Loretta was dying, she had spent hours looking back at her life and listing the ways the world had wronged and cheated her. The main thing she had been denied was "a man who could look me in the eye and swear that he'd be my man forever and that he would always do right by me and my baby." Now, after what Lester had just said to Barbara Jean in his car, she heard the voice of her mother panting in her ear, "This is it, girl, what we been waitin' for."

When she got to her room that night and peered out of the window, she saw that the light was on in the storeroom of the All-You-Can-Eat. But she pulled down her window shade and didn't go to see Chick.

For two days, Barbara Jean kept what Lester had said to her all to herself, hoping that an answer would come if she thought about it long enough. She stayed behind her locked bedroom door and avoided everyone. If asked, she claimed to be sick, which was half true because holding her secret inside made her stomach churn throughout each of those days. And her shade remained drawn, because she knew that if she stared too long at the storeroom light across the street, she would run to Chick and the decision would be made for her.

Finally she had to let it out, so she called a meeting of the Supremes. In the gazebo behind Odette's house, the very one that she and Chick had sneaked off to so many times, she told Odette and Clarice about Lester's proposal.

Clarice was overjoyed. She said, "See? See? I told you Lester was interested in you. You told him yes, didn't you?"

"I told him I'd think about it."

"What's there to think about?" Clarice asked. "There's not a colored woman in town who wouldn't jump at the chance to have Lester. Veronica's been trying to get him to notice her since she was thirteen. You'd better lay claim to him while you can, or somebody else'll beat you to it."

Odette didn't say a word while Clarice went on and on about Lester's proposal as if it were the greatest thing that had ever happened to anyone in the world. Barbara Jean thought that Clarice sounded as excited about this as she did when she talked about herself and Richmond. Clarice stood up from the wooden bench that lined the lattice walls of the gazebo and walked in a tight circle, already planning Barbara Jean's wedding.

Clarice named ten girls from their high school, in descending order of height, who would make the best bridesmaids. She rattled off a full menu of foreign-sounding foods Barbara Jean had never heard of, freely spending Lester's money.

Barbara Jean asked her to stop, saying that she had to think about it. Clarice countered, "Lester is a nice guy, and he has all kinds of money. He's a little on the short side, but he's handsome. I don't see what's holding you back. Do you, Odette?"

That was when Odette said it, just as casual as can be. "Well, Barbara Jean's in love with Chick."

Clarice said, "Chick? What are you talking about?"

"They've been together for months. Don't you have eyes, Clarice?"

Barbara Jean stared at Odette, unnerved by what her friend had just said. Being in love with James seemed to have imbued Odette with a hypersensitivity to other people's feelings that hadn't been there before. This new, greater power of observation, combined with Odette's tendency to say what was on her mind, made her kind of spooky in addition to being a pain in the neck.

Clarice turned to Barbara Jean and asked, "Is that true?"

Barbara Jean was going to lie, but she looked at Odette's face. Odette cast her open, accepting gaze on Barbara Jean and the truth came on out. Barbara Jean described the first time she kissed Chick. She told them about the nights they had shared in the storeroom. She repeated to them what Chick had said to her about the two of them running away together to Chicago or Detroit, how couples like them weren't a big deal there and they could get married.

Odette said, "You should go talk to Big Earl, see what he has to say about it."

"I can't do that. What am I going to say? 'Guess what, Big Earl, I've been sneaking out of the house you invited me into and going over to fuck the white busboy in your storeroom.' I can't have him thinking of me that way. I can't have him thinking I'm like . . ."

Barbara Jean stopped there, but Clarice and Odette both knew how that sentence ended.

Clarice always thought of herself as the most practical of the three of them. She said, "Chick's sweet. And he's good-looking. But he's got no money and no prospects that I can see. Plus, there's his brother to think about."

They had all seen Desmond Carlson driving slowly past the All-You-Can-Eat in his red truck at least once a week over the past several months. He never came inside the restaurant to cause trouble; Big Earl wouldn't have tolerated anything like that, and Desmond knew it. But if he caught sight of his brother through the window as he cruised by, he made obscene gestures and called his brother out to fight before eventually giving up and speeding away.

Clarice said, "That crazy redneck brother of Chick's will track you both down and kill you even if you make it to Chicago or Detroit."

Barbara Jean didn't respond to that because the truth of it was clear. And it wasn't only Desmond Carlson. There were plenty of folks in Plainview, black and white, who'd happily have seen Chick and Barbara Jean dead rather than see them together. That was just how things were.

When the silence stretched out a while longer, Clarice assumed that the debate was over and that Barbara Jean had seen that she was right. She went back to planning a huge spectacle of a wedding for Barbara Jean. Clarice kept it up during the ride from Odette's house and didn't stop until Barbara Jean jumped out of her car in front of Big Earl's.

In her heart, Barbara Jean knew Clarice was right; there was only one choice that made good sense. But the gorgeous picture Clarice painted of a hand-embroidered wedding dress with a ten-foot lace train battled an even more exquisite image in Barbara Jean's head, the vision of what she truly wanted.

In the years that came later, Barbara Jean would

imagine what might have happened if she had been more like Odette when she was young. Maybe if she'd had more courage, she could have told common sense to kiss her ass and run straight at that sweet vision of a life with Chick in Detroit or Chicago or anywhere. Maybe if she had been braver, her boy would have lived.

Chapter 25

On April 4, 1968, the night after Barbara Jean talked with Odette and Clarice in Mrs Jackson's gazebo, Dr Martin Luther King, Jr, was murdered in Memphis. Both Chicago and Detroit, the potential escape routes for Chick and Barbara Jean, went up in flames.

Barbara Jean, Miss Thelma, and Little Earl watched TV as a parade of solemn white male faces tried to explain to white America just what had been lost that day. Big Earl came home late that night. As soon as he'd shut the front door, Miss Thelma asked, "Where you been? I saw the lights go out over across the street almost an hour ago. You had me worried."

"I drove Ray to his brother's place," he said.

"What? You went over there with them crazy-ass hillbillies? Are you outta your mind?"

Big Earl said, "Those folks are too damn happy to be thinkin' about me, or Chick, or anything but their good news. Besides, there was some trouble over at the restaurant, and I didn't want him to be there by himself all night."

Miss Thelma saved Barbara Jean from having to ask what had happened by saying, "What kinda trouble?"

"Not much, just Ramsey and some of his friends actin' stupid. They lost what little sense they have and decided they had to beat down a white man. So Ramsey started in on Ray."

Barbara Jean's heart began pounding so hard that she was sure everyone in the room could hear it.

Miss Thelma asked, "Ray all right?"

Big Earl laughed. "He's fine. Odette and James was there, and they stepped into it. Make that girl mad and you got somethin' fierce on your hands. I had to pull her off of Ramsey myself. And he's gonna have a nasty black eye tomorrow. That'll teach 'im not to act a fool."

"No, it won't," Miss Thelma said.

Big Earl nodded. "You're right. It won't."

"You shoulda brought Ray over here to stay, 'stead of takin' him to his brother," Miss Thelma said.

"I asked, but he said he didn't wanna come. Something's goin' on with him."

When Big Earl said that, Barbara Jean could've sworn he was staring at her. But she told herself it had to be her imagination; she hadn't been able to think straight since Lester had asked her to marry him. As she sat with the McIntyres and took in replay after replay of the ugly story on the TV news, she thought about the boy she loved, sitting in a cold shack in a section of town where people were at that moment firing shotguns into the air in celebration.

Plainview shut down in the days after Dr King was killed. The university was so afraid that its handful of black students would start a riot that classes were canceled. Some white neighborhoods put up barricades. People were afraid to travel about, so businesses temporarily closed their doors. Some business owners who had seen what was happening in big cities around the country stayed in their places twenty-four hours a day with shot-guns on their laps, waiting for looters. Big Earl was one of the few people who understood from the beginning that Plainview wasn't going to explode. He kept his restaurant open every day.

The afternoon after Dr King died, Barbara Jean stopped by the All-You-Can-Eat. Clarice met her just inside the door. She grabbed Barbara Jean's arm and pulled her toward their window table, where Odette sat waiting. After she led Barbara Jean to her seat, words rushed from Clarice's mouth. "I'm so sorry, Barbara Jean. The only person I told was my mother."

Barbara Jean didn't understand what Clarice was saying at first. But she figured it out fast enough when she glanced around and realized that most of the eyes in the room were on her. She realized then that she was looking at a restau-rant full of people who knew her secrets.

"Jesus Christ, Clarice," she said.

"I'm sorry, I'm so sorry. Everybody was so upset last night. I was trying to think of good things to keep our minds off of the bad stuff on TV and it just slipped out. Mother said she wouldn't tell, but she must've told Aunt Glory and Aunt Glory must've told Veronica. And, well, you know that Veronica. She's got such a big mouth."

Odette spoke for the first time. "*Veronica's* got a big mouth?" Then Odette slapped Clarice's arm so hard it made her cry out, "Ouch!"

Veronica and two other girls from school started walking their way. As they came closer, Clarice whispered, "I never said a word about Chick, I swear to God. Just Lester."

Veronica smirked that way people do when they know more of someone else's business than they should. She said, "So your work paid off, I guess. I've got to hand it to you. It didn't even look like you were trying. So, when's the wedding?"

Her friends joined in asking questions. They didn't really care if Barbara Jean responded at all. This was the stage of gossip when getting the facts from the horse's mouth only interfered with the fun of it all.

Barbara Jean couldn't have answered anyway; she was too busy looking around the room for Chick. Until then, the notion of becoming engaged to Lester had been kind of like a fantasy to her, an interesting story to share with her best girlfriends. Now it was out in the world, the property of others, not just Barbara Jean and the other Supremes. It was something real. Now it had the power to hurt people. She excused herself from the window table, brushing past Veronica and her friends on her way to Chick.

He was sitting on the corner of his bed when she walked into the storeroom. He wore his food-stained work apron and his hair was covered with a net. Before Barbara Jean could say anything, he spat out, "Were you going to tell me about it, or were you just going to invite me to the wedding?"

"I didn't tell you about it because I knew you'd get upset. And there was really nothing to say. I didn't tell Lester I was going to marry him."

"What did you tell him, then?"

"I told him I'd think about it."

Chick stood up from the bed then and said, "*Think about it?* What's there to think about?"

"There's a whole lot to think about, Chick. There's my life to think about. There's my future to think about." In the voice of her mother, Barbara Jean heard herself say, "I've got to be a forward-thinking woman. And a forward-thinking woman looks out for herself."

Chick's voice cracked as he spoke. His usual deep, smooth tone went high, almost childlike. "I thought you were going to let *me* look out for you. I thought you were going to be with *me*."

"I can't be with you, and you know it. We've been back here playing around and pretending like it could work out, but we both know it can't."

"We can get married. It's been legal here for two years."

"Legal's one thing. What they'll beat you down and string you up for is another."

"Then we'll get married and go someplace else. We've talked about it before. We could go to Chicago or Detroit. There are couples like us there and nobody even thinks a thing about it."

"Haven't you heard the news? The Promised Lands are on fire. If we tried walking down the street together in Chicago or Detroit, we wouldn't make it half a block before our heads got busted open."

He said, "I'll figure out a way to make it work. There are plenty of other places we can go."

"No, there aren't, and you know it. The best we can hope for is to run away somewhere and find somebody like Big Earl who'd let us hole up in a little dump of a room like this." She gestured around the storeroom. "And what about your brother? He's been driving up and down the street for months now waiting for his chance to catch you outside alone just because you work for a black man. Now you want to tell him that you're going to have a black wife? Do you honestly think he'd let you shame him by marrying me? You think he wouldn't hunt you down and hurt you worse than he ever has? And wherever we go, we'd be lucky to get through a day without getting spit on. Chick, you don't know what it's like to have everybody look down on you, point at you, and treat you like you're less than nothing. You think you know, but you don't. I lived that way almost all my life until this last year and I can't go back to it. I can't."

"What are you saying, Barbara Jean?"

She took a deep breath and tried to hold back the tears that wanted so badly to come out, and then she said what she had avoided saying all week. "I'm saying I'm going to marry Lester."

Chick didn't try to, or couldn't, stop tears from flowing down his cheeks as he yelled, "You love me. I know you love me," making it sound like an accusation.

She answered automatically and honestly without thinking. She said, "Yes. I love you." Barbara Jean felt her will beginning to dissolve. She wanted to grab him and pull him into the bed with her with no thought of who might find them together. But then she felt the hand of her mother pushing her toward the door of the room just as surely as if Loretta had been alive and breathing. As Barbara Jean backed out of the storeroom, Loretta used her daughter's mouth to say, "But love ain't never put a bite of food on any table."

She couldn't face her friends or the gossipmongers in the dining room of the All-You-Can-Eat, so Barbara Jean slipped out the back door. In the alley behind the restaurant, she felt her stomach lurch and she had to bend over and gasp for air. When she got her nerves and her stomach calmed down, she walked around the block. Then she hurried over to the alley behind the next street, so she could enter Big Earl and Miss Thelma's house from the back and not be seen by her friends at the restaurant. By the time Barbara Jean let herself into the back door of the house, she had started to feel a little bit better. She told herself that she had done the right thing for herself, and for Chick, too. This was the first step into a new and improved life, the life she deserved. But she hadn't anticipated what that old comedian God had in mind for her.

Chapter 26

I never thought I'd live to see the day when Clarice walked out on Richmond. I'd thought of them as a couple since we were children and he would tease her by hurling walnuts at her and yelling "Time bomb!" as she ran away. They were lovers before any of us knew what lovers were. Now Clarice had gone and shocked me by moving to Leaning Tree. I couldn't help but join the crowd who studied them like they were a couple of curiosities in a traveling freak show.

Many things were still the same. Clarice and Richmond got together each Sunday to attend morning services at Calvary Baptist. They still came to the All-You-Can-Eat and sat at their usual places at the table.

But Clarice had given up pretending to have a good time at Calvary. The hardcore, fire-and-brimstone services she once used as a yardstick to measure all other churches with – and find the others lacking – weren't bringing her the same satisfaction anymore. She'd started complaining about how judgmental the congregation was encouraged to be – which, frankly, I'd always thought was one of the things she enjoyed most about the place. And she didn't bother to hide her annoyance with Reverend Peterson, who had met with her twice already to remind her of her duties as a Christian wife and to express his disappointment at her "unfortunate recent behavior." She had some especially harsh words for Calvary Baptist and her pastor after she opened the weekly bulletin at church and found her name on the prayer list alongside the names of misfits, troubled children, and other notorious backsliders from the congregation.

There were physical changes, too. I had called upon Barbara Jean's old hairdressing skills one Saturday and had her shave what was left of my hair until it was just a bit of black and gray fluff clinging to my scalp. The second I vacated the makeshift barber chair we'd set up in my kitchen, Clarice hopped into it and ordered Barbara Jean to cut her hair almost as short. She claimed she did it because, after fifty years of dealing with heat, rollers, chemicals, and pins to keep her long hair perfectly styled, she wanted something that required less maintenance. But Barbara Jean and I both thought she did it to get back at Richmond for having her name put on the backsliders' prayer list. She'd kept her hair long for years because he liked it that way. Now Clarice was determined to show him that she had laid claim to her own head in more ways than one.

I could tell that Clarice was filling at least some of her post-Richmond time with music. She had fallen back into her habit of humming quietly to herself and absentmindedly tapping out piano fingerings on whatever surface her hands happened to land on, a practice we'd teased her about back when we were young and she was still performing regularly. Clarice was more cheerful and more relaxed than I'd seen her in years, maybe ever.

Richmond changed even more than Clarice. Without his wife around to dress and tend to him, our stylish, pressed, and polished Richmond was revealed to be a color-blind man who clearly didn't know how to operate a steam iron. Richmond, who had always been so easygoing and relaxed, now spent most of our Sunday suppers staring at Clarice and chewing on his lower lip. Depending on his mood, he either ate the most diabetic-friendly things on the buffet, showing his plate to Clarice for her approval, or he took heaping bowls of sweets from the dessert table and dug into them with a fury while glaring at her. But he couldn't get a rise out of her. The most Clarice would say in response was "Try not to kill yourself. It might upset the kids."

The biggest change, though, was that now it was Richmond, not Clarice, who presented a fantasy to the world about their relationship. He had spread the word that Clarice had rented Mama and Daddy's old house in Leaning Tree because so many of her piano students lived in the new subdivisions over there. Everyone who knew them knew that she had moved out, but he insisted on repeating the fiction that Clarice went to her studio in Leaning Tree to practice and teach every day and then came back to him each night. I always thought I'd enjoy seeing Richmond get a good hard kick in the ass, but it was sad to see the mighty Richmond Baker reduced to spreading such tales.

Like his attitude toward Clarice, Richmond's feelings about me changed from week to week. He didn't know whether he should blame me for Clarice leaving him and react with open hostility or see me as a way back into his wife's good graces and ladle on the sweet talk. That week, as we sat waiting for Barbara Jean to arrive at the All-You-Can-Eat, he was being overly polite to me, inquiring about my health and complimenting a dress he must've seen a hundred times before. It all came across as awkward and forced. Poor Richmond didn't wear desperation well.

I heard Clarice issue a groan and I looked over my shoulder to see her cousin walking across the street toward the restaurant in the company of Minnie McIntyre. Minnie was swallowed up by her new fortune-telling outfit, a dramatically oversized silver robe that billowed out around her in the breeze as she crossed the street. Veronica, all done up for church, moved alongside Minnie with her jerky half-running walk. Together they looked like a Fourth of July parade float and the local beauty queen who'd just fallen off of it.

They entered the restaurant and Minnie headed for her fortune-telling table. Veronica took a detour in our direction. She had her daughter's wedding book under her arm. This was the "official wedding book." Twice as thick as the duplicate book she had given to Clarice, it overflowed with bits of paper and cloth.

Veronica said to Clarice, "I've got all kinds of stuff to tell you as soon as my reading's done." She took two steps away and then hustled back. "Let me show you this one thing, though."

She sat in Barbara Jean's chair and then dropped the heavy book down on the table. It made a loud thud and caused the tableware to teeter so wildly that all of us had to grab our water glasses to steady them. She opened the wedding book and said, "I went to Madame Minnie and told her about the problems I was having over at First Baptist about the wedding. Can you believe that after all I've done for them they refused to let me release doves inside the chapel? I explained to them that the doves were from Boston and were sophisticated and all, and that these doves would just as soon die of embarrassment as make a mess. But they wouldn't listen.

"Well, I talked to Madame Minnie about it and she told me to take a drive and the answer would come to me. I did what she said, and I found my answer at the corner of College Boulevard and Second Avenue. Here it is." She tilted one end of the wedding book so we could all see a brochure she'd clipped in. On the cover of the brochure was a picture of a two-story white building whose entrance-way was framed by several tall columns. Parked outside the building was a white carriage hitched to two white horses with white feathers attached to their heads. The caption beneath the picture read "Garden Hills Banquet Hall and Corporate Meetings Venue."

Veronica said, "Isn't it perfect? The inner courtyard can seat almost as many people as First Baptist. And we can have the ceremony, cocktails, sit-down dinner, and dancing all in the same place."

"The courtyard? Isn't that outside?" Clarice asked.

Veronica rolled her eyes and said, "Of course it is. That's why it's called a courtyard, Clarice."

Clarice ignored the eye-rolling. "You want to have a wedding outdoors in southern Indiana? In July?"

Veronica said, "I have to have it outside. Truth is, the banquet hall wasn't much happier about the doves than the church was. They were going to charge me an arm and a leg for a cleanup fee if I had the wedding inside. Not that money is an object, mind you. I consulted Madame Minnie about the weather and Charlemagne assured her it would be perfect. Also, the laser lights will look better outdoors."

Clarice said, "It's bad luck not to get married in a church."

"No offense, cousin, but you had your wedding in a church and look where it got you," Veronica replied.

Of its own free will, my hand started moving toward an overfilled glass of water that sat dangerously close to the edge of the table just to Veronica's right. I was an inch away from accidentally tipping the glass into Veronica's lap when Clarice grabbed ahold of my arm. She moved the water glass to a safer spot on the table and warned me with her eyes not to give in to immaturity again. Minnie approached the window table then, her silver robe rustling as she swept across the floor. Veronica said to her, "I'm sorry to keep you waiting, Madame Minnie. I just had to tell them about the exciting things happening with the wedding. It's really all her doing," she said, pointing at Minnie. "Everything is happening just like she foresaw it."

Minnie pointed her nose toward the ceiling and said, "I am only partially of this earth. My true essence is already on the spirit plane."

I was glad Mama wasn't hovering around that day. I wouldn't have been able to keep a straight face. Of course, Mama would have started cussing and carrying on as soon as she heard Veronica say "Madame Minnie."

Veronica chimed in, "And get a load of this." She opened the wedding book to a different page and pointed to a newspaper ad that she'd pasted inside. The ad was for a hypnotherapist in Louisville. "Madame Minnie has a friend who does hypnosis. I've been taking Sharon to see him and, let me tell you, it's a miracle. She's dropping pounds right and left. The hypnotist puts her in a recliner, lights some scented candles, whispers in her ear for a while, and she walks out terrified of starchy foods. That girl sees a crouton on top of her salad and she runs scream-ing from the room." Veronica clapped her hands together and grinned so broadly that we saw every filling in her teeth. "Sharon can almost fit into the gown I picked out for her."

Minnie took a bow to acknowledge her latest accom-plishment. The bell on her turban rang, but it was drowned out by the sound of the bell over the doorway of the restau-rant as Yvonne Wilson, one of Minnie's longtime regulars, entered.

Yvonne was pregnant with her seventh child. Two of her older girls, both dusted in powdered sugar from chin to waist courtesy of the Donut Heaven treats they were eating, tagged along behind her. Yvonne had been one of Minnie's fortune-telling customers for years and was one of the few who were dumb enough to actually heed her advice over the long haul. Minnie had told Yvonne a decade earlier that she would have a baby who was so beautiful and talented that he or she would make Yvonne and her boyfriend into showbiz millionaires. Yvonne fool-ishly believed Minnie and commenced to pop out baby after baby, waiting for the miraculous moneymaking child to arrive. With every birth she would run to Minnie and ask, "Is this the one?" Each time, Minnie would take her money and then tell her that Charlemagne said to try again. Now Yvonne had six homely, untalented children, and she still hadn't figured out that Minnie was playing a mean-spirited trick on her.

Yvonne walked up to Minnie and, rubbing her belly, said, "I had a dream last night that this one was tap-dancing on the hood of a gold Rolls-Royce. I need a reading right away."

Veronica said, "You go ahead, Yvonne, I've got some other things to show Clarice. I'll get my reading after you."

Yvonne thanked Veronica and ordered her daughters, whom she had optimistically named Star and Desiree, to sit quietly at a nearby table and wait for her. Then she followed Minnie to the crystal ball in the corner.

When they were gone, Veronica said, "Here's the big news. Sharon's going to be the first in town to have the Cloud Nine Wedding Package." She opened the wedding book to the page with the banquet hall brochure. She removed the brochure from the book and showed us a picture on the back cover. It appeared to be a photo-graph of a huge pink marshmallow squeezing through a doorway.

"That's the cloud," Veronica said. "The party enters and leaves through a lavender-scented pink cloud. Everybody in New York is doing it."

She shared more details about the Cloud Nine Wedding Package, dwelling particularly on its high cost. She told us how every aspect of the wedding had been timed to perfec-tion. She peppered her conversation with catty little comments about Clarice's daughter's wedding that Clarice pretended not to notice.

I'd had just about enough of Veronica and was about to

make another try at dumping the glass of water in her lap when Clarice spoke up during a brief pause in Veronica's monologue. She glanced at her watch and said, "I wonder what's keeping Barbara Jean."

Veronica said, "I figured she must be sick. She didn't come to church today."

Clarice raised an eyebrow and looked in my direction. "Maybe she was just too tired to go today."

Veronica shrugged and said, "I see Madame Minnie is finishing up. I'd better get going. I'll call you tonight, Clarice." Veronica left us and trotted across the room to where Yvonne Wilson was thanking Minnie and corralling her daughters.

Clarice said, "How Veronica can waste her money on such idiocy is a mystery to me."

From across the room Minnie yelled, "I heard that, Clarice!"

That old woman's good hearing never ceased to amaze me.

Fifteen minutes later, Barbara Jean still hadn't appeared. Clarice and I debated whether we should go over to her house and see how she was doing – I was for, Clarice was against. I had just about talked Clarice into getting a quick bite from the buffet and then walking over to Barbara Jean's when we looked out the window and saw her car pulling up on the other side of the street.

The Mercedes crawled slowly into a parking space, thumping the curb repeatedly as she backed up, drove forward, backed up, drove forward in a vain attempt to straighten out the car in a space that could have fit four vehicles of its size. She stopped with the front passenger side tire up on the curb. Barbara Jean sat there for a long while, looking straight ahead. We watched her, wondering what was going on. Then we saw her slump forward until her forehead came to a rest on the steering wheel.

Clarice and I both got up and went out, running across the street to the car. Clarice got there first and opened the driver's-side door. I went around to the other side and climbed in.

Barbara Jean was weeping and rolling her forehead back and forth on the top edge of the steering wheel. She asked, "How could this happen? How did I end up like this?" But she didn't seem to be addressing anyone in particular. When she looked up at me her lovely, exotic eyes were bloodshot and her breath had the sweet, grassy odor of whiskey, something I'd never known her to drink.

It was a raw, early spring day and there were just a few people out on the street, but they were beginning to look in our direction. We were also attracting attention from the All-You-Can-Eat across the way. Clarice shut the driver's-side door of the car and came around to my side. She leaned down and whispered in my ear, "Odette, she's wet herself."

I looked over and saw that, sure enough, the pale green of Barbara Jean's skirt was stained dark with urine from her waist nearly to her knees. I took the keys from the ignition and told Clarice to stay with Barbara Jean. Then I went back to the restaurant to tell James what was happening. I handed off her keys to him and asked him to deal with her car. I went back outside and pulled our car up between Barbara Jean's Mercedes and the All-You-Can-Eat's windows so Clarice and I could transfer her to my car out of eyeshot of the restaurant's curious patrons. Once we got Barbara Jean into the backseat of my Honda, Clarice and I drove her back to her house, cleaned her up, and then put her to bed.

We waited four hours for Barbara Jean to wake up. Clarice and I spent the time chatting about Richmond, the garden at the house in Leaning Tree, the music she was playing now that her piano technique was back, my chemo – everything but what had happened earlier across the street from the All-You-Can-Eat.

When Barbara Jean came down from her room, Clarice headed into the kitchen and began to search through the refrigerator for something to fix for dinner. As Clarice boiled up noodles, she settled into some familiar, comfortable denial. She said, "Barbara Jean, you're going to be just fine. You just have to make sure you get enough rest and enough to eat. It's a nutrition issue, mostly."

I wanted to join in and make the same excuses we had always made rather than deal with what was staring us in the face. But things had changed now. I was a sick woman who saw ghosts. I didn't have the strength or inclination to lie anymore.

I said, "Stop it, Clarice. We've all gotta put an end to this right here and now."

I turned to Barbara Jean, who sat across from me on a chrome-and-leather stool at the butcher-block kitchen island. "Barbara Jean, earlier today you got drunk and got behind the wheel of your car. You could've killed somebody. You could've killed a child." Both Clarice and Barbara Jean gasped when I said that. And, looking back, I suppose that it was just about the meanest thing I could've said. But I was on a roll and I wasn't going to let politeness interfere with what I had to say, what I should have said so many years earlier.

"You drove drunk and you pissed on yourself in public, Barbara Jean. There's no way to pass that off as anything but what it is.

"The way I see it, now that Lester's gone, this is my business." I gestured at Clarice. "*Our* business, because we both love you."

Barbara Jean spoke for the first time since I'd started the off-the-cuff intervention. She said, "Today was a hard day, Odette. You don't understand."

"You're right. I don't understand. I probably can't. My husband's healthy. My children are alive. I'm not saying you don't have cause. I'm saying you're an alcoholic who pissed her panties in downtown Plainview. And I'm saying that I can't watch you do this to yourself. I've got enough on my hands dealing with *my* disease. I can't deal with yours, too. The cancer's all I can handle right now."

"Odette, please," Barbara Jean said.

But I had played the cancer card, and I wasn't ashamed to follow through. I said, "Barbara Jean, I might not live to see you have that moment of clarity that tells you to stop drinking on your own. So I'm telling you, loud and clear. You're gonna put a stop to this shit before it kills you. Tomorrow, Clarice and I will pick you up and drive you to Alcoholics Anonymous."

The AA thing just came to me all of a sudden and I had no idea where we'd find a meeting. But even though Plainview was a small town to those of us who'd grown up here, it was really a small city now, especially if you added in the university. And every city in the country had at least one AA meeting a day, didn't it? I added, "If you're not ready and waiting when we drive up, I'm washing my hands of you."

Clarice cried out, "Odette, you don't mean that." Then, to Barbara Jean, "She doesn't mean that. She's just worked up."

She was right. I couldn't really have washed my hands of Barbara Jean, but I was hoping that Barbara Jean was too messed up to know that. I drove the point home. I said, "Barbara Jean, I won't spend what might be my last days dealing with a damn drunk. I've got too much on my plate."

I couldn't think of anything more to say to Barbara Jean, so I turned to Clarice. "And, speaking of plates, what's with those noodles, Clarice? I didn't get my supper today and I'd better put something in my stomach."

We ate and didn't talk about AA for the rest of the evening.

Aside from putting together a good meal from the odds and ends in Barbara Jean's refrigerator, Clarice did a nice job of keeping our minds off what had happened. She made us laugh talking about Sharon's wedding, which we decided to start calling "Veronica's wedding" since that was more accurate.

Clarice said that, for Sharon's sake, she was trying to inject some small touches of good taste into the spectacle Veronica was designing. The more she talked, the more excited she became. It reminded me of how she'd gotten such big kicks, and big disappointments, out of planning Barbara Jean's wedding and mine.

She claimed to be a fan of understatement now, but decades earlier Clarice had tried to convince both Barbara Jean and me that we had to have at least a dozen brides- maids because it was unlikely you could get your picture in *Jet* magazine with any fewer. She'd also insisted that we had to have our ceremonies at Calvary Baptist instead of our own churches because Calvary's beautiful stained glass and the painting of sexy Jesus above the baptismal pool made for the best wedding photos.

Clarice's wedding to Richmond did get covered in *Jet* – because of his football career and her historic birth and piano prizes. But things didn't go as she'd planned for Barbara Jean and me. I married James in my mother's garden with just Clarice and Barbara Jean as bridesmaids.

The day after our high school graduation, Barbara Jean married Lester in the pastor's office at First Baptist with just Big Earl, Miss Thelma, and Lester's mother in attend- ance. The big wedding Clarice had dreamed of for her was out of the question since Barbara Jean was well into her fourth month with Adam by then and was starting to show.

Chapter 27

AA meetings made Barbara Jean want to drink. She sat and listened to people whine about the hardships that had led them to gather in a basement room of the administration building at University Hospital, where they were served the harshest coffee Barbara Jean had ever tasted – but good pastries, thanks to Donut Heaven. They'd tell their tales of woe and Barbara Jean would think, *I can top that*. But she never said anything herself during those first meetings, nothing honest, at least. She went twice a week, and at the end of each meeting she left feeling that she was fully justified in having a little cocktail as a reward for having sat through it. Still, she declared her AA experience a success because she now drank about half as much as she had been drinking before. At least it seemed like half as much to her.

She patted herself on the back for throwing out most of the alcohol in her house. Though, naturally, she had to keep some beer and wine on hand for guests. And she saw no reason to toss out the whiskey, since she hardly ever drank that anyway. She stopped carrying around liquor in her thermos to her volunteer jobs, most days. She didn't drink before 5:00 p.m., more often than not. And she let the calendar determine the extent of her late-night drinking. She only drank on dates that had some particular importance – holidays, birthdays, special anniversaries, things like that. So, if she was drinking every night, it was just because it was April. That month being a minefield of significant dates was hardly her fault.

On April 11, 1968, one week after Dr King was shot dead, Miss Thelma tired of watching Barbara Jean mope around the house and struggle to keep her food down. So she sent her to the clinic at University Hospital. The next day, which was the day Lester was due back to hear Barbara Jean's answer to his proposal of marriage, she returned to the clinic and learned that she was pregnant.

Barbara Jean was seventeen, no husband, no family – more or less the same situation her mother had faced in 1950. But Barbara Jean was relieved when she found out. By the time she walked the distance from the clinic to the All-You-Can-Eat, she actually felt joyous. The decision she had made to choose Lester was suddenly unmade. She had leaped off a tall building and discovered that the pavement was made of rubber. Marrying Lester was out now. Chick and Barbara Jean would have to create a life together somehow. Detroit, Chicago, Los Angeles. Any city, burning or not, would have to do.

When she got to the All-You-Can-Eat, the after-work rush was on. Barbara Jean saw Little Earl running from table to table taking drink orders and clearing plates, but she didn't see Chick. She walked through the dining room and down the back hallway and looked into the kitchen. Still no Chick. Big Earl was alone there, so busy slinging pots and pans around that he didn't notice her sticking her head in. She went to the storeroom then.

Barbara Jean knocked lightly on the storeroom door and whispered, "Ray?" No one answered. She pushed open the door and walked into the dark room. Groping along the wall, she found the light switch and turned it on. Everything of Chick's was gone. The bed was there, but it was stripped of its sheets and blankets. His books and magazines were no longer stacked on the homemade shelves. His clothes were missing from the hooks Big Earl had screwed into the walls. She stepped further inside and turned in a circle as if she might find him secreted away in a corner of the tiny room. The one thing she did find was the Timex she had given him for his birthday, a day that now seemed as if it were a thousand years in the past. The watch rested atop a stack of cans at the side of the bed surrounded by tiny bits of glass from its smashed crystal. She picked up the watch and squeezed it tight, feeling the broken glass bite into her palm.

She heard Big Earl's rumbling voice behind her. "Barbara Jean, you all right?"

"I was looking for Ray," she said.

Big Earl walked into the storeroom, making the space seem even smaller with his massive presence. He stood there wiping his hands on his apron and said, "Ray quit last night, baby. Said he was movin' on."

Barbara Jean managed not to shout when she asked, "Did he say where he was going?"

"No, he just said he had to go." He put a hand on her shoulder. "Maybe this is the best thing for you two, for now, at least."

Barbara Jean nodded, not knowing what to say. Then she took off. She hurried out of the All-You-Can-Eat and headed up the street. First walking, then running, she went in the direction of Main Street and then over to Wall Road. She had a hard time remembering the way, but eventually she found the winding gravel and dirt route that led to the house Chick had once shared with his brother.

She was covered in perspiration and gasping for breath when Desmond Carlson's place came into view. She saw the big red truck Desmond used to chase people off Wall Road sitting on a bald patch in the center of the overgrown field of weeds that passed for a front lawn. The sun had set by then and the property was dark except for the pulsating blue light of a television shining through one of the windows. She hurried out back and found the run-down old shed that Chick had called home. For the second time that night, Barbara Jean searched an empty room. The moonlight beaming in from the open door provided just enough light for her to see that the few personal belongings she had taken note of on her previous visits when she and Chick had come there to lie together on his narrow cot had vanished. The two posters of eagles in flight, the photograph of his mother and father, the ratty blue sleeping bag covered with crudely cut rectangular patches – all of it gone.

But then, just when she thought she would lose her mind from despair, she turned and saw him standing in the doorway. She shouted, "Ray!" and ran the few steps to him.

Not Ray, she realized when she was close enough to

smell the sour odor of his sweat and feel his breath on her face.

Desmond Carlson reached up and pulled a chain to light the bare bulb that hung from the ceiling so that they could both see each other. The thing that struck Barbara Jean about Desmond, whom she had never seen up close before this moment, was how much he resembled Ray. They had the same height and build, although Desmond was considerably heavier around the waist – a drinker's body. Their features were similar, but the mouth Barbara Jean had known so well as a feature of Chick's face was misshapen on his brother due to a white scar that ran from just below his nose to the cleft in his chin. And Desmond's nose looked slightly off-kilter, the result, she imagined, of a long-ago fight. Still, the life he led had only damaged him slightly. This man, who had caused so much turmoil and become the symbol of everything scary and evil in the world to her, was pretty.

Desmond looked Barbara Jean up and down two times – slowly, making a show of it. Then he snorted and said, "Now I see what it was had Ray goin' over to the coloreds. Didn't know he had it in him. I always figured him for a sissy."

Barbara Jean wanted out of there and away from this man, but she stayed calm long enough to ask, "Where's Ray?"

"Your little boyfriend's gone. Ungrateful bastard ran off and said he ain't comin' back." He smiled at her then. But there was no friendliness or humor in his expression, and she moved away from him as far as the space allowed. He said, "But listen, sweet thing, if it's white meat you've got a taste for, let me show you what a real man's like." Then he lunged at her and pressed her against the wall with his body. He ground his crotch against Barbara Jean's hip, all the while snickering like a mean-spirited child playing a game. He stopped laughing when she brought her hand to his crotch, grabbed him and twisted as if she were wringing out a wet dish towel. He hit the floor with Barbara Jean's fist still between his legs, gripping and turning.

She let go, leaped over him, and ran out of the shed. She flew across the yard, hearing him cuss and threaten as she escaped. "I'm gonna kill you, bitch!" he shouted.

Barbara Jean was back on the gravel road when she heard the sound of an engine firing and knew that he was coming after her. She darted down narrow, muddy streets that she had never seen before, hoping to hide from Desmond. She ducked behind trees and crouched in gullies to stay out of sight. More than once her pursuer's truck passed just a few feet away from her face as she knelt in tall weeds at the side of the road.

Finally, after thinking she would be lost forever in this unfamiliar and inhospitable part of town, Barbara Jean found her way back to Wall Road. From there, it was just a twenty-five-minute walk back to Big Earl's house.

It was probably the thunderous pounding of her heart that kept Barbara Jean from hearing the sound of the engine as it approached from the rear. She didn't realize that she was being followed until the headlights behind her caused her shadow to lengthen on the road ahead. She started to run again, but she only had two steps left in her. She was just too damn tired.

She glanced toward the side of the road where it

sloped down into a deep gully and then dark woods. If she could get out of the light and into the trees, she might be all right. She could hide, maybe even all night if she had to.

No. No hiding, she decided. For just a little while she had to become somebody else. Until this was over, no matter how it ended, she had to be somebody fearless.

Barbara Jean turned toward the headlights that had now come to a stop just a few yards away from her. Then she brought up her fists, ready to fight. She whispered to herself, "My name is Odette Breeze Jackson and I was born in a sycamore tree. My name is Odette Breeze Jackson and I was born in a sycamore tree."

But no one approached. She heard nothing for several drawn-out seconds. Then the quiet night air was filled with the sound of a car horn's blast. The horn played out, "Ooo, *Ooo-*ooo."

Lester.

Inside the blue Cadillac, Lester explained that he had gone to the McIntyres' to see her as soon as he returned to town. He had arrived at the house just in time to cross paths with Big Earl as he came rushing out of the door on his way to look for Barbara Jean. They had talked, and Lester persuaded Big Earl to go back to the All-You-Can-Eat while he tracked her down. After being pointed in the direction of Wall Road, that's just what Lester had done.

Barbara Jean didn't say a word all the way back to the house and Lester asked her no questions. When they pulled up outside Big Earl and Miss Thelma's, Lester performed like the gentleman he was. He opened the passenger-side door for her and accompanied her up the front walkway. As they reached the porch steps, Lester asked, "Have you given any thought to what we talked about?"

She started to laugh then. She laughed so hard at God's good joke on her that she had to hold on to the wrought-iron step railing to keep from falling over. Tears rushed down Barbara Jean's face and she struggled to breathe. When she could talk again, she said, "I'm sorry. But you're going to think this is funny, too, when I tell you . . . Lester, I'm pregnant. I'm going to have Chick Carlson's baby. And I just spent the evening running and hiding behind trees, trying to get away from his crazy-ass brother. So, you can take that proposal back and count yourself lucky." Barbara Jean climbed the three steps to the porch and then turned around, expecting to see Lester scrambling back to his Cadillac.

But Lester didn't walk away. He looked up at her and asked, "What do you want to do?"

"What I want doesn't matter. Chick's gone. Now I've got to make plans for me and my baby. My mother managed to do it on her own. I figure I can't do a worse job of it than she did."

Lester said, "I really meant it when I said I wanted to marry you, Barbara Jean. I've loved you since I first laid eyes on you, and that hasn't changed. We can get married tomorrow, if you want."

She waited for Lester to think about what he had just said and return to his senses. But he just stood there. She could only think of one thing to say. She asked the question her mother would have wanted her to ask. "Lester, can you look me in the eye and swear that you'll forever be my man and that you'll always do right by me and my baby?"

Lester stepped up onto the porch beside her and placed a warm hand on her stomach. "I swear," he said.

So Barbara Jean married Lester, the man who had the right answer to her mother's question.

Chapter 28

Each spring, Calvary Baptist Church held a tent revival. It was a tradition that Richmond's father started during his years as the pastor of the church, and it continued after he moved on. The revival was famous in Baptist circles throughout the Midwest. It attracted a huge crowd of the faithful every year and provided a boost to the church coffers during the long drought between Easter and Christmas. Clarice couldn't remember a year of her life that she didn't attend.

The revival always began on a Friday night with the raising of the tent. A makeshift stage was set up for the choir. Hundreds of folding chairs – ancient, splintering, torturously uncomfortable things Clarice believed had been designed to remind the congregation of the suffering of Christ – were brought in. Then there was a prayer service to get everyone worked up for the thirty-six straight hours of preaching, singing, and soul-saving that would follow. The revival culminated in a mile-long procession from the tent site on the edge of town back to Calvary.

Richmond's status as both a church deacon and the son of the revival's founder guaranteed that he and Clarice always had good seats. On opening night that year they sat in the front row. Richmond was in a snit that day over

Clarice's continued refusal to come back home, so Clarice sat between Odette and Barbara Jean and gave James the honor of sitting next to Richmond. The arrangement had the effect of further worsening Richmond's mood. He sat with his lower lip poked out and only looked in Clarice's direction to scowl at her.

Clarice still saw plenty of Richmond now that she had moved out. He stopped by the house in Leaning Tree a few times a week. "Where's my orange tie?" "How does the oven timer work?" "Where do I take the dry cleaning?" He always seemed to need something.

If he was on good behavior – not too whiny or argumentative – Clarice would invite him in. Richmond was good company. And she loved him. She had never loved any man except Richmond. Well, there was also Beethoven, but he didn't really count. The problem was, just as soon as Clarice started to think about Richmond's good points – how charming he could be, how he made her laugh – he would switch into seduction mode. His midnight eyes would flicker on and his voice would take on a quality that made her imagine that she smelled brandy and felt the heat of a roaring wood fire.

But whenever Clarice thought about having Richmond stay the night – a pleasurable thought – an image came into her mind that made her push him out of the door. It was that picture in her head of James trying, and failing, to style Odette's hair. That image just wouldn't allow her to step back into the life she had lived for so many years.

It was nearly midnight that first night of the revival and Reverend Peterson was wrapping up his sermon. Reverend Peterson always spoke first on opening night before handing off the podium to visiting preachers. His sermon that night was a good one. He told the terrifying story of the Great Flood from the perspective of one of Noah's nonbelieving neighbors. The speech climaxed with a vivid description of the doomed neighbor, knee-deep in swirling, filthy water, banging on the side of the ark and begging Noah to let him in. Reverend Peterson added color to the story by imitating the squawks, neighs, and moos of the animals. Of course, Noah could do nothing but wave goodbye to the terrified sinner as he sailed away with the righteous and the noisy animals.

The Noah's Ark sermon was typical of the Calvary Baptist experience. It was not a gray-area kind of church. Every Sunday, church members sat and listened to their pastor as he gave them the latest message from an angry God. They left the sanctuary certain that Calvary Baptist and Reverend Peterson were the only things standing between them and an eternity of suffering in hell. Calvary's parishioners fully expected that, like Noah, they would be waving goodbye to everyone in Plainview who didn't go to Calvary Baptist when Jesus shipped them all off to join Him.

When Reverend Peterson finished, the crowd was in an uproar of shouting, amen-ing, and speaking in tongues. The church nurses, in their starched white uniforms and white gloves, rushed through the tent to tend to women who had collapsed with the Holy Ghost.

In spite of the barn-busting sermon Reverend Peterson delivered that night, Clarice surprised herself by thinking that maybe it was time she left some of this bad news and rage behind. Sitting there listening to the angriest choir in town as they spat out "It's Gonna Rain," she thought that maybe she should branch out and give something else a try.

Having ended his sermon, Reverend Peterson made a plea to the unrepentant sinners in the crowd to come forward and receive the Lord's blessing before it was too late. He walked back and forth in front of the wailing choir and warned, "It won't be water, but fire, the next time." As he returned to his lectern to introduce the next speaker, there was a commotion in the back of the tent.

A woman's voice shouted, "Let me testify! Let me testify!"

Clarice and everyone else in the front row turned around to look, but there were too many people standing and gawking for them to see all the way to the back. The tent grew quieter and a wave of soft murmuring spread slowly from the rear to the front as the woman moved up the center aisle toward Reverend Peterson.

She was young – around twenty-five, Clarice guessed. The woman's gravity-defying cleavage hovered above a neon-green tube top that was just wide enough that it wasn't illegal. Below her exposed navel, she wore tight-fitting vermillion shorts that were so revealing Clarice imagined the woman had borrowed them from an emaciated eleven-year-old. The tube top and the shorts she wore were both made of shiny, wet-looking latex. With each step she took, the movement of latex abrading latex caused a high-pitched squeaking noise to pierce the air. Her hair was pulled back from her face into a fall of glossy black ringlets that hung down to the middle of her back.

Clarice leaned close to Barbara Jean and whispered, "Hair weave."

She replied, "Implants."

The woman staggered and stumbled up toward the stage and Reverend Peterson. His bushy, silver eyebrows climbed a little closer to his receding hairline with every step she took in his direction. Clarice wasn't sure if the woman's staggering was due to her being drunk or due to the fact that she was only wearing one shoe and had a thick layer of mud up to each ankle.

When she reached the lectern, the woman snatched the microphone away from an astonished Reverend Peterson. "I just had a miracle happen and I need to testify." She yelled her words into the microphone and feedback from the sound system caused everyone to clamp their hands to their ears. "Just a little while ago, after my shift at the Pink Slipper Gentlemen's Club, I was doin' a private perform-ance out in the parking lot in the back of a Chevy Suburban when I heard a voice. Clear as a bell the voice said, 'You are a child of God.'

"Now, at first I just ignored it 'cause I thought it was my customer. He's one of my regulars and he carries on like that – always God this, Jesus that, Sweet Lord the other."

Reverend Peterson's face registered panic and he made a grab for the microphone. But the stripper was faster. She hopped away from him and continued her testimony.

"The voice said, 'You are a child of God. Stop what you're doing.'

"I still thought it was my customer, so I got up off the floor of the Chevy and said, 'Fine. I don't gotta keep doin' what I'm doin'? Just give me my damn money and I'll go home.'

"But then, I heard the voice again. This time it said,

'Your sinful ways will bring a storm of hellfire down upon you. Come to the Lord and you will be saved.'

"I knew then that it wasn't my customer at all. It was an angel sent from heaven to tell me to change my life. So I got out of that SUV and I followed a light I saw off in the distance. I crossed Highway 37 and went through a patch of trees, even lost a shoe walkin' across a muddy field. But I kept goin' until I found this here tent. Now I'm here and ready to give up my sinful ways like that angel's voice told me to. If that ain't a miracle, I don't know what is."

The crowd erupted in praise of the stripper's miracle. People shouted, "Amen!" and the choir started to sing out twice as loud as they had before.

Encouraged by the response of her audience, the stripper went on with her testimony. "The second I walked into this tent, somethin' changed inside my heart. All of a sudden, I started to think about all the fine things God had done for me. I started to think maybe He seen me safely through all the dangerous, sinful things I did for a reason.

"And believe me, there's a lot of scary stuff out there. Hell, you go out for one night's work and you could end up with the herpes, the AIDS, the syphilis, the Chinese chicken flu, or the Ebola virus." She poked long, crimson nails into the air as she used her fingers to count off the diseases.

Reverend Peterson made another attempt to snatch the microphone away from the young woman, but again she was quicker. Like the performer she was, she gave her audience more of what they wanted. She said, "And I tell you, the way some of these men are, they don't care about protectin' themselves, you, or their wives and families.

They only care about their own pleasure. They wanna act like it's thirty years ago, before shit got so serious. I'm tellin' you, you gotta be a safety-first kinda gal if you wanna live long. You know what I do when some asshole tries to talk me into doin' something stupid? I look him dead in the eye and say, 'Honey, you think we're gonna fuck ourselves right back to 1978? This is some magical pussy all right, but it ain't no damn time machine.'"

On that note, several people moved in to restrain her, allowing Reverend Peterson, at last, to retrieve his microphone. The stripper was promptly helped off the stage by one of the church nurses and two representatives of the New Members Committee. As she was led past Clarice, Richmond, and their friends, the woman stopped for a second, turned toward Richmond, and said, "Hey, Richmond, you gettin' saved, too, baby?" before stumbling away with her keepers.

Everyone near the front of the tent, except for Richmond, who had buried his face in his hands, turned to stare at Clarice to see how she would react to the newly saved stripper greeting her husband like an old friend. But Clarice had something else on her mind. She was thinking about the miraculous voice that had summoned the stripper from the back of the Chevy behind the Pink Slipper Gentlemen's Club with the all-too-familiar words, "You are a child of God. Stop what you're doing." Clarice wondered how long her mother and her bullhorn had been back in town.

Chapter 29

The morning after Richmond's stripper friend signed up to have her soul saved, Clarice heard a knock at her door. It was just before nine o'clock in the morning, so she assumed that it was her first student of the day arriving early for her lesson. From the piano bench where she was having her tea, Clarice called out, "Come in." Beatrice Jordan and Richmond marched into the living room.

Beatrice pointed at her daughter's chopped-off hair and grimaced. For several seconds, she stood in the center of the room regarding Clarice as if she'd just discovered her dancing naked in a crack house. Richmond wore a smug expression on his face as his mother-in-law said, "Clarice, would you care to explain yourself?"

In the past, this was the point at which Clarice would revert to behaving like an obedient little girl. She would make nice and apologize to her mother for whatever she had done, just to get Beatrice off her back. But living alone in her own house, even for such a short amount of time, had changed her. Clarice found that she couldn't react like her old self. She said, "I've already explained things to Richmond. And I believe that's all the explaining I need to do."

Her mother spoke softly, as if she believed someone

might be listening in. "Everyone at Calvary Baptist is talking about you. How could you do this? You made a vow before God and everybody."

"So did Richmond. Did you have a talk with him about his vows?" Clarice said, feeling heat rise from her neck onto her face.

"It's different for men, and you know it. Besides, Richmond is not the one who ran out on his marriage; you are. But listen, it's not too late to fix this. Richmond is prepared to go see Reverend Peterson with you to work this out."

"I don't think so," Clarice said. "I've seen where Reverend Peterson's advice leads. And no offense, but I don't intend to spend my golden years shouting at whores through a megaphone."

She felt guilty for that low blow when her mother's eyes began to glisten with tears. But Clarice had been mad for a good long time and a lot nastier things than that were waiting to come out. To keep from saying those things, she took a deep breath and then a drink from her cup of tea. The tea was too hot for the big swallow she took and it scalded all the way from her lips to her stomach. It hurt so much that it took her breath away for a few seconds, but the time she spent recovering from burning her tongue stopped her from saying some of the meaner things that were swirling around in her brain.

Clarice said, "Mother, I love you, but this has nothing to do with you. This is between me and Richmond, and I think I've made it clear to him where I stand. I'm done with things the way they were. I'll go back home, *or not*, when I see fit."

Beatrice whimpered quietly and said, "Honestly, when I think about how hard I fought for us both to live when you were born." She put the back of her hand to her forehead. "It was a horror show." When that didn't produce the desired effect, she changed tactics. In the tone of voice she used when delivering her parking lot sermons, she declared, "Ephesians says, 'Wives, submit yourselves unto your own husbands as unto the Lord.' What do you say to that?"

Clarice snapped, "I say God and I will just have to hash that one out between the two of us. My submitting days are over."

Richmond spoke for the first time. He said, "I talked to the kids, and they're shocked that you've done this. They're very upset and confused."

Clarice said, "You must have talked to four different kids than the ones I talked to. When I told Carolyn, Ricky, and Abe that I'd moved out, they were just surprised that it had taken me so long. And if Carl's upset, it's because he's too much like you and he knows it. The way I see it, I've done him a favor I should have done years ago. Now maybe he'll think about the crap he's pulled on his wife and realize it might come back and bite him in the ass one day."

Richmond turned to Beatrice and said, "See? It's like I told you. She's talking more like Odette all the time."

Beatrice nodded. "I've always known that girl would cause trouble one day."

Clarice's mother believed that a woman showed that she was well brought up by doing three things: dressing impeccably, enunciating like an East Coast debutante, and starving herself to the edge of unconsciousness for the sake of her figure. So, Odette had never made sense to her. But Beatrice had chosen the wrong time to start in on Odette, Clarice's sick friend who had stepped in time and time again when Clarice needed her and had now even supplied her with a home. The little bit of restraint Clarice had managed to get hold of was in danger of slipping away. She narrowed her eyes at her mother and her husband and prepared to let loose. But just as her scalded tongue was poised to toss forth a red-hot string of long-overdue words, Clarice was distracted by the sound of light tapping coming from the front door. Clarice stood from the bench and said, "My student is here."

When Clarice rounded the piano on her way to admit her pupil, Beatrice saw for the first time what her daughter was wearing. Beatrice let out a whimper and turned her face away.

During Clarice's first weekend in the house, she had gone down to the basement to put some things away and came upon a box full of old clothes that had been left behind by one of the previous tenants. Odette had rented the house, furnished, to visiting faculty members at the university. They tended to be an earthy lot and the clothes in the box reflected what Clarice thought of as the academic fashion sense – shapeless, hippie-style items made of cotton and hemp. To celebrate her emancipation, she ran the old skirts and blouses she had found through the washer and dryer and started wearing them.

The skirt Clarice wore that morning was made of a faded blue-and-white-checked fabric. It had a high waist that was embroidered with blue and green stick figures.

Strands of puka shells that hung from the fringed hem grazed the floor when she walked and made a rattling noise.

Beatrice pointed at her daughter and said, "Oh dear Lord, first her hair, and now a peasant skirt. Richmond, we're too late."

It took every ounce of willpower in Clarice's body to keep from lifting the hem of her skirt and revealing that she was wearing a pair of Birkenstock sandals that she had purchased a few days earlier at a shop near the campus where young saleswomen who didn't shave their armpits or wear makeup sold comfortable shoes and artisan cheeses. She continued past her stunned mother and husband and went to the door, where she was greeted by Sherri Morris, a gap-toothed nine-year-old girl whose bad practice habits and resultant sloppy technique gave Clarice fits for an hour each week.

Sherri said, "Good morning, Mrs Baker. I love your skirt."

Clarice thanked the girl and made a mental note to put a gold star in her étude book that day no matter how poorly she played. She told Sherri to go to the piano and warm up on some scales while she said goodbye to her guests.

At the door Richmond whispered, "We can finish this discussion at the revival tonight."

"Sorry, I have students until late in the day today. I'll be too tired to go back to the revival tonight."

Richmond sighed and looked at Beatrice as if to say "See what I've been dealing with?" To Clarice, he said, "Fine, we'll talk at church tomorrow."

"If you really must talk to me, I'll see you at the

All-You-Can-Eat after church. I won't be at Calvary tomorrow. I'm planning to stop by the Unitarian church for services this week," she said.

Clarice said that purely for spite. Although she had talked to Odette about maybe giving Holy Family Baptist a try, Clarice had no intention of going to the Unitarian church that Sunday. She was furious that the two of them had come over to gang up on her and preach at her, so she wanted to shake them up. Besides, there was something about putting on a peasant skirt and puka shells that made Unitarianism pop into your head.

Her mother moaned and leaned against Richmond for support. Clarice felt guilty for an instant. She knew that her mother would just as soon have seen her hook up with one of the polygamist congregations that were rumored to thrive in the hills outside of town as hand her soul over to the Unitarians.

But even though she had said it out of spite, Clarice started thinking that it might not be such a bad idea to try out the Unitarians. Why not? She was certainly in the mood for something different from the bitter mouthful she'd been chewing on for all those years.

As Beatrice crossed the threshold of the front door, still clinging to Richmond, she said to Clarice, "I'll pray for you." Clarice marveled at how her mother had managed to make it sound like a threat.

Richmond mouthed, "See what you've done," and led his mother-in-law back to his Chrysler.

Clarice closed the door behind them and went to her student, who proceeded to brutally massacre a helpless Satie piece. She kept the promise she had made to herself

to give Sherri a gold star, and the girl left happy at the end
of her lesson.

Clarice's roster had expanded since her move. The
wealthy families of new Leaning Tree were thrilled to have
a locally famous piano teacher within walking distance.
And Saturday was her longest teaching day. By that
evening, she was exhausted. She made herself a fresh cup
of tea and went back to the piano to play a little something
to wash away the sound of her students' uneven perform-
ances – a kind of musical sorbet.

She had just settled onto the bench when sharp hammer-
ing at the front door abruptly ended the night's quiet.
When she looked through the keyhole, she expected to see
Richmond or her mother back for another round. Instead,
Reverend Peterson stood on the porch. His dark, wrinkled
face managed to appear sorrowful, beseeching, and pissed
off all at the same time. She reached to turn the knob and
allow him in, but then thought better of it.

Maybe it was more displaced anger, but she couldn't
help but think that Reverend Peterson's counsel was something she was better off without. His track record was
pretty bad, she thought. She had followed his directions
for years and had ended up believing that, in a woman,
self-respect was the same thing as the sin of pride. And his
advice to shut up and pray while her husband made a fool
of her by screwing everything in sight had helped to keep
Richmond a spoiled boy instead of the man he might have
grown up to be. Okay, it might have been a stretch to
blame Reverend Peterson for that, but she wasn't in the
mood to play fair.

Fair or not, thinking clearly or not, hell-bound or not,

Clarice turned around and walked back to her piano. She sat down and, to the beat of the insistent rapping on the door, began to play Brahms's rapturous B Minor Intermezzo. As she played, she felt the stress of the day begin to fade away. Clarice thought, *God and I are communicating just fine.*

Chapter 30

After months of good test results, my medicine stopped working. So my doctor started me on a different regimen. The first treatment with the new medication made me far sicker than I'd been on the worst days with the old formula. And when I stopped feeling sick, I started feeling weak.

My bosses had been real nice about adjusting my work schedule to accommodate my chemo, but with this new treatment kicking my ass the way it was, I had to ask for a leave of absence. They – the principal of the school and the food services coordinator from the school board – were very understanding and told me I could take as much time as I needed before coming back. But I could tell by the looks on their faces that they weren't expecting me to return.

One morning, just after James left for work, I had a bad spell – feverish and achy all over. I was glad it hadn't happened when he was still there. It was next to impossible to get James out the door if he thought I was in trouble. If I didn't look okay to him, he'd dig in his heels and declare that he wasn't about to leave me alone. Then he'd sit staring at me like an orphaned puppy until I convinced him that I felt better.

Of course, James didn't need to worry about me being

alone. The kids called daily to check up on me and kept me talking for hours. Rudy called a couple of times a week. Barbara Jean and Clarice were in and out all the time. And Mama drifted in every day to keep me company. She was there that morning when I shuffled out of the bathroom with a cool towel on my head.

"You've lost weight," Mama said.

I looked down and saw that my nightgown was roomy now where it used to bind me. I was able to grab a handful of cloth at my waist and twist it in a half circle before the material was tight against my stomach.

"Isn't this something, all the time I wasted wishing I was able to take some weight off, and all it took to do the job was the teensiest little touch of cancer. Looks like I'll get the last laugh on Clarice for making fun of me holding on to those old, out-of-style clothes in the attic that nobody ever thought I'd fit into again. I'm gonna wow 'em at the hospice in my parachute pants and Nehru jacket." I laughed, but Mama didn't.

I waved two of my cats away from their resting places on the living room couch. Then I lay down, pulled a quilt over myself, and adjusted the couch pillows to support my head. The cats reclaimed their spots near my feet as soon as I settled in. Mama sat on the floor beside me with her legs crossed, Indian-style.

After lying there in silence for a while, I said, "I guess this is when I'm supposed to start praying for a miracle."

Mama shrugged. "You know, I don't think I much believe in miracles. I think there's just what's supposed to happen and what's not, and then goin' along with it or standin' in its way."

I said, "Hmm, I'll have to think about that. I like the idea of a good miracle every now and then."

She shrugged again and, after a few seconds, said, "I've got to say your James has been more wonderful than I imagined he could be through this whole thing. Not that I ever thought bad of him. I just didn't know he'd be this good."

"I'm not surprised at all. James is being exactly who I knew he'd be. I'm lucky."

"We're both lucky, you and me. I got your daddy and you and Rudy. You got James and those sweet kids."

"And the Supremes," I added.

Mama nodded. "That's what you'll think about when you pass, you know. How good your man was, how you loved your children. How your friends made you laugh till you cried. That's what flows through your mind when the time comes. Not the bad things.

"I don't know if I was smilin' or not when you found me dead in my garden, but I should've been. At the end, I was thinkin' about you and your grandmama and how she'd put you in those horrible dresses she made that you loved so much. And I thought about how good it felt to kiss your daddy.

"I don't recall hittin' the ground after throwin' the rock at that squirrel. I just remember havin' those sweet thoughts and then seein' your daddy standin' over me, stretchin' out his hand to help me up. When I got to my feet, my garden was more beautiful than ever – no damn tulip-bulb-eatin' squirrels in the afterlife. Wilbur and me hadn't walked more than five feet before we ran into your aunt Marjorie. She was doin' one-arm pushups and lookin' more like a man than ever. Her mustache had filled in real nice and she'd taken to waxin' it and twistin' it at its tips. Looked good on her. My big brother was there, too, all decked out in his army uniform, wearing all those shiny medals the government mailed home to us after the war. And the first person to say hello to me was Thelma McIntyre. She handed me a big fat doobie and said, 'Hey, Dora. Take a hit off this. And don't bogart it the way you always do.' It was lovely."

I hoped Mama was right. There had been so many beautiful days with James and the children and the Supremes, so many days I wanted to carry with me when I crossed over into whatever came next. And if I could shed the bad times like a dry, ill-fitting skin, that would be nice, too.

I always feel guilty when I think back to my worst day ever because others lost so much more than I did. Still, that day is there in my memory as the worst. And I believe, no matter what happens to me from here on out, that day will forever have its hooks in my mind.

Barbara Jean had just set out coffee for Clarice and me in her kitchen when the doorbell rang. It was the first weekend of May 1977 and the three of us were planning a birthday party for my Jimmy. All of our children had their parties at Barbara Jean's. Clarice and I had both moved away from Leaning Tree and into new developments with small lawns by then. So letting the kids loose in Barbara Jean's spacious yard, with its topiaries and flowering trees everywhere, was like setting them free in an enchanted forest.

Clarice's children were at home with Richmond. My

three were at Mama and Daddy's house being bribed into good behavior with candy bars and potato chips. Barbara Jean's Adam was at Mama and Daddy's, too – at least that's what we thought. He'd left about half an hour earlier for the fifteen-minute walk to Mama's house. This was a period of time when no one thought twice about a child of seven or eight walking a familiar path alone in Plainview. It was the last day of that era.

Lester answered the doorbell and I was surprised to hear James's voice. In that big house the kitchen was half a block away from the front door, so I couldn't make out exactly what they were saying. I don't know if it was the tone of James's voice or Lester's that drew the three of us into the foyer to see what was going on, but I knew something terrible had happened the second I saw James's face.

The first thing I thought was that it was one of our kids, or maybe Mama or Daddy. Then Lester, who'd had his back to us, turned around. Right away, I knew. So did Barbara Jean.

Lester's skin had gone gray and I could see him wavering on his feet like he was standing in the center of a whirlpool. James, who was wearing his Indiana State Police uniform, stood in the doorway with another trooper, a big white guy with a smooth red face who kept his eyes focused on the floor in front of him. James reached out and held on to Lester's shoulder to keep him upright.

Barbara Jean said, "Lester?" Tears began to fall from Lester's eyes as he stood supported by James. Barbara Jean turned to James and asked, "What's happened to Adam?"

It was Lester who answered her: "He's dead, Barbie. Our boy is dead."

And then Barbara Jean screamed. She screamed like she was trying to cover up every other sound in the world. I had never heard anything like that, and I hope to God I never will again. She started to stumble backwards, her feet losing traction and her arms flailing like she was suddenly standing on ice. The white cop stepped forward to keep her from falling, but I had her already. We fell back together against the wall and then slid down to that elegant parquet floor. She stopped screaming and started making a low, pained moan while I squeezed her against my body and Clarice knelt beside us stroking Barbara Jean's hair.

I heard Lester asking, "Where?" I heard James answer, "North end of Wall Road."

Lester protested that it had to be a mistake. Like all the black children in town, Adam had been warned. He'd been told, time and time again, that bad people drove on that part of Wall Road. It couldn't be Adam.

But James shook his head. "There's no mistake. It's him, Lester. It's him."

Lester stood up straight and knocked James's hand from his shoulder. "I have to go see," he said. Then he started for the door.

The white trooper tried to stop him. "Mr Maxberry, you really shouldn't. This isn't something you want to see." But James pulled a windbreaker from the coat tree near the door – it had started to sprinkle outside – and handed it to Lester, saying, "I'll take you." The men left while the three of us huddled on the floor.

By the time Lester and James came back, Barbara Jean was in her bedroom, lying with her knees drawn up to her chest. We lay beside her in the bed, me clutching her hand

and Clarice praying, while Barbara Jean gasped out Adam's name over and over like he'd hear her wherever he was and come on home. When she heard the sound of the front door opening, Barbara Jean hopped out of bed and ran downstairs, chasing after the one last bit of hope that it had all been a mistake and she'd discover pretty little Adam standing in the front hallway waiting for her.

We found James and Lester in the library. James stood by the fireplace watching his old friend and former boss pace the room and strike his head with his balled fists. Lester's face wasn't gray anymore; his light brown skin was purple with anger.

Lester said, "You know he did it. You know he killed my boy."

James tried to calm him. "Lester, please just take a breath and sit down. They're over at his place right now. I promise we'll get to the bottom of it. I'm telling you, it's not like it used to be."

Lester snorted. "There's nothing to get to the bottom of. You know he did it. If you cops won't do something, I swear to God I'll take care of it myself."

James said quietly, "Lester, please don't let anybody but us hear you say that."

Lester turned to Barbara Jean, his voice almost unrecognizable in his grief and fury. "Desmond Carlson murdered our Adam. He hit him with his truck on Wall Road. Hit him so hard our baby got tossed against a tree." Lester started hitting himself in the forehead again as he croaked out his words. "His neck snapped, Barbie. That fuckin' redneck piece of shit broke our baby's neck."

Barbara Jean let out a grunt and doubled over like she'd

been punched in the stomach. Then she ran from the room. She was up the stairs and back in her bedroom before Clarice or I could get our feet moving. We went up after her when we heard the screaming start again.

Later that night in bed, James and I stared at the ceiling while he explained to me what had happened to Adam. James said Adam had been on his way to Mama's house when he was hit. He was eight years old and knew that he was supposed to go the long way from his house to get to Grandma Dora's, but Adam was an adventurous boy. The temptation of taking the shortcut had, apparently, been too great. And the risk of punishment hadn't stopped him. James said, "I guess we haven't done a good enough job of making them afraid."

James said Lester was right about it being Desmond Carlson. There were tracks in the muddy road that led directly from the place where Adam was hit to the unnamed street that wound through the woods and led to a neighborhood of only five houses, one of them Carlson's place. Desmond, who had been falling-down drunk when the police got to his house, claimed his truck had been stolen the day before and he hadn't gotten around to reporting it. The truck was nowhere to be found and Desmond's girlfriend was backing up his story. Even after the police had located the truck later that evening, hidden in the woods less than a mile from his house, its grille streaked with blood, he'd stuck to his tale that he didn't know a thing about what had happened to little Adam.

Desmond had probably been playing the same game of chicken he had been playing with blacks along Wall Road for years. This time he'd just gotten too close. Or maybe Desmond had simply been so drunk he couldn't keep his truck in a straight line and it was just horrible luck all the way around. After all, Adam was so fair-skinned that most people seeing him would think he was a tanned white child. The *why* of it didn't matter. The result was the same.

"We'll get him, though," James said. But he didn't sound too certain to me.

James was quiet for a while. Then he said, "Adam was lying on his side against a tree. I thought Lester was going to die when he saw him. He made this terrible sound like he couldn't breathe out, just in. Then he dropped down beside Adam and grabbed ahold of him and just rocked back and forth in the dirt and mud with him."

"Oh, James," I said, reaching out to touch my husband's arm.

"When I finally got him onto his feet, he just stood there wheezing and staring down at Adam. Then he said, 'Where's his shoes?' Over and over, he kept asking where Adam's shoes were. He wouldn't leave or let them take Adam away until we found the shoes.

"We poked around, looking in the weeds and underbrush for what seemed like forever, and the whole time Lester's wailing louder and louder, 'Where's his shoes?'

"It was the coroner's assistant who finally found them. They were twenty feet away at the side of the road, little white sneakers, just sitting there side by side, like they'd been polished and set out for him by his mama. Lord, Odette, I've seen some bad things since I've had this job, but as long as I live I don't believe I'll ever forget watching Lester put those shoes on that poor dead baby's feet."

James mumbled, "His face was okay. The back of his head was bashed in and his neck was broken. So was one leg and probably an arm. But his face was okay, so they'll be able to have an open casket if they want to. That's something, I guess."

James and I rolled over toward each other in the bed and we pressed our foreheads together. We both shook with tears of grief over Adam and sorrow for our friends. And we cried with guilty relief that this thing, the monster that all parents fear most, had swiped near to us with its sharp and merciless claws, but had not carried off one of our own babies.

Neither of us got any sleep on the night of that worst day. Both James and I were up and on our feet at least once every hour, prying open the doors of our children's bedrooms to watch them as they slept safe in their beds.

Chapter 31

The second round of chemo with the new drugs gave me an even fiercer ass-whupping than the first round. To make matters worse, in May the great love of my life deserted me. It wasn't James. It was food that left me. I woke up one morning with a sour taste in my mouth that wouldn't be scrubbed away with a toothbrush or rinsed out with mouthwash. Worse than that, nearly everything I ate tasted like tin. And what didn't taste like tin, I couldn't keep down.

Mama and Mrs Roosevelt greeted me when I came into the kitchen. That morning's breakfast was a cup of watered-down coffee – my stomach wouldn't take full-strength anymore – and a small bowl of oatmeal that I couldn't persuade myself to eat.

For the first time in my life, my doctor was concerned that I was losing too much weight too quickly. I wasn't skinny by any stretch of the imagination, but I had lost several more pounds in a short period of time and I didn't see any way I was going to slow down the weight loss. Food and I just weren't getting along.

When I gave up on my oatmeal and rose from my chair at the kitchen table to toss the remainder away, Mama said, "You know what you need? You need some herb."

"What?" I asked.

"Herb. Marijuana, ganja, buda, Tijuana tea, pot, bud, skunkweed, giggleweed, wacky tobacky, kif, reefer."

"Stop showing off. I know what you're talking about."

"Whatever you wanna call it, that's what you need," Mama said. "It'll fix that appetite of yours right up."

I didn't want to admit it, but I'd been thinking the same thing for a few weeks. I'd been on the computer researching it when James wasn't around, and I'd been thinking maybe medical marijuana might be the thing to get me back on track. Unfortunately, I didn't live in a state where I could get it legally.

I said, "You may be right, Mama, but it's not like I can go to the drugstore and order some. And please don't tell me to go over to the campus and hang around at the frat houses. We both know where that leads."

"Scaredy-cat. I thought you weren't supposed to be afraid of nothin'," Mama teased.

I wasn't going to be baited that easily. "I mean it, Mama. James has had enough to deal with lately. I'm not about to get arrested and add to it."

Mama let out an exaggerated sigh. "I won't get you arrested, Miss Priss. Get dressed and come on with me."

Once we were in the car, Mama guided me along the familiar route from my house to her and Daddy's old place in Leaning Tree. She instructed me to park the car on the street, rather than in the driveway, and follow her around to the back. She led me and Mrs Roosevelt behind the house and toward what remained of her once-magnificent garden. It had been a damp spring and my feet sank into the wet ground as we walked. I could hear Clarice playing the piano inside and I was thankful that she was occupied. I certainly didn't want her to see me sneaking through the yard and ask me what I was doing: "Oh, hey, Clarice, my dead mama, Eleanor Roosevelt, and me were just heading out back to fetch some marijuana."

We stepped onto the cobblestone garden path and passed the gazebo. It was already green with clematis and honeysuckle vines, though they hadn't bloomed yet. We passed the roses and alliums and walked through the vegetable garden, which was untended and going wild that season. I hacked with my forearms at the tall reed grass and miscanthus Mama had grown at the back of her garden to keep prying eyes from spotting the illegal crop that James and I had pretended not to know about. A sad thought came to me then that brought our entire journey into question.

With as much gentleness as I could muster, considering I was panting with exhaustion by then, I said, "Mama, you do realize that you've been gone for a long time now and nobody's taken care of your special plants in years. I don't think we're gonna find anything still growing back there."

"Hush," she said. "We ain't goin' there." We trudged on several more yards and then turned. Ahead of us was an old tool shed that I'd forgotten all about. It was a short structure, more the height of a child's playhouse than a work shed. But Daddy had been a small man and he had made this shed for himself. It made me happy to see that it still stood and that, even though the vestiges of its white paint were long gone, leaving the bleached pine boards exposed, it looked solid. My daddy built things to last.

Mama instructed me to open the door of the shed. It took some effort because, although only a sliding wood bolt kept the door shut, reed grass and honeysuckle – which would smell divine in a month, but was now just an invasive pest – had nearly swallowed the building. I yanked repeatedly at the door until it opened just wide enough for me to squeeze inside.

We entered the shed to the rustling sound of small creatures scurrying for cover. Mama said, "Over there," pointing at the back wall.

I climbed over an ancient push mower and a rusted tiller, and then stood staring at the wall. All I saw were cobwebs, mouse droppings, and corroded garden tools hanging from a pegboard. I asked Mama what exactly I was looking for and she said, "Just slide that board over to the left and you'll see."

I curled my fingers around the edge of the pegboard and gave it a vigorous shove. I didn't need to try so hard, as it turned out. The board slid over on its metal track so easily you'd have thought it had been oiled that very day. Behind it, I saw an old plastic spice rack that was screwed into the wall. In the cubbyholes of the rack were small glass jars, each of them filled with brownish leaves and labeled in Mama's neat, loopy handwriting with a name and a date.

I picked up random jars and read the labels: "Jamaican Red–1997," "Kentucky Skunk/Thai Stick Hybrid–1999," "Kona–1998," "Sinsemilla–1996." There were around two dozen of them.

I reached for a jar that read "Maui Surprise," and Mama said, "Oh no, no, honey, put that one back. That Maui'll blow the top of your head clean off. We'll start you off with somethin' tamer." She pointed an index finger at a jar in the lower right-hand corner of the rack and I pulled it out.

"Soother–1998," I read aloud from the jar. "They're all kind of old. You think they'll still be good?"

"Trust me. An hour from now you'll wanna kill anybody standing between you and a bag of pork rinds."

I slipped the jar into my pocket and was about to slide the pegboard back in place when Mama stopped me. "Wait a minute. We need that and that." She gestured toward a small shelf below the rack. On the shelf, I found rolling papers and a box of wooden matches. I grabbed them, covered Mama's secret stash with the sliding pegboard, and left the shed.

Mama suggested that I take my herbal cure in the gazebo, but I had another idea. I stomped through more reeds and climbed the hill at the back end of the property. I stopped when we stood beneath the sycamore tree where I was born fifty-five years earlier.

Mama and I sat on the cool ground and rested our backs against the tree. Mrs Roosevelt, who seemed to have been energized by our walk in the spring air, spun in a circle like Julie Andrews at the beginning of *The Sound of Music,* and then did some cartwheels.

Mama said, "Pay her no mind. If she gets your attention she'll never stop."

When I opened the jar, the vacuum seal broke with a noise that sounded like someone blowing a kiss. I lifted it to my nose and inhaled. It smelled like rich soil and newly cut hay, with a dash of skunk spray laid on top. It was as fresh as if it had been picked that day. Mama might not have been able to cook worth a damn, but she sure as hell knew how to can.

Mama started in instructing me. "What you need to do is grab ahold of one of the bigger buds and roll it between your fingers to get the seeds and stems out. Then—"

I interrupted her. "Mama, I think I watched you do this enough times over the years to figure it out." Then I began to roll the first joint I'd rolled in my life.

To my embarrassment, it turned out to be a lot harder to do than I'd imagined. Mama had to guide me through the entire process. It was made worse by the fact that the papers were so old that they cracked whenever I bent them, and the saliva-activated adhesive refused to activate. But I finally produced a functional cigarette. The old sulfur matches worked just fine, and soon enough I found myself inhaling the sweet, pungent fumes of Mama's Soother.

I had never smoked marijuana before and had only smoked tobacco once in high school, when Clarice and I had proclaimed ourselves bad girls for a day and each coughed our way through a quarter of a cigarette before giving up. But in ten minutes that tinny taste in my mouth was fading away, and I was starting to feel pretty damn good. I had to hand it to Mama: she had named the Soother just right.

I looked up at the leaves of the tree. They were still the pale green of spring, and they shivered in the breeze against the background of the blue sky.

"Beautiful," I said. "It looks like a painting. You know, Mama, I think it's *all* like a painting."

"What is?"

"Everything. Life. It's like you're filling in a little bit more of a picture every day. You stroke on color after color, trying to make it as pretty as you can before you reach the edge of your canvas. And if you're lucky enough that your mama had you in a sycamore tree, maybe your hand won't shake with fear too bad when you see that your brush is right up against the frame."

Mama said, "You're stoned."

"Maybe, but I think this is the loveliest spot on my canvas. When the end comes, I think this is where I'd like to be. Right back here where I started out," I said.

"I don't like to hear you talk like that. Makes me think you're givin' up. You probably won't have to think about dyin' for a long time."

Mrs Roosevelt, who now knelt beside me after tiring of turning cartwheels, shook her head and frowned as if to say "Your mother may think you've got time, but I say you're a goner." Then with the grace of a jungle cat, Eleanor Roosevelt hitched up her skirt and scrambled up the trunk of the sycamore and into its branches until she was nearly at the top of the tree. She put a satin-gloved hand up to her brow to block out glare from the sun and proceeded to scan the horizon – looking for mischief to get into, no doubt.

I said, "I don't dwell on it, or anything. But when I think about it, this is always the place that comes to mind when I imagine the end. I like the idea of making this big ol' jumble of a life into a nice, neat circle."

Mama nodded and looked up at the sky with me.

I don't know how long we sat under the sycamore staring up at the passing clouds, but I called a halt to it when my behind started to go numb and the damp of the ground began seeping through my hose. I pushed myself up, using the tree trunk for leverage. After I straightened and stretched, I brushed the dirt from my rear end and said, "Well, I guess we'd better head on home."

Mama and I – Mrs Roosevelt chose to stay up in the tree – began to walk back through the garden. My first few steps on the soft, uneven ground were not too steady. Mama commented, "I think your nerves might be a little too soothed for you to drive right now. Let's go sit in the gazebo for a spell." I agreed, and we walked back toward the house.

The open side of the six-sided gazebo faced the rear of the house, so we couldn't see into it as we approached it from the back. Even from the front, it was impossible to make out more than a narrow slice of the dim interior from outside. So we had no way of knowing who was inside when we heard the unmistakable sounds of lovemaking – a man's low grunts, a woman's sighs – emanating from the gazebo as we came closer to it.

Mama said, "Sounds like Clarice and Richmond are gettin' along better these days."

I turned away from the gazebo and walked as fast as I could toward the house and the driveway that led back to the street. I was even less eager to come across Clarice and Richmond in this situation than I was for Clarice to catch me foraging for marijuana.

I had just about made it to the driveway when I heard

the back door of the house open and then heard the sound of Clarice's voice. She called out, "Odette! Glad you came by. I was just going to call you to ask you over for lunch."

Confused, I looked back at the garden. Clarice followed my gaze and then we both heard muffled voices. A head stuck out from the entrance of the gazebo and looked back at us. Clarice came and stood beside me and we watched a young man come in and out of view inside the gazebo as he hopped from one side of the structure to the other, struggling ungracefully to get back into his drawers. The young man was Clifton Abrams, the fiancé of Clarice's cousin Sharon.

Mama shook her head with pity as she watched Clifton hurry to cover his nakedness. Holding up her thumb and forefinger spaced about two inches apart, she said, "Poor boy has the curse of the Abrams men. Did you notice?"

A woman's head popped out and peered at us, then receded into the shadows. We heard more shuffling as the two of them bumped around, climbing into their clothes. The young woman was not Sharon.

I glanced at Clarice, wondering, but not saying, *Who the hell is she?*

Clarice read my mind. "Her name is Cherokee."

"Like the Indian tribe?"

"No, like the Jeep. Come on in and I'll tell you all about her. I've got some leftover turkey breast. You hungry?"

My stomach growled at the mention of roast turkey and I was surprised that I was able to honestly answer, "Yes, as a matter of fact, I am hungry."

We left the garden and strolled back toward the house. Mama came along, saying, "Told you your mama knew how to fix up that appetite." With that, the three of us stepped together through the back door of Mama's old house.

Chapter 32

Barbara Jean's AA sponsor was a man named Carlo who taught speech therapy at the university. A pudgy tanning booth devotee whose carrot-colored skin had the texture of an alligator purse, Carlo was a few years younger than Barbara Jean, but he looked a lot older. He had an unusually long, pointed nose, a wide jaw, and eyes that bulged a little. Still, in spite of having an odd collection of features that seemed to be fighting for dominance of his face, Barbara Jean thought he wasn't a bad-looking guy. Somehow it all worked together, the different unpleasant facets canceling each other out.

Carlo lived with his partner, another former drinker who sometimes came to meetings with him. Barbara Jean chose him to be her sponsor because he was gay. During some of her late nights, she watched television shows that featured gay guys who were perpetually shopping and making witty conversation. She thought a sponsor like that would be a lot of fun. Barbara Jean was disappointed to discover that Carlo must have been watching different TV shows. She liked him enough, but, blunt and serious, he was as different from those men as she was from the sassy, wisecracking black women who populated TV Land. Carlo, as it turned out, was a big gay pain in the neck.

Right about the time Barbara Jean convinced herself that she had fully mastered the AA thing, Carlo called and asked her to meet him. They arranged to get together at a coffee shop near the campus. It was a dark, cramped place with bookshelves lining every wall, designed to cater to the student population. Their meeting took place early in the day, just after the morning rush of harried graduate students had left. Barbara Jean came armed with a shopping list, ready to begin the fun part of their relationship.

She arrived at the coffee shop first and found a seat at one of the tables, which were all made from recycled industrial cable spools. When Carlo sat down across from her, she greeted him by saying how happy she was that he had called and that she had been thinking it would be nice for the two of them to get together for brunch, but hadn't gotten around to asking him over to the house.

He interrupted her. "Barbara Jean, it doesn't appear that I'm the right sponsor to help you to take your recovery seriously."

"Why do you say that?" she asked.

Carlo crossed his arms over his chest and stared at her. One of his eyebrows rose. "Your eyes are fucking bloodshot and you're drunk right now."

She put her hand to her chest and gasped to let Carlo know how offended she was. She would have stood up from her chair and stormed out of the place if she hadn't been just the tiniest bit buzzed and afraid that she might fall on her face in front of him.

"I can't believe you would say such a thing to me."

Barbara Jean slipped her sunglasses onto her face, blowing a quick breath into her hand to check for the telltale odor of liquor as she adjusted the frames. "I don't know how much more seriously I can take my sobriety. That damn Serenity Prayer is on my lips practically all day long. And I've been going to three meetings a week for two months now. *Three* meetings."

He scrunched up his long nose and said, "Are you sure you haven't been going to one meeting a week, but getting there so drunk you're seeing triple?"

Barbara Jean felt a tear trickle out from behind her sunglasses and travel down her cheek. She grabbed a napkin from the table and wiped it away as quickly as she could.

Carlo softened his tone, which was contrary to his nature and, she knew, hard for him. He said, "Look, Barbara Jean, I like you a lot. You're good company and you're a nice lady. But I'm not helping you. And, frankly, it's not good for me to be around someone who continues to drink the way you do. Especially someone I like as much as I've come to like you."

Barbara Jean struggled to find something to say. She mumbled a few words about how wrong he was and how it hurt her that he didn't believe her. But her heart wasn't really in the lie anymore. She leaned back in her chair and said, "Some folks have a good reason for drinking, you know. A damn good reason. I want to tell you a story. And after I'm done, you look me in the eye and tell me that I shouldn't take a drink every now and then."

She took a sip of the coffee she had spiked with a healthy splash of Irish whiskey from her silver flask before he'd arrived at the coffee shop. Then she told Carlo a tale she had never told Odette or Clarice.

The night of Adam's funeral, Odette and Clarice stayed on after everyone else had left Barbara Jean's house. After they'd helped her maid to clean up after the guests who had filled the house with far more food and sympathy than Barbara Jean could handle, she rushed them out the door. Lester, who was just a few weeks away from the first of many hospitalizations that were to come, collapsed onto the bed the second he was out of his black suit. As soon as he began to snore, Barbara Jean slipped out of the house.

She went to see Big Earl. It was cool and misty outside that night, but there he was, smoking a cigar and rocking on the porch swing, when she came up the walk to the house. It was as if he'd been waiting for her. When she stood beside him, he looked up at her and said, "Baby, you should go on home."

"I need to know where he is," she said, not bothering to say his name. Though Chick never set foot in the All-You-Can-Eat or made any attempt to see her, Barbara Jean knew that he had been back in Plainview for at least two years. She had spotted him coming and going from the McIntyres' house, and she had overheard Little Earl saying that Chick was a frequent visitor now that Miss Thelma was sick.

Big Earl said, "You and Ray ain't talked in nine years. Won't nothin' be helped by talkin' now."

"I need to see him. And I know you can tell me where to find him."

"Be careful, Barbara Jean. You ain't in the shape to make a

good decision right now. You need to give it some time before you do anything that might cause you more heartache."

"*More heartache?*" She laughed at the thought of that, and Big Earl winced at the sound of her laughter, which to his ear sounded like a shriek of hysteria. She said, "I've got to talk to Chick and I'm going to do it tonight. Will you tell me where he lives? Or do I have to drive out Wall Road past the place where my little boy died and ask Desmond Carlson where I can find his brother?"

Big Earl stared down at his feet and slowly shook his head. Then he looked up at Barbara Jean and told her the address. As she left, he said, "Be careful, baby. Be careful."

Chick lived on a block near the university that was mostly student housing, little square boxes painted dinner-mint colors. Was he in school? She didn't really know anything about his life since he'd returned to Plainview. Was he married? Was she about to awaken a family? She sat in her car across the street from his house, staring at the place until a light came on in back. She decided that was her signal, just like the light in the storeroom of the All-You-Can-Eat she had once watched for from her bedroom. She crossed the street and knocked on the door. The noise of her fist striking wood was the loudest sound on the street at that late hour.

Chick opened the door and drew in a sharp breath when he saw her standing in the harsh light of the yellow bulb that hung over the front stoop. "Barbara Jean?" he said, as if he thought he might be seeing things. He didn't move, so she opened the screen door and walked in, brushing past him.

She stepped into a small, tidy living room that was furnished with two metal folding chairs, a beaten-up old couch upholstered in cracked brown patent leather, and a desk that was piled high with neatly stacked papers and books. Against one wall were two tables that supported six cages and an elaborate system of lights. Each cage contained an identical small bird with gray, red, and white striped feathers, pretty little things whose sad cooing echoed in the quiet room.

Chick saw her looking at the birds and said, "I'm studying them at the university. I'm working on this project . . ." His voice tapered off and they stared at each other.

There he was, just inches away from her again after all those years. Ray Carlson. Ray of light. Ray of sunshine. Ray of hope. Ray, who had danced naked for her to an old, dirty blues song.

The room was hot, warmed by the lights over the cages, and he was shirtless. He was still thin, but broader across the chest than he'd once been. *He's still beautiful*, she thought, *just like our son was*. She turned her back to him, afraid all of a sudden that she wouldn't be able to say what she had come to say if she was looking at him.

"Barbara Jean," he said, "I heard about your—"

Still with her back to him, she interrupted. "I just want to know one thing. Did Desmond kill him because of us? Did he kill Adam because he was your son?"

She waited for his answer, but he said nothing. After several seconds, she turned around and looked at him. His mouth hung open in a face that was slack with shock. His jaw twitched with little movements, but no words came out. When he finally said something, it was so quiet she could hardly distinguish it from the cooing of the birds. "I didn't know."

"You didn't know?" she cried out, surprising herself that she had any more anger left inside of her. "How could you not know? Didn't you ever look at him?"

Every time Barbara Jean looked at Adam, she saw Chick. His profile, the shape of his body, the way he moved. It was all Chick. Clarice and Odette saw it, too. She could tell by the way they stared at Adam sometimes. If other friends and acquaintances didn't see the resemblance, it was probably because they couldn't have imagined a man doting on a child who wasn't his the way Lester had doted on Adam. And Barbara Jean understood Lester's family not seeing it. They had taken their cue from Lester's late mother, who saw her light-skinned grandchild and thought of nothing but rejoicing over the new infusion of café-au-lait-colored blood into the veins of her family line. But how Chick could not have known that Adam was his son was impossible for Barbara Jean to comprehend.

Chick said, "I couldn't look at him. When I came back and heard that you and Lester had a son, I couldn't look at him. Or you either." His voice growing more tremulous, he said again, "I didn't know."

She knew then that she should just go home. She knew that words could only make things worse. But Barbara Jean couldn't stop herself from speaking the truth to Chick, just like she couldn't stop herself from telling him the story of her life in the hallway of the All-You-Can-Eat back when she had first realized that she loved him.

"I married Lester because you took off and I had to make a life for myself and your child. I married him because it was that or die because I couldn't be with you. Maybe I was wrong to marry him. Maybe I was cruel to you. Maybe this is my punishment for spending nine years waiting for you to knock on my door and come take me and Adam away, even though Lester loved our son as much as any father could and loves me more than I deserve. Maybe this is God's judgment for every bad thing I ever did."

He stepped toward her then and wrapped his arms around her. He pulled her into his body and she inhaled the scent of him, familiar and strange, perfect and wrong. She wanted to embrace him and squeeze him to her, but her body wouldn't cooperate. She stood stiff and straight with her arms crossed over her chest like a corpse inside a coffin.

He asked in a voice ragged with sorrow, "What can I do, Barbara Jean? What can I do to make it better?"

It just came out, the simple truth of what she wanted at that moment. "Kill him. If you want to do something for me, if you want to do something for our son, you'll kill Desmond." Barbara Jean twisted out of his arms and stepped away from him. Brushing off the stray gray, red, and white feathers that had transferred from his body to her black sweater, she said, "I've got to get back to my husband. He's not well." She left him standing with his arms reaching out for her.

The police were back at Barbara Jean's house the next day. They were Plainview police officers this time instead of the Indiana State Police. They talked to Lester for a while in the foyer and told him they wanted him to come with them. Barbara Jean refused to let him leave the house without her. She made such a fuss that they put her in the squad car along with her husband. The police drove them out of downtown Plainview and onto Wall Road. She closed her eyes as they passed the place where Adam had been found.

The Plainview chief of police stood in the side yard of Desmond Carlson's house, one of a dozen cops milling around – the entire Plainview police department back then. Three of the policemen were loading Desmond's body onto a stretcher when the car carrying Barbara Jean and Lester drove up. At least Barbara Jean thought it was Desmond. She hadn't seen him up close in nine years. And he was barely recognizable now, with half of his face gone.

They separated Lester and Barbara Jean then. The chief of police talked to Lester ten yards away from her while a patrolman asked Barbara Jean where her husband had been the previous night and early that morning.

That was when James drove up along with the white state trooper who'd come to the house with him to tell Barbara Jean and Lester about Adam. They moved fast, their police cruiser skidding in the mud. The questioning ended as soon as James approached. Lester came over and stood next to Barbara Jean while James spoke with the police chief for several minutes. Then James walked over to his friends and said he would drive them home.

On the way back to the house, James apologized for the trouble and explained that he didn't hear about it right away because Desmond's neighborhood was part of the Plainview cops' jurisdiction, while Wall Road, owned by the university, was the territory of the state police. He assured them that, after the investigation, it would be concluded that Desmond, overcome with guilt, had killed himself with a shot to the head. James said, "That'll turn out to be the best thing for everybody."

When the car pulled up in Barbara Jean and Lester's driveway, the white trooper shook Lester's hand and whispered, "I would've done the same thing if it'd been my boy."

It began that day, the rumor that Lester had killed or engineered the death of Desmond Carlson. Eventually, Lester seemed to believe it himself. But Barbara Jean knew the truth. Out at Desmond Carlson's place, while the policeman questioned her about her husband's whereabouts, she had stared down at her feet and watched several delicate gray, red, and white feathers, just like the ones she had brushed from her sweater at Chick's the night before, float across the ground.

That night was the first Barbara Jean spent curled up on Adam's little bed and the first time in her life she had been drunk.

When she finished talking, Carlo looked at Barbara Jean with an expression of pained empathy on his face. "Whatever happened to this guy Chick?"

"What do you mean?"

"I mean did he get arrested or anything?"

"No. He just disappeared. I found out later that he went to Florida, but I never heard from him. And I didn't see him again until this past summer."

"Is he here now? In Plainview?"

She nodded.

Carlo reached across the table and patted her hand.

"You can do something about this, you know. You can work your eighth and ninth steps."

When he saw that, even after months of going to meetings, Barbara Jean had no idea what the eighth and ninth steps of AA were, he sighed with exasperation. In a voice that made his annoyance clear to her, he said, "Make a list of all persons you have harmed, and become willing to make amends to them all. Then make direct amends to those people wherever possible, except when to do so would injure them or others.

"This Chick guy seems to be on your list, so you should go see him."

She agreed that she would, not knowing if she meant it or not.

Carlo said, "I'll see you at the ten-thirty meeting tomorrow." Then he got up and left the coffee shop. She watched her sponsor walk away, this chunky man who was so comfortable doling out unpleasant truths. Barbara Jean thought, not for the first or last time, that she must have some special kind of bad luck. She'd gone searching for a witty shopping companion and ended up with a gay Italian version of Odette.

Two nights after her meeting with Carlo, that moment of clarity Odette had tried to knock into Barbara Jean's head after she had embarrassed herself so badly outside the All-You-Can-Eat finally came. And to her amazement, it came in her library, in her Chippendale chair.

Without alcohol, her body fought sleep. Feeling ants crawling beneath her skin and unable to even imagine rest, she returned to her beautiful Chippendale chair and the Bible Clarice had burdened her with decades earlier. She did what she had done more times than she could count. She opened the book to a random page and dropped her finger. Then she read what she had landed on.

John 8:32. "And ye shall know the truth, and the truth shall make you free."

Common as salt, as the old folks used to say. And Barbara Jean had found her fingertip pointing to this passage often enough over the years that it ordinarily held no meaning for her. But that night, John 8:32 started her thinking.

Maybe if she'd had a couple of good stiff drinks in her at that moment or if she'd had one more day of sobriety, she would have ignored this familiar verse. In either case, Barbara Jean might have simply closed up the book and gone back to bed for another stab at sleep. But she was freshly dried out and ready for a revelation. She thought later that it was likely any verse would have done the job, but that night it was John 8:32 that rolled around in her mind until it transformed from an adage into a command. Before she returned to her bed, that verse demanded and received a promise from her that she would face Chick. She would acknowledge out loud that she had used him, that she had transformed him, the father of her child, from the sweetest man she had ever known into her instrument of vengeance against his own brother. Then she would have to ask him, "What can I do to make it better?" just as he had asked her all those years earlier.

Chapter 33

Before things turned ugly, Clarice, Veronica, and Sharon sat enjoying iced tea and friendly conversation beneath a patio umbrella on the enormous redwood deck that wrapped around the back of Veronica's house. The deck was the first in a long series of alterations Veronica had inflicted upon her redbrick ranch house after she and her mother split the money they received for the property in Leaning Tree. It occupied two-thirds of her backyard and rightfully belonged on the Pacific side of a California oceanfront mansion. The other changes were fashioned after Barbara Jean's huge Victorian. She had added on a small turret, two colorfully painted front porches, and a widow's walk. The result of the renovations was a structure that combined the worst aspects of a Southern California beach house and a San Francisco bordello. Behind her back, Clarice called Veronica's home Barbie's Malibu Whorehouse.

With the words "Sharon, there's something I have to tell you," the atmosphere of conviviality evaporated. After Clarice told Veronica and Sharon the story of finding Clifton Abrams nude with a woman in the gazebo, she was called a liar in stereo. Then Veronica began to pace the deck, her heavy footsteps echoing like hammer blows as she stalked across the redwood beams.

Veronica recited a list of offenses Clarice had committed against her over the years. She started in 1960 and worked her way forward, spelling out just how Clarice had wronged her in each decade of her life. The most heinous crime, Veronica said, had been Clarice keeping her at arm's length while publicly embracing Odette and Barbara Jean as if they were her sisters. "It says a lot about your character, if you ask me, throwing over your own family for a foul-tempered, smartass fat girl and a whore's daughter."

Sharon said, "Mmm, hmm."

Clarice knew from experience that a young woman in love could derive great comfort from sticking her head in the sand. So instead of addressing Sharon, she said to Veronica, "This relationship between Sharon and Clifton has come along pretty fast. I'm just saying that there are things she hasn't learned about him yet, and she should learn those things before she marries him."

Veronica shrieked, "Minnie warned me you would try to interfere with things. I bet you've been itching to pull this for months. You can't stand for anybody else to be important. It always has to be about you." She singsonged, "Clarice and her piano. Clarice and her football star." Then she coughed out a rough-sounding laugh and said, "You're a fine one to come around here with marriage advice. Why don't we ask Richmond how he appreciated coming in third on your list behind *the Supremes*?" She put her finger to her chin, pretending to be deep in thought, "Oh yeah, that's right, we can't ask him. He put you out. Didn't he, Miss Marriage Expert?"

Clarice turned to Sharon. "I really didn't come by to

upset you or cause trouble." Sharon responded with a groan of skepticism. "The thing is, I *am* the expert on this. I know what it means to spend your life with a cheating man. And the only reason I'm here telling you this is that I care about you and I don't want to see you go through what I've been through."

Veronica put her hands on her hips and cocked her head to one side. "Because you care so much about Sharon, I won't un-invite you to our wedding. But your services as assistant wedding planner will no longer be needed. I'll have your wedding book back now, thank you very much." She dramatically extended her arms and held out both hands, palms up, as if she thought Clarice had the twenty-pound book in one of her pockets and might conceivably slip it out and hand it to her.

When Clarice pointed out that she didn't have the book on her, Veronica said, "Well, you can bring it by later. Leave it on the front stoop, if you please. I don't think you and I need to have any further interaction." Then she opened the sliding glass door and strode inside with Sharon at her heels.

As she disappeared into the house, Sharon called out over her shoulder, "People will be talking about my wedding for years to come."

None of them knew then just how right Sharon was about that.

When Clarice got back to Leaning Tree, she did some work in the garden to sweat the lingering frustration from her tussle with Veronica out of her system. Then she bathed and started to cook her dinner. She cracked eggs and pulled leftover potatoes and fried onions from the refrigerator for a frittata. Since she'd been on her own, her meals tended toward that kind of thing – simple dishes that Richmond had refused to eat because of their foreign-sounding names or had rejected as "girl food" because they lacked red meat.

Clarice was whisking eggs when Richmond knocked on the front door. She saw him on the porch and thought, *Lord, this is the last thing I need today.* She opened the door and prepared herself for a fight.

"Hello, Richmond. What do you want?"

He smiled and said, "Is that any way for a wife to greet a husband who comes bearing a gift?"

He held up an envelope in his right hand and waved it back and forth in front of his face.

"What's that?" she asked.

"Like I said, it's a gift. A birthday gift."

"It's not my birthday. You must have me confused with some other woman."

He pouted. "Come on, Clarice, give a man a break. I know when your birthday is. This is an *early* present."

"Sorry. It's been kind of a rough day. Thanks for the present." She held out her hand to take the envelope.

"Aren't you going to invite me in?"

Clarice sighed, still not in the mood to be bothered. But years of childhood etiquette training kicked in and she couldn't be rude any longer. She said, "Come on in," and he followed her into the living room.

They sat together on the couch. Like most of the furniture in the house, it dated back to the 1960s. The springs beneath the cushions had long since given up the ghost, and Richmond's weight caused him to sink so far into the couch that his knees came close to his chest. He handed Clarice the envelope and she tore it open.

She began to read the letter he had given her, but she couldn't make sense of what she was seeing. "What *is* this?" she asked.

"It's what it looks like."

What she held in her hands was a letter from Wendell Albertson, the music producer who had invited her to record all of the Beethoven sonatas for his label more than thirty years earlier. She said, "Is this some kind of a joke? Wendell Albertson would have to be a hundred years old, if he's alive at all. And I know his record company is long gone."

"The record company is gone, all right. But Albertson's alive and well. He's not that much older than we are. You were only, what—twenty, when you first met him? Everybody over thirty was old to us then. Anyway, as you can see, he's still working and still remembers you."

In the letter, Mr Albertson expressed his surprise and pleasure that Clarice had contacted him after all these years. He also thanked her for the "wonderful recordings" that had accompanied her letter to him.

"What letter? What recordings?" she asked Richmond.

He said, "Well, the letter is what you might call a 'loving forgery,' but the recordings are yours. I took the tapes from your recitals over to the audio lab at the university and they made them into disks for me. And I sent the disks to Albertson." He leaned back and sank even further into the couch with a self-satisfied smile on his face.

Clarice shook her head. "Oh Richmond, I know you

meant well, but you really shouldn't have done this. Those tapes are ancient. I don't play like that anymore."

"No, you play better than you did," he said. "I've been listening. Every time I come by here I sit outside on the porch before I knock, or sometimes after I say goodbye, and I listen to you. You play better than ever, sweetheart, you really do."

The last part of the letter from Wendell Albertson discussed possible dates for Clarice to come play for him in New York. Assuming that went well, they would talk recording dates and discuss his idea of marketing her as a resurrected prodigy.

She put the sheet of paper down on the coffee table in front of her and said, "I honestly don't know whether to kiss you or spank you."

Now was the time for Richmond to test the waters by saying "You could do both," or something along those lines. Because he didn't, she leaned over and kissed him on the mouth. Then she gave him another kiss because, even though what he'd done was crazy, it was also the kindest thing he had ever done for her. She picked up the letter and read it again just to make sure she hadn't imagined it.

"So, do you like your birthday present?" he asked.

"You know, I think I do like it. It'll probably blow up in my face. But I like it. Thank you, Richmond."

"You're welcome. I'm glad to see I can still make you happy."

Clarice kissed him once more, on the cheek this time. Then she thanked him again.

Richmond said, "Well, I'd better get out while I'm

ahead." He scooted forward on the couch, beginning the process of extricating himself from the cushions. He stood, grunting as he put weight on his bad ankle.

Clarice walked a few steps toward the door with him, but then stopped him with a hand on his arm. "You don't have to go. Stay for dinner. I'm making a frittata."

"That sounds nice. You know how I love fri-tta-ta." He pronounced it "free tah-tah," drawing it out so that it sounded both silly and dirty. She gave his arm a playful punch and he accompanied her into the kitchen.

After dinner, they sat on stools at the kitchen counter and talked. Clarice described her afternoon at Veronica's house to him. He filled her in on the latest about the football team and how their prospects looked for the upcoming season. She told him that Odette was getting worse and that it scared her. He bragged that he was on schedule with his diabetes medication nearly every day now and was becoming a champion clothes ironer. She told him about going to the Unitarian church and how she thought maybe it was just right for her. Clarice even related to him the tale of finding his girlfriend Cherokee in the gazebo with Clifton Abrams.

Richmond laughed until tears came to his eyes at her description of Clifton hopping around naked, trying to get back into his underpants. But he took exception to her calling Cherokee his girlfriend, insisting that he had given up all of his women in an effort to become a better man. This included, he claimed, the girls at the Pink Slipper Gentlemen's Club. He said that his only recent visit to the club had been for purely theological purposes.

In response to her laughter, Richmond raised his right

hand as if he were taking the Boy Scout Oath. "No, really. Tammi, the girl who showed up at the last revival meeting, has been doing biblically themed pole dances on Monday nights at the club. Last week she danced the tale of Eve's expulsion from the Garden of Eden and gave every cent she made to the New Roof Fund at church. What kind of Christian would I be if I didn't show up and support a young convert preaching the Word?" He swore that he had left the club, alone, the second the dancer and her python exited the stage. He said, "You told me to evolve, remember?"

"I remember. But please don't change everything. You've still got your good points," Clarice said. She wondered if she was flirting with him now from force of habit or because she actually sensed something was different about him.

She thought back to her conversation with Veronica then. She said, "Richmond, tell me something. Do you feel like I neglected you or made you a low priority in my life because of Odette and Barbara Jean?"

The expression on his face said that he thought she had thrown him a trick question or was laying a trap. "Why do you ask that?"

"Something Veronica said to me today made me wonder."

He thought about it for a while and then said, "You know, if you'd asked me that question a few weeks ago, I'd have said yes. But that would have been to get you to feel guilty and maybe come back home. But, honestly, I was always glad you had the Supremes. I think it made me feel okay about running with Ramsey and all my other . . . well, *activities*, let's say. When it came to you and me, I never felt anything but loved, and that's the truth."

"Thanks, Richmond. I appreciate you saying that. That was really sweet of you."

"What can I say? I'm a sweet guy. That's why you married me, isn't it?"

Remembering the early years of their courtship and the fever that had swept over her whenever she looked at Richmond or even thought about him, Clarice said, "Not exactly."

"No, I suppose it was having your mother on my side that sealed the deal for me."

"Partly. But, to be honest about it, the thing that really made up my mind for me was something Big Earl said."

"Big Earl?"

"Mm-hmm. I had already talked to Mother, Reverend Peterson, even that old fraud Minnie, and I was still wavering. So I went by the All-You-Can-Eat one night to talk to Big Earl. Odette and Barbara Jean both swore the man was a genius, and I had always liked him. So I figured, *why not*?"

"Big Earl stuck up for me, did he?"

"He said that when you grew up you'd be a fine man."

Richmond swallowed hard and his mouth spread into a slightly sad smile. "Damn, I miss that old man."

Clarice had done a little paraphrasing for the sake of the evening's mood. What Big Earl had actually said was, "Clarice, honey, I truly believe that in about twenty-five years, Richmond Baker is likely to show himself to be as fine a man as this town ever turned out. Till then, you might be in for a rough ride." With that fever in her blood,

Clarice had decided to hear what Big Earl said as a glowing endorsement. It was years before she realized that she had ignored a warning in favor of an optimistic prediction. And that prediction had been quite optimistic. Big Earl had seen Richmond's turnaround coming in twenty-five years. As usual, Richmond was dragging himself in late.

Neither of them said anything for a while. Then Richmond glanced at his watch. "I guess now I've really got to go."

Clarice reached out and patted his cheek with her hand, allowing it to rest there for a few seconds to enjoy the familiar sensation of his beard stubble against her open palm. She thought for a moment and then said, "Don't go. Stay over."

His eyebrows rose and he asked, "You mean it?"

"Yeah, why not? We're married, aren't we?"

As he hopped off of his stool, he smiled that fun, nasty smile she had always loved. Then he hooked an arm around her and pulled her to him. They kissed through the kitchen, the hallway, the living room, and up the stairs.

Clarice had thought that it would be like old times, she and Richmond together enjoying that type of married folks' lovemaking that was a mixture of passion and efficiency gained from familiarity. But it was better than it had been before. Living alone for the first time in her life had changed her perspective. She didn't have to see Richmond as a disappointing husband anymore. In her house he was her lover, there at her request, for her pleasure. In that department, Richmond never disappointed. And without the burden of having to play the wronged wife, Clarice could be his lover, too – a free woman who wore peasant skirts and comfortable shoes and gave as good as she got in bed.

She woke up in the morning to find Richmond already awake. He was lying on his side, his right elbow on the mattress, his head propped up by his hand. "G'morning," he said.

She stretched and yawned. "Good morning to you, too."

He pecked her lightly on the lips and whispered, "Glad you're awake. I didn't want to take off before you got up. I have to be at a meeting in a couple hours."

Clarice nodded. "Sorry you have to go."

"Me, too." He slid out of the bed and went across the room retrieving his clothing, which they had flung from wall to wall in the heat of the moment the night before. Once he had gathered all of his clothes, he sat on the edge of the bed and started to dress. It was a reverse striptease Clarice had seen thousands of times. It was always done in the same order. Right sock. Left sock. Underwear. Pants. Belt. Shoes. Then, finally, the undershirt and shirt were slipped over his massive and still firm upper torso and arms. Richmond had a strong sense of what his best features were and he didn't like to cover up the good stuff too quickly.

He was just about to pull on his pants when he said, "Listen, while you were sleeping I was thinking there's no need for you to have to pack up all your things. We can hire somebody to box up your clothes and whatever else you brought over. And later in the week we can have the piano movers come. How's that sound?"

"What are you talking about?"

"Your move back home. We can hire someone to pack your things."

"I'm not moving back home, Richmond."

He'd had his back to her; now he stood and turned around. Richmond, clad in his boxer shorts and socks, stared at Clarice with an astonished look on his face. "What do you mean you're not coming home? I thought – well, after last night and what happened . . ." He gestured back and forth from his bare chest to her naked body in the bed to illustrate his point.

She sat up in the bed. "Richmond, last night was a lot of fun, but I see no reason to come back home. I like it here. And this short amount of time we've been apart isn't enough to fix forty years of both of us making foolish decisions. You know that."

His eyes grew big and he raised his voice. "You knew that if we went to bed together I'd think you were coming home, and you went ahead and let me think that."

"I'm sorry if that's what you thought. But nothing's changed, except we had a really good night."

Richmond stood beside the bed with his mouth opening and shutting. He looked like a giant brown fish that had been thrown onto dry land. He clutched his pants against his chest as if he had suddenly grown modest and was trying to cover himself. With his empty hand, he pointed at Clarice and stammered out, "Y-y-you led me on and used me. That's what you did. You made me think we were going to be together again and you used me."

She thought about it for a few seconds and realized that he was right. She had known what he would think about the two of them after last night, and she had pushed that knowledge aside because she wanted him, the way she had always wanted him. Some other day, maybe she'd have felt guilty. But that morning, she was completely unable to keep herself from grinning, and then giggling at the thought that she had used Richmond.

Towering over her beside the bed, Richmond looked as indignant as Clarice could remember seeing him. But then she saw his face gradually break into a smile and he began to chuckle along with her. He laughed harder and harder until he wobbled on his feet and collapsed onto the bed next to her.

"You had me over for dinner, screwed my brains out, and now you're getting rid of me at sunrise. I can't believe this. You turned me into a one-night stand. No, it's even worse. You actually had me believing we were going to be together. Holy shit. I'm not your one-night stand; I'm your mistress." He whacked his forehead with his hand and shook his head. "Ramsey's always telling me, 'Man, Clarice is gonna turn you into a woman if you give her half the chance.' And after forty years, it's finally happened."

Still snickering, Clarice put a leg over him and straddled his hips. "We don't have to tell Ramsey about it. We can keep it our dirty little secret." Then she kissed him hard.

He stayed for another hour.

On his way out later that morning, she told him she would call him about getting together for dinner soon. At the door, she swatted him on his firm, round ass and kissed him goodbye.

After she put the teakettle on and popped bread into the toaster, Clarice reread the letter Richmond had brought her the night before. She thought to herself that if this was what it was like to have a mistress – a night of thoughtful gifts and good sex, then your lover is out of your hair by breakfast time – Richmond's behavior over the past few decades made a lot more sense to her.

Chapter 34

Sharon's wedding took place on the hottest day south-ern Indiana had seen in decades. Spring had come early that year and the trend of record temperatures that had begun in February continued into the summer. The mercury registered right at one hundred and five degrees that afternoon and the humidity was just as awful. Only Richmond wasn't panting from the exertion of climbing the slight incline that led to the Garden Hills Banquet Hall and Corporate Meetings Venue from its parking lot. The Supremes and James began gasping for air within yards of their cars. The journey from the parking lot to the banquet hall was made worse by the fact that the high temperature had caused the tar on the asphalt of the lot and driveway to become tacky so they had to work hard just to lift their feet from the ground.

They stopped at the front steps of Garden Hills to take in the enormity of the place. The pictures from Veronica's wedding book hadn't done it justice. The building was a half a block long. The huge white columns supporting the second-floor verandah that stretched across the width of the structure were far more massive than the photo had let on. Nothing else in town, aside from the larger buildings on the campus, approached this place in size.

The banquet hall was a part of "the other Plainview," the Plainview that those who had grown up there didn't recognize. This imposing tribute to Greek Revival belonged to the new town that was being built by the university and by Plainview's newer residents, people who worked in Louisville and saw little of the town outside of the routes from their bloated homes to the pricey specialty shops of modern-day Leaning Tree. Every one of the people gathered in front of the building thought the same thing. They were becoming outsiders in their own town.

Barbara Jean said, "It looks like something straight out of *Gone With the Wind*."

Clarice snapped her fingers. "That's it. I've been trying to think what this place reminded me of, and that's it. It's Tara, caught in a fun-house mirror. What a sight."

Odette said, "Would somebody please explain to me why any self-respecting black couple would want to get married in a giant plantation house? That's messed up."

Barbara Jean shook her head. "I tell you they're asking for trouble not getting married in a church. Everybody knows that's bad luck."

"My words exactly," Clarice said.

Two young men exited the building and gawked at Barbara Jean as they passed by. Clarice and Odette silently agreed with their judgment. Barbara Jean looked fantastic. She had toned down the color palette of her clothing over the previous few months. She hadn't exactly turned into a wallflower, but the days of the wild outfits seemed to have come to an end. And it wasn't just her clothes that were different. Sobriety seemed to be doing wonders for her. Who could have imagined that Barbara Jean could become more beautiful? But a few months without liquor had managed the impossible. Odette and Clarice both told her all the time how proud they were of her, but in typical Barbara Jean fashion, she refused to take any credit for what she had accomplished. She would mutter some catchphrase like "One day at a time," and then change the subject. But Barbara Jean had been resurrected and that was plain to see.

"Let's get inside. It's too hot out here," James said, meaning that it was too hot for Odette to be outside. James was more vigilant than ever that summer – part nurse, part mother bear, part prison guard. He was also more aware than anyone that Odette had lost more weight and more strength. She fought on like a champion, though, refusing to acknowledge that anything had changed. Her husband and her friends admired her warrior spirit, but couldn't help but feel like Odette was rubbing her legendary fearlessness in everyone's faces. When they looked at Odette, they all knew it was time to feel scared. They battled with the urge to shake her until she came to her senses and was as frightened as they were.

The lobby welcomed the Supremes, James, and Richmond with a blast of frigid air that made each of them sigh with relief. A pretty young hostess with bright red hair and an exaggerated English accent greeted the wedding guests at the reception desk. She said, "Good afternoon. We are delighted to have you here at Garden Hills Banquet Hall and Corporate Meetings Venue. Please follow the corridor to the doors that lead out to the courtyard for the Swanson-Abrams nuptials," and pointed out the way for them. Her instructions were accompanied by flamboyant arm waving. She wore a tight gray skirt and a very low-cut frilly white blouse. Her breasts jiggled with each of her grand movements. Richmond did an admirable job of staring at the ceiling instead of ogling the girl as his nature would surely have had him do. Clarice had to give the man an A for effort.

Unlike Richmond, who was going all out to prove that he was a changed man, Clarice wasn't certain what degree of exertion on her part was appropriate where her marriage was concerned. The new Clarice enjoyed having Richmond as her secret lover – she hadn't told her friends that he'd been spending nights with her. But the old Clarice, the one who knew all of the rules and yearned to follow them, had staged a reappearance. Somehow Clarice had gone from reveling in her newfound freedom and sensuality to feeling guilty about her vain pursuit of pleasure. She had even begun to take pride in sending Richmond away at the times she most wanted him to stay. Funny how easy it was to tap into all of that – the guilt, the shame, the anger. *You can take the girl out of Calvary Baptist, but you can't take Calvary Baptist out of the girl,* she thought.

At the end of the hallway, two young men in white uniforms stood stationed beside massive oak doors. When the Supremes, Richmond, and James approached, the men shoved open the doors, exposing a vast and spectacular courtyard. Second – possibly – only to Barbara Jean's prizewinning gardens, this was the most elaborately land-scaped property in town. Intricately sculpted evergreens lined the courtyard's redbrick walls. Lacy vines trailed from stone pots that sat atop pillars that had been distressed in the style of Roman ruins. Luridly bright flowers of every variety surrounded the wedding guests.

Barbara Jean grabbed Clarice's arm. "This is incredible. They must swap out these plants every week to keep them looking like this."

The garden was something to see, all right. Unfortunately, the direct sunlight that helped the flowers remain so beautiful was not greeted with much approval from the wedding guests. The sun beat down on them and, as more people arrived, their shared suffering soon became the number one topic of conversation. Erma Mae and Little Earl McIntyre stepped into the courtyard just behind the Supremes, both of them frantically fanning themselves with their hands. Erma Mae grumbled, "Outdoor weddin' in July. Your cousin's tryin' to kill us all, Clarice."

Erma Mae wore a violet straw hat that Clarice thought was cute. But that hat didn't provide a bit of shade to her great, round head. Erma Mae's cheeks and ears baked in the afternoon sun. She continued to curse Veronica as she and her husband headed to their seats.

To ensure Odette's comfort, James had been toting around an enormous insulated bag full of just-in-case supplies all summer. By the time the Supremes and their spouses had traveled down the brick path that divided the courtyard in half and seated themselves on creaky white wooden chairs, James had dug into the bag and pulled out five chilled bottles of water and a couple of battery-operated personal fans. He handed each of his friends a bottle of water and gave fans to Barbara Jean and Odette. In return, James received heartfelt thanks and an apology from Richmond for having teased him about carrying a purse for the past month.

Refreshed by the water and puffs of air from the tiny fans they passed back and forth to each other, Barbara Jean and Clarice ventured from their seats to take a closer look at the flowers. They took a few steps toward the nearest bed, but stopped when they were still about five feet away after discovering that they weren't the only admirers of the flowers. Dozens of bees floated from bloom to bloom in lazy arcs – a picturesque summer scene, best appreciated from a safe distance. When they discussed it later, they all agreed that the bees had been an omen.

The two uniformed employees who had opened the courtyard doors for the guests reappeared, each carrying an oscillating electric floor fan. When they placed the fans in opposing corners of the rectangular seating area and turned them on, the crowd burst into applause. The effect was mostly psychological, though. Humid hundred-degree air was still humid hundred-degree air, even with a two-mile-per-hour gust behind it. But the slightest of breezes was cause for celebration on that day.

The tiresome elevator music that had been piped in via speakers placed throughout the flower beds stopped. The redhead who had greeted everyone at the front door entered the courtyard and asked the crowd to be seated in order that the service might begin. James glanced at his watch and nodded his approval. "Right on time."

The speakers blasted out music again. This time it was Pachelbel's Canon in D. Clarice muttered to herself, "How unimaginative can you get." Then she admonished herself for being mean.

The large oak doors opened again and Reverend Biggs stepped through. He was followed by Clifton Abrams and his groomsmen – Clifton's shoe freak brother Stevie and two shifty-eyed, scowling young men. The groomsmen slouched in their ill-fitting, rented tuxedoes with matching green cummerbunds and emerald bowties beneath a bridal arch that was covered in chartreuse carnations. Behind them, a fountain in the shape of a gigantic fish spat water high into the sticky air.

Odette leaned toward Clarice and said, "Is this a wedding party or a police lineup?" Clarice responded, "You are just awful," even though she had been thinking the same thing.

The doors opened again and Veronica's mother walked out on the arm of her favorite granddaughter's husband, a heavyset young man who stopped every few seconds to wipe perspiration from his eyes with his free hand. Glory's green dress wasn't very flattering, but she seemed unaffected by the heat. In fact, she looked far healthier and cheerier than when Clarice had last seen her. Glory and Clarice's mother, who was boycotting Plainview until Clarice left "that Unitarian cult" she had joined, hadn't spoken in several weeks due to yet another theological spat. From the looks of things, not talking to Beatrice had been good for Glory. There was, Clarice thought, a lesson to be learned in that.

Minnie McIntyre strutted down the aisle after Glory. In keeping with the color scheme of the wedding, Minnie wore a kelly green suit, making it the first time in months she had been seen in anything other than one of her fortune-telling outfits. She slowly walked, unescorted, down the brick path toward her chair in the front row. On her way, she acknowledged acquaintances in the crowd with a slight dipping of her head. She frowned each time she did it. It was clear to all spectators that her signature move was unsatisfying to her without her turban and bell.

The groom's parents, Ramsey and Florence Abrams, came next. Ramsey grinned as if he were filming a tooth-paste commercial. Florence smiled, too, though it was difficult to tell with her. For years, Florence had twisted her facial features into an expression more suggestive of having encountered an unpleasant odor than experiencing joy. The muscles responsible for smiling had atrophied long ago. However, her customary pained smirk seemed to be less agonized than usual that day.

Just after Ramsey and Florence were seated, the music changed to Handel's "The Arrival of the Queen of Sheba," which had been Clarice's suggestion for use as the bridal march. Veronica appeared.

Clarice was forced to admit that Veronica looked nice. Green wasn't a good color for anyone else in the wedding party so far, but it looked good on her. Veronica smiled, waved, and occasionally mouthed hello to guests as she proceeded down the aisle with her jerky, fast gait. When she passed Clarice, Veronica made a show of pointing her chin toward the sky to remind her cousin that she had not forgotten the clash they'd had on Veronica's backyard deck when Clarice passed along the story of catching Clifton in a compromising position with another woman.

Veronica's grand procession was marred by a sudden outburst when she was nearly at her seat. Florence Abrams began to scream and run back and forth in front of the bridal arch. No one could hear what she was yelling at first. But the cause of the commotion became evident when Florence ran past Reverend Biggs, who was outfitted with a lapel microphone. She yelled, "I'm stung. I'm stung!" and she clutched her left forearm where a bee had just stung her. A few seconds later, Florence was down on the ground, still screaming. It was very frightening because everyone who knew Florence at all well knew that she was severely allergic to bee stings.

Ramsey promptly fetched his wife's EpiPen injector from her pocketbook and administered a shot of epinephrine so Florence wouldn't choke on her tongue in front of three hundred wedding guests. After tending to his wife, he walked over to Reverend Biggs and shouted into the pastor's lapel that they'd been through this many times before and that Florence would be just fine. Florence remained on the ground for a while, though, until the injection took effect. All anyone could see of her was her feet sticking out from a bed of sky-blue phlox.

Odette leaned across Clarice, who had the aisle seat, in order to get a better look. Always immune to hysteria, Odette said, "I sure do like her shoes."

To a round of applause, Florence was hauled up from the ground and helped back into her seat. Then the reverend, groom, and groomsmen took their places and the speakers came to life again, blasting out a loud drumroll.

The doors opened and suddenly the scent of lavender overwhelmed the fragrance of the flowers. Out came the pink cloud. It wasn't quite the round, cottony ball it had appeared to be in the brochure advertising the Cloud Nine Wedding Package. Because of the fans blowing on it, the cloud looked more like an undulating blob of fiberglass insulation, tendrils of which flailed threateningly in the hot air and then evaporated.

One at a time, Sharon's sisters filed out of the fog. Each of them wore the same neon-green crushed-velvet dress with balloon sleeves and puffy bows ringing the waistline. Only Veronica would conspire to make those homely young women wear such terrifying monstrosities. Watching the bridesmaids lumber down the aisle, Clarice thought, *I know I can't be the only one here thinking "Gorillas in the Mist."*

The bridesmaids were followed by the flower girl, Veronica's nine-year-old granddaughter, Latricia. Veronica had chosen Latricia because she was the prettiest of her three granddaughters and consequently her favorite. Clarice had tried, as diplomatically as she could, to talk Veronica out of that decision. Latricia was a cutie, but no one would ever accuse her of being the least bit intelligent. Latricia's flower girl technique amounted to running several quick steps, then stopping suddenly. Every time she stopped, she dug her hand deep into the green toile-covered wicker basket she carried, took out a fistful of green carnation petals, and flung them as hard as she could directly into the face of whoever sat nearest to her. She kept this up until her mother, the matron of honor, bellowed, "Latricia, cut it out! Now!" Latricia completed her walk at a steady pace. But along the way, she glared at the wedding guests and stuffed flower petals into her mouth.

Odette said, "That is not a bright child."

A trumpet fanfare began and Reverend Biggs raised his

arms to let the guests know that they should stand for the entrance of the bride. Sharon emerged from the pink cloud on the arm of her father, Clement.

Her appearance was greeted with oohs and ahhs from the guests.

"My goodness, she's so thin I wouldn't have recognized her. She looks adorable," Barbara Jean said.

It was true. Sharon looked divine. With the aid of her hypnotist, Sharon had wiped fifty pounds off her figure in just a few months. The gown her mother had purchased several sizes too small for her now fit perfectly. Though Clarice had sworn to herself that, as a part of her new life, she had given up on diets forever, she couldn't help but think that when she and Veronica started speaking again she would have to ask for that hypnotist's phone number.

The trumpet music ended and a syrupy, string-heavy tune began to stream from the speakers as the doors closed behind Sharon and her father. A few steps beyond the pink cloud, Sharon slowly raised her bouquet to her veil-covered face and began to sing "We've Only Just Begun" into a microphone that was hidden among her flowers.

The song was clearly a Veronica touch, Clarice thought. A girl of Sharon's age would never have chosen an old Carpenters' song, popular long before her birth, to sing at her wedding. And Sharon certainly wasn't singing it as if it were a personal favorite. All around the courtyard, people squirmed in their seats and grimaced in response to the bride's voice. The newly slimmed Sharon may have looked like an angel in her ivory-colored, form-fitting bridal gown, but she sang like a screeching demon freshly released from the deepest pit of hell. Clarice thought, *Why, oh why, didn't Veronica spring for a few voice lessons in addition to Sharon's hypnosis?*

Right on cue, a dozen white Bostonian doves fluttered away from a cage hidden behind the spitting fish fountain as Sharon wailed, "A kiss for luck and we're on our way." About ten feet up in the air, the doves formed a circle and flew in formation in response to whistled cues from the bird wrangler, who crouched behind one of the taller pseudo-Roman pillars. The effect was impressive enough to draw scattered applause.

Unfortunately, that impressive moment didn't last long. As Sharon caterwauled her way toward her groom, a dark blur appeared overhead and streaked toward the doves. In a scene reminiscent of *Mutual of Omaha's Wild Kingdom*, an enormous gray-and-brown falcon snatched one of the doves away from the formation and zipped off with it clasped in its talons. The dove wrangler began frenzied tooting, presumably calling the other eleven birds back to their cage. But the doves kept flying higher. They had already sensed the arrival of the second hawk. It descended upon them an instant later and reduced their number to ten.

The remaining birds, shrieking loudly, returned to their trainer. He secured them inside a large cage and then hustled them away from the courtyard. The location of the two missing doves was made clear to the assemblage by the twin streams of white feathers that lazily drifted down from a tall maple tree just on the other side of the wall. Occasionally a feather floated onto the courtyard and was struck by the red light of the laser that spelled out "Sharon and Clifton," imbuing the white feathers with an eerie, bloody-looking tinge.

Shocked, Sharon gave up on her vocalizing and walked the rest of the way down the aisle with her father to the sound of the instrumental accompaniment of the song.

Reverend Biggs tried to get things back on track. He began his homily with a brief reference to the circle of life. Then he artfully segued into his prepared speech.

But, like so many things that day, the reverend's remarks went unfinished. Not long after Reverend Biggs began speaking, the big oak doors creaked open once again. All of the guests turned their faces toward the back, hoping they might feel the sweet breath of cool air escaping from the indoors for a moment. No one got any relief from the heat, but they did get another look at the pink cloud. Then they saw four uniformed policemen step through the fog and onto the brick path. The policemen appeared to be embarrassed when the doors shut behind them and they realized that hundreds of wedding guests sat staring at them. The policemen moved off to one side, trying to make themselves less conspicuous. But they'd been seen, and their effect was immediate.

One of the groomsmen shouted, "It's the cops, man!" Then he and the unsavory-looking character next to him took off running. The groomsmen leaped over shrubs and bushes, finally escaping the courtyard through an emergency exit. Opening that door activated an alarm, and the thick air was filled with shrill screeching. Clarice turned toward her friends and said, "I don't know about you, but I prefer this to the singing." Odette and Barbara Jean nodded in agreement.

The police didn't make a move to pursue the grooms-men. They stared directly at the groom. Clifton Abrams responded to their attention by shoving Reverend Biggs out of his way and running through the tea roses and across a perennials bed. He made a dash for a clematis-covered trellis that stood against an outer wall. Once there, he began to climb. The police chased after him. They grabbed him by his ankles before he could make it over the wall and wrestled him down into a patch of black-eyed Susans.

Florence Abrams let out a loud cry and fainted. She crumpled to the ground so that, once again, all that could be seen of her was her feet sticking out of the phlox bed. Clarice said, "You're right, Odette, those really are cute shoes."

The policemen handcuffed Clifton and carried him out. Sharon followed them, howling, "Clifton! Clifton!"

Little Latricia skipped along after Sharon, tossing green petals high into the air.

Odette said, "They really should get that child some help."

Veronica let loose a stream of obscenities the likes of which none of the Supremes had heard since Odette's mother passed. Veronica cornered Minnie McIntyre near the bridal arch and made quite a scene shouting about the faulty information her oracle had provided. She yelled, "Where's my perfect day, dammit?!" Veronica's husband and daughters had to restrain her while Minnie escaped, running into the pink cloud after the cops, the groom, the bride, and the flower girl.

Rather than stick around Garden Hills for canapés and

quiet gossip, Odette, Barbara Jean, and Clarice decided to adjourn to the All-You-Can-Eat for ribs and loud gossip. They stuck around just long enough for James to put on his law enforcement hat and get the lowdown from one of the cops who had arrested Clifton. Then they walked to their cars in silence, each of them trying to digest what they had just witnessed.

They were in the parking lot when Barbara Jean interrupted the quiet that had fallen over the group, saying, "Well, that just goes to show you what happens when you don't have a church wedding. It was bound to end badly."

Clarice said, "No, that's what happens when you're foolish enough to listen to Minnie McIntyre's advice."

James said, "No, that shows you what happens when the groom is dumb enough to mail a wedding invitation to his pissed-off ex-girlfriend when she knows he has outstanding felony warrants for drug possession and grand larceny in Louisville. The detective said some girl named Cherokee walked into the police station last night waving the invitation in the air and saying, 'If you'd like to apprehend a fugitive felon, I know where he'll be tomorrow at three.'"

Clarice stopped where she was standing and began to laugh. She said, "I feel sorry for Sharon, I really do. But I've been holding in a giggle ever since Florence got stung by that bee."

The floodgates opened. Barbara Jean joined Clarice, laughing so hard that she cried. Richmond chuckled into one hand and held his stomach with the other.

They all stopped laughing when they noticed that Odette had slumped against James. The two of them slowly sank down onto the hot pavement. Odette appeared to be only half-conscious. And James looked even more stricken than she did as he cried out her name.

Clarice and Barbara Jean rushed to Odette's side and saw that her eyes were flickering open and shut. Before she completely lost consciousness, Odette mumbled something that they could have sworn was "Back off, Mrs Roosevelt."

Chapter 35

I was on my feet hooting and howling and preparing to lie about feeling sorry for Veronica when the air around me turned to milky water. Then I was sitting on the asphalt. Everyone except for Mama and Mrs Roosevelt, who both popped up just as the air went to liquid, began to move in slow motion and fade away. I told Mrs Roosevelt to back off, but she cast sorrowful puppy eyes at me and moved closer.

Then I was in the ICU. For six days I lay there, not exactly awake and not exactly asleep. I wasn't in pain. I wasn't frightened. And Lord knows I wasn't lonely, not with the constant stream of guests who came and went – James, my pastor, the other Supremes and Richmond, my doctor, nurses, to mention a few. And that was just the living. Sometimes the room was packed to bursting with Mama, Eleanor Roosevelt, Big Earl, Miss Thelma, and other friends from the spirit world.

Mostly, I felt tired and blazing hot, hotter than I had ever been when I'd had those bad night sweats at the start of my illness. I had a powerful urge to shake off my tired body like it was a heavy, scratchy wool coat and walk away from it feeling light and cool.

Sometimes the air around me would clear and I'd

mumble a few words. Always James was there to respond. He'd grin down at me in my bed and say, "Hey there. I knew you'd come back," and then we'd exchange a few words. But the flood would come again and he'd suddenly be unable to hear what I was saying to him even though I was shouting at the top of my lungs. Whenever that happened, Eleanor Roosevelt would frown and cover her ears and Mama would say, "Stop all that yellin'. You'll wake the dead." Then, each time she made that joke, she'd giggle like it was the first time she'd said it.

On my first day in the hospital, I learned from listening in as Dr Alex Soo talked to James that, for the first time in months, cancer wasn't my most serious health problem. I was suffering from an infection. My heart and lungs were distributing sickness throughout my body and the antibiotics weren't halting it. I was, in Alex's words, "gravely ill."

The rooms in the Intensive Care Unit formed a square around a large nurses' station. Every room was the same: one bed, one chair, one window on the outside wall, three inner walls made of glass. Unless the curtains that lined the walls of each room were pulled shut, I could see into every room in the ICU. I didn't need to peek to know who lay in the other beds, though. My neighbors were up and about every bit as much as they were in their beds. The lady confined to the bed next door to mine regularly left her physical self behind and roamed the corridors performing elaborate dances with a fan of white ostrich plumes. The ancient man across the way from me withered away as a ventilator breathed for him. But I also saw him as a broad-chested, yellow-haired fisherman who politely tipped his lure-covered cap at his fan-dancing neighbor whenever he passed by her on the way to his secret fishing hole. They stepped out of their diseased or broken bodies and had a good old time until they were drawn back to their flesh by a rush of hormones or some medication that suddenly kicked in.

I only left my body behind when I slept. When I was truly asleep, not just incapacitated by sickness or floating in a fever dream, I always traveled to the same place. I relaxed, alone, at the foot of my sycamore in Leaning Tree. Leaving that spot, with its view of the silvery creek I'd played in as a child and the twisted trees that bordered Wall Road, and returning to ghosts and grief in my hospital room was the hardest part of those six days.

I learned from those days in the hospital that if you really want to hear the secret details of people's lives, all you need to do is lapse into a coma. It's like opening up a confessional booth and inviting all comers. People kept showing up and telling me things that they couldn't bring themselves to tell me when I was responsive.

Clarice started the confession ball rolling when she stopped by on my second day in the hospital. She walked into my room all full of optimistic chitchat. She told James about people she'd known who had recovered after being in far worse condition than I was in, and she went on about how she was sure I'd be up and about in time to accompany her and Barbara Jean to New York City when she went to play for the record producer there. Then she took a good look at James, baggy-eyed and haggard, and ordered him to go to the cafeteria for something to eat. As soon as he was gone, she sat on the edge of my bed and confided that she was sleeping with Richmond again.

Barbara Jean and I had long since figured that one out, but Clarice was having such a nice time with her secret that we didn't want to ruin it for her by letting on that we knew. Unfortunately, Clarice had made the mistake of talking to her mother about it. Now Mrs Jordan had Clarice worried that she was headed for hell. Her mother put it in her head that having sex with her own husband while refusing to be his wife in any other way was the height of wantonness.

Clarice said, "Maybe I should just go back home. I love being on my own in Leaning Tree, but it can't be that simple, can it – just doing what you want because it feels good? Mother always says, 'Happiness is the first sign you're living wrong.'"

Mama, listening in, said, "I've always liked Clarice, but right now I wanna slap the shit outta her. Don't she know how lucky she is, havin' that good-lookin' man at her beck and call like she does? She needs to stop this damn whinin' and get to work on a how-to book. There's about a billion women who'd pay good money to learn how they could be in her position. Your father was a good man, but if I coulda had him when I wanted him and then sent him away when I'd had my fill, I'd have been too busy thankin' Jesus to worry whether I was committin' a sin. Poor Clarice, that mother of hers did a real number on her."

Considering the peculiarity of Mama's legacy to me, that struck me as the pot calling the kettle black; but, out of respect, I didn't say so.

Clarice also confessed to trying to outdo my daughter Denise's wedding when she planned her own daughter's ceremony more than ten years ago. She said the guilt had been preying on her mind ever since she'd started helping

Veronica put together that mess of a wedding for poor Sharon. If I could've, I'd have sat up and said, "Tell me something I don't know, why don't ya?" Then I'd have said, "We've been together too long to worry over trivial shit like that, sister. Forget about it."

Richmond came by later that same day and showed that side of him that made Clarice, and so many other women, melt in his presence. He rattled off jokes and stories until he coaxed a genuine smile from James. Then, just the way Clarice had done, Richmond practically tossed James out of the room, insisting that he go get some dinner.

Once we were alone, Richmond got to confessing. And, let me tell you, when Richmond Baker started listing the whos, whats, and wheres of the wrongs he'd done, he drew quite a crowd. The dead, Mama and Mrs Roosevelt, and the almost-dead, my colleagues from other beds in the ICU, couldn't get enough of him. They bellowed with laughter and giggled from embarrassment as Richmond confided some of the carnal sins he'd committed. Mama was quieter than I could ever remember seeing her, uttering only the occasional "Oh my." Mrs Roosevelt pulled a bag of popcorn out of her oversized black alligator pocketbook and munched away like she was at a Saturday matinee. Every now and then someone grunted in disapproval, but they all stuck around to hear every single word of it.

When Richmond was done telling a string of the dirtiest tales I'd ever heard, he stroked my hand and told me that he couldn't imagine the world without me, which touched my heart. Then one last confession. He told me that he'd been terrified of me for years, which made me even happier.

He finished up by talking about Clarice. He went on about how he was so in love with her and how he didn't think he could go on living if she didn't come back home. "I love her so much, Odette. I don't know why I do the stuff I do. Maybe it's an addiction, like alcohol or cocaine."

Mama thought the addiction theory sounded like an excuse. She'd never had patience for what she called "the navel-gazing of philanderers." Mama slapped the side of Richmond's head with the bong she'd been sharing with Mrs Roosevelt – he didn't feel it – and said, "Shut the hell up. You're not addicted. You're just a horndog, you stupid sonofabitch. Odette, tell him he's a dog and that he should just do the decent thing and carry a Victoria's Secret catalog into the bathroom and take care of business when that mood strikes, like every other God-fearing married man in America. Tell him, Odette."

Of course, I wasn't about to tell Richmond something like that, even if I could have. There are some things even I won't say.

It turned out that even the dead still had things to confess. On my third day in the hospital, Lester Maxberry visited me. Or rather, he came to watch Barbara Jean visiting me. He strolled into my room dressed in a spring walking suit that was the color of orange sherbet. His short pants were cut mid-thigh and he wore knee socks and suede espadrilles that were the same shade of light blue as his old Cadillac.

Barbara Jean sat in the visitor's chair while James sat on my bed beside me. The ICU allowed two visitors at a time but, oddly, provided just one chair per room. I did notice, though, when the fan dancer passed away surrounded by six family members, that they relaxed the two-visitor rule when they figured you were about to die. James and Barbara Jean talked about my condition, the weather, and the new volunteer job Barbara Jean had taken. She taught reading to poor kids from the tiny hill towns outside of Plainview. "There are so many more hours to the day when you stop drinking," she said.

While they talked, I took the opportunity to converse with Lester. I said, "Hey, Lester, you're looking sharp."

"Thanks, Odette. Clothes make the man, you know."

"Nope, it's the other way around, my friend. Have you been doing all right?"

Lester nodded, but he wasn't really paying any attention to me. He watched Barbara Jean with the same affection and longing he'd had for her when he was alive. "She's still the loveliest thing I've ever seen. And I've seen some amazing sights over these last eleven months."

"Has it been that long, Lester? I swear it seems like yesterday the six of us were together at the All-You-Can-Eat."

"Sneaks up on you, doesn't it? It's been almost a year." He continued staring at Barbara Jean. "I should never have married her."

"Why would you say that?" I asked.

"It wasn't right. She was practically a child and I was a grown man. I should've known better. Did know better. But when I saw that she was desperate because of the baby, I couldn't stop myself. I told myself it was okay because she'd come round to loving me over time."

"I'm pretty sure she did, Lester."

"Maybe, but mostly she was grateful. And gratitude's not a thing to build a marriage on. I was old enough to know that. She wasn't. Odette, I felt bad about that every day we were together, but it didn't stop me from holding on to her."

"Did you ever tell her that?"

He said, "No." Then he grinned at me. "But you can. The next time you talk to Barbara Jean, you can tell her I'm sorry, that I should have been stronger. Will you do that for me?"

Only someone as over-gentlemanly and overly moral as Lester Maxberry could let a thing like that eat away at him for decades. Any other man would say, "All's fair in love and war," and spend the rest of eternity bragging about how he'd managed to get the most beautiful girl in town to be his wife. I told Lester that I had it on good authority, both medical and ghostly, that I probably wouldn't be talking to Barbara Jean again in this life. But he kept at me until I promised I'd say something to her if I got the chance. Then he thanked me and went back to silently watching Barbara Jean.

The next morning, Chick Carlson dropped by and caused an even bigger fuss in the ICU than Richmond had. The nurses at the station, all full-grown women, fanned themselves and fell against each other in mock swooning after he walked by. When he came into my room, Mama eyed him up and down and nodded her approval. Even Mrs Roosevelt sat up straight and fluffed up her fox stole. Decades had passed, but Ray Carlson was still the King of the Pretty White Boys.

Chick gave my hollow-eyed, gaunt husband the once-over, and then did what all my friends had done. He badgered James into abandoning his vigil long enough to go get something to eat while Chick watched over me.

When James left, Chick sat in the visitor's chair and began to chat with my silent body. He started talking about the All-You-Can-Eat and Big Earl, all that stuff from the distant past. He'd been by my house several times over the months since he'd first visited with me in the chemo room, and every time he sat down with me he'd wanted to relive or analyze the old days. He was just as caged up in the past as Barbara Jean.

That day in the ICU, he also shared a tale with me that made me wish I could sit up right then and call Clarice on the phone. He told me all about how his tower project at the university had successfully released two rehabbed peregrine falcons just that previous Saturday. He described in beautiful detail how his birds had taken flight in front of news cameras and impressed donors. The birds, he said, were majestic and awe-inspiring.

I thought about the two hawks who had swooped in on Sharon's wedding that same Saturday and said to myself, "Majestic, awe-inspiring, and *hungry*."

Outside at the nurses' station, I heard one of the nurses saying, "Hi there, Mrs Maxberry." The staff all knew Barbara Jean from the many visits she had made to the ICU when Lester was in the hospital to have something removed, reattached, repaired, or replaced. When Barbara Jean entered my room, Chick hopped up like the seat of his chair had been electrified. They exchanged greetings and then stood there staring at each other. They were like teenagers at a school dance – both of them eager to say something, neither of them knowing how to say it.

Chick claimed that he'd just been leaving, even though he'd told James he would stay until James returned. He said, "It's nice to see you, Barbara Jean." Then, through my glass walls, I watched him walk past the giggling nurses on his way to the elevator. Every fifth or sixth step, he looked back over his shoulder for another glimpse of the most beautiful woman in town.

Barbara Jean sat in the empty visitor's chair and chewed her lip for a while, then she began to talk. The bedside confessional was open for business again.

"My sponsor, Carlo, says I need to talk to Chick. He says I need to make amends; it's one of the twelve steps. See, I did something terrible that I never told you about."

Then Barbara Jean told me a story about going to see Chick on the night of their son's funeral and how what she'd put in motion that night had eaten away at her soul for all the years since. When she got to the end of her story, she was crying hard. Her tears caused her makeup to streak and rain down onto her powder-blue blouse in brown and black droplets that she never made a move to clean up.

Just when you think the world can't hold any more surprises for you, I thought. Unlike most of the people I knew, I had never believed the rumor that it was Lester who'd shot Desmond Carlson. Even though Desmond had killed little Adam, Lester Maxberry couldn't have pulled that trigger. Former soldier or not, Lester was no killer. Truth was, I had always assumed it was Barbara Jean who'd done it, probably because that's what I would have done. Also, the way she'd fallen apart right after, with the drinking and all, she'd seemed as much guilt-ridden as grief-stricken. I had just misjudged where the guilt was coming from.

James came back as Barbara Jean attempted to put her face back together, cleaning up trails of mascara with a handful of tissues. Misreading the situation, my good James knelt on one knee beside my friend and patted her shoulder. He said, "Don't you worry, Barbara Jean. She'll pull through."

She stuffed the tissues back into her pocketbook and said, "I know she will. It all just gets to you sometimes." She pecked James on the cheek and left the room, making her way through the crowd of people, all invisible to her, who'd been eavesdropping on her conversation.

Mama wept as she watched Barbara Jean go. "All that pain. That part of livin' I surely don't miss."

I closed my eyes, though I can't really say for certain that they'd actually been open, and fell asleep. I journeyed again to Leaning Tree, the glistening creek, and my sycamore.

When I woke up, it was dark outside and James was snoring in the visitor's chair. Mrs Carmel Handy, the retired schoolteacher who'd once set her husband on the path to righteousness with the aid of a cast-iron skillet, stood at the foot of my bed. I was surprised to see her. I'd never had anything against Miss Carmel, but she hadn't had much use for me when I was a student in her classroom, and that hadn't changed in the decades that passed afterwards. But there she was, all dressed up, visiting me in the hospital. Then I saw her talking to

Mama and knew that Miss Carmel had taken the boat across to the other side.

I said, "Hello, Miss Carmel. I didn't know you'd passed. I would've sent a ham to your family, if I'd known."

"Just happened today. And, let me tell you, it came as quite a surprise. I was in the middle of cleaning up after supper and I came down with what I thought was a touch of indigestion. Next thing I knew I was getting up from the kitchen floor and my arthritis was gone and my real teeth were back. Then, something drew me right here. And now I know why. Listen, I have a small assignment for you."

The Skillet Lady came closer and whispered a message that she wanted delivered to James. Just like I'd explained to Lester, I told her that I probably wouldn't be talking to any living people again. But she got me to promise I'd try.

I slept and dreamed through the fifth morning – I was doing more of that every day. But I was aware of my kids' presence in my room that afternoon. Denise, Jimmy, and Eric walked in, all full of hope and good cheer. They updated James on the grandkids, their spouses, their lives. They did all the things I'd have wanted them to do to make their father feel better. I was so happy and proud that I used every bit of strength I had to swim up through the water and fog in my mind so I could thank them. It worked for a little while. I got out a few words – my only words to live people that whole day. But after I spoke each of their names aloud, I faded away again. Then my children's composure wilted like the straggly flowers of my garden. Eric's lip began to tremble. Jimmy started to sniffle. Denise's eyes leaked tears. My big boys each laid their heads on one of their sister's shoulders and sobbed. The spectacle was made even more heartbreaking by the fact that Jimmy and Eric had, respectively, seven and eight inches of height on Denise, so they had to crouch down to be comforted. This was the sight I had feared seeing. I was relieved when they dissolved into gray as I fell asleep again.

When I woke up, my room was filled with the warm light of the afternoon sun. It was also packed with people. James held my hand. He had such thick stubble on his face I wondered if maybe more than one day had passed while I slept. My three kids stood next to their father with their hands linked like they used to do when they crossed a street together as youngsters. Barbara Jean and Clarice were perched at the foot of my bed, both of them massaging my legs. Richmond and my brother, Rudy, stood behind Barbara Jean and Clarice with bowed heads. My pastor stood on the opposite side of the bed from James, reading from the Bible in a voice that sounded way too loud in the small space of my crowded hospital room. It was clear from the miserable expressions on everyone's faces and the fact that the nurses had suspended the two-visitor rule that all of these folks were there to say goodbye.

Beyond the ring of sniffling, praying people, my dead acquaintances gabbed without bothering to lower their voices. Among the chatting ghosts stood my father, fit and hardy in his sawdust-sprinkled coveralls. When Daddy realized that I was aware of my surroundings again, he made his way through the crowd to my bedside. He said, "Hey, sweetheart, I see you're back. You had a rough night, baby."

Lester, looking dashing in a rust-colored three-piece

suit and leaning on a gold walking stick, took his place next to Daddy then and said, "I hate to bother you, Odette, but I think maybe this might be a good time to talk to Barbara Jean like you said you would."

Daddy snapped, "This is hardly the time for her to be thinkin' about that, Lester."

Carmel Handy disagreed. "She made promises and she needs to keep them. That was one of the most important lessons I taught my students. *Honor your word.*"

Mama said, "If she's going to talk to anybody, I think she should start with that cheater." She pointed at Richmond. "I got my request in first."

They all started to argue. All those dead folks putting in their two cents about what I should or shouldn't do with the end of my life. Mrs Roosevelt was the only one who kept out of it. She just sat cross-legged atop a steadily beeping machine to the side of my bed and hummed to herself.

I tried to ignore them and concentrate on my own plans. During that last long nap, I'd been thinking about the way this endgame should play out. If I could work it right, these needy ghosts might get some satisfaction, too.

I had to wake up, completely, just for a little while. But that was a tall order. My body didn't want me anymore. The more I tried to wake up, the more my flesh tried to push me out. I wrestled and wrestled, latching on to every reviving thought I could muster. I reached way back and pictured Mama, young and brassy, shouting for me to get my ass out of bed for school. I smelled the bad coffee James distilled on cold mornings. I splashed my face with the frigid water from the creek behind Mama's garden. I thought about the one thing I wanted to do more than anything else and I tried to draw strength from it.

In front of me, a tiny pinpoint of clear air appeared in the haze. In my mind, I ran for that open spot and pulled at it with my fingers until I could stick my head through. Then I kicked and pushed back toward my old life while Lester, Miss Carmel, and Mama shouted out encouragement.

The first thing I said was "Everybody, shut up."

My pastor looked surprised and offended and stopped reading. I was actually talking to the dead people in the room, still fussing and yakking, but I didn't know how many words I had left in me, so I didn't waste them on the reverend's hurt feelings.

At the sound of my voice, creaky and hoarse, James shouted my name and started kissing my face.

Denise ran out and fetched Dr Soo. A few seconds later, Alex squeezed into the room with a nurse at his side and probed me with a cold stethoscope.

James said to the doctor, "See, I told you my girl wasn't done yet." But the frown on Alex's face as he reviewed my vital signs said that he didn't believe there was any need to celebrate.

The bucktoothed, tipsy Angel of Death agreed with the doctor. When we made eye contact, Mrs Roosevelt shook her head solemnly. Then she whispered, "It will happen today."

But she didn't need to warn me. I could see that milky water, thicker and darker than before, forming again at the edges of my vision. So I got down to business.

With a voice weak from not being used, I croaked out,

"James, you look terrible and you smell bad. Alive or dead, I won't have you going to seed. And listen, Carmel Handy is here and she wants you to know that she died yesterday."

"Day before," she corrected.

"Sorry, day before yesterday. She's on her kitchen floor. She wants you to talk to your cop friends and see to it that none of them start the rumor that she died with a skillet in her hand. She refuses to leave this world with people making jokes about her."

Of course, I knew full well that the time for Carmel Handy to worry about people joking was in the seconds before her skillet met the side of Mr Handy's head. But she seemed satisfied with what I'd said to James. She said, "Thank you, dear."

Now that I'd completed her assignment, I waited for her to leave. I figured once you did a ghost a favor they would fade away or maybe pop like a soap bubble that had been pricked with a pin. That was how it worked in the movies, at least. But Miss Carmel was no Hollywood ghost. She stayed put, looking relieved but excited about what might happen next.

Worried expressions spread around the room like a virus. James was frightened. His concerned gaze went back and forth from me to Alex Soo. "Sweetheart, did you say Carmel Handy is dead, *and* she's here?"

"Yes," I said. "I didn't want to worry you with it, but I've been seeing dead folks for a year now. I know it's probably not what you want to hear, but I think we both knew it might happen sooner or later."

From the back of the room, Mama hollered, "Hey,

Odette. Tell Richmond what I said about taking care of those urges!"

"Richmond, Mama says . . ." I stopped to think about what to tell him. I was not about to utter the words "carry a Victoria's Secret catalog into the bathroom" to Richmond Baker. I said, "Mama says you need a new hobby. She suggests you take up reading.

"And, Clarice, Mama also says you should count your blessings for having Richmond around to do the thing he's best at and not having to deal with the bullshit that comes along with living with him. Right now she wants to slap you, but I think she'll get past it if you promise to forget about what your mother says and just use Richmond till you use him up."

Clarice looked mortified, and it pleased me to see that I could still embarrass her after so many years. When she recovered enough to speak, she said, under her breath, "Barbara Jean, I think she's got brain damage."

"Call it brain damage if you need to, Clarice. Just do what Mama says, or we'll both haunt you."

I spoke more carefully to Barbara Jean. "Lester's here and he wants me to tell you something. He feels bad that he got you to marry him when he knew you didn't love him. He says it wasn't right and he should've done better by you since he was so much older. He's asking you to forgive him."

Barbara Jean didn't look the least bit surprised or upset by what I'd said. I knew that she was worried about me, but I could also see that she still wore the remnants of the despair I'd seen on her face two days earlier when she'd talked to me about Chick and his brother Desmond. And

I supposed that, after the haunting she'd gone through over the years, a message from her dead husband was nothing.

Barbara Jean said, "Tell Lester he was good to me . . . to us. He's got nothing to feel bad about. I'm glad I married him."

Lester let out a sigh. He tipped his hat to me and then, like Miss Carmel, sat watching.

James said, "So, you say you've been seeing dead folks for a year?"

"Just about," I answered.

Big Earl, Miss Thelma, and Daddy yelled out in unison, "Tell James we said hey."

I relayed the message. "Daddy, Big Earl, and Miss Thelma all say hey."

James twisted his mouth and rubbed at the scar on his face, the way he often did when he was deep in thought. No doubt he was remembering Mama and her endless public conversations with dead folks. But my James is as adaptable as any of those bowing trees along Wall Road. The frown melted from his face and he nodded his head. "Okay then." Addressing the room, he called out, "Hey, Pop Jackson. Hey, Big Earl and Miss Thelma."

James never ceases to amaze me.

I felt like I was drifting away again and I forced myself to breathe deep and concentrate on staying in this world a little while longer. When I got a second wind, I spoke again, my voice even fainter and hoarser than before. "Now I'd like to have a little family time. Reverend, Alex, nurse, would you mind giving us some privacy?"

They didn't look pleased about it, but they cleared out

like I asked. After they left the room, I said, "The rest of y'all can go, too," talking to the ghosts. But only Lester and Miss Carmel complied. Lester performed a low, courtly bow and then offered Miss Carmel his arm. She wrapped her hand around his elbow and walked toward the door with him. As they left the room, I heard her say, "Lester, did I ever tell you that your wife was born on my davenport?"

I talked to Rudy and my children. "I need y'all to do something." When they stepped forward, I said, "I need you to take my husband home and make sure he's fed and bathed."

James shook his head no. "I'm not leaving you."

I said, "James, I promise you won't come back here and find me dead." I could see that he was mulling it over, wanting to believe me. For insurance, I issued commands to Rudy and my giant sons. "Carry him out if you have to, but take him home."

Eric, Jimmy, and Rudy glanced at each other and then at James, wondering what to do. James let them off the hook, like I thought he would. He said, "Okay, I'll go home and get cleaned up. But I'm coming right back." He said to the Supremes, "Call me if anything happens." Then he kissed my forehead and left with Denise, Jimmy, Eric, and Rudy.

"Clarice, I want you to pick up a couple things for me. I want you to get that violet housecoat you gave me last Christmas from my bedroom chest of drawers. I'd have asked James, but Lord knows what he'd bring back. And I also would kill for a piece of Little Earl's peach cobbler. Would you run by the All-You-Can-Eat and get me a piece?"

Thrilled to think that my appetite had returned, she said, "Sure, I'll go." Then, to Barbara Jean, "I won't be long."

When Clarice was gone, I said to Barbara Jean, "I've got one thing to say to you, Barbara Jean, and it's not coming from any dead person. It's coming straight from me. You need to go see Chick. And not just for the 'making amends' stuff." Her mouth dropped open then as she realized that I had heard and remembered the things she'd said to me a couple days earlier while I was swimming around in that world between worlds.

She wrung her hands for a moment and then, recovering, said, "I'll talk to him soon. I promise. I've just been waiting till I'm strong enough."

"Go now. And after you've settled the past, deal with the here and now. It's time to see how this thing between you and Chick is supposed to play out, once and for all."

Barbara Jean said, "It's too late for any of that, Odette. Years and years too late."

The dead people in the room with us piped up, yelling that I should tell my friend she was wrong. It was never too late, not until you've passed out of this life and maybe not even then.

I told Barbara Jean, "My mama and daddy and Big Earl and Miss Thelma all say you're wrong." I left out Eleanor Roosevelt because I knew the mention of her would tilt the whole thing from eerie and otherworldly right over into crazy. Then, just like I'd played the cancer card to send her off to AA, now I played the dying card. "Barbara Jean, you've got to talk to Chick and set it all straight. Lay every bit of it out in the sunlight, the whole truth. I won't rest in peace unless you do this one last thing for me." I was shameless.

Barbara Jean tugged and twisted the fabric of the loose skirt she was wearing as she sat thinking at the far end of my bed. For a while, I wondered if she still might refuse. Then she walked over to me and kissed my forehead. "Okay, I'll go." She didn't sound eager, but she did at least seem resigned to doing what I'd asked. And that was enough. When she left, Mama, Daddy, and the McIntyres accompanied her, pressed close to her sides like they were propping her up.

I was alone then with Richmond Baker and Mrs Roosevelt.

Richmond rocked back and forth on his heels, looking like he'd rather be anywhere else on the face of the earth at that moment. He said, "Listen, why don't I go get the doctor for you." Then he moved toward the door.

"No, Richmond. I need you to stay."

Eleanor Roosevelt whipped out her popcorn bag again, preparing to hear more juicy stuff from Richmond.

He slumped back in my direction. "Odette, I don't know how much of the stuff I said the other day you remember, but let me just say that I know I've been a bad husband, and maybe I've been a bad friend, too. Can I just tell you I'm sorry for everything and leave it at that? You don't have to tell me what *they* say." He looked around the room like he was expecting floating white sheets to emerge from the walls and shout "Boo!"

With the little bit of voice I had left, I said, "Oh, for God's sake, Richmond. I don't want to talk to you. I just want your muscles. I need you to close the door and all the curtains. And then, when I get these tubes out of me, I need you to grab that wheelchair out in the hallway, bring it in here, and help me get in it. Then you can take me to your car. And if anybody tries to stop you, I need you to be big, black, and scary."

A loud sigh of relief escaped Richmond when he realized that I hadn't kept him around so the two of us could have a heart-to-heart. As he reached for the curtains that were clustered in one corner of the room, he said, "Thank God. I just about pissed my pants wondering what you and your ghosts might come up with next."

Chapter 36

It wasn't until Barbara Jean walked the short distance
from the hospital to the tower where Chick worked and
saw the puzzled, slightly alarmed expression on the face of
the young woman at the reception desk that she remembered what she was wearing. When James called that
morning, she had just gotten dressed for a volunteer shift
pretending to churn butter in front of a busload of school-
children in the Plainview Historical Society Museum's
frontier farmhouse re-creation. James had hardly been
able to get the words out, but he told Barbara Jean that
Odette's doctor had said she was too weak to fight off the
infection. She wasn't expected to live through the day.
Without changing clothes, Barbara Jean headed straight
over to the hospital as soon as she hung up the phone.
Now, hours later, she followed the receptionist's directions
to the elevator through a maze of workstations and found
herself on the receiving end of even more curious looks.
People swiveled around in their desk chairs to watch her
pass by in her high-collared blouse, long gingham skirt,
and tight, pointy-toed leather boots.

The ground floor of the tower was so cluttered with
small work cubicles, file cabinets, and tall shelving units
that the round shape of the building was completely

obscured. But when Barbara Jean stepped out of the elevator, the space she entered was as different from the first floor as it could have been. The fifth floor of the tower was one large open room with a fourteen-foot ceiling that was supported by massive rough-cut wooden beams. The tall windows that dominated the exposed brick walls allowed in so much afternoon sunlight that she had to squint for a moment so that her eyes could adjust to the brightness.

She saw a long wooden desk at the far end of the room. It was very old and a little beaten-up, but freshly waxed. Behind the desk, which was crowded with stacks of books, Ray Carlson stopped shuffling papers when he caught sight of her.

Two beautiful and haughty peregrine falcons scrutinized Barbara Jean from inside their large cages as she passed by them on her way to Chick. The plank flooring creaked beneath her old-fashioned boots with each step, providing an accompaniment to the soft rustling noises of the birds flexing their wings and moving along their perches.

Chick stood and came around the desk to greet her. "Hi, Barbara Jean. This is a nice surprise." A quizzical expression crossed his face as he looked her up and down, taking in her anachronistic outfit.

She saw him staring and said, "I'm supposed to be pretending to churn butter."

He had no idea what she was talking about, but he nodded as if what she said had made sense.

For several awkward seconds, Barbara Jean stood in front of Chick regretting that she hadn't rehearsed something to say to him during her walk from the hospital. She was struck now with a strong urge to run back to the elevator. But she thought about the promise she had made and, instead of running away, looked directly into Chick's eyes, hoping the force that had always moved her to give voice to her feelings when she was near him, whether or not she should, would take over. She said the first thing that came to mind: "Odette—"

He put his hand to his heart and interrupted her. "Is she gone?"

"No, no, she's not gone. She's awake, even speaking. But she's saying some strange stuff."

He smiled. "Well, being that it's Odette we're talking about, saying strange stuff could be a good sign."

"Maybe, maybe not. Her doctor was sure she wouldn't make it through the day and I don't think he's changed his mind."

"I hate to hear that," he said. "Well, let's hope she surprises him." He gestured toward two high-backed, copper-colored leather chairs that sat facing his desk. "Would you like to sit down?"

She answered, "Yes, thank you," but her feet carried her past the chairs and on toward one of the tall windows instead. Chick followed her and stood by her side, so close that their arms almost touched.

From the window, Barbara Jean could see the hospital where Odette lay. She thought about Odette, and she tried to draw strength from imagining how her brave friend would approach this. Odette would get right to it, Barbara Jean thought. So she did the same.

She said, "I'm an alcoholic, just like my mother was. It's a struggle, but I haven't had a drink in a while." That was something she hadn't meant to say, something she had never said outside of an AA meeting. But, after it had been said, it felt like as good a way to start as any.

He furrowed his brow, as if he were searching for the proper response to what she had just blurted out. He settled on "Congratulations. I know how hard that is."

"Thank you. I came to see you because they tell us at AA that we have to make a list of the people we've harmed and try to make amends."

His head jerked back a little and he looked confused. "You want to make amends? To me?"

Barbara Jean nodded. "I know how bad I hurt you and—"

He interrupted her again. "You don't need to feel bad about any of that, Barbara Jean. You were just a kid. We both were." He paused. "And we were in love."

"That's what makes it worse, Ray. That's the thing I used to think about when I sat up at night drinking. I knew you loved me, or at least that you had loved me once upon a time, and I used that. I think maybe I could have gotten past the guilt if I'd done the honest thing and shot Desmond myself. But, instead, I took your love for me and I twisted it to make you pull the trigger. Now, both of us have had to live with it. I can't even imagine what that must have done to you."

Chick remained silent. His only response was to slowly shake his head back and forth.

Barbara Jean wondered why she wasn't crying or shouting, or something. Lord knows she felt as if she were bursting at the seams. But at the same time, she was strangely calm. Well, not calm, she thought. More like purposeful. She could feel something, or someone, willing her on. She imagined voices whispering in her ear saying that every word she spoke was moving her incrementally closer to a place she wanted to be.

She went on. "According to the twelve steps, making amends shouldn't injure the person you've harmed. So I hope and pray that saying this and dredging it all up again doesn't hurt you more. It's just that I want you to know that I'm sorry for what I made you do. And if there's a way I can make it up to you, I'd like to."

Chick's shoulders slumped and his face looked weary. In a tone of voice that sounded as if he were apologizing, he said, "I didn't kill Desmond."

His words took a moment to register and, when they did, Barbara Jean still couldn't accept them. She found herself focusing on his eyes again. She felt sure that, even after all of the years that had passed, she could still read the truth there if she stared hard enough.

It was there, all right. Her throat went dry and she brought her hand to her mouth to smother an escaping gasp. She whispered, "Oh Lord, you're telling the truth."

She took a few steps and fell into the chair he had offered her earlier. Part of Barbara Jean accepted that what Chick had said was true. But another, maybe stronger, piece of her had memorized every second of the morning the police had taken her and Lester to Desmond Carlson's place. That memory, as vivid to her that afternoon as it had been decades earlier, made her mistrust anything that threatened to alter the script of the movie she had played over and over in her head for years.

She said, "But I saw feathers from those birds in the

cages at your house. They were all over the ground at Desmond's place that day. Gray, white, and red feathers. There was nothing that looked like that just flying around town. You had to have been there."

Chick came away from the window then and slid the other leather chair closer to hers so that, when he sat, their knees were just inches apart. The room had grown warmer since she had arrived, the air-conditioning unable to compete with the July sun, but her hands had gone icy. They trembled as if she had laid them onto the surface of the frozen river in her dreams. Chick surprised Barbara Jean by reaching out and pressing her cold fingers between his warm palms.

Speaking quietly and slowly, Chick said, "I was there. But I didn't kill him. I went over to see Desmond late that night after you left my house. I didn't really know what I was going to do. In my mind I pictured strangling him with my bare hands. But when I got to Desmond's place, he was already dead on the porch with his rifle lying beside him. I don't know for sure what happened, but his girlfriend Liz's father walked up to me at Desmond's funeral and bragged right to my face that he'd shot Desmond for beating Liz one time too many. He was falling-down drunk when he said it, so maybe it was true, maybe not. My brother spread a lot of misery in his life, and a long list of people wanted him dead. I suppose it's even possible that Desmond did it himself, like the police decided. But I doubt it.

"All I can tell you for sure is that what you believed . . . Well, that's what I hoped you'd believe. I thought maybe that way you wouldn't hate me, maybe you would believe I'd done at least that one thing for our son."

Barbara Jean sat frozen in the leather chair, going over what he had just said. She sat motionless for so long that Chick asked her if she was all right and offered to go get some water for her. She said, "I'm fine, Ray." But in her mind, she was trying to sort out her new role as an exonerated prisoner. What do you do when your cell door suddenly swings open? How do you embrace freedom when you've never known it? How do you forgive yourself for serving as your own jailer for three decades?

The easiest thing – and the smartest thing, she suspected – would have been to leave then. But being cut loose from the familiar ground of her guilt somehow made going further less scary.

She took a deep breath and said, "Odette told me I had to come talk to you and see how this thing between you and me is supposed to end. She said it was time to tell the whole truth, lay everything out in the sun once and for all. And she said Big Earl and Miss Thelma agreed with her."

Chick looked confused. "What?"

She continued without explaining. "Tomorrow I'll call my sponsor, Carlo, and I'll tell him about today. He'll probably say, 'Barbara Jean, you should have stopped at making amends. You can't trust what you're feeling right now. Years of drinking have pickled your brain and left you stuck where you were when you were a kid.' Or he might say that I'm like a lot of drunks, nostalgic for a sweet past I just imagine I lived.

"But Odette and Big Earl never led me wrong. And since I know the truth, I'm going to say it. That way I can go back over to the hospital and tell my friend that I did what she told me to do. And if that's the last thing I get to tell her, I think I'll be able to look back and not have any regrets. And believe me, I've learned about regret the hard way."

At that moment, Barbara Jean felt that it wasn't just Odette pushing her to talk. All of that ghost business must've gotten under her skin because the voices she had heard whispering in her ear from the time she walked into Chick's office were louder now. The voices encouraged her. "Tell it, girl." "Preach!" "Speak the truth and shame the devil." And Barbara Jean would have sworn on that Bible in her library that had been her companion and nemesis for so many years that one of those voices was Big Earl's.

She kept her eyes on Chick's handsome face and said, "Ray, I loved you that day I kissed you that first time in the hallway at the All-You-Can-Eat and I've never stopped. I loved you when I was sober and when I was drunk. I loved you when I was young and still love you now that I'm old. I thought it would change, or I'd grow out of it one day. But all these years later, after all kinds of people and things have come and gone in my life, that one fact, foolish or not, hasn't changed even the tiniest bit."

She stopped and, except for the occasional chirp or caw from the birds, the room was quiet. There was really nothing more to say. She let out the breath that she hadn't been aware she was holding.

While she talked, Chick had aimed his gaze downward and stared at the floor. Now he released her hands and slid his chair away from hers. As he got up and moved away from her, Barbara Jean told herself that it was fine, *she* was fine. She had done what she needed to do, what Odette had insisted she do. If it ended with this, with Chick stepping away from her, that was okay. At least this time they would part with the whole truth being the last thing spoken. What mattered was that she would know how the story ended, like Odette had said.

Barbara Jean lifted her eyes from the empty chair Chick had vacated. He had moved a few feet away and now stood just to the side of his desk. The afternoon sun blazing into the windows backlit him, turning him into a silhouette. She couldn't see his face. But she heard his voice, strong and exquisitely out of tune, when he opened his mouth and started singing.

"My baby love to rock, my baby love to roll. What she do to me just soothe my soul. Ye-ye-yes, my baby love me . . ." He sang louder and louder, gyrating his hips and pivoting around until he was wiggling his narrow rear in her direction.

She heard herself let out a howl that had been waiting too, too long to come out. She applauded, clapping her hands together until they ached, as Ray Carlson, King of the Pretty White Boys, swayed in the sun and danced the blues.

Chapter 37

By the time Richmond brought me to the house in Leaning Tree, I was holding on to just a tattered corner of the world of the living. I had used up all of the energy I had left in me explaining to Richmond what I needed him to do, and I spent most of the drive from the hospital resting my head against the car window, watching the scenery go by.

Throughout that short ride, I kept picturing James and how he was going to react when he found out I'd run off the moment I got the chance. He'd be good and mad at first. He would ask Richmond why he helped me do this foolish thing and Richmond would shrug those big shoulders of his and say, "She told me to." James would cuss, maybe even take a swing or two at his friend. But he'd think it over and forgive Richmond, eventually.

I hadn't exactly lied to James. I'd promised him he wouldn't come back to the hospital and find me dead. And that was the truth. He would be angry with me for a while, but then he'd admit to himself that I would have found a way to do what I wanted no matter what. And then he'd acknowledge that he couldn't have brought himself to help me do it. Yes, James would understand what I'd done. He couldn't stay married to me for thirty-five years without learning to roll with the punches. He might even laugh about it someday, maybe turn it into a funny story to entertain the grandkids with when they're older: "Hey, did I ever tell y'all about that last crazy thing your Grandma Odette did?"

Richmond helped me out of the car and into the wheelchair we'd borrowed from the hospital. When he wheeled me back behind the house we crossed paths with my father. Daddy looked up from the 1960s-style riding lawn mower he was tinkering with. He saw me and smiled. Then he wiped his hands on a red shop rag that was covered with black oil stains and he waved at me.

Richmond and I bumped along the cobblestone path that led past the gazebo. Clarice, bless her heart, had been good about taking care of Mama's garden. It looked better that year than it had in ages. The climbing roses that Mama had trained onto trellises and an arch were in full bloom. The pink and white flowers and rich green foliage provided shade for Aunt Marjorie, who sat under the arch smoking a cigar and sipping gold-colored liquor from a mason jar. She called out, "Hey, Dette." It cheered me to hear that wonderful, unique voice of hers again, that sound that made you imagine she gargled with pine tar and rock salt. But I didn't have time to say more than a quick hello to her. Richmond, a good soldier who knew a thing or two about breaking rules, was intent on accomplishing the mission I'd assigned to him. He quick-stepped behind my chair as fast as his bad ankle would allow.

When we got to the far end of the garden, where it was too over-grown for him to continue to push the wheelchair, Richmond stopped. He came to my side, slid one arm under my back and the other beneath my knees, and lifted me. Then he carried me up the hill toward my sycamore tree.

At the base of the tree, Richmond put me down with my back pressed against the warm bark of its trunk. He saw that I didn't have the strength to keep my head from falling forward, so he adjusted my position against the tree. Then he lifted my chin so I could look up into the branches and see the green leaves against a blue sky unbroken by a single cloud.

I thanked him, but he couldn't hear me.

I let go then of that little bit of the world I'd been holding on to. When hazy liquid flooded in from the corners of my vision, I didn't try to swim against it. I let the tide carry me up toward the branches of the tree where my mother had given birth to me after following a witch's advice so many years earlier.

"Hello, tree, my first cradle, my second mother, the source of my strength, the cause of my struggles. I'm back home."

I saw Mama then. She was wearing her best dress, the light blue one with embroidered yellow flowers and green vines. Her legs were crossed at the ankle, and she kicked her feet out in front of her like she was on a swing set. She shared her tree branch with Eleanor Roosevelt.

I breathed deep and inhaled the smell of the soil, the aroma of the honeysuckle that drifted up the hill from the garden, the faint odor of Aunt Marjorie's foul-smelling cheap cigar. I felt good. Felt like whatever happened next would be just fine. I floated and waited.

I looked around for that welcoming light I'd heard

about, but I didn't see it. Instead, everything around me seemed to glow and shimmer in the sunlight. I heard beautiful sounds – not the voices of dead loved ones, but the laughter and singing of my children when they were tiny. I saw James, young and shirtless, chasing them through Mama's garden. Off in the distance I saw Barbara Jean and Clarice, and even myself when we were kids, dancing to music pouring out of my old pink and violet portable record player. Here I was with my fingers brushing up against the frame of the picture I'd been painting for the last fifty-five years, and my beautiful, scarred husband, my happy children, and my laughing friends were right there with me.

I looked up then to tell Mama how overjoyed I was to see that crossing over was just like she had said it would be. That was when I saw Mrs Roosevelt reach out, pick something from the tree, and then pass it to Mama. I watched as Mama rolled whatever she'd been handed around in her palms before letting it go. It fell from her hands, through the branches and leaves of the tree. Finally, it came down to me where I sat on the ground – or floated in the air, I wasn't quite sure which I was doing. I felt the thing land on my lap.

The object Mama had dropped rested just above my knees. It was small and dark green with blackish-brown spots. I felt the heat it had absorbed from the summer sun coming off of it so strong that I wondered if it might burn clean through the thin robe I was wearing.

Then I felt and heard it tick. Like a time bomb.

I looked back up at the tree again. This time I studied it more carefully. I focused on the shape of the leaves. I squinted and saw that there were clusters of little round fruit covering the tree. I watched as Eleanor Roosevelt tugged another one from the tree and let it fall. This one landed on my head and then bounced off to my right.

"Damn you, Richmond Baker. This is just you all over. I give you one thing to do and you screw it up. And, to top it off, you do it when I'm too gone from the world to yell at you about it. Any fourth grader can tell a sycamore from a time bomb tree. Now here I am with walnuts falling on my head while I'm trying to die the way I want to."

I picked up the walnut from my lap and tossed it at him.

To my surprise, Richmond ducked. Then he backed away several feet.

He started apologizing. "I'm sorry, Odette. A tree's a tree to me. They all look the same."

Another surprise. What I'd believed I had shouted out in a place far beyond Richmond's hearing, I had apparently bellowed directly at him. And he'd heard at least enough of it to know that I was truly pissed. Richmond kept his distance, afraid I might find the strength to toss something else at him.

Throwing something else at Richmond wasn't on my mind, though. I was too busy trying to figure out why I was alive when all the indications were that I was done for. I put my hand to my forehead. I felt hot. But it was the heat from the sun now, not the fire that had been roiling in my blood since the day of Sharon's wedding.

I called up to Mama, "Is this a miracle?"

She raised and lowered her shoulders. Her voice drifted down: "Maybe. Or maybe this is just what's supposed to be."

Richmond assumed I was talking to God, so, preacher's son that he was, he bowed his head. I started to feel bad for yelling at him. He'd done me a big favor, one I couldn't have asked anyone else to do. And it wasn't his fault he screwed it up. That was just his nature.

"I'm sorry, Richmond. I shouldn't have yelled at you, or thrown that walnut either. You've been a good friend, and I appreciate it."

Sensing that the danger had passed, he came closer. Then he sat down next to me in the shade of the walnut tree. The summer afternoon heat was getting to him and he wiped his forehead with a handkerchief he'd pulled from his pocket. "Umm, so do you want me to carry you somewhere else? If you point out the sycamore, I can take you to it."

I pondered what I should do and couldn't come up with a decent answer. "I've gotta tell you, Richmond, I'm not quite sure what to do. I'd only planned the day as far as this. I had it on what I'd taken as good authority that I'd be dead by now."

I turned my face up toward the top of the tree and cut Mrs Roosevelt a dirty look. I was happy to still be a part of the world of the living, but I'd gone to a fair amount of trouble to get myself to my sycamore tree – no, walnut tree, thanks to dumb-ass Richmond – so I could pass in peace. Now it looked like it was all for nothing.

I looked around and saw my sycamore tree about fifty yards away, as twisted and beautiful as ever.

Richmond saw where I was staring. "You want to go over there?"

"I don't think so. It appears I won't be dying just yet.

Let's go back to the hospital. If we're lucky, we might make it before James gets back. If he finds out about this, I might die on schedule after all."

Richmond chuckled.

"I wouldn't laugh if I was you. After James is done with me, he'll want a piece of you, too."

"Well then, we'd better get a move on." Richmond got up on one knee and then bent and scooped me up from the ground.

"Really, Richmond, I don't think you have to carry me. I can probably walk, if you help me."

He began to climb down the hill with me in his arms. "No, no, you're as light as a feather," he lied, grunting with every step.

"You know, Richmond, I see why all the women love you so much. You talk a bunch of shit, but you make it sound good." I wrapped my arms around my accomplice's thick, muscular neck and enjoyed the bouncy ride.

Over Richmond's shoulder, I smiled up at my mother in the walnut tree. She gazed back at me, looking as pleasantly surprised as I was to see me leaving this place alive. Then I focused my attention on that bothersome Eleanor Roosevelt, who had caused me so much concern and vexation throughout the year. I wanted her to know, before Richmond carried me out of sight, that she might have had me worried, but she never had me scared.

I balled my hand into a fist and shook it at Mrs Roosevelt. And, just before Richmond and I reached the tall reed grass at the back end of Mama's garden, I shouted as loud as my hoarse throat would let me, "I was born in a sycamore tree!"

Chapter 38

My first Sunday back at the All-You-Can-Eat came three weeks after I didn't die beneath my tree. The restaurant was packed. Every chair in the place, except the ones waiting for James and me, was occupied. And from the unusual amount of trouble even skinny James had squeezing between the patrons, it seemed to me that Little Earl had added some tables to the dining room to handle the increased numbers.

As we made our way through the crowd, folks greeted me like I'd just returned from the battlefield. Erma Mae rushed up to me and kissed me on each cheek. Ramsey Abrams hugged me – a little too tight and a little too long, as usual. Florence Abrams shook my hand and contorted her face into that wince she believed was a smile. Every step we took, somebody stopped me to say how glad they were that I was on the mend. People had done the same thing when I'd returned to church that morning, and I have to admit I was flattered by the attention.

When we finally got to our window table, I took my seat between Clarice and Barbara Jean. James sat down at the men's end of the table, and we both launched into conversations with our friends.

It was like things had never changed, and it was

completely different at the same time. Clarice, bold and braless in a gauzy, shapeless white dress that she wouldn't have been caught dead in six months earlier, was still the most dedicated gossip I knew. But, courtesy of the Unitarians, she wasn't so filled up with fury now that every story or observation had to have a bite to it. And Barbara Jean was as beautiful as ever in a pearl-gray dress from her new toned-down and sobered-up collection, but she had a way about her that said maybe her soul was truly at peace for the first time in all the years that I'd known her.

I could hear the usual sports talk coming from the other end of the table. But they'd shuffled up things a bit there, too. Richmond had moved over one chair and now sat in the space that Lester had occupied for years. James sat where Richmond used to sit. And Chick Carlson sat in James's old spot.

Barbara Jean didn't talk about the future. She said she planned to take each day as it came. But if you got her alone and pressed her about it, she'd tell you that what was happening – her and Chick together, trying to learn to be happy – was a miracle.

I didn't argue with Barbara Jean, but I'd grown partial to Mama's take on that topic. What we call miracles is just what's supposed to happen. We either go with it or stand in its way. It seemed to me that Barbara Jean had just finally stopped getting in the way of what was meant to be. But what did I know? I'd chosen to go with the flow and I'd ended up letting the drunken ghost of a former first lady convince me that I was about to die.

When we headed to the buffet line, we found the pickings pretty slim. Erma Mae saw me spooning the last of the braised short ribs from a tray. She said, "We'll have some more soon. We thought we'd have a busy day today, but we didn't plan on this kinda crowd showin' up. It's like they all marked the date on their calendars and ran straight over here from church to see the show."

That was when I remembered. One year ago, Minnie McIntyre had announced to everyone that her spirit guide, Charlemagne the Magnificent, had put her on notice that she had a maximum of 365 days to live. Now the All-You-Can-Eat was full of people who'd come to see how Minnie was going to deal with waking up alive a year later.

Little Earl hustled out of the kitchen with an overflowing tray of short ribs. He saw me and said, "Hey, Odette, good to have you back." He put the tray on the steam table with one hand while sliding out the empty tray with the other in one smooth, practiced motion. He said, "It's crazy in here today. Sorry I can't stay and talk." Then he rushed back into the kitchen.

Erma Mae shook her head. "He's not sorry at all. He's tickled pink to have this crowd. Maybe we can persuade Minnie to predict her death every Sunday. That way we could retire in another year." Then someone waved at her from the cash register and she hurried away.

All six of us filled our plates and headed back to our table. As soon as we sat, Clarice said, "I talked to Veronica last night." Veronica had started speaking to Clarice again immediately after everything went so wrong at the wedding. She'd been calling Clarice just about every day since then to vent some steam about what Minnie had done to her with her bad predictions.

"Is Veronica doing any better?" Barbara Jean asked.

"A little. She's still too embarrassed to leave the house, but she got a new prescription for nerve pills and she doesn't talk about murdering Minnie quite so much. Now she does a fair amount of inappropriate giggling instead. It's creepy, but I suppose it's an improvement."

"I'm surprised she isn't here today. I'd think she'd want to be on the scene to hear Minnie try to explain being alive. It might give her a bit of satisfaction," I said.

Clarice said, "No, she's determined to lay low until people forget about the wedding."

"She'll have a hell of a long wait on her hands," I said. "I heard a rumor that the wedding photographer was selling his footage to *America's Funniest Home Videos*."

Clarice and Barbara Jean both squealed, "Really?"

"Well, no," I confessed. "But a girl can dream."

Barbara Jean asked, "What about Sharon? How's she doing?"

Clarice said, "Not so good. I haven't seen her, but, according to Veronica, she's locked herself in her room and only comes out to shoot evil looks at her mother. On top of that, her hypnosis is wearing off, so she's struggling to stay away from the sweets. It's not easy for her, depressed as she is, living with three hundred servings of wedding cake in the deep freezer down in the basement."

Then Clarice said, "Excuse me for a second." She lightly rapped on the table with her knuckles and cleared her throat. When she had everyone's attention, she said, "Richmond," then she extended her right hand, palm up.

Richmond tried his unconvincing innocent look for a few seconds. Then he slid a large serving of banana pudding out from beneath his napkin where he had been hiding it. He stood and brought the pudding to the other end of the table, depositing it in the hand of his part-time wife.

Chick and James laughed at him and started in with the teasing as soon as Richmond sat back down in his chair. But Richmond just grinned and said, "What can I say? My woman wants me to live."

Clarice and Richmond seemed to have come to an understanding. Clarice had gotten over worrying about going to hell for wanting love without misery, and Richmond had given up fighting for a return to the life they had led before she left him. I was happy to see it. I loved Clarice, of course, and Richmond Baker was all right by me, too.

The main reason I'd chosen Richmond to take me out of the hospital and to my sycamore tree was that he was physically the strongest person I knew. Fifty-seven years old and every inch of him still bulged with muscle. Also, of all my friends, Richmond had shown himself the most willing to do things that other people thought were wrong. But it turned out he had some other valuable qualities.

For one, years of sneaking around had taught Richmond how to keep his mouth shut. We made it back to the hospital that day before anyone else returned. I did some apologizing to my doctor and Richmond did some flirting with the nurses. And by the time James, the Supremes, my brother, and my kids came back, an agreement had been struck with the hospital personnel to pretend my escape had never happened.

I thought about telling James what I had done. But I decided it would be better for everyone, especially me, if I didn't. The way I figured it, James had enough on his plate. He was a good husband whose wife had cancer. He was a lawman who had to go on pretending, at least a little while longer, that he didn't know I was smoking marijuana every day. And now James also had to deal with having a chorus line of dead folks dancing in and out of his life. No, that whole thing about my escape to Leaning Tree was something me and my new buddy, Richmond, would keep to ourselves.

Someone shouted, "There's Minnie," and Clarice lost any concern for Richmond's diet, Barbara Jean quit gazing at Chick, and I stopped mulling over my own little secrets. Along with everybody else in the All-You-Can-Eat, we stared out the window at the house across the street.

I scanned the front of Minnie's house and still didn't see a thing. "Where is she?" I asked.

"Look up," Barbara Jean said. "She's on the roof."

Sure enough, there was Minnie. She was crawling, rear end first, out of a second-floor window and onto the wedge of roof above the front porch.

"What on earth is she doing?" Clarice asked as we watched Minnie gain her footing on the slanted shingles. Balancing up there had to have been a tough task since, in addition to her purple fortune-telling robe with the signs of the zodiac pasted all over it and her white turban, she was wearing her satin Arabian slippers with the curled-up toes.

"I believe she's fixin' to jump," I said.

Barbara Jean said, "That's a long way to go to make a prediction come true. If she goes through with it, you have to admire her dedication to her work."

Clarice rolled her eyes. "Oh please, she'll never jump. You know as well as I do that Minnie McIntyre won't die until she contracts some lingering mystery disease that she can whine about for decades till somebody snaps under the strain of listening to her running her mouth and smothers her with a pillow." She snatched a chicken finger off my plate and bit into it.

I said, "Sounds like you've given this a bit of thought, Clarice. What happened to that fresh, mellow outlook on life you said the Unitarians were giving you?"

"I haven't been a Unitarian long," she responded, waving the stub of the chicken finger. "I've still got some work to do."

Always the most charitable of the Supremes, Barbara Jean said, "Someone really should go over there and talk her down."

But no one moved. I'm sure Barbara Jean knew even as she said it that she'd be hard-pressed to find a soul in town who would try to talk Minnie McIntyre out of leaping. In that very room was an assortment of people who would gladly climb onto that roof with her, but only to give her a shove, convinced that they were doing the world a favor by hastening her departure. No, these folks were not a crowd of likely suicide prevention counselors.

Minnie stood now with her arms outstretched like Jesus on the cross, her purple robe billowing in the breeze like the sails of a ship. A particularly strong gust came along and snatched the turban off her head. When she tried to grab for it, she pitched forward so awkwardly that everyone gasped. Minnie wobbled for a few seconds, but soon righted herself. Then she stuck her arms out and struck her martyr pose again, looking angry and defiant as the little wisps of gray hair that poked out from the hairnet she'd worn under her turban danced in the wind.

We all watched for a while longer. Then Little Earl, who had been summoned from the kitchen by his wife, let out a groan. "I guess I better go have a talk with her." He took off his apron and came out from behind the steam tables. But he halted at the front door when he saw that someone had appeared on Minnie's lawn and was having a lively conversation with her.

A slim young woman carrying a pale pink cardboard box labeled "Donut Heaven" under her left arm stood in the center of the lawn. She was wearing a long white dress that looked like it had seen better days. Strips of cloth hung from the ragged hem of the dress, like somebody had taken scissors to it. Stains of assorted sizes and colors dotted the fabric. At first it seemed she and Minnie were having a casual conversation, but then the young woman began to shake an upraised fist in Minnie's direction. Suddenly it was clear that the exchange they were having was anything but casual.

Clarice said, "I can't believe it. It's Sharon."

I squinted and saw that it was, indeed, Sharon, the almost-wife of the now re-incarcerated Clifton Abrams. As I watched, Sharon's movements graduated from testy to furious. Now, instead of a fist, she jabbed her middle finger up toward the old woman.

Clarice said, "I should call Veronica." She twisted around to get at the pocketbook that hung on the back of her chair and fished inside until she found her phone. Then she dialed her cousin.

"Hi, Veronica, it's me. I'm having supper at the All-You-Can-Eat and Sharon just showed up . . . No, she's not having supper with us. She's across the street and it appears she's having words with Minnie . . . Uh-huh . . . And, Veronica, she's in her wedding gown . . . Really? Every day? . . . Well, right now she's just standing there yelling at Minnie with a Donut Heaven box under her arm."

The shriek that came from the other end of the phone line at the mention of Donut Heaven was so loud that Clarice jerked the phone as far away from her head as the length of her arm would let her. When the wailing subsided, Clarice put the phone back to her ear. She listened for a moment and then told Veronica, "I can't really say for sure from this distance, but my guess would be it's the family-size box." Another shriek. This one came and went too quickly for Clarice to pull the phone away. She listened for a few seconds longer and then turned off her phone. Then, to us, Clarice said, "She'll be right over."

We continued to watch the spectacle across the street. The restaurant was so quiet now and Sharon was yelling so loud that we could hear an occasional word even though she was dozens of yards away and separated from us by a thick pane of glass. Her gestures got bigger as she became angrier. She escalated things by opening the donut box, removing a long chocolate éclair, and lobbing it at Minnie like a javelin, which drove the audience in the restaurant to hoots of amusement and shock. The pastry sailed wide of its target and missed by two feet. Minnie made an obscene hand signal back at Sharon and then they screamed at each other for a while longer. Little Earl sighed again and opened the restaurant's front door to go outside and play referee.

Clarice, Barbara Jean, and I glanced at each other, each of us trying to come up with an excuse for following Little Earl across the street that didn't seem like pure nosiness.

Barbara Jean got there first. She said, "I hope Veronica gets here soon. Sharon needs family with her."

Clarice said, "I would love to offer her a shoulder to cry on, but I'm afraid she'd believe I was just butting in. And I wouldn't want Veronica to think I was overstepping. You know how she can be."

"Nonsense," I countered. "When you're a blood relative it's not butting in. It's a family responsibility."

"And a Christian duty," added Barbara Jean.

Clarice asked, "Do you really think so?" She said it like she still had to be persuaded, but she was already standing up to leave, her eyes fixed on the front door.

Barbara Jean said, "I'll go with you . . . for moral support."

Not one to be left out of a mission of Christian mercy, I tagged along. In fact, I nearly beat Clarice to the door.

When we got to Minnie's yard, Little Earl had taken off his All-You-Can-Eat cap and was fanning his face with it. He said, "Miss Minnie, please, just go on back inside the house. We can have a cool drink and work this out."

She said, "Oh, you'd like that, wouldn't you?" Then, addressing us – the Supremes and the other spectators who had decided to leave the All-You-Can-Eat and brave the heat for a closer look at the goings-on – she said, "You'd all love that, wouldn't you. You'd love to have me live through this day and have everybody calling my gift for prophecy into question."

Sharon cried out, "Gift? That's a laugh." Then she flung

a powdered donut at Minnie. Her aim was true that time. She got Minnie in the chest, leaving a chalky white circle of confectioner's sugar on Minnie's purple robe.

Just then, I heard the screeching of car wheels behind us. I thought, *Veronica got here fast.* But when I looked over my shoulder, instead of Veronica's sharp gray Lexus, I saw a rusted old Chevy shuddering to a stop. Yvonne Wilson, the most devout believer in Minnie's fortune-telling abilities, hopped out of the car with a baby in her arms. Her boyfriend and the six underachieving child stars she'd given birth to after Minnie's prediction that one of them would make her rich piled out of the car after her.

Panting for breath, Yvonne sprinted in front of Sharon and gasped, "Don't jump, Madame Minnie! Please don't jump. When I heard you were up on the roof I just about keeled over dead. You can't jump until you see the new baby." Then she raised the infant she was holding high above her head, turning the baby's scrunched-up little face toward Minnie and the sun. "Don't jump until you tell me if this is the one!"

Minnie snarled, "Go away, Yvonne. I can't be bothered with you now."

Yvonne waved the now-crying child in the air. "But I really need to know."

Minnie put her hands on her hips. She twisted her mouth in annoyance and then hollered down, "Charlemagne says no. Try again." Then she extended her arms back out to her sides and scooted the curled toes of her slippers even closer to the edge of the roof.

Yvonne handed off the yowling baby to her boyfriend, who was already carrying another of their offspring. She said, "Dammit! Let's go home." The nine of them piled back into the rusty Chevy and rattled off.

As I watched Yvonne's family disappear in their shivering, smoke-belching car, I found myself thinking of Mama. I wished I could share this with her. If she'd been there, I'd have said, "Mama, this is one of those moments, one of those times that is so good I'll want to carry it with me when I really do cross over one day." I also wished that I could've shared that feeling with Clarice and Barbara Jean in a way that would make sense to them. They did their best with the topic of Mama and the community of ghosts I'd started keeping company with, though we hadn't really talked much about it since I left the hospital.

But maybe there are some things that you don't need knowledge of an unseen world to understand. Just as I was thinking of how I'd like to talk about the wonders of this day with Mama, I felt Barbara Jean hook her left arm around my right. Then, on my other side, Clarice's elbow wrapped around mine.

The three of us stood there on Big Earl's lawn, regarding each other with the kind of expression that could have broken out into a face-splitting grin just as easily as it could have collapsed into tears. A feeling passed between us that didn't need words, an understanding that there was no other place on earth that we should be right then, no one else we could quite so fully share this strange and beautiful day with. We squeezed closer to each other and leaned our foreheads together, forming our own tight, private triangle. Finally, Clarice said, "Let's get back across the street where we can laugh out loud. You don't need to be out in this heat, Odette. And we all know that old fake isn't about to jump."

From the roof, Minnie, with that good hearing of hers, shouted, "I heard that! Don't you call me a fake!" We turned toward her just in time to see her launch herself out into the open air with her long purple painted nails aimed at Clarice, ready to scratch her eyes out.

It seemed to me that it wasn't until Minnie's feet had parted with the metal gutter that she remembered she was up on the roof and not on ground level with Clarice. I clearly recall seeing the expression on her face transform from white hot fury to surprise and terror as she fell. Minnie screamed as she came hurtling down toward the lawn, her purple robe fanning out all around her like a parachute.

As it happened, she didn't hit Clarice or the lawn. She landed on Sharon. The impact caused Sharon to fall back against Little Earl, and all three of them tumbled across the lawn in a purple and white blur. Because the yard sloped slightly toward the street, the Minnie-Sharon-Earl bundle tumbled downhill until it came to a stop against the low yew hedge that lined the front of the property.

The three of them were immediately set upon by rescuers. The first challenge was untangling them from the purple robe and the torn lace of the wedding gown. Then, as a throng of people asked if they were hurt, Minnie shoved helping hands away from her and hopped right up, still ready to take a swipe at Clarice. But as soon as she took one step in Clarice's direction, she crumpled back to the ground and grasped her foot. She howled, "Oww!" Then, pointing at Clarice, she wailed, "You broke my ankle."

Erma Mae, who had come running when she saw Little Earl hit the ground, was checking her husband over for injuries even though he kept insisting that he was just fine.

Tearful and grass-stained, but unhurt, Sharon crawled across the yard on her hands and knees picking up crushed pastries and tossing them back into the pink box.

I heard tires squealing again and I looked toward the street and saw Veronica leaping from her shiny gray car. She trotted over to where Sharon crouched in the grass in her ruined wedding gown and, getting onto her knees, embraced her daughter. She kissed the top of Sharon's head and tried to comfort her, while at the same time attempting to pull the Donut Heaven box from her daughter's grasp.

From the edge of the growing crowd in Minnie's yard, I heard a voice say, "Now that was somethin' to see." I turned, and there was Mama.

Everyone else was occupied. Clarice was trying to prevent a tug-of-war between Veronica and Sharon over the Donut Heaven box. Barbara Jean was playing nurse-maid to Minnie. The rest of the crowd was busy discussing what they'd just seen, already starting to exaggerate. So I walked away from the commotion and took off down the street with Mama.

I had seen my mother milling around the hospital during the days between my leaving the ICU and my being released to go home. And later I had noticed her roaming through my backyard, frowning over the condition of my flowers. But we hadn't talked since that day in Leaning Tree when I thought I was going to join her in the afterlife.

Mama said, "You're lookin' good."

"Thank you. I'm feeling all right, considering middle age and cancer."

She said, "Well, you won't have to deal with cancer too much longer. I've got a feelin' you'll be past that soon."

"No offense, Mama, but I think I'm done listening to predictions about whether or not I'll be recovering."

Mama made a face like my remark had stung her. "I'm so sorry about that. Believe you me, I gave Eleanor a piece of my mind for misleadin' you. She swears up and down it wasn't a prank. And I'm inclined to believe her. It was a big blow to her confidence, bein' wrong about you. She took it real hard." Mama whispered, "She's drinkin' like a fish."

I said, "You can tell her I'm not mad. If there's one thing I'm not going to get too angry with somebody about, it's them being wrong about me dying."

Mrs Roosevelt appeared at Mama's side then, like she'd been waiting nearby to hear that all was forgiven. She favored me with a wide, bucktoothed smile and a shy wave.

I nodded to her and we kept walking.

At the corner, we turned around and headed back. When we were about a half a block away from Minnie's house, I saw an ambulance pull up to the curb. I watched paramedics take over tending to Minnie and saw Barbara Jean return to the All-You-Can-Eat now that she wasn't needed. Veronica climbed into her Lexus with Sharon in tow, and Clarice walked back across the street, too.

I told Mama, "Hey, I'm having my last round of chemo on Tuesday – leastways I hope it's my last."

Mama said, "Wonderful. We should have a party. I'll get

everybody together to celebrate – your daddy, Big Earl, Thelma, Eleanor, and maybe your aunt Marjorie."

I said, "How about just you and Daddy. I'd like to keep things a little quieter from now on."

"You're right. That probably would be nicer." Her voice dropped so low I could barely hear her as she added, "Besides, you can't have your aunt Marjorie at the same party with *this one*." She pointed at Mrs Roosevelt, who weaved along beside Mama, sipping from a silver flask that was emblazoned with the presidential seal. "Put the two of them in the same room and it's nonstop arm wrestlin' and drinkin' games."

The paramedics were strapping Minnie onto a gurney as we approached. The hot weather had driven the spectators away. Now only Little Earl remained. As they wheeled her off the lawn, Minnie told her stepson, "Be sure to tell everybody that I had a near-death experience when I hit the ground. And tell 'em all I said it counts as fulfillin' my prediction." I waved goodbye to Minnie as the back doors to the ambulance closed. Little Earl hurried off to his car to follow his stepmother to the hospital.

Now that all of the action was over, I started to feel the sun scorching my skin. I said to Mama, "I've gotta get out of this heat."

"I'll see you on Tuesday, all right?" Mama said.

"All right."

We parted ways then. Mama and Eleanor Roosevelt walked toward the swing on the McIntyres' front porch. I crossed the street and headed back to my friends.

Through the window I saw Barbara Jean and Clarice with their heads together. I suspected they were arguing about whether or not they should ask me if I'd wandered off alone in order to talk to ghosts. At the men's end of the table, Richmond drew laughs from Chick and James as he tried and repeatedly failed to coax small cubes of sugar-free cherry Jell-O onto his spoon without losing them down the front of his gold silk shirt.

James must have felt me looking at him. He turned away from his buddies and made eye contact with me through the glass. He winked.

This was a pretty picture I'd been allowed to paint – my man and my friends all together. It was the best it could be, really, even though the hand that had sketched it was unsure and in spite of the fact that age had washed out some of the colors. And I wasn't about to worry over my picture's frame, not when there was so much more good painting to do.

I reached out to open the door to the All-You-Can-Eat.

Acknowledgments

My most sincere and heartfelt thanks to:

Julia Glass, for her incredible kindness and generosity. My phenomenal agent, Barney Karpfinger, for his encouragement and advice. My editor, Carole Baron, for allowing me to be the beneficiary of her immense talent. My first readers, Claire Parins, Harold Carlton, Grace Lloyd, and Nina Lusterman, for their patience. My father, Reverend Edward Moore, Sr, for a lifetime of lessons in real strength and true goodness. My mother, Delores Moore, for that first library card. And Peter Gronwold, for absolutely everything.

The best books live on in your head long after they are finished. As you read, you are turning the pages faster and faster to find out what happens next, only to feel bereft when you reach the end.

If that is how you feel now, you might like to join us at www.hodder.co.uk, or follow us on Twitter @hodderbooks, and be part of our community of people who love the very best of books and reading.

Whether you want to find out more about this book, or a particular author, watch trailers and interviews, have the chance to win early limited editions, or simply browse our expert readers' selection of the very best books, we think you'll find what you're looking for.

And if you don't, that's the place to tell us what's missing.

We love what we do, and we'd love you to be part of it.

www.hodder.co.uk

@hodderbooks

HodderBooks

HodderBooks